THE FRENCH DECEPTION

By Linda Steinberg

Linda Steinberg

The French Deception

ISBN 978-0-9897546-1-3

Printed by Create Space

Acknowledgements

Special thanks to my fantastic critique partners, Pamela Stone and Juliet Burns, for brainstorming, critiquing, hand-holding, and most of all, for keeping me focused on this journey. Also to Chris Keniston for being my Beta reader, to Yvonne Jocks for her help with the scenes in the Paris catacombs, and to the Plotting Princesses for blazing the trail.

Linda Steinberg

Chapter One

Late! Paul Bernard dashed out of the Metro station and bolted up rue de Faubourg de St Honore toward the British Embassy, holding his jacket over his head to ward off the light morning mist.

Just as he got to the corner the traffic light changed. Bloody hell! Paul shifted his weight impatiently from one foot to the other as Smart cars, bicycles and the occasional luxury sedan swooshed past him, dodging potholes and pedestrians. He was way past due at work, thanks to an unexpected but very pleasurable morning romp in the sack.

He'd woken when it was still dark to Colette's arousing hand on his pecker, and half-dreamed her riding astride his responding erection. After the brief but immensely satisfying encounter, she'd rolled out of bed to shower and dress before hurrying off to an early call for an important audition. "You don't have to get up yet," she'd said in her bedroom voice, kissing his ear. "Go back to sleep."

And he had. So blissfully knackered that he'd slept past his alarm, so dead to the world he didn't even remember hearing it ring. He smiled, thanking whatever beneficent force had seen fit to bestow upon a mild-mannered computer geek the favors of that incredibly sexy French coquette.

The crowd of pedestrians shoved at him from behind and Paul stepped off the curb. Blinding light flashed and a deafening boom sent shockwaves strong enough to knock him backwards. Debris flew past, burning chunks of plasterboard and metal. The dark, billowing smoke twined around his neck, thick and choking.

Paul blinked and wiped the soot from his eyes. He stared at the British Embassy, half destroyed, in flames.

Someone had bombed his bloody offices. And if he'd gotten to work just five minutes earlier...he could be dead.

* * *

Breaking away from her tour group to meet her friend, Megan Adele Chandler rounded a corner inside the Musée d'Orsay and came face to face with...herself.

She stopped short. The young woman in the turn-of-the-century painting wore a purple felt hat adorned in flamboyant feathers, swathed in tulle. The wide brim nearly obscured her forehead. But the midnight blue eyes staring out at Megan were unmistakably her own. As were the high cheekbones, the wispy brown ringlets framing the face, and tiny cleft chin.

Megan's breath ebbed away. If the artist had copied the facial details from last year's college graduation photo, he could not have been more exact.

A shiver tensed her spine. This would explain why Nicole had chosen this place to meet, though the Paris museum was the last itinerary item of Megan's European tour. Her Facebook friend must have seen this painting and noticed its eerie similarity to Megan's profile photo.

She glanced at the title. *Mademoiselle Adele Jarreau.*

Reading her middle name caused Megan's heart to skip a beat. Just one. Adele was a common French name. The last name, Jarreau, meant nothing to her. The likeness could be mere coincidence.

Or not.

Her heritage on her mother's side was French, which was one of the reasons Paris had always intrigued her. Could the woman in the portrait be Megan's ancestor?

She dropped her black backpack and summer trench coat on a bench and stepped closer to read the date and the artist's name. 1910. Eduard Dubois.

Mom's middle name was Dubois. Megan's heartbeat quivered again before resuming its normal beat. Another common French name. But not of any artists she'd heard of. Writing her master's thesis on European works of the early twentieth century had familiarized Megan with many artists of this period, but she'd never heard of Eduard Dubois. Maybe Nicole knew something about him.

Where *was* Nicole? She'd said she'd be wearing a yellow scarf. Megan hadn't seen anyone wearing a scarf, yellow or otherwise.

Anxiously she checked her watch. Nicole was fifteen minutes late. They'd have barely an hour to visit before Megan's tour group left for Charles de Gaulle airport. And home.

A wistful sigh escaped her lips. Three weeks had flown by in a minute. And she still hadn't decided how to respond to Fletcher's proposal.

She started to turn away, but the eyes in the portrait called her back, the flecks of paint glinting as if they could actually see her. Megan swayed to either side. Like the Mona Lisa's, Adele Jarreau's eyes seemed to follow her, focus on her. She shut her eyes but the portrait's image imprinted in her brain, swirling like colors in a kaleidoscope.

A rustling noise made her lids flutter open. Megan looked up to see a woman in a yellow scarf dart out of the gallery into the next room.

She slung her backpack over one shoulder, grabbed her coat, and headed after the scarf. "Nicole?"

The next room was crowded, but the flowing yellow scarf wasn't difficult to pick out. Megan approached the woman, but when she got within a few feet the elusive figure moved again, disappearing into another gallery.

"Nicole. Wait up. It's Megan."

Hadn't she heard her? Her quarry kept moving, vanishing from one room and appearing again in another, never speaking or seeming to notice she'd been spoken to. Megan weaved through galleries of portraits and early modern art, feeling like Alice chasing the White Rabbit down a Wonderland rabbit hole.

"Hey, Megan." Two women from her tour hailed her as she passed through a room of wild-colored Fauvists works by Matisse, and lost sight of her prey. "Did you find your friend?"

"Hi, Jessica." She skittered across the polished wood floor, stopping in front of a young woman wearing black jeans and tank top, and black nail polish. "Did you see a woman in a yellow scarf pass by?"

Jessica pointed to a curtained doorway. A sign dangling above read *Employees Only.*

Seeing no museum guards, Megan made for the curtain.

"Don't forget," the other girl called after her. "The bus leaves exactly at two. Madame Richard will have a fit if you're late."

"I'll be there." Megan slipped through the curtain into a small hallway lined with closed doors. Offices? Did Nicole work for the museum?

She tried one door, then another. All locked. Megan glanced at the floor, half expecting to find a key that would fit one of the locks and make her grow bigger or smaller.

At the end of the hallway was a door marked *Femmes*. The Ladies room. Megan marched ahead, pushed open the door and walked in. "Nicole? Are you--?"

A hand shoved at her back, and something wet and spongy clapped over her nose. Flailing helplessly, Megan choked on the sweet, cloying scent. Her eyelids weighted and closed. Cold tile smacked her back and bottom as she slid to the floor.

*   *   *

She roused herself out of a dark fog, forcing one heavy eyelid open. A gray metal wall loomed in front of her. Two others at her sides imprisoned her in a cramped room. Something hard jammed into her back.

Megan opened the other eye and blinked. She was on the floor in a toilet stall. But she couldn't remember coming in here. Had she passed out?

Oh.

Struggling to stand, she coughed out the remnants of whatever she'd been drugged with, then nudged the door, which was wedged shut, with her shoulder. Blinking, she stepped out of the stall. Her legs wobbled, but she managed to place one in front of the other.

Her stomach jackknifed. Lurching to the sink, Megan retched until weak and even more light-headed, but puked nothing out.

She washed her face. The mirror above the sink reflected no cuts or bruises, but her mouse brown curls hung limply to her shoulders and her eyes were dilated to twice their normal size.

How long had she been out? She checked her wrist for the time, but her watch was gone!

Frantically she checked the stalls. It wasn't in any of them. Megan snatched up her coat and backpack and ran out into hallway. No watch.

Trembling, she backed against a wall. Her parents had given her the diamond-crusted Cartier watch when she'd graduated Princeton last year. She should have been more careful. Fletcher had warned her thieves in Europe were bold and canny, but who would expect to be drugged just for a watch? Even an expensive watch.

She remembered coming in here after Nicole. Was her friend all right? Had the same thief accosted her? Or was Nicole...? No. She swallowed hard. Surely not.

Megan slipped back through the curtain and retraced her steps until she reached the grand staircase. She stopped a museum guard. "*Excusez-moi, ou est la* Lost and Found?" It was worth trying.

"Downstairs, Mademoiselle. Off the main entrance."

Her shaky French obviously tagged her not only as a tourist, but as an English speaker. Nodding gratefully, she descended the staircase of the grandiose museum that had once been a railway station. At the service desk, her gaze skimmed the cathedral ceiling and lit on the gilded clock in the great hall. Two-thirty?

Her heart froze. "That clock can't be right."

The desk attendant checked her own watch. "It is, mademoiselle."

Panic dug its fingers into Megan's stomach. The bus! Scanning the lobby for anyone from her group, she raced to the front of the museum and out the doors.

Think positive. The bus would be waiting at the riverbank. Having searched for Megan unsuccessfully, their guide would be angrily tapping her foot and her tour mates would playfully harass her for almost making them miss the plane. She hoped.

The Quai Anatole France on the Seine's Left Bank teemed with tour buses. Megan ran from one end of the line of parked vehicles to the other, but none were hers. Her throat gagged. The bus had actually left without her.

How could they do this? The tour guide always counted heads before moving on. True, they were always cautioned to be prompt or get left behind, but that was an empty threat, wasn't it?

The downside of being an incurable optimist was that she rarely considered a Plan B.

A muffled thunderclap sounded in the distance. Megan looked up at darkening clouds. The air hung heavy with the scent of impending rain.

She clutched her coat to her body. *You're an adult now, Megan.* She could help herself. She just had to think logically.

With her pack bouncing against her back, she ran down the Quai to the nearest taxi stand. Her plane was scheduled to leave at four-thirty. With luck, she could still make it. Hopefully--she had to have hope--Madame Richard would be waiting for her at Security with her luggage.

A taxi pulled up just as she reached the stand. Hope validated, Megan climbed in. *"Charles de Gaulle. Dépêchez-vous, s'il vous plait."*

Catching a long, serene, breath, she sank into the patched leather seat cushion. The tears she blinked away cast a filmy haze over the historic bridges and tourist-packed boats along the Seine. Focusing her positive energy, she envisioned herself with her tour mates at the Air France gate. Her heart beat out an encouraging rhythm to the cab's wheels. *Faster, please. Go faster, s'il vous plaît.*

This would turn out all right. Terrible things didn't happen to Megan. She'd always followed the safe, familiar, close-to-home path, surrounded by friends and family. But she'd always longed to visit Europe, especially Paris, and when Nicole had suggested this tour...

A vise squeezed the breath in her lungs.

"You're too trusting, Megan," Fletcher had said of her Facebook friendship. "You don't even know what this Nicole person looks like. Your 'girlfriend' could be a two hundred pound con man who's planning to rob and rape you."

She'd told him he was too cynical. That not everyone posted their photograph on Facebook. So what if Nicole's profile photo was a picture of Venus de Milo? It just showed her passion for art.

God, she felt naive.

She yelled through the opening in the Plexiglas separating her from the driver. "*Quelle heure est-il?*"

"*Quatorze heure quarante-cinq.*" Two forty-five. She could still make it. Breathing heavily, Megan foraged in the backpack for her phone. Maybe the tour guide had left her a message.

Her hand probed aimlessly. Where was the darn phone? She stretched the backpack all the way open, pushing aside an unfamiliar blue sweatshirt, and fumbled about. There was no cell phone. And not much else except cosmetics. Her wallet wasn't there. Nor was the huge sheaf of papers with her itinerary and contact numbers. Nor was--

Her passport.

Her positive energy evaporated into a cloud of doom.

"This isn't my backpack," she wailed, terror swelling her lungs. It looked like it from the outside, same Jansport logo, same color, but this one was newer, and the contents obviously belonged to someone else.

The driver's monosyllabic grunt was probably French for I-couldn't-care-less.

"My passport is gone."

"*Quelle dommage*," he said flatly. The taxi sprinted forward onto the bridge at Pont de la Concorde, swerving around slower vehicles toward the Right Bank.

Megan tried to summon her trademark optimism but failed. She dove into the backpack, sweeping through tubes of lipstick and bottles of nail polish, searching for a wallet, any wallet. A dark realization unleashed a flood of tears even Pollyanna couldn't have held back. "I...I have no money."

The cab screeched to a stop at the other side of the bridge. The driver came around to Megan's door, and yanked it open. "Twenty Euros," he said in perfectly accented English.

"For a five minute trip?"

"Minimum fare."

"But I just told you. I have no money." She scrubbed a tear off her cheek. "Someone must have switched backpacks with me by mistake."

The cab driver seized the pack.

"What are you doing?" Megan stepped out onto the sidewalk. "Please, take me to the airport. My plane leaves in an hour. My tour guide will pay your fare."

His snort said he'd heard that story before. Unzipping the backpack, he upturned it and dumped the contents onto the cement.

"Stop! That's not my bag." Tubes of lipstick rolled among half a dozen loose tampons, nail polish in shades of shocking pink and purple, and an *Elle* magazine.

He shrugged. "No matter. Maybe they have twenty Euros." He kicked at the bag's contents. Finding no money, he spat in the street. "Americans," he sneered.

He dropped the empty pack on the ground. Instead of landing on its flat bottom, the bag listed to one side and fell over.

Brows knitted, the driver righted the bag and unzipped the side pocket. His pupils dilated to the size of two Euros. Color drained from his face. He dropped the bag, fled to his cab, and drove off as if pursued by a demon.

Megan knelt beside the bag, her heart hammering. She reached into the pocket. The breath stalled in her lungs as her fingers closed around the hard metal of—

A gun.

Chapter Two

Paul edged open the door of the conference room. His boss sat alone at a large oval table, wiping his face with a handkerchief. "Am I the first one here?" Paul asked.

His boss grunted, avoiding Paul's eyes, and motioned for him to sit. "Would you like tea?"

"Sure."

"Back straightaway." Nigel shut the door behind him.

Paul looked around the sparse, windowless room. It looked more like an interrogation cell than a conference room. But under the circumstances, this room at the Canadian embassy was probably the best place Nigel could arrange for a team meeting.

Nervously he fingered his shirt pocket. Why had Nigel asked him to bring his passport? Were they evacuating British citizens home to London?

Some terrorist group Paul had never heard of had claimed responsibility for the attack. According to the news reports, there were four confirmed dead, their identities withheld pending notification of relatives.

His hand dropped automatically to the front pocket of his trousers, forgetting his security card wasn't there. Blimey. He'd never misplaced his badge before. And of all days to lose it. He was quite sure he'd placed it on the dresser last night as usual, but he hadn't found it this morning. After a cursory look beside the dresser and under the bed, he'd opted not to risk being any tardier than he already was and left without it.

He pulled out his cell phone and dialed Colette's for the third time today, only to have the call go straight to voice mail once more. Hadn't she heard about the bombing? It was all over the Internet and on every telly and radio station. Surely she would have phoned to make sure he was alright.

Paul checked to see if he'd missed a text, but there were no messages. He drummed his fingers on the scarred metal table. Had Colette forgotten to turn her phone back on after the audition? Why hadn't she returned his calls?

He laid his phone on the table and checked the time. Twenty minutes of waiting was hardly 'straightaway.' The tea was surely ready by now.

Another fifteen minutes passed before his boss returned, without the tea, and without any of his colleagues in tow. Instead, three gentlemen in dark suits followed Nigel inside.

"Bernard."

Paul stood for the introductions.

"This is Agent Claude Moreau of Interpol, and Officer Pierre Dumond of the French police."

Paul shook both men's hands, trying to keep his face impassive despite the uneasy feeling in his gut.

"And this is James Kendall."

Mr. Kendall's title wasn't given but his somber, scary

16

expression suggested to Paul that the third man might be from MI6. What the hell was going on here? "Where's the rest of my team?" he blurted out.

Once again his boss motioned for him to sit. Nigel, Dumond and Moreau seated themselves in a row at the opposite side of the long table. Mr. Kendall remained standing. Intimidating silence ensued.

Finally, his boss spoke. "May I see your security badge, please?"

Shit. "I don't have it," he confessed. "I must have misplaced it."

The men flanking his boss exchanged knowing glances. Moreau fastened an icy glare on Paul. "How convenient."

"When do you last remember having it?" Nigel asked gently.

Last night? But he couldn't be sure. It had been after midnight when he'd left the office; perhaps in his exhausted state he'd forgotten it on his desk.

When he suggested that, Nigel shook his head sadly. "I'm afraid you won't find it on your desk. There's nothing left of your desk." He took a long time clearing his throat. "The bomb detonated in the data center."

At his workplace? Paul's stomach muscles clenched. His eyes raked frantically over the empty seats. "Ian? Peter? Will?"

"All three were killed by the explosion."

A sharp spear of pain hacked through Paul's body, then all his muscles went numb. God must have a cruel sense of humor. Just a few days ago, weary from the overtime worked on the current project, they'd all joked about setting fire to the building and calling it a terrorist attack. And now all his mates were...dead.

He clenched his fingernails into his palms. Will's wife had just given birth to their first child. Peter had been planning a holiday to London, as soon as this project was over. Ian had arrived in Paris about the same time Paul had, and they'd shared many a pint at a Parisian pub and played bridge every Tuesday with Malcolm from public relations and Roger from the Passport Division. How could they be gone, just like that?

A cold, crisp voice sliced into his grief. "Where were you at seven-twenty-two this morning?"

What? Paul slowly raised his gaze to face Agent Moreau, the Interpol detective. "In bed. I...overslept." Guilt thudded in Paul's chest. "We've all been working long hours on a special project. I sent the rest of the team home at eight last night. I stayed until midnight. We were all supposed to return at five a.m..."

Which the others, apparently, had. A silent howl coursed through Paul's lungs. He was the only member of his four-man team to survive.

"Can anyone verify that you were home at seven twenty-two?" This from the Paris police officer.

"Well, yes. My--" He paused. Colette had probably already left by that hour. "Perhaps not exactly at that time." He glanced at his boss. "Why is this important? Why are you asking me these questions?"

Nigel sighed and looked away before returning his gaze to Paul. "Because at seven twenty-two this morning your security card was used to enter the embassy. Thirty minutes before the explosion."

Paul's mouth went dry. "That's impossible. It...I..."

The men stared as if he were a fish floundering on a river bank.

A vise of panic gripped his chest. They were accusing him of...of...? Bracing his hands on his thighs, Paul focused on his boss, steadying his gaze. "I don't know how my security badge went missing. But it wasn't I who used it today. I told you, I overslept. I only arrived at the embassy just as the building exploded."

Nigel and the police officer exchanged looks, then glanced at the MI6 man. If that's what the quiet Mr. Kendall was. The Interpol agent glared at Paul with eyes so cold he might have kept them in the icebox at night. "Who else might have access to your badge? A wife? Friend? Girlfriend?"

"I'm not married." His cheeks grew hot. "My girlfriend lives with me, but she would never..." He trailed off, realizing how naïve that sounded. "I mean, she's an actress. She has no political interests whatever. I doubt if she even knows the name of Britain's prime minister."

Moreau's steely gaze never wavered. "And where is your girlfriend now, Mr. Bernard?"

Damn. If he said he'd been unable to reach her, they'd think he was covering for her. Not that there was anything to cover. "She went to audition for a part. In Rouen. I don't expect her home until tomorrow."

Moreau looked at his colleagues, and then back at Paul, as if 'bald-faced liar' were stamped on his forehead. The agent opened the briefcase he'd carried in with him and pulled out a photograph. "Is this your girlfriend, Monsieur Bernard?"

Paul held it by its edges. The photograph was grainy, a crude download, apparently, from one of the security cameras. It showed a young woman, in profile, carrying a vase of flowers. He'd wager ten pounds it held an explosive in a false base. The woman wore a low-necked black tank top of the same sort he'd often seen Colette wear. And had shoulder length brown hair.

He let out his breath. "No. My girlfriend has short hair." He handed back the photo.

"The suspect could be wearing a wig." The Interpol agent handed it back to Paul, urging him to look again.

He forced himself to focus on the familiar features, his heart pumping at double speed. "It's a poor quality photo. I can't make out her face very well."

Breathe slowly. There was no way Colette was involved in this. She didn't even read a newspaper, only those silly fashion magazines. Terrorist? Murderer? He considered laughing out loud, dismissing the accusation for its ridiculousness, but thought better of it. This was a serious charge. Colette would eventually be cleared; the photo had to be of someone else who looked like her. But he'd been careless with his security badge. If he'd facilitated a crime, he'd be sacked straightaway, with a permanent ugly cloud on his reputation. And his family's good name.

The Interpol agent's stone eyes bored into him. "Are you familiar with a radical group called The Community?"

He tried not to flinch under the drilling gaze. "Only from hearing it mentioned on the news reports. Are they the perpetrators?"

His boss nodded. "Taliban sympathizers," he added, earning a black look from Moreau.

Officer Dumond turned to Paul. "Has your girlfriend ever mentioned that name, or made any reference to a group of friends?"

He shook his head lamely. The project his team had been working on involved decoding data about suspected leaders in various terrorist organizations. "Is The Community one of the organizations on our project list?" he asked Nigel. Paul remembered now seeing that phrase several times but had assumed it was a generic term, not a name. "Was that why the data center was targeted?"

He was given no answers. Nor any enlightenment as to when the embassy might reopen, and what would happen to what used to be the data center.

Instead, the policemen asked for Colette's name and cell phone number. They grilled Paul about her friends, her hangouts, her daily routine. Her past history as far as he knew it. He didn't know much. Colette appeared to be a free spirit, without roots in the past, with no plans for the future.

"Do you have a picture of your lady, Monsieur Bernard?"

"Not with me."

He eyed Paul's cell phone sitting atop the table.

"New phone," he said. That much was true. He'd just upgraded last month.

His boss rose, crossed to Paul's side of the table, and clasped his back. "Paul, I'm sorry, but until this matter is cleared up, you're suspended from duty." Nigel held out his palm. "I'll take your passport, please."

A cold shiver snaked down Paul's spine. This was really happening. He, Paul Bernard, who'd never been detained for so much as a traffic violation, had unwittingly become an accessory to a terrorist plot.

Dumond and Moreau handed him their cards. Kendall still stood silently as if he were part of the room décor. "Contact us the moment your girlfriend returns but don't tell her she's a person of interest or make any mention of this conversation." Moreau's hard gray eyes locked on his again.

He nodded, pocketed the business cards, and stood. He wanted to ask if they were pursuing any other leads. If they had fingerprints or DNA samples. But his questions might be interpreted as other than idle curiosity.

Don't push your luck, Bernard. They could have locked him up and held him for days until they had another suspect. Probably didn't have enough evidence for that.

At least he was walking away a free man and, as yet, employed.

But as he shuffled back to the Metro station he felt naked without his passport, and in the city he'd come to love as home, he suddenly felt like a stranger.

* * *

No phone. No passport. No money. A gun in her backpack. And it was starting to rain.

Megan slipped her arms into her trench coat and belted it tightly around her waist as she walked the Paris streets in a shocked daze. Whose bag was this? Why had they stashed this gun in it? Had the weapon been used in a robbery? Or worse?

A rain drop landed on her trembling hand. She should find a police station, turn in the gun, and explain what had happened. But what if the police didn't believe her story? She shuddered. What if the person who'd switched the backpacks had planted the gun to frame some unsuspecting tourist for a crime?

And now it had Megan's fingerprints on it.

She needed to get rid of the gun. But how? In movies, a criminal might drop his weapon in a river, but it was a long walk back to the Seine from here. And she couldn't just chuck a loaded gun in a trash container.

Stopping at a lamppost, she hitched the bag on her hip, unzipped it, and gingerly reached inside. Touching that cold metal gave her the creeps—she'd never held a gun before in her life--but she needed to figure out how to take the bullets out. Where was the ammunition compartment? How was a city girl supposed to know about guns, anyway?

She tapped a finger to a protrusion on the bottom. Would the bullets just slide out or was there a button to press? Her bones chilled. What if she did something wrong and the gun discharged? She could shoot herself in the leg. Or maim, even kill, someone else.

Heart pounding, she slowly eased the weapon out of her hand and zipped the backpack. Who was she kidding? She was in way over her head here. How quickly her world had changed with a random twist of fate.

But she hadn't been chosen at random. A woman she knew--or thought she knew--had lured her into that bathroom. How had she been so naïve to trust a Facebook friendship?

Naïve and gullible. *Rich American tourist*, Nicole must have thought, and easily taken advantage of her. But why not steal just her money and credit cards? Why take her passport? And what was up with that gun?

Rain spattered Megan's backpack and then the sidewalk, the dark cloud hovering above her like proverbial doom. She walked on with no destination. Cars dodged and weaved in the narrow lanes of the boulevard. Shoppers browsed the fruit and vegetable stands that dotted the sidewalks, ducking occasional raindrops. Yesterday Megan had thought the paintbrush-stroked tableau romantic, and yearned to be part of it. But today, she just wanted to go home.

Well, she wasn't going to get there by clicking her heels together and wishing. She'd have to call her parents, get them to wire her money and documents.

The rain finally broke through its cloud and landed in a downpour. Megan shrugged out of her trench coat and held it over her head. Spotting a rare phone booth on the next corner, she ran toward it. As a card-carrying optimist, she rifled through the pack's small zippered pockets for coins. But as a pessimist would have expected, she found none. Not that it would have mattered. The phone didn't take coins. Only cards.

Megan stood dripping in the booth when the next dismal thought hit her: she didn't know her parents' new phone number. She'd never memorized it when they'd moved to the city last spring, because it was in her cell phone.

As were the cell phone numbers of her brother, her boyfriend, and practically everyone else she knew.

Helplessness curdled her stomach. It was easy to be an optimist in the sheltered environment in which she'd grown up, where you just followed the rules and good things were handed to you. The real world was a different ball game.

For a minute she was back in third grade, on the dreaded school playground. Un-athletic, always the last one chosen, she'd hated physical education. The one game she'd been good at, or so she'd thought, was Dodge ball. It was easy to jump aside to avoid the haphazard throws. Until the day Bobby Goodwin aimed right at her stomach, knocking the wind out of her. And forcing her to face a tough reality: following the rules of the game doesn't make one a skilled player.

So much less so when you don't know the rules. Today she'd been thrust without warning into an experience she wasn't prepared for, with dodge balls coming at her from every direction, and no place to hide. For the first time in Megan's life, she had no one to rely on but herself.

When the shower slowed to a sprinkle, she edged out of the

phone booth. Heavenly smells of bread and croissants from a patisserie taunted her, reminding her she hadn't eaten anything since the buffet brunch at the hotel.

Hotel. *Duh.* Better hotels had business service centers for their guests' convenience. She could get on the Internet and look up her parents' phone number.

But the snooty desk clerk at the nearest hotel chirped, "I'm sorry, our services are for guests only," even after Megan assured him that her parents would wire her the money for a room. The manager was even less accommodating.

Megan shook out her wet locks, fuming behind her polite smile. In her bedraggled state she might not look like she could afford this hotel, but her family was accustomed to staying at five star establishments. But good luck getting anyone to believe her. Without money or identification she might as well have been a penniless bag lady.

Frustration walled her gut, but she'd been brought up not to make a scene. So she snagged a complimentary city map off the counter, threw her head back, and marched outside into a full-fledged downpour.

Fingers of anxiety dug into her stomach. The cruel scent of heavy rain brought back a long-buried memory, but she shoved it back into her subconscious. She wasn't a powerless three-year-old and this wasn't a flash flood. She could take care of herself.

Ducking into an alcove beside a produce stand, Megan took cover under the flimsy awning. Rain clanged against the cheap tin and sloshed puddles at her feet. The smell of overripe fruit mingled with the odor of wet paper bags as shoppers hurriedly shoved purchases into their carts. Workers at a sidewalk café folded chairs and dragged tables inside. Cyclists chained up their bikes and mothers huddled children safely into doorways. Everybody seemed to have someplace to go.

She'd never felt so alone, so helpless. Maybe she did need Fletcher to take care of her. She obviously wasn't capable of managing alone.

Something wet and furry rubbed against her ankles. Megan looked down. A small dog, probably part Yorkshire terrier, was using her legs for a towel. She bent down and patted its damp coat. "Poor thing, are you lost too?"

The puppy sniffed her sandals, then stared soulfully into her eyes. Megan wished she had crackers or cookie crumbs to feed the mangy mutt, but if there'd been any food in this backpack at all, she would have eaten it herself by now.

She reached under the dog's shaggy coat and found a collar, with a name tag attached, just as a voice rang out halfway up the block. "*Henri! Viens ici!*"

The terrier gave Megan a poignant parting look, and then trooped obediently after his mistress.

An odd sense of loss enveloped her. Even the scruffy dog had someone come for him, while she could disappear in this city for days without anyone knowing where she was. If she couldn't contact her family, how could they help her?

What was the closest thing to family away from home? The American Embassy. They'd replace her stolen passport, help her find a way to call home and get money for a hotel. Megan's heart lightened. She unfolded the map and raised her eyes to the sky. In the dark clouds overhead, a patch of light glimmered.

Holding her coat above her head, she crossed the Place de la a Concorde and headed toward the Champs-Elysees. Her wet leather sandals slapped against the pavement as she skirted around beautiful fountains and a few hardy tourists.

By the time she reached Avenue Gabriel, her feet were pads of ice and her stomach cramped in hunger. But those were the least of her worries. At the wide sidewalk in front of the embassy, Megan stopped dead. She'd expected to see a sentry or two at the entrance. But the wrought iron gates were shut and cordoned off. A line of armed soldiers guarded the perimeter.

"Is it closed?" she asked a somber-faced marine at the entrance. "What's going on?"

His facial muscles barely moved. "A precaution because of the terrorist attack."

"Terrorist attack?" She glanced about wildly, half expecting gun-wielding radicals to rush at her and mow her down.

"A bomb at the British Embassy," the marine explained, his eyes focusing somewhere over her head. "We're on high alert until further notice."

Until further notice? What did that mean? Megan's heart sunk. "Please, this is an emergency. My passport and wallet were stolen, and my ticket home."

"I'm sorry, ma'am. But nothing can be done today. You can make an appointment online."

"But I don't have a computer. I don't even have a cell phone."

No response.

She tried again. "Please help me. I know no one in Paris. I have nowhere to go, no place to stay."

The marine finally looked at her. "I'm sorry, ma'am. Truly. But there's nothing I can do. Have you tried the police?"

"I--never mind." There was no use in explaining about the gun.

She'd almost managed to forget she had it. Almost.

She shouldered the backpack again, the gun weighing even heavier at her side. Weary and hungry, Megan shuffled dejectedly back toward the Place de la Concorde under a dark cloud that had no silver lining.

"Colette!"

She turned to look behind her. A man sprinted toward her, gesturing wildly. Megan moved aside to let him pass, but he veered intentionally into her path. His six-foot, football player frame skidded to a stop and almost collided with her body in a full frontal assault. Brawny arms encircled her in a bear hug.

"Colette, thank God you're safe," the man said to the top of her head. "Where in the bloody hell have you been?"

Chapter Three

Wriggling in his arms, Colette twisted out of Paul's embrace. "Let me go. I'm not Colette. My name--"

"Save it, love, we need to talk." Releasing his grip, Paul stared into eyes that didn't look at all relieved to see him. They looked terrified. "I've been ringing you all day. Did you lose your phone?"

She startled. "Yes. How did you know?" She narrowed her eyes at him. "Who are you?"

"Colette, this is serious. Have you not heard that the embassy was bombed?" He drew her closer and ran his fingers through the long strands of a wig he didn't remember seeing before. He didn't remember her wearing that trench coat before either. But it looked well-worn and one of the brown leather buttons was blatantly missing.

"Stop!" She shook off his hand. "You've mistaken me for someone else. My name is Megan--"

"Please, enough." He grasped both her hands. "And you can drop the American accent." He winked. "Tonight, if you like, we can play the wanton American and the stuffy Brit."

Instead of returning his wink, or grabbing his ass as she normally would, she dug her nails into his palms. "Let. Me. Go."

Heavy footsteps sounded in the direction from which he'd come. Paul whirled to see two men in suits striding across the pavement toward them. They glanced at Colette, narrowed their eyes, and broke into a run.

"Shit." He grabbed Colette's arm, and, despite her protests, led her toward the curb. Plainclothes detectives, he'd wager, assigned to follow him in the hope he'd lead them to Colette.

Which he had.

The detectives called out to him to stop. Paul's ingrained sense of duty warred with his desire to protect his lady. Chivalry won. He hailed an approaching taxi, and let out a groan of relief as it skidded to a stop. "Get in," he directed Colette.

"Are you crazy?" Again she tried to shake him off. "I'm not going anywhere with you."

"Do you see those stiffs running toward us?" He opened the back door of the cab and tried to nudge her in. She struggled, kicking him in the shins and poking her fingernail into his neck. "Dammit, Colette, get in." He grabbed her by the waist, tossed her onto the seat, and scrambled in beside her.

"*Allons-y. Vite*," he yelled at the driver, and the cab shifted into gear and took off just as the two Bobbies approached and banged on the door. Paul instructed the cabbie to cross the river at the next bridge. In the late afternoon traffic, perhaps they could lose their trackers before they were able to get to their vehicles.

When the driver slowed for a red light, Colette yanked on the opposite door and tried to alight into traffic. "Stop here," she yelled to the driver. "I'm getting out."

"No! *Continuez*." Paul countermanded.

He grabbed Colette, pulled her close and held her arms to her sides so she couldn't escape. "Listen to me. Those men we saw?" he whispered in her captive ear. "They're Interpol police." He tightened his grip. "And they think *you* bombed the British Embassy."

She stopped fighting him. Her eyes took on a blank glaze, and then hardened into stone. "Mister, I don't know who you are. And I don't know who you think I am. But I am not this Colette. And I certainly didn't bomb any embassy. My name is Megan Chandler. I'm an American."

She almost had him going for a minute. And then it all clicked. The wig. The accent. He'd been so focused on the upheaval in his own life he'd totally forgotten about her big audition. "You got the part!" he exulted. "Congratulations, love." He tipped her chin up and kissed her, imprinting his mouth on hers, his tongue savoring the sweet taste of her lips.

She didn't resist him, but she didn't kiss back, either. Typically she would have plunged her tongue down his throat halfway to his stomach. Paul pulled away. Her eyes brimmed as if she were about to cry. Maybe she'd finally comprehended the gravity of her situation.

He studied her face. In that wig, she looked alarmingly like the woman in that security photo. A chill passed through his lungs. He tugged at the hairpiece, but Colette yelped and batted his hand away.

"Where are we going?" Fear tinged her voice.

Where indeed? Paul hadn't thought that far ahead. "We need a lawyer," he decided, his mind racing faster than the taxi. Usually he'd rely on the embassy in a legal situation. But this was no ordinary situation. Colette was an alleged criminal, and if Paul hadn't been considered an accessory before, whisking her away from the authorities had made him one.

"Your friend Jacques, the gay actor," he said to Colette. "Isn't his partner an attorney? Solicitor or barrister?"

She glared at him for a full minute before speaking. "I don't know any Jacques. Because I am not Colette."

Blimey, she was going to be no help at all.

* * *

The man was either blind or crazy. And he was definitely not blind. Those piercing brown eyes seemed to notice everything, except, of course, the fact that Megan was not his girlfriend Colette.

Which left crazy. Why else would he stubbornly refuse to believe her? Maybe his girlfriend--he wore no ring so she probably wasn't his wife--looked somewhat like her, but Colette would have to be Megan's identical twin for him to be this confused. And she didn't have a twin, identical or otherwise.

The painting. Megan's stomach muscles tightened. That museum portrait had looked exactly like her. What if the portrait was a trick mirror of some sort? And after looking into it, every other woman appeared to look exactly like Megan? She looked uneasily at the solemn man at her elbow, guiding her toward a three-story, century-old apartment house. Maybe *he* wasn't the crazy one here.

Why was she here at all? When the cab had let them out, her captor hadn't grabbed her or prevented her from running. She could have walked away, chalking this up to a misunderstanding, never to see the nameless, hard-faced Brit again.

But it was getting dark outside. And Megan had no place to go. And so far the man hadn't killed her. All of which were pretty poor reasons for humoring him. But whether it was some magical influence of the painting, or the chemical effect of whatever she'd been drugged with, Megan's brain seemed to be functioning well below normal. And despite his physical strength and hard-headedness, her gut sensed that this man posed no threat to her.

Of course, her gut had been wrong before.

At the second floor, the man rapped on a door knocker. An eye appeared at the peephole, and the door flung wide open.

"*Ma Cherie*! "A lean man of medium height embraced Megan and kissed her on both cheeks, nearly knocking the backpack off her shoulders. He spoke rapidly and animatedly in French. She roughly translated his remarks as inquiring after her welfare, and demanding to know why she hadn't shown up somewhere.

My god, did he think she was this Colette woman too? Or had she fallen into some Wonderland rabbit hole, where nothing was what it seemed? Or were the two of them playing some sick joke on her? "Look, I don't know what kind of game you're playing, but I'm not--"

"You missed the audition?" The big British man cut her off as if she hadn't spoken.

The Frenchman ignored her as well. "It was such a perfect part for her, Paul," he said in English, with expansive gestures. "Now it will probably go to that melodramatic bimbo who's sleeping with the director and can't remember to smile without a cue card."

Paul. So that was the British man's name. It fit him somehow, though Megan wasn't sure why since she knew nothing about him except that he was overbearing and obstinate. And a damned good kisser.

The lean man invited them inside, motioning to a flame red sofa in an otherwise traditional drawing room. A stone fireplace dominated one wall of the room, and a spinet piano sat opposite the sofa. An intricate Oriental rug accented the polished hardwood floor.

Megan paused in front of the sofa before shrugging out of her backpack and trench coat and sitting at one end. She placed the black backpack next to the arm of the sofa.

"Love your shirt," Jacques exclaimed, admiring the rhinestone pattern of a cat against a red background. "Did you get it at La Boutique?"

"No, at Macy's, in the Princeton mall," Megan answered but he paid no attention to her answer.

Paul stood hesitantly, then perched at the other end of the sofa. "Sorry to disturb you, Jacques, but we need the advice of an attorney."

Jacques lifted a brow, but didn't question him. "Marcel's only just arrived home, he'll be out in a minute. Can I get you a soda or a glass of wine?"

Against her better judgment, Megan accepted the glass of red wine. She should be trying to keep her wits sharp, but her nerves were frayed to the edge. She'd just drink a tiny bit to calm them.

Jacques darted into the bedroom, then to the kitchen. He set a tray of crackers in front of her next to her wine. "You're looking well, Colette."

She was almost too tired to continue protesting. "Excuse me, but I'm not--"

"You look like you've gained a few pounds since I last saw you." Jacques winked at Paul. "Something you're not telling me? Have you managed to get our Colette pregnant?"

Megan wouldn't have thought Paul could blush, but he did, a beet red that made him look refreshingly vulnerable. "No, I...at least I'm quite sure..." He turned to look at Megan, really scrutinizing her, from her stomach to her face and back down, slowly over her body. His hard eyes filled, for the first time, with questions.

"Bon soir, mes amis." An attractive, dark haired man, taller than Jacques but not as large as Paul, appeared from the hallway that

apparently led to the bedrooms—or bedroom. Wearing jeans and a tight-fitting polo shirt, sporting a dark goatee, Marcel looked very masculine, but in a gay sort of way. When he made eye contact with the more effeminate-featured Jacques, Megan could see their affection for one another.

Her gaze drifted to Paul. Definitely straight. A hulk of a man, he had to weigh north of two hundred pounds, but there was not an ounce of fat on him. Were she to use him as a model for a portrait, Megan would paint him as a noble Roman warrior, his bearing strong, his stance solid, with thick dark chest hair peeking out of his armored breast plate. Tanned, tree-trunk thighs rooted in the earth. If she *were* Colette...

Paul cleared his throat. Megan swallowed, fearing he'd caught her imagining him half-naked, but his gaze was directed at the man who'd just entered.

The other man spoke first. "Paul! Thank goodness you're all right. I heard about the bombing at your embassy. Terrible, terrible."

Jacques's eyes flew wide open. "Oh my God, I didn't hear. What happened?"

Paul seemed to struggle for composure. "The bomb exploded in the data center where I work--worked. All of the other programmers were killed."

Megan gasped. No wonder Paul was so somber--and paranoid.

He moved close to Megan, his eyes moist. "You saved my life, love. If you and I hadn't...this morning..." He lifted her into his arms, his grip strong, but achingly gentle.

Megan started to push away, then changed her mind. Despite his tough facade, the man was hurting. And possibly just as scared as she was. Without direction from her brain, her arms slid around him and caressed his sturdy back. The scent of manly French cologne--

what else?--permeated her air. His body was warm against hers, reassuring. The embrace seemed so natural she forgot for a moment where she was.

Paul pulled away first. He resumed his place on the opposite end of the sofa. "Marcel, we need your legal help."

Marcel sat in the brocaded wing chair. "So Jacques tells me. What's the problem?"

Paul pressed his hands together and cracked his knuckles. "The person who entered the embassy minutes before the explosion used a stolen security badge. Mine."

Megan blinked. Jacques gasped. Marcel stared without expression at Paul, apparently used to strange confessions.

"It gets worse." Paul bit down on his lower lip. "They showed me a download from the security camera at the point of entry. The woman in the photo looked amazingly like Colette."

Jacques gasped. Marcel narrowed his eyes at Megan.

She took a breath. "Paul." She reached out her hand to him. "I'm so sorry for what you've been through. I can only imagine how upset you must be. But, please. Look at me." She stood, turning to Marcel and Jacques for support. "I'm not Colette."

Marcel and Jacques exchanged glances, then eyed her suspiciously. And why shouldn't they? If the man who'd presumably been intimate with Colette had confused Megan with her, why wouldn't these casual friends?

"My name is Megan," she said firmly. "I'm an American tourist stranded in Paris." She glared at Paul. "Why do you—why does everybody—think I'm Colette?"

Silence. Had she turned mute and invisible again? Slowly Paul took a cell phone out of the pocket of his long-sleeved, pinstriped shirt. He powered it on, touched a few icons, and handed it to her.

She stared at her own image. "When did you take this? While we were in the cab?" But the woman in the photo wasn't wearing the tee shirt Megan wore today. She wore a low cut black tank top that nearly exposed her petite breasts. And her hair was short and wavy.

Oh. My. God. She glanced at Paul, who eyed her with silent indulgence. Megan swallowed. "Is this...Colette?" she croaked.

No one answered. Three anxious faces stared at her as if she were a mental patient who'd gone off her meds. Swiftly Megan scrolled through Paul's other photos, her jaw dropping lower at each picture of a sexier version of herself. Colette on a park bench near a pond, throwing bread crumbs to the ducks. Colette wearing a beret and a skirt with less material than the hat, striking a sultry pose at the Arc de Triomphe. Colette dancing in a bedroom--Paul's?--wearing a diaphanous shawl and nothing else.

"I'm not crazy!" she shrieked. "I'm not Colette." Had that drug she'd inhaled driven her mad? Or had Megan Chandler ceased to exist and become someone else in another world?

Paul stood, his dark eyes hard. "Take off that wig."

"It's not a wig. Ouch!" She grimaced as his heavy hand yanked her hair. "I am not losing my mind." She reconsidered. "Well, maybe I am losing my mind, but I am not and have never been Colette. You have to believe me." She looked hopefully at Paul.

He grabbed her wrists and hoisted her to her feet as if she were a feather. "There's one way to prove it."

He dragged her to a door off the foyer, and then shoved her inside the small half bathroom. He locked the door behind him. "Take off your shirt," he demanded.

"I will not." She struggled to free herself from his grasp. "Take your hands off me."

He complied with her request, but backed her up against the door, propping his knee between her legs, his arms at her sides. His breath heated the neck of her shirt. "Are you going to take it off or shall I?"

Surely he wasn't planning to...have his way with her here in this cramped bathroom within earshot of Jacques and Marcel. "Help!" she screamed, but no help came.

"Shirt," he said dispassionately. "Off." He backed up an inch, allowing her room to move her arms, but kept his knee nudged into her groin.

"Please don't hurt me," she whimpered. Why she had ever felt safe with this man? How had she naively imagined two gay guys would protect her? Her fingers quivered as she touched them to the edges of her shirt, and slowly lifted the hem to expose her white cotton bra. Fortunately, it was full coverage.

Maybe not so fortunately. Paul yanked the shirt out of her fingers and over her head. "Bra," he said.

She swallowed. Praying that her nipples hadn't stiffened from fear, she reached behind her and unhooked the clasp. The bra slipped off her shoulders and fell to the floor.

Paul stared as if he'd never seen breasts before. "Where's the dragonfly?" he bellowed. "What happened to it?"

Dragonfly?

"There's not even a scar." His voice wavered. "You couldn't have had it removed that quickly."

A tattoo. He must be looking for a tattoo. Which she didn't

38

have. And Colette apparently did. Megan let out half of a shaky breath. "I've never had a tattoo," she said deliberately when his gaze finally lifted to her face. "Do you believe me now?"

His cheeks drained of color. He looked too shocked to speak.

A rap on the door, followed by Jacques' voice. "Is everything all right in there?"

Paul unlocked the door. Megan grabbed her shirt and threw it over her head, bunching the bra in her fist. Preceding him out, she strode to the sofa, unzipped her backpack, and dropped the bra inside.

She turned to see Paul facing the two curious men, his face white, his chest heaving. "She's not Colette," he said.

Megan took a slow, deep breath, filling her lungs with joy and relief. Marcel and Jacques would take their cue from Paul and hopefully, help her get home.

Paul eyed her warily. "Who are you?" he said in a voice that could cut steel.

Not the reaction she'd expected. She began her story again. "My name is Megan. I--"

"Megan Marchand? Colette's evil twin?"

Breathe calmly. Speak slowly. "Megan Chandler. I don't have a twin. I'm American. I was in the museum and--"

"Where's Colette? What have you done with her?"

What? "I don't know where she is. I've never met the woman."

"Then how did you get my security card?" Hot rage filled his cheeks but his tone was cold and deliberate.

39

Was the man out of his mind? "I don't have your security card. Why would I want--oh." Megan drew in a quick breath. If anyone could gain access to his security card, it had to be his live-in girlfriend. "Oh my God." Her lips quivered. "Colette really did bomb the embassy." She looked to Paul's face but reality hadn't grazed it. "I mean, isn't that what you think?"

"No." His barely contained wrath exploded. "I think you did."

The bottom dropped out of Megan's stomach and plummeted to the floor.

"Colette has short hair." Paul paused dramatically. "The woman in the embassy security photo had long hair." He glanced at Jacques and Marcel for their reaction, and then glared needles at Megan. "As. Do. You."

"And that makes me a terrorist?" Megan's cheeks flushed with indignation. Was there no fairness, no justice in this world? "Using your logic, you might be Jack the Ripper."

He lifted a brow. "How's that?"

"The Ripper was British and had a penis. *You're* British and *you* have--"

"Thanks for noticing. However, I'm alive and he's dead. Two out of three." Paul grabbed her arm and twisted it behind her back. "Marcel! Get her other arm," he directed. "Jacques! Call the police."

Megan whirled to avoid Marcel's grasp, struggling to free her arm from Paul's viselike grip. The adrenaline of desperation gave her strength she hadn't thought she'd possessed. With one painful twist, she wrenched her wrist out of Paul's grip, reached into the backpack and pulled out the gun.

"Stop! Nobody move." Breathing erratically, Megan pointed the weapon at Paul's chest.

Chapter Four

Shit! Paul stared down the barrel of a nine millimeter Glock. Why hadn't he anticipated this?

She's a damn terrorist, Bernard. Of course she would have a gun. Acting confused and misunderstood, the woman had played him for a fool. Colette couldn't have done a better job herself.

If they weren't twins, they were cloned copies.

He glanced at Jacques and Marcel, seated beside him on the sofa as the woman had directed. They were both ashen-faced. Another wave of guilt besieged him for having gotten them involved in this.

As if the pistol were too heavy for her, the woman supported her right arm with her left hand. "You are going to sit quietly," she said, "and you are going to listen to me." The gun wavered in her hand and her voice shook with unshed tears.

"My name is Megan Adele Chandler," she said, panning the weapon slowly over each of them. "I'm an American. I live in New Jersey. I'm working on my Master's degree in Fine Arts and I teach freshman art at Princeton University." The gun dipped and danced in her hand.

Paul took a breath. "Could we fast forward through your unhappy childhood and get to the part about where you bombed the

41

British embassy?"

Marcel and Jacques gasped, darting frightened looks at him. *She's not going to shoot you,* he wanted to assure them. *She doesn't even know the proper way to hold a gun.* In fact, she seemed almost afraid of her weapon. Not that he'd stake his life on that. Inexperienced shooters could be far more dangerous than those who knew what they were doing.

"I didn't bomb your embassy," she said, her voice only slightly steadier than her gun hand. "I'm an artist, not a terrorist. A Facebook friend who lives in Paris recommended this tour of Europe's great art museums, so I signed up. Paris was our last stop, and I was supposed to meet Nicole today at the Musee' D'Orsay just before my group was due to fly home."

Paul listened with half an ear, watching her eyes and her hands. And her body. Now that he actually looked at her, he wondered why he hadn't realized straight off that she wasn't Colette. Megan was probably twenty pounds heavier, and the calories had taken residence in all the right places. Colette had a great figure— small waist, pert little breasts—but Megan was rounder, fuller, and he'd bet, softer. Not that he intended to find out. Even if she turned out to be innocent, this woman was trouble.

As if she'd read his lecherous mind, she steadied the Glock and pointed it inches above his family jewels. "While I was waiting for Nicole, I saw this painting." Her voice quavered. "And everything changed after that."

"What painting?" Paul asked, hoping to rattle her. The memory of what she'd seen seemed to frighten her, and he intended to take advantage of that.

"A portrait of a nineteenth century woman who looked exactly like me," she said ominously. "It was called Mademoiselle Adele Jarreau."

"Mon Dieu!" Jacques gasped.

She turned to him. "You know the painting?"

"*Bien sur*, you and I--I mean, Colette and I--saw it when we visited that museum last March. We both marveled at how much the woman looked like her." He gulped. "And like you, I suppose."

"Maybe you're both descended from that woman," Marcel said. "Do you come from French ancestry?"

"Yes, on my mother's side. My maternal grandmother was a French war bride."

What was going on here? Were these two buying her story? Jacques and Marcel seemed utterly entranced by this wily woman. Completely forgetting she had murdered four people.

Possibly five. As yet he'd received no text from Colette.

Megan—if that was really her name--backed toward the piano. When her knees hit the bench, she sat, then lowered the gun and laid it across her lap.

"My friend said she'd be wearing a yellow scarf," she continued. Fingers clenched, she went on to fabricate an entire story about following a woman down a rabbit hole, being drugged and knocked out in a bathroom, her watch stolen. A pretty good yarn if she were making it up on the spot. More likely, she'd been given this cover by her terrorist friends and rehearsed it to present in the event of capture.

Of course, there was a third option: that she was telling the truth. But that would mean Colette had bombed the embassy and murdered his friends. And Paul would need rock solid proof, not fairy tales, before he'd believe that.

"And then, in the cab to the airport, I found out somebody had switched out my backpack and stolen my passport, ticket, phone, and credit cards. And money," the woman added.

Jacques looked horrified. "Do you think it was your friend?" he asked.

"I don't know. I didn't see her face. And even if I had..." She hesitated.

Paul took a guess. "Do you even know what Nicole looks like?"

"No." She'd been playing to Jacques and Marcel, but now she turned her attention back to him. "I--she didn't post a profile picture."

Whoa. Paul's scam radar tingled. "This friend Nicole--she set you up on this tour?"

Her eyes narrowed. "No, I arranged it myself."

"But you sent her a copy of your itinerary."

She nodded, completely clueless. Or perhaps trying to appear so. Megan was either the victim of a clever con or its perpetrator.

He studied her eyes, trying to determine which. "Let me get this straight. You made a trip across the ocean on the recommendation of a woman you never met and hadn't even seen a picture of." His heart raced in his chest. This story had more holes than Swiss cheese. Nicole could be pure fiction. The only thing real about Megan Chandler was that gun.

Megan glared at him. "You sound just like Fletcher."

"Who's Fletcher?"

"My boyfriend. He always tells me I'm too naïve and trusting."

Paul snickered. "Excuse me if I don't believe you."

Her cobalt blue eyes flashed. "I do so have a boyfriend. I may not be as sexy as your hot French sweetie, but--"

"I believe you have a boyfriend." Why wouldn't she, she was quite attractive in a girl-next-door-way. Although 'Fletcher' was probably another fictitious name; more likely it was Abdul or Mohammed. "However, I'm a bit skeptical on the 'naïve and trusting' part. That's what you'd like us to think, because you want us to trust *you*. But your story doesn't hold water."

"It's the truth," she insisted. She steadied the gun with both hands and aimed it at him once again.

"I'm a particular fan of the truth," he said, ignoring the anxious flutter that had returned to his heart, his liver, and parts south. He pushed forward to the edge of his seat. "Where did you get the gun?"

"It was in the backpack."

"Nicole's backpack."

"I guess." Her face scrunched up as if it took all her strength to hold the weapon. Megan crossed her legs and braced it against her knee, still holding it with both hands.

"What else was in the backpack?"

"Not much. Lipstick, nail polish, a magazine. No money or ID." Her chest heaved out and her breathing turned erratic.

"Does Nicole work for The Community?"

"What community?"

"Do you?"

"I don't know what you're talking about." She took her right

45

hand off the gun and shook out her fingers. Paul calculated how long it would take him to leap off the sofa and wrest it from her hands.

About a half second longer than it would take her to shoot him. "Then why were you hanging around the British embassy?"

"I was at the *American* embassy." She leaped to her feet. "Trying to get a new passport." Tears appeared in her eyes.

Dammit, not the waterworks. A crying woman could soften Paul's brain faster than a naked woman. Colette never cried. Nor had Allison, except one time. When she'd told him she couldn't marry him.

"I didn't know what else to do." Megan's lip quivered. "I tried to call my parents but I don't know their new number. All my contacts are in my cell phone. I can't reach my brother or my friends and I have no money or any place to go and I don't know anyone else in Paris except Nicole and --"

Gasping for breath, she touched her throat. The gun wavered. Paul's eyes followed it as her aim swerved wildly, from the floor lamp to the windows, to the bright gold and blue carpet. Megan grabbed the gun with both hands again, but with her hair hanging in her face and eyes filling with tears she looked more like a lifeless rag doll than a terrorist. "I just want to go home."

Paul swallowed his breath and stood. "Megan." He took a step toward her.

"Stay where you are." She refocused her aim, blinking back her tears.

Praying silently for courage, he moved close enough to touch her. "Please. Give me the gun."

"No," she whispered. But her hand shook. Barely breathing, keeping every other part of his body still, Paul reached out, placed one hand over hers, pointed the weapon down, and gently tugged it from her grasp.

Her knees buckled. Her body went limp. Paul caught her just as she collapsed and fell forward, to his surprise, into his arms.

* * *

After two delicious helpings of Jacques' fortifying vegetarian stew, Megan almost felt like herself again. The two gay men had been quite solicitous, almost nurturing, after she'd fainted. Marcel had even let her use his computer to look up her parents' phone number. But it was Paul she sensed she needed to persuade, and despite the strength and comfort he'd provided when she'd humiliated herself by collapsing in his arms, he still seemed dead set against believing anything she said.

She couldn't entirely blame him. If he believed in her innocence, then he had to believe his girlfriend Colette was guilty. And Paul was nowhere near ready to accept that.

Megan cleared her throat. "May I use somebody's phone to call the States? My parents will be expecting me to arrive home tonight. I promise I'll pay you for the call as soon as they wire me some money." She looked hopefully at Marcel, but he excused himself, saying he had to call a client, and carried his phone out of the room. Jacques, who was loading plates into the dishwasher, appeared not to have heard her. To Megan's surprise, it was Paul who volunteered his phone.

"Thanks." She took the phone from his hand. Dad was probably not home from work yet. Summoning positive energy, she punched in the international code, then the ten-digit number, and waited for her mother to pick up. The phone rang four times and then went to voice mail. Even as a recording, the sound of her mother's voice almost made her cry.

What message to leave? Megan cleared her throat. "Hi, Mom, it's me. I don't want you to worry, but my bag was stolen with my passport and money and cell phone and credit cards and I missed my flight. I'm okay," she said, trying for a reassuring tone. "But I'll need you to wire some money to--" Damn. She didn't know the address of the American Embassy. Her parents could probably look it up, but she'd also need some documentation for a new passport, and she wouldn't know exactly what until she visited the Embassy in the morning. "I'll call you back tomorrow and tell you where to send the money. Tonight, you can reach me at this number."

She handed back Paul's phone. "Thanks. I will pay you back. I'm sorry about leaving your phone number, but I didn't know any other way--"

"No problem," he said. "Unless you've just put my number on a terrorist's speed dial."

She narrowed her eyes, trying to decide if was joking. His face was expressionless, but his dark brown eyes twinkled. It made Megan wonder what he'd look like wearing an actual smile.

"Have you tried calling your own cell phone?" he asked. "Maybe someone found it."

More likely it had been tossed into the Seine, but Megan dutifully took the phone again and tried her number. It went immediately to voice mail. "Dead or turned off," she said. She handed Paul's phone back again.

"Damn," he said, staring at the display. "Battery's low." He switched it off.

"The news is on." Jacques turned up the volume on the television. With a video of the burning British embassy in the background, the announcer gave the hourly update. Megan stole a look at Paul as photos of three of the victims flashed on the screen.

His colleagues, no doubt. Again, his face didn't change expression, but his eyes filled with grief.

The fourth victim was the security guard at the point of entry. He'd been shot. Megan glanced at the gun Paul had placed on the mantel. Could it be the murder weapon?

According to the newscaster, the international police were pursuing all leads and arrest of the suspect or suspects was imminent. But there was no mention of ballistics. Nor the security photo Paul had mentioned of the woman who supposedly looked like her. The authorities must not yet have Colette in custody. Then where was she? And why hadn't she answered Paul's calls?

"Any luck phoning home?" Marcel asked, returning to the room."

Megan shook her head.

"Quelle dommage. Is there anyone else you can call for help?"

"My brother, but I don't know his cell phone number by heart. It was in my phone."

"Boyfriend?"

"Ditto."

"What about your French relatives?" Paul asked.

"I wish," she replied. "The rest of my grandmother's family died in World War II." What wouldn't she give to be able to meet someone from the French side of her family?

"What about that friend you were supposed to meet at the museum?" Jacques suggested. "If she *wasn't* the person who drugged you, she'll be worried that she didn't connect with you. Maybe you can stay with her until you get your passport reissued."

"Nicole's number is in my phone too." Megan brightened. "But I met her on Facebook. Maybe I can contact her that way."

She logged into Facebook and danced her thumbs over the keys. "That's odd."

"What is?" Marcel asked.

"I can't access her page. She must have un-friended me." A lump formed in Megan's stomach. "We emailed each other just this morning."

"Let me try." Paul logged into his Facebook account and searched for friends. But he found no one named Nicole Reneau.

Had Nicole deleted her profile? "It's as if she disappeared off the face of the earth," Megan said bleakly.

"Or she never existed," Paul said dryly. "Do you have any friends in common? Has anyone else ever heard of her?"

"You think I made her up?" Like a stubborn child with his fingers in his ears, Paul seemed determined to challenge everything she said. "I notice they didn't show that security photo on the news. You're the only one who claims to have seen it. You could have made that up."

"To what purpose?" His cynical brown eyes glared.

"To throw suspicion off yourself." She met his glare with one of her own. "*Your* security card was used to enter the embassy. Why did the authorities just let you go?"

Paul hesitated before answering. "I'd thought at first it was due to lack of evidence." He sighed. "But apparently they hoped I'd lead them to the woman suspect."

"Which you did," Marcel inserted. "Which brings us back to

the reason you are here. You two are wanted fugitives." He flexed his hands behind his neck. "You came to me for help. But there's nothing I can do for you legally unless you turn yourselves in."

"Turn myself in for what?" Megan wailed. "I haven't done anything."

"Nor have I." Paul raked his fingers through his dark hair. "Look, I'm sorry I got you two chaps involved." He stood. "I should leave."

"What about me?" Megan asked.

Paul glanced at her and then at the gun that still lay on the mantel. Did he plan to grab it and turn on her? Should she lunge for it first?

"It's probably not safe for you to go home," Marcel said to Paul. "The authorities may be waiting for you there. Can I drive you to the train station? Perhaps you both should leave the country."

"I have no passport," Paul and Megan said in unison.

"Besides," Paul added, "the police have probably set up roadblocks, and guards at the train stations and airports."

"Let's sort this out in the morning," Marcel said. "I'll go with you to Interpol and make your case. Tonight, you'll stay here. We only have one guest room, but..."

"I'll take the sofa," Paul volunteered.

Megan shot him a silent *thank you*. At least he was that much of a gentleman.

"I'll get linens for the sofa," Jacques said. "Megan, I'll show you to your room."

She started to follow Jacques, then backtracked toward the

sofa. In the distance she heard a raucous, repetitive sound. "What was that?"

"What was what?" Marcel fingered his sparse mustache.

"Sounds like sirens. Ambulance or fire--or police." The knot in her stomach bunched harder.

"Don't worry, *ma Cherie*." Jacques returned with an armful of sheets and a blanket. "We live off a main boulevard. We hear them all the time."

The old, go-along-to-get-along Megan would have been placated. But the new, on-her-own Megan was more suspicious. The chilling sounds didn't fade away. Whatever it was, was heading in this direction.

She walked to the window. "Look!"

Three marked police cars pulled up directly in front of the apartment building and six uniformed policemen got out.

Chapter Five

Paul wedged his body into a dark, narrow space between two dryers, squinting as his eyes became adjusted to the dark. Hiding in the laundry room had been Marcel's idea, until the police finished their rounds of the building.

He tugged at Megan's waist. "Here," he whispered.

Megan slipped beside him and kicked him in the shin. "You called them, didn't you? You phoned the police."

"Ow!" He edged back, cramming his shoulders between the wall and the whirring dryer. "How could I? I was with you the whole time."

"You could have called when you went to the bathroom."

"But I didn't."

Not that he hadn't considered it. He was so ruing the moment he'd grabbed Megan and hauled her into that taxi. Before that, he'd merely been a person of interest to the authorities. After his uncharacteristically impulsive act, he'd become an accomplice. "Why would I call the police? I might point out that they're looking for me too."

"Only because of your connection to Colette." She inched closer to him, trapping him between the scents of fabric softener and strawberry shampoo "You still think she's innocent, don't you? You still don't believe me."

Beyond the closed laundry room door, he heard heavy footsteps pounding the apartment stairs. "Quiet." He crouched low so his head could not be seen. "Get down."

She scooted in closer and squatted. "Well, this is uncomfortable."

"How do you think I feel?" His knees and chin fought for the same space. He waited until the sound of footsteps faded away, then spoke in a whisper. "Megan, I've known Colette six months. I've known you barely six hours. You seem to be a nice person, but..."

"If I were a terrorist," Megan persisted, "why wouldn't I be with my friends now? Why wouldn't I have left the country?"

"Maybe that was your plan until I apprehended you."

"Right. You 'apprehended me.' You manhandled me and threw me in a cab thinking I was Colette. No wonder she hasn't called you back."

He winced. "I didn't manhandle you. I was trying to protect you from being arrested and you weren't complying. How was I to know you weren't Colette?"

Her words stung. He'd never hurt Colette. He treasured her. Every man he knew envied him, but deep down he'd always wondered why she'd chosen him, when she could have charmed any other man as easily. Handsomer men, richer men, more exciting men. What did Paul have that others didn't?

Access to the British embassy.

A vise squeezed his chest. Could he have been that stupid? There had to be another explanation. "If you're not a terrorist, why did you hold a gun on me and threaten to kill all of us?"

"I just wanted to make you listen to me!"

"Shhh." Paul cupped his hand over her mouth. A door rattled. Apparently locked. There'd been no lock on the entry door so there must be another exit, perhaps to a back alley.

They waited silently, breathless, until the rattling stopped. When he released her mouth, Megan let out a gasp. "Do you think they've left?"

"Maybe. But stay quiet."

She pushed against the dryer and raised herself to her feet, keeping her head bowed. Paul thought his knees were going to crack but he held his position, trying to ignore the fact that his face was right next to, and on the same level as, Megan's breasts.

Moments later a flash of light lit the laundry room like a thousand candles. Megan ducked back down. Footsteps sounded at the entrance. One step, two steps, each closer to the crevice in which they hid. Megan gripped his thighs with both hands, as if stifling a scream.

And then the steps backtracked. The light switched off. Once again the room was dark, silent except for the whooshing of a washing machine and the whirring sounds of a dryer.

Paul waited one more painful minute and then drew himself up to his full height. Megan disengaged her fingers from his khaki pants. "Do you think they saw us?" she whispered.

"If they had, we wouldn't be having this conversation." Paul nudged her slightly, and Megan edged out of the cramped quarters into the relative openness of the aisle between the washers and dryers. She straightened her tee shirt which had ridden up to reveal her navel. "Should we go back up or wait for Marcel to come get us?"

"Neither." Paul stepped out of the hiding place. "We should get the hell out of here."

"But Marcel--"

"--is probably the person who called the police. Did you notice he left the room for a long time and seemed a little embarrassed when he came back?" He strode to the back door and fiddled with the rusted hasp on the door until he was able to push it open. "Let's go."

"Wait." Megan tugged open a dryer door and pawed through the hot clothes. "If Marcel called the police, he also gave them our descriptions. We should change clothes."

He looked at his nondescript, tan windbreaker. "Marcel wouldn't have noticed what we wore."

"But Jacques would." She pulled out a jean jacket. "Try this on."

Grumbling under his breath, not wanting to give her credit for forethought, he shrugged off the windbreaker and forced his arms into the tight sleeves. "This is about four sizes too small."

"Sorry, sir. Shall I check the other dryers for something your size?" Sarcasm dripped from her lips. "Perhaps a more tailored jacket? Gray? Blue? Black?" She eyed the entry light switch.

"Forget it." Reaching into his windbreaker, he transferred the bottles of stage makeup and disguises he'd pilfered from Jacques and Marcel's bedroom to the smaller pockets of the jean jacket.

Megan's eyes widened. "What's that?"

"Something I thought we might need." He tossed his

windbreaker to the floor and helped Megan out of her trench coat. "You'd better lose that Rudolph the Reindeer blouse."

She tunneled through the dryer again, scooping out golf shirts and tee shirts, but everything seemed to belong to an adolescent male.

Paul grabbed a plain blue-gray tee shirt. "Just put this on. Fashion can wait another day."

She fingered the hem of her own shirt. "Um... My bra is in the backpack. Please turn around."

He chuckled. "It's dark in here. Besides I've already seen what you've got."

"For ten seconds!" she protested.

"I have a photographic memory," he quipped, but he turned his back to let her change. "Now ditch the coat. Does our clothing donor have one of those hooded sweatshirts?"

"I have one here." She dug into her backpack. "Courtesy of whoever left me the gun." She donned the sweatshirt, which fit almost perfectly.

"Let's go."

He grabbed her arm but she insisted on stuffing her coat and shirt, and his jacket, in an empty dryer at the end of the row. "Maybe we'll come back and get them later."

Sure we will. In a few short hours he'd lost his girlfriend, probably his job, and possibly his freedom. He was going to worry about a ten-Euro windbreaker?

They stepped outside to the alley, hiding behind a bush until they were sure no one was watching the door, and then strode out to the street. "Where are we going?" Megan asked.

"Damned if I know." The evening air was warm and the sleeves of the jean jacket threatened to cut off his circulation, but at least they somewhat covered his long-sleeved pinstriped shirt. "Just keep moving."

He spotted a sign for a Metro station and walked toward it, switching his phone back on. Maybe Colette had called while it was off.

No Colette, but there was a missed call from his bridge buddy Roger.

Paul phoned him back. "Hello, mate."

"Paul." His friend's voice was hushed. "Are you all right?"

"Quite all right, thanks. Not a scratch."

"I can't believe Ian's gone. Your whole team. You must be devastated."

Paul bit down hard on his lip. "Something like that."

"How did you manage to escape uninjured?"

He confessed to having been late for work and just outside the embassy when the bomb hit.

"You're a lucky man," Roger said.

"Lucky to be alive, absolutely. But I've been temporarily relieved of my post. My section head thinks I may have had something to do with the bombing."

"Just because you survived?" Roger sounded horrified.

"There's a bit more to it." He told Roger about his missing

security card and its use to gain access to the embassy. He didn't mention the photo of the woman who looked like Colette.

"That's terrible," his friend replied. "Any notion who might have gotten hold of your badge?"

"No clue. Maybe I dropped it somewhere."

From Roger he learned that the embassy would re-open for emergencies only on Thursday. As passport supervisor, Roger and his team would have only two days holiday before going back to work.

Paul would have given anything to change places with him.

"Again, I'm so sorry about your mates." Roger signed off. "Keep in touch."

Which meant either 'Keep in touch' or 'Since you're under suspicion, don't contact me.' Paul switched the phone off again. Without his charger on hand, he had to make his battery last as long as possible.

"Who was that?" Megan asked as they stepped into a crosswalk. "Someone you work with?"

He nodded but didn't share any more information. If Megan *was* the person who'd killed his friends, he wouldn't give her access to any others.

If? His brain spun with ambiguous cognitions. If he still suspected this woman might be the perpetrator, why was he walking with her, protecting her?

They were half a block from the metro station when Paul saw the flashing lights. About two streets east and moving at a steady pace, no sirens. "Run," he directed Megan.

Within ten seconds, he heard the sirens. In another twenty, they arrived at the subway entrance. Bloody hell. No one had followed them from Jacques and Marcel's, Paul was sure of it. He'd kept a cautious lookout, eyeing the side streets, watching the traffic behind him. The police must have been cruising the general area. And he'd gotten careless while on the phone.

The phone.

They bounded down the Metro stairs. Paul purchased a three-day pass for Megan and hustled her to the turnstiles, then swiped his own commuter card and passed inside.

"Don't look back," he cautioned as they jumped on the escalator that descended to the train tracks. "Keep moving." Adrenaline flooded his veins. He heard boots or heavy footsteps above him, also jumping the escalator steps. And he didn't dare hope it was just a couple of passengers late for their train.

The escalator went on forever. The footfalls behind him sounded louder, then were drowned out by the blessed horn of an incoming train.

When he and Megan reached the bottom, the arriving train had stopped. Passengers rose from benches to board the northbound subway as the doors opened. Across the platform, another train faced the southbound direction, engine revving, warning its doors were about to close.

Paul bounded across the platform. In the last seconds before the door's closing, he pulled his cell phone from his pocket, activated it, and tossed it into the departing southbound train.

Then he nudged Megan into the crowd across the platform and holding her hand tightly, blended with the swarm and boarded the northbound train.

Chapter Six

"What did you do that for?" Megan yelled as the train started up with a lurch. "Are you out of your mind? How is my mother going to call me back?"

"We'll find another way." Paul guided her toward an empty double seat and motioned for her to sit.

She slid in next to the window and he sat beside her, his large body taking up too much of the seat, rubbing against her. His musky cologne invaded her breathing air. His body heat...

She crossed her ankles to stop his leg from touching hers. "Now all your contacts are gone, too. And neither of us has any means of communication with the world."

He shrugged noncommittally. Her first impression of him had been correct: the man was insane.

She rubbed her eyes to make certain she was awake. "This whole day has been a nightmare." She leaned forward and held her face in her hands. "First, I'm robbed, then you mistake me for a terrorist, then the people you assure me will help us turn us in, and now--"

"Maybe not."

She lifted her head. "Maybe not what?"

"I don't think Marcel called the police. Nor Jacques."

"Then who did? How did they find us?"

"My cell phone."

The train stopped at a station. A woman with a walker got on. Paul scooted even closer to Megan to allow room for her to pass. "My phone has a GPS tracker on it. The police probably got my number from my boss and followed the signal to the apartment building. From the length of time we were in that laundry room, they searched every flat in the building, trying to pinpoint the signal. If Marcel or Jacques had called them, they would have come directly to their flat."

"But you turned off your phone after I called my parents."

He nodded. "To save battery. But the police were already on their way. When they searched the building and didn't find us, they drove around the area hoping I'd turn on my phone so they could pick up the signal again."

"And when you did, they located us."

"Yes, and that's when I realized what had happened."

So that's why he'd ditched his phone. "Did you turn it off before you tossed it?"

"No, I turned it on. Hopefully the police will follow that train to the end of its southbound line. Whereas we are headed to the opposite end of the city."

Megan almost felt like hugging him. "You're a genius."

He chuckled. "You just told me I was out of my mind."

"Okay, you're a crazy genius."

He patted her hand, then reached across her to pull the stop cord. "We're getting off here."

Megan didn't challenge him. He knew the city better than she did. And though he still might not believe her, he'd had numerous chances to turn her over to the authorities and he hadn't. Meekly, she followed him out onto the platform.

"What's here?" she asked as they rode the escalator toward the street.

"ATM," he said when they reached the top. He inserted his card and withdrew a fistful of cash.

"Not to retract your genius status, but the police have probably gained access to your financials. Won't they be able to track you through the transaction you just made?"

"Yes. They will know that I was at this Metro station at ten forty-five tonight." Paul nudged her toward a different set of escalators than the ones they'd ridden up. "This station is a major transit area for three separate subway lines." He preceded her down the escalator.

"Let me guess, we're going to get on a different line and go in a different direction."

"Righto."

After another hour of aimless riding, during which they switched lines two more times, they finally rode up to the street and scrambled up the steps into a night full of twinkling lights.

Paris at midnight. "It's like all the travel brochures," Megan exclaimed. But those didn't take into account the sounds and smells of the city. Whispers between strolling lovers. Exotic perfumes. Even the air had a special Parisian aroma.

Paul hailed a taxi and settled her in the backseat, then slid in beside her, directing the driver to the intersection of two streets unfamiliar to Megan.

She peered out the window as the City of Light rolled by, blinking and winking like a thousand stars. "This is so romantic."

Paul made no comment but he was probably rolling his eyes.

Megan sighed. Her group had done the nightlife tour, visiting the Moulon Rouge and other historic tourist spots. But sitting in a bus with a bunch of chatty women was a lot different from a midnight taxi ride with a man. She closed her eyes and tried to envision Fletcher sitting beside her, but his face refused to fill the picture.

Realizing she'd leaned into Paul's shoulder, she jerked back.

"It's okay," he said. He pulled her against him, nestling her in the crook of his arm. For no logical reason, Megan relaxed. There was danger all around, inside the cab as much as out. And yet, in this moment, she felt safe.

The taxi pulled up in front of a very European, very posh hotel with a doorman. Paul took her arm. "When we go inside, please keep mum. Let me do the talking."

Waving away the bellman who hurried to meet the cab, Paul sauntered inside to the reception desk, asked for a room, signed the registry, and paid with cash. "Traveling back to Britain and I want to get rid of my Euros," he explained to the desk clerk in well-accented French.

The clerk nodded perfunctorily and looked over the counter at their lack of luggage, but didn't mention the absence. "*Bienvenue aux Hotel Denise, Monsieur Potter,*" the clerk said, handing him two plastic room key cards.

"*Merci.*"

"Mr. Potter?" Megan whispered as they waited for the elevator. "Please tell me you didn't sign that registry Harry Potter."

"Of course not, love." He winked. "Mr. and Mrs. George Potter."

Mr. and Mrs. One room. Of course, how could she expect him to spring for two? Even one room in this old world hotel was probably well beyond the price a government employee could afford to pay for a night's lodging. And truthfully, Megan was glad not to be alone tonight.

The room was lovely but small, with the look and feel of two hundred years of history. Megan's eyes darted to the half dozen assorted silk pillows sprawled across the slightly-larger-than-full-but-nowhere-near-king-sized spread.

Paul caught her eye. "This was all they had." He sat at the foot and stretched his arms over the opulent spread. "It's quite large, though."

Megan pictured herself in bed with this stranger, his body inches from hers. Her cheeks heated. "At Marcel and Jacques' you offered to sleep on the sofa."

"Do you see a sofa here?" He waved his hand at the small quarters. There was barely enough space between the bed and the dresser for one person to pass. "Don't worry, love, you'll be quite safe." He shucked off his jacket and removed his shoes and socks.

If she pressed the issue, he'd think she was a silly little virgin. He was paying for this room, she couldn't ask him to sleep on the floor. If they both slept in their clothes...

But Paul was already unbuttoning his shirt, revealing a muscular chest of dark, dense hair. A woman could warm her nose in that comfortable forest all night. Megan chastised herself for staring, but couldn't turn away. Slipping out of the sleeves, Paul tossed the shirt on the straight hard-backed chair and unselfconsciously tugged at the zipper of his khaki pants.

"What are you doing?"

"Undressing." He looked nonplussed. "I'll have to wear these same clothes tomorrow. You might consider that fact in determining your own sleep attire." And without further warning, he dropped his pants. Wearing nothing but black briefs, he strode past her into the bathroom.

Megan swallowed. This was going to be a long night.

She set the backpack on the floor next to the side of the bed he hadn't touched, slipped off the navy blue hoodie, and examined herself in the bureau mirror. The tee shirt she'd purloined from the dryer was pale blue rather than gray, and showed the outline of her nipples. At least it was clean. But it wouldn't be after a night of sleeping, possibly sweating in it. The room had no air-conditioning and it was a warm night.

"The loo is all yours." Paul brushed past her, a towel wrapped around his waist. Megan swallowed, guessing he no longer wore even those very brief briefs. Scooping her bra out of the backpack, she darted into the bathroom.

The black briefs hung from a towel rack. Megan pursed her lips. She should rinse out her underwear. At least she'd feel somewhat fresh in the morning. But...

"There's a robe hanging on the back of the door," Paul called from the bedroom, as if he'd read her thoughts.

She stepped out of her jeans and shirt, and washed bra and undies with the hotel-sized soap, then laid them over the tub to dry. The white spa robe was long and comfy, but as she padded back to the bedroom, Megan was very aware of her nakedness underneath.

The light had been turned off. Megan groped her way to the unoccupied side of the bed and slid under the covers.

"Comfy?"

His voice was too close, but its direction told Megan he was facing away from her. She turned her back as well, one foot touching the edge of the bed, prepared for escape. "Goodnight, Paul."

"Goodnight."

She couldn't tell how long she lay there, the day's events jumbling in her mind like recurrent bad dreams, uncomfortably aware that a strange man's bare back lay inches away. He was presumably bare everywhere else. What if, consciously or in his sleep, he rolled toward her and... Her skin tingled. It would be natural, in the dark of night, for him to assume she was Colette, wouldn't it?

And those tingles were apprehension and not arousal, right?

Paul never stirred. She would have expected by now to hear light snoring, or heavier breathing, but he was quiet as a stone.

"Paul?" she whispered. "You still awake?"

"Yes."

She'd expected maybe a sleepy grunt. His deep voice, so clear and close, sent sensuous prickles up her arms. "I'll bet you wish you were home in your own bed right now."

"At least I'd have my toothbrush and razor."

Megan giggled. He did have a sense of humor, British humor, designed to deflect discomfort. What was going through his mind right now? His day had been even worse than hers. At least she hadn't lost any friends to a terrorist bomb.

They lay quietly a few more minutes, strangers from different worlds, inches apart. "How long have you and Colette been a couple?" she asked when the silence threatened to drown her.

"Six months."

Quick romance. He'd said he'd only known her six months. "How did you meet?"

"On the train. We had coffee, she came home with me, never left."

Wow. It must have been love at first sight. "What does she do, besides acting? Does she have a day job?"

"A little waitressing. I think she's done some modeling," Paul replied. "Not sure what else she did before I met her."

"You don't seem to know much about her." The unintended tartness surprised her.

"Colette's always been a woman of mystery." He chuckled. "Every man's fantasy, you know?"

She didn't know. And wasn't sure she wanted to. But something propelled her to ask. "Are you still in love with her?"

Protracted silence. "Sorry," she said after almost a minute. "Was that too personal?"

"No, not at all." He shifted his position but still faced away from her. "I just hadn't thought about it."

Hadn't thought...? Fletcher had told Megan he loved her after they'd dated only six weeks. Of course, back then he was still trying to get into her pants.

"Colette is like no one else," Paul said quietly, as if he were talking to himself. "Vivacious. Charming. You never know—knew-- what she was going to say or do next." His voice abated to a whisper.

Megan edged closer until her back almost touched his.

"Eye candy and bedroom entertainment in one petite package. Any guy would give his left ball for a woman like that. But, love?" Paul breathed heavily, so close Megan could almost feel his ribs. "No. I never loved Colette."

Megan's feminist dander arose. "So it was just sex? You spent six months of your life with a psychopath for sex?"

"It was damned good sex," he said sheepishly. He turned toward her, not moving any closer, but still near enough that she felt his breath on her neck. "How about you? How long have you dated the boyfriend?"

"Fletcher," she clarified. "About a year."

"Do you live together?"

"That's none of your business," she said hotly.

"I'll take that as a yes."

"Take it as a no." Why had she bristled? His question was no more personal than those she'd asked him. "He stays over at my place sometimes, but that's all."

"How did you meet the lad?"

"He's a salesman for my father's company. Fletcher's ambitious and hard-working," she added proudly. "He's up for a promotion to district manager."

"I'd wager his chances are quite good, seeing as how he's dating the boss's daughter."

"Don't go there," she said, gritting her teeth. Why did people always think Fletcher was after her money? When they went out, he always paid.

"Fletcher and I are good for each other," she explained, although she wasn't sure whom she was trying to convince. "He's romantic." At times. "He brought me flowers for my birthday."

"How lovely," Paul said dryly.

"He...looks after me," she added, despite Paul's obvious indifference.

His cool breath danced down the neck of her bathrobe. "You love him?"

"Of course." Had she said that too fast? Too slow? "Just before I left for this trip, Fletcher asked me to marry him.

"Oh." That seemed to give him pause. "I guess congratulations are in order, then."

Megan sighed. "Actually, I told him I'd think about it while I was away and let him know when I returned."

"Really? And the poor lad's been awaiting your decision for-- what, three weeks? Are you going to put him out of his misery?"

"Meaning, am I going to marry him?" She winced. "I still don't know."

Paul chuckled in her ear. "Lack of a decision sounds like a decision to me."

She gritted her teeth. "It's more complicated than that."

"Is it? Does the complication have anything to do with the place you didn't want me to go?"

Damn his arrogance. She loved Fletcher, she did. He protected her from impulsive decisions, reining her in when she got flaky and irrational. Keeping her from making stupid naïve mistakes. But Megan's stubborn romantic streak yearned for a passion that would fill her mind and senses, a lover she couldn't bear to live without.

The room was getting warmer. The bathrobe lay heavy on her shoulders, but it would be a hot day in hell before she'd take it off. "We should try to get some sleep."

"Right." His shoulder--she guessed it was his shoulder— brushed her back as he turned away again. Megan inched closer to her edge of the bed. And yet there remained an unbidden, uncanny feeling of intimacy.

She hadn't told anyone else, even her best friend Amber, about Fletcher's proposal. She wasn't sure why. Maybe in her heart of hearts she'd hoped it would go away and she wouldn't have to deal with it. Was it wrong to want something more from a life partner than a decent income and occasional sex?

Correction. In Fletcher's case, it was more than occasional. The man was a horny dog. When, after three months of fending him off, she'd finally 'let him' make love to her, Megan had been overwhelmed by his size and his rampant lust. Of course he claimed there was something wrong with *her*. "Frigid," he'd called her on more than one occasion when she hadn't managed to become aroused quickly enough. "Ice queen." And even though he was right, the taunt stung.

Was that all men cared about? Paul had lived for half a year with a woman who was surely a dangerous terrorist, totally clueless about whom he was sharing his bed with. As long as she provided him with hot, frequent sex, he'd been a happy camper.

Paul rolled over onto his stomach, then, with a groan, turned on his side again. Megan's head ached from closing her eyes and opening them again, hoping to find herself somewhere other than here.

"Paul?"

It took a second, but he answered with a groan. "Hmmm?"

"If you really believe Colette is innocent, then why did you help me? You could have left me on my own when we got to the Metro. You didn't have to take me with you, put me up in this nice hotel."

He was silent another second or two. Then, "I couldn't leave you on your own. Yes, I'm hoping Colette is innocent. Can you blame me? But as long as there's a chance you really are who and what you claim, then I couldn't in good conscience leave you friendless and penniless to fend for yourself in a strange country. That's not who I am."

Meaning, he was giving her the benefit of the doubt. But there was no way an intelligent man would befriend a woman he even ten percent suspected had murdered his colleagues. Let alone share a bed with her. Megan's heart lightened. *His* heart might be fighting it but in his head, Paul had as good as told her he believed her.

Relief shuddered through her body. More than anything, she'd wanted to earn Paul's trust. She wasn't sure why it was so important to her. But she sensed he was the kind of man who was loyal and devoted not only to his country, but to his friends.

She touched his arm, reassured by its warmth. "Where do you think Colette is?"

He sighed. "If she has your passport and credit cards, she could be halfway to Afghanistan."

Chapter Seven

"Bienvenue aux Etats-Unis," the loudspeaker at Kennedy airport announced. "Welcome to the United States." Breathing a relieved sigh, Colette followed the hordes of arrivals into the terminal. New York City. The Promised Land. The passage point to her new life

At passport control, she was heading briskly to the short line of foreign nationals, when a hand clasped her arm. "Megan."

Colette recognized her chatty, dressed-all-in-black seatmate from the plane.

"Wrong line. This way." The woman led her toward the snaking, corded lines where ninety percent of the Air France passengers stood, in front of the signs that said, *USA Citizens and Residents.*

"Thanks." She grinned what she hoped was a sheepish smile. "That line looked way shorter."

"It always is. No matter whether I'm entering a foreign country or coming home, the other line is always shorter."

Well, that was incredibly stupid. After all her rehearsing to act American, she'd almost blown her cover by standing in the wrong line.

The woman—Jennifer? Jessica?--stayed at her elbow in the line, babbling away about Superheroes and her visits to comic con conventions. Colette's head ached from trying to make small talk with her. One could only pretend to sleep for five or six hours of a nine-hour flight. She'd meant to bring a magazine to bury her face in, but she must have left it in the other backpack.

At last she reached the counter and handed over her passport and landing card. She had no idea what was in Megan Chandler's suitcase, since the first time she'd seen it was at Charles de Gaulle airport before the flight, but she'd listed a few souvenir-type items of minimal price so she'd look like a proper tourist.

The inspector glanced briefly at the passport and then at her face. Colette held her breath, hoping he wouldn't turn to that list of names he must have in his drawer. Should she smile and distract him with conversation? *Don't call attention to yourself.*

After an hour-long minute studying the passport, the inspector stamped the visa page authoritatively and said, "Welcome home."

"Thank you," she said in her practiced American accent. Stifling her sigh of relief, she slung the black backpack over one shoulder, unbuttoned the tan trench coat, and followed the signs to Baggage Claim.

She was tempted to leave the tacky orange suitcase on the conveyor belt, but since she had no other clothes and these would fit her, loosely, she hauled it off the belt and rolled it toward the green door marked *Nothing to Declare.*

The customs agent waved her on with a bored nod, and she sailed blithely through to the other side.

She'd done it! An ocean separated her from the Community and the French police. She glanced at her newly acquired Cartier watch and reset it for New York time. Barely past seven. But probably too late to catch a flight out tonight. She'd have to stay overnight in a nearby hotel. Tomorrow she'd fly out to a warm Caribbean destination where drinks flowed at the snap of her fingers and every day was a party.

She headed straight to a bathroom, and, after washing up, examined her face in the mirror. The wig had inched backward making her hair look thinner from the scalp to the crest. She yanked off the hairpiece and scratched her itchy head, then stuffed the wig into the backpack beside the yellow scarf.

So much for planning ahead. She'd had her hair cut weeks ago in exactly the style of Megan's profile photo, only to find her American cousin had let her hair grow since that had been taken. Good thing she'd scoped out the situation when Megan's group had toured the Louvre two days ago. Buying a matching backpack and coat had been easy. The trench coat was a particularly useful cover-up, since she couldn't have predicted the kind or color of the blouse Megan would wear today.

She turned her phone back on. Five missed calls: one from Cyrus, one from Salim, and three from Paul. She didn't bother listening to the messages. The time stamps on Paul's indicated he was alive, and that was the extent of her concern. He probably hated her, or he would soon, but he should thank her. If she hadn't screwed his brains out this morning and then turned off his alarm clock, he'd no doubt be splattered into little pieces like his less fortunate colleagues in the data center.

Colette logged onto the Internet, then into her secure, confidential bank account. No deposit yet. She logged out and switched off the phone. The less time online, the less opportunity for someone in the Community to track her.

At the currency exchange desk, she traded in enough Euros to pay for her night's lodging and then asked directions for the international ticket counter. It was tempting to use Megan's credit card to pay for tomorrow's flight, but the money trail would be easily traceable, and the card might already have been reported stolen. Fortunately, she'd brought enough cash to buy the ticket and handle any emergencies over the next few days. By the time she arrived at her final destination, the payment for the embassy job would be in her account.

Fifty thousand dollars was hardly a fortune, but it was enough to get her settled, and then she'd do whatever work came her way. She would have fled the country penniless, months ago, if she could have. But the Community didn't take kindly to Believers walking away from the Family, especially if they knew secrets. If Colette hadn't performed her assignment as ordered, they would have killed her.

That was probably their plan anyway.

She shuddered. In the future, she'd be much more careful about who she hooked up with. If only she hadn't confused passion for a man with passion for his cause, she wouldn't be running for her life.

"Megan!"

Don't turn around.

"Megan, over here." The chorus of voices came from somewhere behind her.

Keep walking. There must be thousands of Megans in New York City.

"Meggie, is that you?" A man's hand grabbed her arm and spun her around. "You cut your hair." The young blond man pointed to another man and a woman, a matching pair in their fifties, smiling and waving frantically.

Mon Dieu. Megan's parents. Colette turned warily to the good-looking man who'd grabbed her elbow. The boyfriend? Should she give him a believable homecoming kiss?

She decided on a quick peck on the cheek. He responded with a bone-crushing hug, then dragged her over to the happy senior couple. The three enveloped her in a four-way hug that made her feel like a kindergartener.

"Your brother insisted on driving us out here to meet you," the woman said. She smothered Colette with kisses from cheeks to forehead. "You know I don't like your father driving after dark, especially in the city. Donnie promised he'd have us all home before ten."

Donnie, then, was the brother. Thank goodness she hadn't frenched him. "It was good of you all to come. But I can get home by myself." Megan, Colette knew, had her own apartment.

"Oh, no we wouldn't hear of you traveling all the way to Jersey at this hour. Daddy can drive you home in the morning. Tonight you'll stay with us." The woman slobbered another kiss on her for good measure. "It will be so nice having you stay under our roof again."

Colette forced a smile. "I am so looking forward to it." She tried not to gaze longingly at the ticket counter as Donnie grabbed her suitcase and the father shouldered her backpack.

Merde.

* * *

Waking from a delicious dream, the first thing Megan noticed was the mid-morning sunlight streaming into the hotel room and warming her bed.

The second thing she noticed was that she was not alone in the bed.

She sat up carefully. Paul lay on his back, snoring softly. The blanket in the warm room had slipped just below his waist. Mesmerized, Megan watched his brawny chest rise and fall. Thick dark hair zigzagged around his flat nipples and washed over his stomach in a haphazard pattern before arrowing down toward his navel and--well, the blanket cut off her view of below.

Megan glanced at the clock on her nightstand. Ten twenty-five! Wrapping her robe around her, she took small quiet steps to the bathroom. The American Embassy was surely open by now. And the day was running away from her.

The bra and panties she'd laid across the tub were fully dry. After pulling the shower curtain and negotiating the old-fashioned faucet, Megan breathed in the invigorating steam and let the warm water caress her body. Energizing needles cascaded over her head and down her breasts. Her nipples peaked.

The morning of her flight to Europe, Fletcher had joined her in the shower. Standing behind her, his horse's erection poking between her legs, he'd tweaked her nipples with his long, thin fingers. Lightly at first, then harder and harder until she'd yelped in pain and nudged him away. Disgusted, he'd left her alone and gone back to the bedroom to pleasure himself.

What was wrong with her? It was their last intimate opportunity for three weeks and she'd blown it. How long did a normal, healthy woman need to become aroused?

Three weeks, apparently. Today under the shower her nipples stiffened without effort, and her mouth was wet with desire. Megan touched her breasts, imagining larger hands gently cupping and kneading them, thick thumbs teasing her nipples to tingly, needy peaks.

She gulped. Was that the result of breathing in a man's scent all night? Mercilessly Megan scrubbed her breasts and then washed herself thoroughly from head to toe, trying to cleanse her improper thoughts.

She toweled herself slowly, erotically, her mind drifting. Had Paul even wondered what her body would feel like, pressed against his? Would she be a second-rate version of Colette or—

Stop it. Hurriedly she stepped into her panties, hooked her bra, and slipped on her jeans and the tee shirt she'd worn last night.

Paul was still flat on his back in the bed, still lightly snoring, but the blanket which had provided such an enticing view was now tucked modestly around his neck.

Megan sat in the one chair to put on her socks and shoes, slammed the sweatshirt over her head, and then grabbed the backpack from the floor. It felt lighter. She unzipped it and glanced inside. The gun was gone.

Frowning, she studied Paul's motionless figure. Halfway down his body, the blanket rose provocatively. Either he had a monster morning hard on or--

"Looking for this?" He sat up, pointing that gun at her. He was fully dressed except for his shoes.

Megan let out a whimper, trying to keep her heart from jumping out of her rib cage.

Paul raked his gaze over her body, from her hooded sweatshirt to her shoes. "You thought you'd just sneak out?" His gun hand was much steadier than hers had been last night.

Megan tried to breathe and speak at the same time. "I'm going to the American Embassy. I didn't want to wake you." She glanced at the door and then back at his intense eyes.

"What have you done with Colette?"

Not this again. She'd thought he was finally beginning to believe her. Last night...

"Recognize this?" He reached into his shirt pocket with his free hand and pulled out a laminated card. An ID badge. With his picture on it.

Megan swallowed. "Where did you find it?" she asked, although she was pretty sure she knew the answer.

"In your backpack. Don't act like it's the first time you've seen it."

"I swear, it is. It must have been in one of those zippered pockets." That seemingly-empty backpack was like Mary Poppins' carpet bag where strange items kept appearing.

He yanked the backpack from the floor and drew out the Elle magazine. "What about this?"

"I told you there was a magazine in the backpack. What does that matter?"

"Don't play dumb. Colette reads these fashion magazines." If eyes were swords, his would have cut her to ribbons. "This is her backpack."

Colette's backpack? Not Nicole's? Megan's brain bounced like an errant rubber ball.

Paul aimed the weapon at her chest. "I'll give you one more chance to tell me what you've done to her."

"Nothing!" She swallowed but there was no liquid in her throat. "I didn't know Colette existed until you kidnapped me."

"Do I look stupid? Did you mug Colette after you bombed the embassy and try to frame her by planting a gun in her backpack?" He sneered. "She got the better of you, didn't she? She got away and you were left literally holding the bag."

"That's not what happened." Had she really had erotic thoughts about this man just this morning? Maybe she should have shot him while she had the chance.

Paul's dark eyes flashed. "Or did the two of you plan this together?"

Megan weighed her options. She could make a dash for the door, hoping he wouldn't shoot her. She could grab for the gun, pretty much guaranteeing she'd shoot herself. Or she could try to reason with him.

"Paul." She sat in the chair, a little farther from the gun. "You know what happened. Colette stole your badge and bombed the embassy. She knew I looked like her so she sought me out, mugged me, and framed me for her crime."

"How would she know you looked like her? Unless--"

"Colette is Nicole." It made sense. They'd both disappeared at the same time.

Paul's face drained of color.

Megan's heart hammered. Nicole hadn't just happened on her profile, and friended her to discuss art. She, that is, Colette, had sought out Megan for a different purpose. But how had she found her?

The painting.

"We know Colette saw that museum portrait," she said, her pulse racing. "What if she searched the Internet for the same image and found my profile photo? Or what if she *is* related to me somehow? She might look up her American relatives, see that we are virtually identical, and pose as Nicole to lure me to Paris."

Paul set the gun beside him on the bed. "You have a vivid imagination, Megan. You haven't yet convinced me that there ever was a Nicole, except in your twisted mind. But let's say, for the sake of argument, that I believed your story. Even if Colette is the mysterious Nicole, how does that prove she bombed the embassy?"

"Why else would she suggest I take that particular tour, at this particular time?"

"You're reaching." He dismissed her theory with a wave of his hand. "Nothing connects Colette to the bombing."

Megan's head swam, searching for that puzzle piece. "Your ID badge. Who else but Colette had access to it?"

He folded his arms across his chest. "Maybe I left it on my desk at work."

"Then how did it end up in this backpack?" Despite her adversarial tone, her heart went out to Paul. His mind knew the truth, but his emotions were still fighting it.

And *he* was fighting his emotions. "It's an interesting theory," he said coolly, as if they were discussing some unsolved TV mystery. "*If* Colette stole my badge. What's her motivation for bombing the embassy? Why would she have gotten involved with some terrorist agency?"

Megan took a shallow breath. "That I don't know."

"Then all you have is speculation. I need proof."

Of course he did. Paul was a logical man. And the police were rational civil servants. Until something or someone proved Colette's guilt, Megan was just as likely a suspect.

The gun was still within Paul's reach but he was no longer holding it or aiming it. Megan walked to the dresser, picked up the remote control, and turned on the TV. "It's almost eleven. Maybe there's a news update." Would it be too much to hope that the authorities had already located and apprehended Colette?

The broadcast was the same as they'd heard last night. Until the news anchor described two fugitives, a man and a woman, who were being sought in connection with the bombing. Paul's picture flashed on the screen. And then Megan's.

"Oh my God." Of course it couldn't be her photo. It had to be Colette's. But the woman with brown, shoulder-length hair actually looked more like Megan than the photo Paul had shown her of Colette.

She turned to Paul. "Is that the security photo you saw?"

He was staring at it, rapt. "Yes. It's been enlarged and enhanced." He moved close to the television, zeroing in with his finger on Colette's right breast. His mouth was open and his face intense.

Megan's gaze followed his finger. The skin of the woman's cleavage showed a couple of stray marks. To someone who didn't know her, it might be creases in the photo or natural blemishes. But Paul knew what he was looking at.

And so did Megan.

"Proof!" He jabbed his finger onto the screen, at the ink marks protruding from Colette's black vee-necked shirt. The edges of a dragonfly tattoo.

Chapter Eight

Damn Salim! Restless and unable to sleep, Colette kicked off the lacy blue and white comforter and slammed her fist against the matching pillow sham. The man had seduced her with his radical agenda and she'd jumped on board as easily as she'd jumped into his bed. Her body had followed wherever he led, her heart and mind trotting along for the trip.

And he'd used her the same way she'd used Paul-the-geek.

What was Salim doing now? Banging the new starry-eyed recruit and whispering sweet Arabic nothings into her ear?

The sun was just coming up, a red ball rising beyond the skyscrapers over the East River. Or was it the Hudson? When her class studied American geography, she'd been out in the halls smoking cigarettes with the guys.

For the second time since she'd arrived, Colette scrolled through her Smartphone and logged into her Swiss bank account. No new transactions.

She sighed and shut it off, staring at the frilly blue and white curtains, which matched the spread and the pillow shams. Had this been Megan's childhood bedroom? She could just imagine prissy Megan Chandler playing with her dolls here, or making up stories of fairy tale princesses. No cares or worries in her charmed life.

Well, now she'd know how it felt to be on the other side. Now, without friends or family, she'd be struggling to survive in Colette's world.

And wouldn't she try to call her parents for help?

Merde. Colette lunged for the desk phone. As she'd feared, a message had been left on voice mail. But as luck would have it, the voice mail number had been taped to the phone's base. She dialed it, listened to Megan's whiney plea for help, and then deleted the message.

Close one, Colette. She sank back on the bed, smiling, but then relief morphed into alarm. The number Megan had dialed from had looked familiar. *Merde.* Paul Bernard's cell.

How had those two found each other? In a city as large as Paris?

Don't panic. This could work for her. The authorities would learn that Paul's security card had been used, and question him. If they found Megan with him, she'd be arrested. And the cops would stop looking, temporarily at least, for Colette.

Again her relief was short-lived. The authorities might stop looking for her, but Paul wouldn't. She picked up the land phone again and tweaked the settings to block any call from Paul's number. Then she yanked the wire to the phone, burying the receiver among the bed linens to muffle that beep-beep disconnection sound. That would buy her time, but not much.

Unzipping the suitcase she'd transported across the Atlantic Ocean, she looked for something to wear. Most of the clothes were suitable for a schoolteacher or a nun, definitely not Colette's style. But if she were going to be Megan right now, she supposed she ought to look like Megan.

Along with a handful of pastel-colored tees, she found a pair of straight black jeans and a couple of pairs of khaki Capri's. Colette pulled on the loose-fitting jeans, then stuffed the Capri's and a few plain tee shirts into the backpack with her own jeans and black shirt, selecting one of the shirts to wear over her jeans. Then she zipped up the orange suitcase and stuffed it as far back as she could in a closet the size of Colette's last apartment. Before anyone noticed it, she'd be lying on a beach where the only attire necessary was a bikini. If that.

She glanced at the Cartier watch that was now feeling so comfortably at home on her arm. It was only a little after six and still dark. If she sneaked out the front door and walked a few blocks to a main intersection, she could call a cab and head back to the airport.

Hoisting the backpack over one shoulder, she opened the bedroom door and stepped out into the hallway. The grandiose mid-town apartment was as quiet as a cemetery.

Glad she'd worn her old tennis shoes, Colette tiptoed out to the main living area. She didn't dare switch on a light. Taking care not to bump into furniture, she edged toward the corner curio cabinet she'd seen earlier, bursting with impressive miniature sculptures. It wouldn't hurt to take a few expensive souvenirs.

Carefully she opened one of the glass doors and switched on the mini light. She lifted out a couple of Hummel figurines, a bronze horseman statuette, and what looked to be a Lladro porcelain angel, and buried them amid the clothes in her backpack.

She set the much-heavier bag down gently on the floor beside the front door. The predawn glow through the sidelight windows fell on a family photograph perched on an end table. Megan at about age ten, Donnie, already buff and handsome in probably his mid-teens, Mommy and Daddy and an older woman, presumably Grandma. Colette blinked in the dim light. The woman looked like *Grannimere,* her mother's grandmother. Not that she'd seen the old bag more than a couple of times. But Maman had kept a picture of the ancient woman on a high shelf as if she were some sort of queen, and the resemblance to this American woman was striking. Like her and Megan?

She ground her teeth. How was life so unfair? They were both descended from the same aristocratic woman. But for arbitrary circumstances, Colette might have been the one growing up in luxury with a loving family. Instead of a slut mother who'd pretty much left her to fend for herself.

She headed to the kitchen. To minimize contact with the family, she'd begged off on the deli sandwiches they'd ordered last night, claiming a bad case of jetlag. But when grabbing a soft drink to take to her 'room,' she'd seen a refrigerator magnet with the phone numbers of local cab companies.

Skirting inside the kitchen doorway, she switched on the overhead light.

"You couldn't sleep either?"

She jumped at the voice. Donnie Chandler sat at the solid oak kitchen table, wearing sweat pants and a Boston University T-shirt, a can of diet soda in his hand. Dr. Donnie Chandler. She'd learned that last night in the car by pretending to be too tired to talk, picking up whatever information she could about the family she was supposed to be part of.

"You startled me." She glared at him, invoking the stratagem that the best defense was often an offense. "Why are you sitting here in the dark?"

"It relaxes me." He slid his leg off the chair it had been resting on. "This is the most wonderful part of the day." He glanced outside at the dawn creeping over the horizon.

Should she agree or disagree? What would Megan say? "I'm so jet-lagged I'm not sure if it's day, or still night." Colette grabbed a soda from the fridge and sat in the chair his leg had vacated.

"I know how it is. I always feel wired when I return from an overseas trip. Anxious to reconnect with normal life, I guess."

What did a doctor do that took him overseas so often? Oh, right. *Doctors without Borders.* Megan's brother was not only Ivy League educated and a brilliant surgeon, he was a damned do-gooder.

"So how was it?" He sipped his soda. "You barely said a word in the car last night. Was 'The Grand Tour of Europe' all it was cracked up to be?"

"Definitely. The Louvre was amazing. The Prado...it defies words." For Colette. Because she'd never been to Madrid.

"Did you meet up with Nicole?"

How to answer? 'No' would require some plausible explanation. And then awkwardly end the conversation. 'Yes' would invite more questions, but at least the subject was one she could totally wing. "I did. It was so great to finally meet her." She went on to describe the appearance and personality of the mythical Nicole, inventing a café near the museum where they'd had lunch.

"Sounds like you had a great trip."

"I did." She patted his shoulder with sisterly affection. "But honestly, Donnie, it's good to be home."

"Donnie?"

Panic leaped to her throat. Wasn't that his name?

He grinned. "You haven't called me that since you were twelve years old."

But the parents had called him that. "I'm sorry--" She said a silent prayer and plunged forward. "--Don." When he didn't react, she affected a yawn. "I guess I'm just tired and being in Mom and Dad's house makes me feel like a little kid again."

"I absolutely know how that feels."

Because he lived here with his parents? Colette surreptitiously scanned his face. Megan, she knew, was twenty-three, but based on the age difference in that family photo, this man was probably in his thirties. And as a doctor, even a do-gooding, not-drowning-in-money doctor, he undoubtedly could afford his own place. Maybe he meant that he felt the same way she did staying under his parents' roof last night.

"So," he said, patting her knee, "Are you ready to get out of here?"

Colette's stomach plummeted. He couldn't have seen her backpack parked by the door. She forced out a giggle. "What do you mean?"

He crushed his empty soda can with one hand and tossed it into the chrome can marked Recycle. "You know how the folks are. Mom'll get up and fix a four-course breakfast, then sit you down for the play by play day by day, complete with photographs. Then she'll drag you to MoMA for whatever must-see art exhibit is there now, and by the time you get back, it'll be too late for Dad to drive you home, so you're stuck here for another night, and tomorrow, it starts all over again."

Not if you go back to bed so I can sneak out as I planned.

"So why don't we slip out now?" he asked.

What? She feared she hadn't hid the shock in her eyes.

"Neither of us is tired. I've got to move my car by seven anyway to the other side of the street before the street cleaners start working. I'll just drive you home."

"But--"

"It's not too far out of my way. I've got to go to East Brunswick, anyway, on my way home." He stood. "We can stop at that greasy spoon on the turnpike for breakfast."

So he didn't live here. He'd driven a couple of hours just to meet Megan at the airport. Colette couldn't imagine her own brother crossing the street to meet her. Not unless there was something in it for him.

"It's decided, then." Donnie—Don stood and embraced her with a one-armed hug. He smelled like Irish Spring soap. Not as exotic as the Moroccan-spices cologne Salim used, but pleasant. "Grab your stuff. I'll leave Mom a note."

Colette cast a longing eye at the front door, wondering if she could make a run for it. The backpack! Had he noticed it?

He didn't comment, but remained like a guard dog in front of the door, so she had no choice but to go back to the bedroom, retrieve Megan's suitcase from the closet, and drag it out front.

A two-hour drive? With a man she was supposed to know well? Megan's emails had rarely mentioned her brother.

Normally Colette had no problem enticing men to talk about themselves, and that kept them from asking too many questions about *her*. But Don was her 'brother.' Her seduction routine was off the table.

Ask about his work. Hopefully, Donnie Do-gooder was just full of stories to share about the diseased and downtrodden.

As they walked outside to his Jeep Cherokee parked at the curb, she thought one more time about giving him the slip and running. But flight would arouse immediate suspicion, and she couldn't afford to have the authorities alerted until she was safely out of this country.

So she let herself be imprisoned in the leather seat, and watched the lights dim and traffic thin as they drove farther and farther from the city, JFK airport, and freedom.

New Jersey? Seriously?

Chapter Nine

Paul stared at the television long after the images had disappeared from the screen. God, he'd been a bloody fool. He should have been more wary, but he hadn't wanted to question his good fortune. He hadn't worried about exposing state secrets during pillow talk, because he didn't know any. But he'd paraded Colette around his office, shown her the data center, where the tapes were kept. *Dammit, Bernard, why didn't you just make her a blueprint of the place?*

"I'm sorry, Paul." Megan's warm palm tucked into his.

"Nothing for you to be sorry about. You're not responsible for the murders of four people."

"Neither are you."

He sighed. "I didn't put a gun in Colette's hand, but I was careless. And stupid." He let go of Megan's hand, which was beginning to feel too comfortable in his. "I actually thought the woman cared about me. How big of a moron does that make me?"

"You're not a moron." She smiled encouragingly. "You're just a man. Most men would have fallen for that combination of sex and guile."

"Is that supposed to make me feel better? I thought I was

smarter than that. But I guess I'm no better than the average clueless idiot who thinks with his dick instead of his brain."

She giggled. "Now there you have me, Paul."

Despite his dour mood, he grinned. "I'm sorry I doubted you and gave you such a hard time."

"It's okay. I get it. You were trying to remain loyal to a woman you thought you knew well."

He spoke through the bitter taste in his mouth. "Apparently I didn't know her at all."

Megan moved toward the side of the bed he'd vacated, where the gun still lay undisturbed. "If we're done pointing this at each other, let's put it away. Makes me jittery."

She reached for the weapon and lifted it easily. She frowned. "Either I was awfully weak last night, or this gun was heavier then." Crystal blue eyes narrowed at him. "You took the bullets out, didn't you?"

"Yes." There was no longer a need for subterfuge. "Last night." If he'd been dumb enough to close his eyes with a possible terrorist *and* a loaded gun in the room, he really should have his head examined. "I was afraid someone might get hurt and I didn't want it to be me."

She giggled again, an easy, spontaneous laugh that brightened the room. Megan retrieved the backpack and placed the weapon inside. "Where are the bullets?"

"In a safe place."

She raised her brows.

He wiggled his. "If I told you, it wouldn't--"

"--be safe anymore," she finished for him.

Paul smiled. Though in the midst of the worst predicament of his life, he was having something akin to fun. The adrenaline rush was exciting, and now that he knew they were on the same side, being with Megan was not altogether unpleasant.

He opened the nightstand drawer, took out the bullets, and shoved them into a zippered pocket of the bag.

"I wish I'd thrown that damn thing in the Seine when I had the chance," Megan muttered.

"It's good you didn't. If this is the murder weapon, it might have fingerprints."

"*My* fingerprints," she pointed out. "And yours."

True enough. But in that video, he hadn't noticed the woman—Colette—wearing gloves. A print might give the police the evidence they needed. Paul already had all the evidence *he* needed.

Megan sat in the single chair. "Well, what do we do now?"

"*We?*" Just because they were no longer at each other's throats didn't mean they'd become a partnership. "*You* are going to lie low for the next few days. I'll give you enough money for another night or two in the hotel, until you can have your family wire you money and the documents you'll need for a new passport. By then, Colette should have been apprehended and it'll be safe for you to go to your embassy."

Her face wrinkled like a petulant child's. "So what are you going to do until they arrest Colette?"

"Go back to my flat. Turn myself in." He fingered the card still in his shirt pocket. "Offer my help to find Colette."

She stared at him as if he were daft. "Did you see the same newscast I did? The authorities believe you've already found Colette and helped her escape."

"But I didn't find her. I found you."

Her face paled. "You're going to tell the police about me?"

Paul frowned. He hadn't really thought this through. Would the police believe he'd 'happened to' run into Colette's exact double? Doubtful. More likely they'd come after Megan, and lock her up until they captured Colette. Or maybe, eager to close the case, they'd stop looking for Colette. And prosecute Megan. "You're right, I can't tell them about you."

Color slowly returned to her face. "Then you won't leave me?"

Whoa, where did that come from? "Megan, you'll be perfectly safe here. Don't leave the room, have food services leave your meals outside the door. You have a telly, you'll be able to follow the case."

She jutted out her attractive-when-determined chin. "It's not safe for you in your apartment. Stay here. I can help you. We can work together to find Colette."

"You think an art teacher and a computer programmer can catch a terrorist better than Interpol, MI6, and the French police?"

"Yes," she said stubbornly. "You know Colette--her friends, her haunts, her habits. I'm convinced she's related to me in some way, and if we can figure out that connection, we may be able to discover why she did this, and how she pulled it off."

On that, he was of the same mind. But..."If we stay together, it's twice as likely someone will recognize us."

"All the more reason for you not to leave," she said. "When we checked in as Mr. and Mrs. Potter, our pictures hadn't been televised

95

yet. We're safer here."

He thought about spending another night--or two or three-- lying beside a strange woman whose body seemed so familiar. It had been difficult enough last night not to reach out. "Megan..."

She folded her arms. "When you thought I was a terrorist, you wouldn't let me out of your sight. Now that you know I'm innocent, you're going to just abandon me?"

Damn, she knew exactly which button to push. The honorable one, ingrained in generations of Bernards, that wouldn't allow him to forsake a damsel in distress.

What the hell, his life was already so bollixed... He scratched his head. "Fine," he agreed. "I'll stay with you until you're safely on your way home."

"Thank you." She leaped out of the chair, arms outstretched, as if she meant to swallow him in a hug, then stopped a foot away from him. "But..."

There was always a *But*. With every woman he'd ever loved, shagged, or even started to care about.

"How am I going to contact my family? My parents' number was in your cell phone."

He opened the nightstand drawer and handed her the information he'd printed out at three this morning. "Here's your parents' phone number. And the list of documents you'll need for a new passport."

Her face scrunched up as if she were going to cry. "How did you...?"

"I couldn't sleep last night so I went down to the business center and used the hotel computers." He reached into the drawer for another set of papers. "I also started researching Adele Jarreau and her descendants."

Megan's eyes brightened. "Did you find anything?"

"I did." He sat at the edge of the bed and motioned for her to sit beside him. She sat close enough to peruse his notes. Close enough for her hair to brush his shoulder.

He read. "Adele Jarreau was the only daughter of Emile and Genevieve Jarreau, French aristocrats."

Megan grinned. "Well, if I am descended from them," she said affectedly, "it's nice to know I'm upper *clahss.*"

"Not all it's cracked up to be," Paul said dryly. He turned back to his notes. "Mademoiselle Jarreau was married in nineteen nineteen. To an Eduard Dubois."

"The painter!" Megan bounced excitedly on the bed. "No wonder I hadn't heard of him. He must have been some obscure commercial portrait artist. Her eyes sparkled. "Perhaps Monsieur and Madame Jarreau hired an artist to paint a portrait of their daughter, and in the course of the sittings, they fell in love."

The woman was definitely a romantic. Not that that was necessarily a bad thing.

Megan's face scrunched up in a thoughtful little pout. Same face as Colette's, but where Colette was seductive, Megan was...cute. She jumped off the bed. "Adele Jarreau might have been my great-grandmother!"

Paul had come to the same conclusion, but he was missing some of the connecting dots. "What was your grandmother's name? The war bride?"

"Sophie Jameson. But that's her married name." Megan

drummed her fingers against her stomach. "Grandpa was a fighter pilot in Normandy. Captain John Jameson. Grandma told me they met in 1944 and married when the war ended."

"You don't know your grandmother's maiden name?"

"Not for sure. But I'm guessing it was Dubois."

He sighed. "That would be my guess too, but that's conjecture, not deduction."

She grinned slyly. "Does it help the conjecture to know that my mother's middle name is Dubois?"

Paul tried to contain his excitement but he couldn't help a self-satisfied smile. "Did your grandmother have any siblings?"

"One sister."

Yes! It felt so good when puzzle pieces started coming together.

Megan narrowed her eyes. "What are you grinning about?"

He leaned toward her, folding his arms triumphantly. "Adele Jarreau and Eduard Dubois had twin daughters. Marie and Sophia."

Her mouth dropped open. "My grandmother was an identical twin?"

"A twin, not necessarily identical. But that could indicate that identical twins run in your family." Paul stood and paced the length of the small room, adrenaline pumping through his veins. "Was the sister's name Marie?"

"I don't think so." She frowned. "I think she called her 'Champignon.'"

"Mushroom?" He sank into the armchair.

She shrugged. "I guess it was some childhood pet name."

Paul thrummed his fingers against the chair arms. Even without her great-aunt's name, it seemed quite likely at this point that Megan was Adele Jarreau's great-granddaughter. But that still didn't explain the likeness of both to Colette.

Megan shoved his hand to his lap and leaned a butt cheek against his chair arm. "So how are Colette and I related?"

"I don't think you are."

"But--"

"Your grandmother and her sister were probably in their twenties during the war." Paul snaked an arm around Megan's waist to keep her from sliding off the chair arm. "Let's say for argument that they *were* Sophia and Marie Dubois. If Marie died childless, the French side of the family tree stops. There's no way you and Colette are related."

Megan sighed. "Well, at least I don't share a gene pool with a psychopathic killer." She wrinkled that cute pug nose. "But if we're not family, then why do Colette and I look so much alike?"

"Random coincidence?"

She looked pensive. "I just don't believe that."

"Nor do I. Would you consider the theory that you and Colette really are twins separated at birth?"

She shook her head emphatically. "That is absolutely not true." She studied him. "How old is Colette, anyway?"

"Twenty-seven." If that wasn't a lie like all the rest.

"Well, I'm twenty-three," she said triumphantly. "Not. A. Twin. What else you got?"

There was only one other explanation. "Perhaps Marie Dubois gave birth to a child before she died." He sighed. "I'll do some more digging after I retrieve my laptop."

Her eyes widened. "Your laptop? From your apartment? Why can't you use the computer here?"

"There's a risk, even at three in the morning, that I'd be recognized. But mainly, I want my own laptop because Colette used it. If I search the history of the websites she visited, I may be able to find who she's been in contact with, or how she planned this operation. And we could use some changes of clothing." He studied her delectable curves. "A few of Colette's things should fit you."

Megan pursed her lips. "It's too dangerous, Paul. What if the police arrest you before you even make it to your place?"

He retrieved the jean jacket he'd acquired last night and emptied the pockets onto the bedspread. Stage makeup. Hair dye. A fake mustache. "Hopefully they won't recognize me."

Chapter Ten

"Got your keys?" Don/Donnie swerved his Jeep Cherokee into a parking space in front of an apartment complex.

Colette rummaged through Megan's bottomless backpack before finally finding her house keys in an inside pocket. She peeked at her driver's license to find the apartment number. Two sixty-eight. Did that mean second floor?

She looked up, but the upstairs hallways looped and turned in all directions, and the only numbers visible from the lot were one-nineteen and two-twenty. How could she just march toward the right one looking like she knew where she was going? She'd have to wait until Don drove away.

But he was too gentlemanly to do that. Before Colette could unbuckle her seat belt, Dapper Don was at her side of the vehicle. He actually opened the door and helped her out! Salim would barely come to a rolling stop and expect her to jump.

"Damn!" Don's mild curse surprised her as he hoisted the big orange suitcase out of the back. "What's in here, bricks?"

She'd transferred the bronze Remington statue and the other booty she'd lifted from the Chandlers' display cabinet into the big bag while he was paying the check at Denny's. "I brought home part of a Greek column as a souvenir," she said saucily, hoping that would sound like Megan's brand of humor. Assuming she had a sense of humor.

"You're a card, Kid." Don carried the bag up the stairs, and then wheeled it down one of the long outside hallways of the garden apartment complex.

Colette followed his lead. One problem solved. Another possibly on the way. What if he decided to stay awhile? She was all out of small talk. Her face hurt from two hours of showing interest in the poor people of Kazakhstan and Katmandu. Although she hadn't minded the view. Don Chandler was handsome and sexy enough to make her want to jump his bones.

If he weren't her 'brother', of course.

It wasn't far to two sixty-eight. Colette pulled out the key, inserted it in the lock, and breathed a quiet sigh of relief when the door opened. Funny, she hadn't been this nervous about blowing up a building.

But then, she hadn't planned to kill all those people. If the security guard had believed her story about bringing flowers to surprise her boyfriend on his birthday, she wouldn't have had to shoot him. And what was up with those workaholics in the computer room so early in the morning? If they'd stayed home until a reasonable hour, they wouldn't have gotten hurt.

Killed. She was wanted for murder now. Good thing there was no death penalty in France. If captured, the worst she'd get would be life in prison.

Women's prison. Colette groaned inwardly. She might have to live fifty or sixty lonely years without ever seeing a penis again.

She'd rather face the death penalty.

"Want me to stay a few minutes while you check around, make

sure nothing's missing?"

The irony struck her but she refrained from a chuckle. "No, I'm fine. Thanks for driving me."

"No problem."

She pecked Don's cheek and started to pull away, but he grabbed her with both arms and enveloped her in a bear hug.

Mon Dieu. She tried not to act startled. The Chandlers were, apparently, a very affectionate family. Hesitant, she leaned into the hug. Don Chandler's chest was more streamlined, less husky than Paul Bernard's, but his body exuded the same sense of assurance and security.

Just as she got comfortable in the embrace, Don wrenched away, and she realized her hand had strayed from his back to his hip.

"Megan, are you all right?"

She straightened and flounced back her hair. "Sure. Why do you ask?"

"You've just been acting a little strange since you got home. Nervous. Uncomfortable."

"Probably jetlagged. I'm not as used to intercontinental flying as you are."

"You're not worried about starting back to school?"

School? She'd thought Megan had already graduated college.

"You've got a year of teaching behind you. And your students last semester loved you. You'll do great."

Teacher. Now she remembered. Megan taught Art History. The art interest was how she'd lured her on that European tour. "I'm not worried. But thanks for the vote of confidence."

Don smiled. "You know if there's anything you need, I'm only forty minutes away." He glanced at the tan, comfortable-looking sofa.

Please don't make yourself comfortable. Please believe your sister is fine and just leave.

As if responding to her silent vibes, Don chucked her under the chin and left.

Before he could change his mind, Colette closed the door behind him and quietly locked it. Then she looked around the apartment. Kitchen to the left, bedroom to the right. Beyond the kitchen, a large open living area, with a round dining table in one corner and in the center, a small television and a mid-range sofa and chair. As nice as could be expected on a teacher's earnings. It would do for the short time she'd be here.

A thought struck her. Did the boyfriend live here? Colette searched the neat apartment looking for a closet of men's clothes, empty pizza boxes, rotting food in the refrigerator. She found a clean kitchen and only a few men's shirts hanging in the walk-in closet. The boyfriend had his own place.

No matter. By tomorrow, she'd be gone from this forsaken excuse for a state and on her way to a tropical island with no extradition policy.

She sank into the serviceable sofa, grabbed her I-phone and logged, once again, into her bank website. Her breath caught in her throat as silent computer bytes chugged their way into the confidential page and onto the screen.

Yes! There it was. Today at one thirty-six p.m. Switzerland time, a deposit of fifty thousand Euros had been made into the coded, unnamed account.

And at one fifty-five, the same amount had been zipped right out.

Merde! Colette stared unblinking at the small screen as if some technical error had occurred, as if she could reboot or just wait and it would all be righted. But sixty long silent seconds later, vain hope turned into anguished misery.

The Community could not have recalled its deposit. The routing and account numbers were encrypted, a one-way trip for money to flow into the account. Never out. Only she had the password which decoded the shadow account number and entered the real one, and she'd never written it down or uttered it aloud. No one else in the world knew that password.

Salim.

Nausea taunted her stomach. She'd logged in once, in his room, still naked from a night of amorous pleasure. He'd been playing with his cell phone, taking videos of her nude body, scanning all over the room. Including her fingers as she typed in the password numbers for her account. She'd protested and demanded he delete it. He'd laughed, said he was just playing with her. Then he'd clicked a button on his phone and deleted the video.

Except, obviously, he hadn't.

"Son-of-a-bitch!" Colette yelled at the screen, at the walls, at her own stupid heart. She'd risked her life and snuffed out the lives of innocent people, and he'd absconded with her money. And he was probably now on his way to that island they'd both dreamed about.

Paradeo. The romantic isle in the South Pacific where they'd once planned to live off coconuts and their love for each other. *Son-of-a-cock-sucking-bitch.*

Could she have been any more stupid?

Yes, considerably. She'd almost confided to Salim her discovery of her American look-alike, and her plan to switch places with her and leave Megan to face the consequences of Colette's actions. But after she'd seen him cozying up to that new female recruit, she'd kept that plan to herself. Thank goodness her head was smarter than her heart, or the two-timing bastard might have anonymously tipped off Interpol that Colette Marchand had escaped to New York. As it was, he probably thought she was still expecting to see him, eventually, in Paradeo.

"I'll see you in *Hell*, Salim!" Her body quivered with adrenaline, burning for action. She wanted to shoot the son-of-a-bitch. Hurl a grenade at something. Or have angry, heart-stopping sex.

She had to settle for slamming the backpack onto the floor, wishing it were Salim's face. If she were a woman who cried, tears would have filled the room. What the hell could she do now? She had Paul's five hundred Euros and a few pricey knickknacks she might be able to pawn toward a new life in the Caribbean. But then what? How would she live? Apply to the Haiti Department of Terrorism?

She stalked the small apartment, looking for something of value she could add to her meager possessions. Megan's only 'treasures' were a Barbie Doll collection and a bunch of cheap art prints. Colette should have stayed at the parents' house. At least they had some good stuff to sell.

She dragged Megan's suitcase from the front door into the bedroom and tossed all the clothes out onto the floor. After stripping down to her bra and panties, she searched the closet for clothes that were, if not fashionable, at least less ugly. She might be on the lam a long time. One thing was certain. She would not live out the rest of her life in a cheesy garden apartment in New Jersey.

While she was stuffing jeans and shirts into the suitcase, the doorbell rang. Colette caught her breath. The brother returning for a chatty visit before he went home? Surely not. Probably just a neighbor mooching coffee. Colette smoothed the clothing over the hidden contraband, zipped up the suitcase, and stood it upright on the floor.

She listened for the bell to ring again, but it didn't. Instead, she heard a metallic sound as a key turned in the locked front door.

Merde.

Another woman might have felt fear, but that emotion held no contest for the fury in Colette's soul. Grabbing a robe from the closet, she threw it over her and cast around for a weapon. She found nothing more lethal than a nail file. But she'd wring this intruder's neck with her bare hands if she had to, and picturing him as Salim would make her triumph even sweeter.

Standing behind the partially opened bedroom door, she listened to the front door open. Heavy footsteps padded into the main room. "Megan?"

Not the brother. Colette peeked out to see a suit jacket draped over a barstool. The matching pants had been dropped on the floor beside it.

She edged out of the bedroom, following the trail of a man's shoes and socks, a blue tie, a white dress shirt, and black silk boxers.

A naked, thirty-ish, dark-haired man turned to face her. Grinning. Colette's gaze dropped from his semi-handsome face, to his pale, sparsely tufted chest, to his impressive, locked-and-loaded package.

He walked toward her. "Hi, honey, I'm home."

Chapter Eleven

Megan held a towel around Paul's neck as he bent over the bathroom sink, massaging yellow hair dye into his scalp. "I can't believe you stole this stuff from Jacques and Marcel."

"Borrowed," he corrected.

"Without their knowledge," she teased. Yet, she was impressed by his resourcefulness. Like hers, Paul's life had changed in a heartbeat. There'd been no time to plan even minutes ahead.

"How long am I supposed to leave this on?" He straightened, dabbed at his forehead with the edges of the towel, and washed his hands.

"I don't know. The instructions are in Dutch."

"I guess an hour should do it." Paul draped the towel around his neck, dragged the armchair next to the bed, and sat with legs propped on the spread. Bare-chested, wearing only pants and the white towel, he looked like a prizefighter resting between rounds. A prizefighter with yellow-orange hair tufts clumped about his head. Hopefully that neon color would wash out in the rinse.

Megan walked to the bed, where the remains of their room service meal still sat on a tray. "You going to finish your *croque monsieur*?" she asked.

"Nope. It's yours."

She wolfed down the remainder of the sandwich under Paul's amused gaze, then reached for a leftover chip. "What's so funny?"

"When it comes to food, you and Colette have nothing in common. You attacked your sandwich—and now mine--as if you hadn't eaten for days. Colette would have ordered a salad and picked at it for an hour without actually consuming much at all."

"When it comes to anything, Colette and I have nothing in common," Megan snapped. They'd been getting along so well, and then he had to go and compare her to the lovely Colette. She lifted the tray off the bed, carried it to the door, and, after cautiously peeking outside, placed the tray out in the hall.

"No need to get huffy," Paul said. "The comparison wasn't an insult."

"Just a preference for stick-figure women?"

His gaze roved approvingly over her body. "Not necessarily."

Determined not to blush, Megan walked to the nightstand where the silent telephone sat and looked at the clock. It was eight a.m. in New York. She fingered the phone hesitantly. Surely Mom would be up by now.

"You've left two messages in the past hour," Paul reminded her.

"I'm sorry, I know it's expensive to use a hotel phone to make an international call." Not that there was another choice, since both of their cell phones were AWOL. "I'm going to owe you so much money. I promise, when this is all over, I'll pay you back. With interest."

He shrugged. "The money's not the issue, Megan. But you're

driving yourself crazy."

Waiting and doing nothing would make her crazier. "Mom has to be home at this hour. Why doesn't she answer?"

"You're calling from a different phone. Perhaps your mother doesn't pick up if she doesn't recognize the number."

"But it went straight to voice mail." As if the phone was off the hook. "Anyway, why wouldn't she pick up *any* strange number? She knows I'm stranded in Paris."

"*If* she got your earlier message."

He had a logical answer for everything. "Obviously you've never met my mother. I was supposed to get home last night. Mom would have called me the minute the plane landed to make sure I got in okay."

He clicked his tongue against his teeth. "So you moved all the way to New Jersey yet still haven't left your parents' nest."

She glared at him. "My parents used to live in New Jersey," she said. "*They* moved away. Downsizing, wanting to be closer to the city so Daddy doesn't have to drive, all that."

"Do you speak to your mother every day?"

"Usually." It made her feel childish to admit it, but she liked sharing her day with her family.

Paul flicked a loose orange hair from his brow, examined his finger, cursed, and then wiped the stained finger on the towel. "Perhaps she's been calling and leaving messages on your cell phone. What would she do if *you* didn't pick up?"

"Call my home phone."

He raised a dark bushy brow. "You have a land line?"

Why did his every word make her feel like a child? "I'm probably the only person under thirty who does. My parents insisted they have a way to contact me if I forget to charge my cell phone."

He chuckled. "I rest my case."

She strode to his chair and punched him playfully in the shoulder. Her fist connected with hard muscle. She drew back, rubbing her hand. "How often do you see *your* parents?"

"Two or three times a year."

"They live in London?"

"Yes. He paused, then, as if feeling the need to contribute something personal, added "My father is retired. My mother retired the day she married my father. Her life revolves around the social season."

His face made an interesting study when he wasn't angry, sarcastic, or joking. She had to capture this on paper. Megan foraged in the desk drawer for a page of hotel stationery, a pen, and the room service menu to lean on.

She settled herself on the bed, back propped against the headboard, toes not quite touching Paul's. Her fingers began to sketch with her brain barely aware of it. "Do your folks ever come here to visit you?"

"Once a year. Mom's annual Paris shopping trip."

He had such expressive eyes. They were probably the reason she'd trusted him even before she knew she could. "How did you choose your career?"

"I've always been a logical sort. I like puzzles, and computer programming appealed to me in college."

"I meant the civil service."

His smile took her by surprise. It lit up his face, softened his expression, and was potentially heart-stopping. He moved his leg, only slightly, but his bare toes now tickled hers. "Since I was a lad, I've wanted to live abroad and serve my country. It sort of runs in the family. My father served the Crown, and my grandfather before him."

"That sounds a lot more glamorous than my family's business."

"Which is?"

"Liquor distribution."

He quirked a brow. "Not bootlegging, is it?"

"Of course not." She bristled. "Perfectly legal."

He grinned. "Just yanking your chain, love. Isn't that what you Americans say?"

Megan filled in the details of Paul's face on her sketch paper, then drew in his torso. Though proportionate, his brawny chest filled the rest of the page.

Curious, he leaned over and grabbed the sketch paper before she could jerk it out of his reach. "What the hell? Is this me?"

Her face flamed. "It's not very good. Just a quick sketch."

"It's damned good." He grinned. "I almost look like a hunk."

"You are a hunk," she blurted before she could stop herself. She giggled. "If you ignore the orange hair."

"Hair!" He jumped to his feet. "It's probably time to wash this stuff out." He ran to the bathroom sink, turned on the faucet and plunged his head under the water.

"You might have left it on too long," Megan said after he'd rinsed three times. His hair was now mostly yellow-blond, but with a few orange lightning-bolt streaks.

"It'll wash out," he said philosophically. "Won't it?"

She couldn't help grinning. "After about twenty shampoos."

"Bloody hell." He brought the rest of the makeup into the bathroom and began applying a beige blush. It was not particularly flattering, but it did add a little color to his pallid, indoor cheeks. He held up a fake, brownish gold mustache. "Do you think it's too much?"

She cocked her head to one side. "No more outrageous than the hair."

He plastered it on, took a last look in the mirror and then strode out to the bedroom. His gaze lit once again on the sketch she'd made. "What does your boyfriend look like?"

"Fletcher?" The question took her by surprise. "He's tall, though not as tall as you. Thin. Brown hair, brown eyes."

"Hairy chest?" He looked again at the drawing.

"Um...no."

He grinned.

Despite the yellow hair, with or without the shirt, that grin was incredibly sexy. But she didn't share that thought with Paul. He was already ego-tripping because she'd called him a hunk.

Paul grabbed his shirt off the headboard and stuffed his arms into the sleeves. He buttoned his cuffs, and then fastened the rest of the buttons without watching what he was doing, managing to skip a buttonhole and get the whole row out of line.

"You missed one."

He let out a frustrated growl.

"Let me help." Megan moved close to him and re-buttoned his shirt, her fingers almost-but-not-quite touching his skin. An odd sensation enveloped her. The domestic gesture felt every bit as intimate as an embrace.

She backed away, her eyes refusing to meet his.

Paul grabbed the jean jacket and slung it over his shoulder. "I'll stop at the reception desk and pay for another night, then head to my flat. Be back in a couple hours." He touched her chin, forcing her to look at him. "Stay in the room and don't open the door for anyone."

Megan reached for her blue hooded sweatshirt. "I'm going with you."

"No." His voice was soft, but uncompromising. "You're not."

"But what if--?"

"You'll be perfectly safe here." He shrugged into his jacket, then placed his hands on her shoulders and leaned forward, lips puckered.

Megan stiffened. Would he kiss her? She closed her eyes, but he planted his kiss on her forehead instead.

"I'm so glad you're not a terrorist, Megan Chandler." He straightened, but his warm breath stayed on her skin.

"I'm glad I met you, Paul--" She swallowed, realizing she didn't even know her rescuer's last name.

He smiled. "Bernard."

Nice name. Playfully, Megan extended her hand. "Nice to meet you, Paul Bernard."

"Nice to meet you too." He grasped her hand, holding it a little longer than customary. Then, before his warmth had faded, he strode to the door. "Lock this behind me," he said, yanking the Do Not Disturb sign off the doorknob and moving it to the outside. And then he was gone.

Megan's gaze circled the room. Without Paul's imposing presence, it seemed so much bigger. Emptier. With nooks and crannies she hadn't noticed before.

What if somebody had planted a bug in this room? What if the evening reception staff came on duty and, having seen the TV news, recognized the fugitives' resemblance to the Mr. and Mrs. Potter they'd checked in last night? What if, ignoring the Do Not Disturb sign and her protests, they walked in and found the gun in the backpack?

She shuddered. Moments ago she'd felt secure, almost comfortable with her situation. Suddenly she was terrified again. She didn't feel safe here. She didn't feel safe anywhere.

Adrenaline stoked by panic, Megan shoved the black backpack under the bed, donned her sweatshirt, and bolted out the door.

Chapter Twelve

Colette stared at one of the biggest cocks she'd ever seen. And she'd seen plenty. "What are you doing here? Darling," she added. Since the man had a key, he must be the boyfriend. Or some other man in Megan's life who felt comfortable barging in and dropping his drawers in the middle of the living room.

"The last segment of my route was cancelled so I came on home. God, I've missed you so much."

He didn't ask about her trip, or waste time with small talk. He just grabbed her, slipping his hands inside her open robe. Squeezing her butt to lock her against his imposing erection.

Another woman might have panicked, but Colette excelled at handling this kind of situation. Horny men were the easiest to manipulate. With his brain temporarily disabled, this man wouldn't ask a lot of questions.

"It's good to be home." She moved into the embrace, grinding her pelvis against his hips, mashing her breasts to his chest. When she dug her fingers into his buttock he gasped, though whether in surprise or delight, she wasn't sure.

"Baby."

She shushed him by inserting her tongue deep in his mouth,

but he didn't appear anxious to say anything else. Colette let him take over the kiss, moving her hands down his sides, cupping his balls. He was *so* ready. He'd probably gone without for a couple of weeks. It'd been only a couple of days for Colette, but she wouldn't mind sampling this big stud's talents.

"Oh, baby." He sucked a hickey onto her neck and yanked her robe off her shoulders. It puddled on the floor like fluffy clouds. His eager erection strained against her hand, poking and pushing toward her pleasure spot.

"Whoa, tiger. Not ready." To slow him down, she stepped back and thrust her chest forward, encouraging him to suckle at a black-lace covered breast. Big mistake.

"Wow." He raised his head to cluck appreciatively. "Megan Chandler got a tattoo? Who are you, Woman, and what have you done with my girlfriend?"

Colette froze. *Breathe*. It was just a saying, she told herself. An idiom. She'd heard a character on American television say something similar.

"I thought you'd like it." His leering smile said he did, so she went with it. "I wanted to make myself into a new woman." She fondled her breasts for his pleasure. "Just for you."

As his eyes filled with desire, she dropped to her knees, grasped his member and applied her lips to its swollen yearning.

"Ooh. Baby. I like it. Oh, yeah."

She licked and sucked until Boyfriend couldn't even emit those words, just primal groans.

Men were so easy. With the proper technique, you could lead them around by their penises and play them for all they were worth. Fortunately, Colette was a virtuoso on that organ.

She performed a skillful sonata on his instrument, her solo enriched by the percussive background of his groans and gasps, bringing him just to the brink. Then she withdrew her mouth.

He dug his fingers into her shoulders. "Don't stop."

He'd barely gotten inside the apartment, and already she had him eating out of her hand. Colette enjoyed having a man where she wanted him. And right now, she wanted him inside her, filling up that hole of anger and despair.

He tried to mount her right there, but she slipped out of his grasp. "Protection," she hissed. "Now." She didn't care how enticing his dick was, no way was she going to risk having this bastard's bastard child.

He rushed to the bedroom, his member still pointing straight up. Colette followed, unsnapping and removing her bra and letting it dangle from her wrist. She positioned herself on her back in the center of the king sized bed as the boyfriend suited up.

Fletcher. His name, she remembered from Internet conversations, was Fletcher. Strong-looking face, though she hadn't spent much time looking at his face.

"Fletcher, come to me," she whimpered, only partly for effect, as he climbed over her and finger-pleasured the damp desire between her thighs. "I want you now."

The first thrust was always the best. Colette let him grunt and rut inside her until he was stiff enough to keep a boner in church. Then she braced her elbows, reared up, and forced him over onto his back. "My turn, cowboy."

Fletcher seemed surprised at her taking command. But not displeased. She rode him hard and wet, bouncing her breasts with each stroke. *Fuck you, Salim. May your tight sexy ass rot in the lowest corner of Hell.* She punched Fletcher's chest. She leaned low and bit his nipple. She slapped his balls with her thrusts and stuck a finger in his asshole.

And he seemed to enjoy every second of it.

* * *

Which direction? Megan threw her hood over her head and glanced both ways down the sidewalk. To the right, halfway down the block, a head of bright yellow hair loomed over the dozen or so people that separated them.

Megan charged forward, then skidded in her tracks. If she caught up with him, Paul would insist she go back to the hotel. And she'd demand to go with him. They'd argue. Possibly attracting the attention of a gendarme. The beat cop could become Paris's new hero for arresting two dangerous fugitives that Interpol hadn't been able to apprehend.

Her stomach spasmed. It was too dangerous for her and Paul to be seen together. And she probably *would* be safer in the hotel. But she didn't feel safer. Being alone reminded her of her first hours on her own in Paris. Paul had become a lifeline she couldn't bear to let go of, even for a few hours.

So she tailed him to the Metro station, hanging back far enough so that half a dozen people separated her from Paul, but following close enough not to lose sight of him. Using the pass he'd purchased for her yesterday, she entered the subway station twenty yards behind him and kept her distance until a train roared into the station. When Paul boarded it, Megan entered the doors of the next car behind his.

Over the next few stations, the train filled up. Megan gave up her seat and held onto a strap near the window so she could see the passengers who'd exited. A huge crowd got on at the Boulevard Voltaire station, and almost as many got off. As the doors started to close, Megan took a last glance out the window. Paul stood on the station platform.

She leaped off the train just in time to see him swallowed up in a throng of business suits and shopping bags. When the crowd dispersed, he had vanished.

Damn! Had he exited to the east or west? Or hoofed it upstairs to transfer to another line?

As Megan debated her options, a hand clamped over her mouth and a large body shoved her behind a pillar. "What the hell are you doing?" rasped a man's voice.

Paul's voice. As he released her mouth, Megan let out a relieved breath. "I'm sorry. I know I shouldn't have followed you but--"

"'But' and 'I'm sorry' are incompatible." His body pressed against hers.

"Okay, I'm not sorry. I followed you because I was scared."

"If you'd stayed at the hotel--"

"I didn't feel safe there."

His breath warmed her ear. "And you feel safer here with me, exposed on the streets?"

"Yes." There, she'd said it. "You're my only friend in Paris. I was afraid you wouldn't come back."

Paul's cheeks puffed, but she couldn't tell if he was pleased or angry. He brought his face close to hers. "I promised I wouldn't leave you, that I'd stay with you all the way to the airport. I never go back on my word."

"Good to know." She stared silently into his solemn eyes, not knowing what else to say.

He returned her gaze. Finally he drew back and scanned the crowds in the station. "Keep that hood up over your face. Don't talk. And try to keep your boobs from sticking out. Maybe people will mistake you for a boy."

And be less likely to recognize them as the man and woman whose faces had been plastered across the television screen.

Megan hunched her shoulders, pulled the hood drawstring snug around her chin and followed Paul, at close range now, out of the metro station and onto the Boulevard Voltaire. They tramped past majestic hotels and small pensions, which gave way to three story apartment buildings.

"Wait here." Paul stopped at a small patisserie wedged between a dry cleaners and a bicycle repair shop. "They have wonderful croissants." He nudged her inside, yanking a ten euro note from his pocket. "I'll be back before you can eat your way through this." He left the bill and loped down the sidewalk.

Megan took a seat next to the window and watched his retreating figure shrink. But she kept squinting to view it until he turned off onto a residential street.

He'd be back. He'd said he would. And it might be naïve and trusting, but Megan believed him.

After eating three buttery, flaky pastries, she had to agree with Paul's assessment. The croissants were to die for. She bought another half dozen to take back to the hotel and stepped outside to watch for Paul's return.

It wasn't raining, but the afternoon clouds had darkened and a distant roll of thunder threatened. Megan paced to the corner and crossed the street, then headed back to the bakery/cafe. A few steps from the door, footsteps pounded behind her. Arms seized her around the waist and warm breath tickled her neck.

"Paul, stop. Enough." She tried to shrug out of his arms but his grip tightened.

"Ma cherie." A man breathed against her neck.

Not Paul. Megan's muscles froze. "Let me go."

The lecher pressed his chest into her back and kissed the nape of her neck. She'd heard Frenchmen were bold, but this man's persistence in almost-broad daylight on a public street was unnerving.

She bucked her backside into his front. "*Arrete.*"

But he didn't stop. His tongue licked her ear lobe. His fingers brushed against her lips, seeking entry. When Megan tried to scream, he clamped his hand over her mouth. And hissed French nothings into her ear. One phrase she couldn't quite make out sounded like 'Serious attention.' Then he murmured one that did. "*Colette, mon amour.*"

Colette?

Terrified, Megan sunk her teeth into his palm, kicking and struggling. "I'm not Colette!"

Heavy footsteps charged up behind them. A wonderfully familiar voice yelled, "*Dégage tes sales pattes d'elle!*"

At being told to take his dirty paws off her, the lecher released her. He faced Paul with his dukes up, his olive-toned face flushed with rage, but when he took in Paul's size and his menacing glare, he dropped his hands to his sides.

"*Dégage d'ici!*"

Cursing in French, the dark-skinned man spat on the ground

and took off down an alley.

Megan let out her breath and hugged Paul's neck.

"Can't seem to stay out of trouble, can you?" Frowning, he linked his elbow possessively through hers as they walked back to the station.

She noticed his other arm was empty. "Where's your laptop?"

"I couldn't get to my flat. I expected maybe a patrol car halfway down the block staking out the place, but there was a uniformed officer at the entrance to the apartment house, checking IDs as people went in."

Megan gasped. "Did he see you?"

"No, because I saw him first."

"I guess it's lucky for me you did, and came back to the bakery so quick. If you hadn't..."

"You would have been fine on your own. Don't all women know how to kick a man where it hurts?"

"Kind of hard when he grabs you from behind." She hugged Paul's arm. "My hero," she said playfully.

He wrinkled his face. "I'm not a hero, Megan."

"No, you're a saint." She giggled. "Saint Bernard."

"Clever," he said sarcastically. "That's the first time I've heard that--today." He steered her toward the subway entrance and down the underground escalator.

"Paul," she said when they were waiting for the train, "did you know that man?"

"No, should I?"

"He thought he knew me. He called me Colette."

Paul's body stiffened. "Are you sure?"

"My French isn't that bad."

"If Colette knows him," Paul said uneasily, "wouldn't *I* know him as well?"

Not if she were two-timing him with this other man. Which seemed likely, given the man's amorous attentions. But Megan didn't mention that to Paul. He was already devastated at having been used for Colette's nefarious political purposes. Suggesting she'd also betrayed him in the sack wouldn't help his frame of mind.

Had that man recognized Paul? The look he'd fastened on him had been pure wrath. Had Colette told him she was also seeing another man? Or had he only just discovered where Colette lived, and with whom?

Maybe they should all join forces to find Colette and bring her to justice. Or not. Megan recalled the lecherous look in that man's dark eyes and his tight grasp on her arm. What if he was part of the terrorist organization?

Chapter Thirteen

Colette lay on her back in contented exhaustion, Fletcher's snores droning beside her. He ought to be damned tired. Three times in two hours was a record, even for her. But he'd sailed through like a champion training for a marathon.

She shifted cautiously, too damned sore to stay in one position. The man was a fucking battering ram.

Not that she hadn't enjoyed the battering. But the sooner she got rid of the naked man in her bed, the sooner she could get out of this town. Out of this country. She didn't dare risk another encounter with Megan Chandler's family.

A phone rang somewhere in the apartment. Hers? His? Fletcher didn't stir, so she dragged her exhausted body off the bed and into the living area.

No sound from his pants, which still lay on the floor. Colette reached into the black backpack and drew out Megan's phone, which warbled some vaguely familiar tune. The display registered 'Mom Calling.'

She'd barely left the Chandler home a few hours ago. Megan's mother really was as smothering as Don had hinted. Or had she discovered that some of her treasures were missing? Colette disconnected the call and pushed the phone into the bottom of the backpack.

The cotton floral robe sprawled seductively on the floor next to the black boxers. Colette slipped it on and belted it loosely at her waist.

A phone rang again. This time with a more traditional ring tone. Colette found a standard wall phone in the kitchen, and raced for it before it woke Fletcher. She checked the Caller ID. Mom again. Two times in two minutes. Maybe she should answer it.

She lifted the phone from its cradle. "Hi, Mom," she said brightly. "What's going on?"

"Hello, dear. Is everything all right?"

No, and I suspect it's going to get worse. "Of course. Why wouldn't it be?"

"Well, you left so early without even saying goodbye."

"Didn't Don leave you a note? He had some early meeting and he offered to drive me home. Save Daddy the trip."

"Yes, I saw the note." Mrs. Chandler sighed. "I was just hoping you'd stay a little longer. We could have gone to the museum and had lunch in Manhattan..."

Brother Donnie had definitely called it. "Some other time, Mom." She yawned audibly. "It was a long trip and I was just anxious to get home to my own place."

"I completely understand. Maybe next weekend."

Colette grinned. Next weekend she planned to be on some Caribbean beach.

"Megan, did you realize you left the phone off the hook?"

"What? Oh, I guess I did," she said innocently. "Someone phoned looking for Don and I went to get him and I guess I forgot to hang it up. Sorry."

"No problem, dear. I couldn't understand why I couldn't get a dial tone just now."

"Well, that's why. See you on the weekend." Colette clicked off the phone before Mama Dear thought of something else to say.

This was getting too complicated. So many details required to keep her cover. Colette stared at the phone in her hand. Mrs. Chandler had only just reconnected the phone. So she probably hadn't yet checked her voice mail for messages.

Thankful she'd memorized the number printed on the Chandler's phone, Colette dialed into their voice mail system. When the robotic voice asked for the phone number she was trying to access, Colette dug into the backpack for Megan's cell phone, found the last missed call, and then typed that number into the other phone.

"Password?" the machine asked.

Damn. How could she possibly guess what four numbers they would use for their password? Somebody's birthday, maybe? Don's? Megan's?

She visualized Megan's profile page. Birthday, October 28. It was worth a shot. Colette keyed in one-zero-two-eight and was rewarded with the robot's voice. "You have two unheard messages."

Unheard. *Merci.* After listening to the messages, Colette jotted down the number Megan had left for the Hotel Denise. Why wasn't she using Paul's phone now? Had he been arrested? Or just dumped her whiny ass?

She deleted both messages, well aware that this action, like the others, was only a temporary solution. Megan would phone again.

And the next call might reach her mother. Colette was tempted to call the French police herself and leave an anonymous tip leading them to Megan's arrest.

Hmmmm....

To confirm the twit's whereabouts, Colette used Megan's cell phone to call the Denise Hotel in Paris. "Megan Chandler, *s'il vous plait*."

After a long wait, the desk clerk responded. But there was no Megan Chandler registered.

Merde. She switched off the phone and tossed it back in the bag. Had Megan already moved on?

"Hello, Beautiful."

Colette jumped at Fletcher's voice behind her. How much had he overheard?

His hand snaked inside her robe. "So what did your mother want?"

"She was just checking to make sure I made it home okay."

"Mama Bear worried about her baby bear." He squeezed her ass. "Sure makes it tough on baby bear's sex life."

Clearly he was not completely worn out.

Fletcher slid both arms inside the robe and anchored his hands to her buttocks while he pushed his erection between her thighs.

She nudged his hands away and belted her robe. "I need to go grocery shopping. I'm out of everything." Hopefully, Mr. Horny would consider that a boring errand, dress and leave.

"You've got frozen pizzas." Fletcher swirled his tongue inside her ear in a motion that affected her more than she cared to admit. "Let's spend the afternoon getting...reacquainted."

If his hardening erection had any say in it, the only scarcity that would interfere with Fletcher's plans was a condom shortage. If that. Colette plastered on a seductive smile. "Sure, baby."

The man had to get tired eventually. And then she'd leave him sleeping happily, as she'd left Paul, and make her escape.

Fletcher strode to the refrigerator. "I'm getting a beer." He grinned. "Energy for the workout. You want one of your flavored waters?"

"Sure." She dropped the robe on the floor and sashayed into the bedroom.

The boyfriend was a tiger, Colette had to admit. He knew how to use what he had, and he had a lot. He hadn't asked about her satisfaction, but that didn't surprise her. Men like this rarely did. In the short intervals between their multiple sexual congresses, he hadn't asked her anymore about her trip either.

When he joined her moments later, the beer bottle was half-empty, and his prick was fully erect. Colette took a swig of strawberry flavored water and then stretched out on her back, knees slightly bent, hips raised to give him a full view.

He climbed onto the bed and sat on his haunches beside her. With no further foreplay, he plunged one long finger inside her. "You are so naughty, baby." He fingered his erection with his other hand. "Look what you do to me."

She reached for him, but he knocked her hand away and flipped her onto her stomach.

"Get up on your knees."

Colette complied without protest. Doggy style could be fun.

Fletcher slapped his hands against one buttock, then the other. "Naughty girl." He spanked her harder. "Megan is a very naughty girl."

The stinging pain was tantalizing at first, but as he smacked harder and harder, 'hurts so good' became just 'hurts.' "Stop!"

He climbed on top of her, his chest grazing her back, and whispered in her ear as he slapped her thighs. "Ask me nicely."

She groaned. "Please stop."

For an answer, he grabbed her butt cheeks and, again with no foreplay or warning, rammed into her.

Colette screamed and tried to wriggle away. This wasn't fun. With no condom or lubricant, a cock this size was damned painful. And Fletcher made no effort to be gentle.

"You like this, don't you, baby?" He pulled out and rammed into her again. "You like it when I hurt you."

A sadist. And Colette was no masochist. She ground her teeth, cursing silently in French. *Get this over with and get the hell off of me.*

"Tell me you like it."

"Bastard!" She struggled to crawl forward, out of his grasp.

"You know you like this." He dug his fingernails into her butt cheeks to hold her in place and forced another thrust. "Say 'Yes, Master, please hurt me,' and I'll stop."

Like hell. With all her strength she bucked, not exactly toppling him over, but freeing his dick, at least, from the place where it had gotten way too familiar. She liked sex on her own terms. She rolled to her back and tried to scoot off the bed, but he grabbed her and pinned her down. Damn, he still had a stallion-sized erection.

Sweat ran down Colette's breasts as she wrestled with him. Though wiry, the man was stronger than she would have thought. She slapped at his arms and legs, and reached for his penis.

He grabbed her wrist and pinned her elbow onto the bed. "So you do want it?"

Before she could reply, he'd slipped on protection and was moving in for a frontal assault. His magnificent member teased the places where she liked being stroked, until she was wet with undeniable desire.

When she raised her hips to meet him, he pulled back. "Beg me for it, bitch."

No way would she ever beg a man for anything, least of all his penis. "Game over." Colette struggled to push him away. *Then tussled to pull him closer.* She was so damned angry. And so turned on.

With rage and desire boiling in the same pot, she twisted and clawed, bucking and inviting. He met her thrusts and dared her to fight him. She raised her head and bit his nipple. He plastered his mouth onto hers, crushing her lip against her teeth in a bruising kiss.

Grabbing his butt, she pulled him close for a deep, powerful thrust. Her heart pounded so hard she thought it might burst as her body exploded. A whimper of ecstasy followed as his orgasm shuddered inside her and rocked her once again.

She lay on her back panting, unable to catch her breath. What had just happened? How had this turned into the best sex of her life?

After what seemed like a very long time, she opened her eyes. Fletcher was arched over her on knees and elbows, his tired penis curled on her stomach. His piercing brown eyes bored into hers like a knife.

"Now that we've gotten that taken care of," he said with shallow breaths, "Who the hell are you?"

Chapter Fourteen

Reckless, irritating, woman. Paul grabbed the overhead strap as the train jostled him against the other standing passengers, but kept his eye on Megan seated in the middle of the car. She'd endangered herself and put him at risk, as well.

How had he gotten so entangled in this dubious mission?

Paul had always played by the rules. He'd been a good, though not exceptional, student at public school and university, participated on the debate squad and the wrestling team, and followed his father and grandfather in a career of public service. He enjoyed his work. Hadn't kicked up any fusses or started any revolutions. How had he become embroiled in a debacle that could cost him his career, and possibly his freedom?

Cherchez la femme.

Quite right, it was always about a woman. Colette had used her wiles to deceive him, and anxious to believe a woman like her could find a guy like him attractive, he'd unplugged his critical thinking unit. But he was over that. And should now know better. Why had he continued on this path toward his own destruction?

Because Megan was in trouble. And it wasn't in his nature to refuse help to someone in need. That guy who'd accosted her was no everyday French flirt. If he knew Colette, he was likely a member of the Community. Colette's 'handler'? From the way he'd confidently groped Megan, Paul guessed the relationship was more than professional. Had Colette used him too? Or had Paul been the only patsy in this equation?

His stomach churned. Roger had once told him he was too easygoing, that he let women walk all over him. That wasn't quite true. At least not with Colette. Paul had provided her with food and lodging, but he'd been more than compensated for his generosity. Quid pro quo, and all that.

Allison, however, had broken his heart. He'd believed she loved him. Yet in the end it was, "You're a nice guy, Paul, but..."

There was always that 'but.' Nice guys finished last. He would not put his heart out there again.

He studied Megan's face as she glanced out the window. She was a tough bird. Gutsy. Now that she had a place to sleep and eat, she needed nothing more from him. Yet she'd dashed rashly after him without even a disguise, as if her world was incomplete without him.

I was afraid you wouldn't come back.

That tugged at the damned heartstrings he'd determined to pay no heed to. But he wouldn't get emotional this time. He felt responsible for Megan, that's all. He'd promised to help her get home, and he would. Even if she disregarded his sage advice.

As soon as they got back to their hotel room, Megan raced to the phone. There was no red blinker indicating a voice message. Her whole face drooped like a wilted flower. She shuffled to the window and pulled back the curtain a few centimeters. Wistfully staring outside.

Despite his vow to keep things impersonal, Paul yearned to make it all better for her. "I get why you went out. It must be hard to spend your time in the world's most beautiful city imprisoned in a hotel room."

She turned to him, acknowledging his appraisal with a sad smile. "This is not how I would have planned an extended vacation."

He joined her at the window. "How long have you been in Europe?"

"Three weeks on the tour. London, Amsterdam, Florence, and Madrid. Paris was our last stop."

He clasped a stray curl that had fallen onto her cheek and tucked it behind her ear. "I assume you've been to all the usual tourist spots."

"Oh yes, Notre Dame, the Eiffel Tower, the museums."

"And your favorite?"

She sighed. "I'd say the Eiffel Tower, but I only got to see the outside. I've always thought it would be so romantic to go to the top, look out over the city."

Paul had gone to the top when he'd first arrived in Paris. A nice view, but he hadn't found it particularly romantic. Perhaps he hadn't seen it with the right woman.

Maybe after Colette was apprehended and Megan had arranged for her passport and flight home, they'd visit the top of the Eiffel Tower together...

Don't even go there, Bernard. He fortified his mind against his feelings. Once she had her passport, Megan would be on the first plane back to the States.

"What time is it?"

He checked his watch. "Almost six."

"Almost noon in New York." She glanced longingly at the telephone. "Do you mind?"

"Go for it."

Her fingers fairly danced through the numbers. Paul stood at the ready to comfort her if she was disappointed again, but this time, Megan's face brightened as the call apparently connected.

"Mom! It's Megan. I've been trying for two days to reach you. I--what?"

Her brow furrowed.

"No, I didn't just talk to you. What do you mean? Didn't you get my messages that I'm stranded in Paris?"

She looked like she was going to choke. "Mom, it's me. I swear. I need you to wire me money and--No, this is not a scam. This is your daughter. I—no, don't hang up! Please! Mom!!"

The phone dropped out of her hand. She looked like she was going to faint.

Paul grabbed her. "What's wrong?"

Her body trembled in his arms. She pushed out a word at a time through a cascade of tears.

"Mom...hung up...on me..." Another torrent of tears. "She thought...I was...some scammer."

Paul stroked her hair, pressing her face against his chest. If he'd had anything useful to say she wouldn't have heard him anyway. Her mournful cries filled the room and echoed against the walls.

He held her until her sobs subsided, then, in a violent aftershock, began again. This time accompanied by a shriek that pierced Paul's heart.

"She's there!" Megan wailed.

He lifted her chin and wiped tears off her chin with the flat of his hand. "Who's there?"

"Colette. She's in my apartment!"

A chill ran down Paul's spine. That couldn't be. Megan was overreacting to something her mother had said. A terrible misunderstanding.

"How would Mom not recognize me, unless she'd already talked to another Megan?" She pawed at his shirt, her fingernails raking his neck. "How could she fool my own mother?" Convulsive sobs racked Megan's body. "It wasn't enough to steal my identity," she blubbered. "She's taken over my life!"

Paul settled her on the bed and grabbed a tissue to blot her tears. That made no sense. Colette would never risk exposure and capture by embedding herself in Megan's life. There had to be a much more plausible explanation, but discussing it would be quite useless until she calmed down. "Megan, please don't cry."

"My mother said she'd just spoken to her--me!--on the phone. Colette could be in my apartment right now," she choked out through sobs. "Driving my car, wearing my clothes, sleeping in my bed." Her tear-brimmed eyes widened. "With my boyfriend!"

She grabbed Paul's hands and tugged him down beside her. Her fingernails dug into his wrists. He winced but bore the pain silently, patiently waiting for her to run out of tears. When she coughed out the last of them, he handed her another tissue and said, "Let's talk this out rationally."

She dried her eyes and sniffed into the tissue.

"We know Colette has your cell phone," he said, removing Megan's nails from his wrist. "Your mom probably called it. Colette could have answered it from anywhere. That doesn't mean she's in your house."

"That's true," Megan said, recovering a little. "I just assumed Mom would call my home phone to check on my arrival."

"Your parents wouldn't have picked you up at the airport?"

"No, my Dad doesn't drive at night. Fletcher's out of town on business, so I'd planned to take the train from JFK airport to Princeton."

This was making more sense now. "So, what if your mother called your cell and Colette answered, pretending to be Megan so as not to arouse worry and suspicion. Your mother would have no reason to suspect anything was amiss, correct?"

Megan's face scrunched up. "But she does know something's amiss. I called and told her."

"*If* she got the message. She might not have even checked voice mail once she was satisfied that you'd returned home safely."

Megan still looked doubtful.

"Pretend you're your mum," he said. "Your daughter is due in from Paris. You call her cell phone, probably just after she's arrived and on her way home to New Jersey. Someone who sounds exactly like Megan—and Colette does, trust me—answers and says all is well, great time, etc. etc."

Megan's expression didn't change.

"The next day you get a call from someone who sounds exactly like Megan—because she *is* you—saying she's stranded in Paris, please send money." He looked her straight in the eye. "What

138

would you think?"

Pain lanced her eyes. "That someone is scamming me."

"Precisely." He took her hand and laid it in his lap, caressing her fingers. "If you'd ever met Colette, you'd know the last place she'd want to spend her life is New Jersey."

"Hey." Megan seemed to be trying for a chuckle, but it came out as a sob. "What's wrong with New Jersey?"

Paul lifted her hand to his lips and kissed her cold fingers. He'd made the snarky comment in an attempt to lighten Megan's mood. But it helped dispel his own doubts and lead him to a more logical supposition.

Instead of some terrorist-infested country in the Middle East, Colette might have actually gone to New York. Since she possessed not only Megan's passport but, undoubtedly, her airline ticket, all she'd have had to do was hook up with Megan's tour group at the museum and get on their bus to Charles de Gaulle. In New York, she could catch a flight to anywhere. Presumably some country with no extradition policy.

But New Jersey? Not in a million years.

"Nevertheless," he cautioned, "it's probably best if you don't try to phone your mother again."

"Why not?" Her blue eyes threatened another rainstorm.

He stroked her fingers aimlessly, having almost forgotten he still held her hand. "If I were a betting man, I'd wager your mother called your cell phone as soon as you hung up. Colette probably answered it with another reassuring lie."

"Damn that bitch!" Megan slapped her hand over her mouth. "I'm sorry, I know you once had feelings for her."

"I still do. Rage, revenge, and the determined desire to bring her to justice." He stood and went to the bathroom to grab a towel, which he blotted against his tear-dampened shirt. "We have to find another contact to help you get home. How about the boyfriend?"

"I told you, he only has a cell phone and I never learned the number by heart."

"You also told me that *you* have a land line."

"So?"

His wet shirt still clung to his skin. Paul unfastened the buttons, opened the shirt, and pressed the towel directly to his chest. "When Boyfriend gets home from his business travels, wouldn't he go first to the home of his almost-fiancée whom he hasn't seen in more than three weeks?"

She beamed through a residue of tears. "Yes! Fletcher has a key to my apartment. And he's due home today."

He smiled, relieved to see her hopeful again. Regretful it was at the thought of reconnecting with the blackguard who was obviously using her--at least it was obvious to Paul--to finagle himself into a more comfortable life situation.

Megan checked the clock on the nightstand. "He might be at my place right now. I'll call him. He'll talk to my mother and explain everything, and he'll make sure I get the documents I need." She raced to Paul, smacking against the wet towel as she hugged his neck. "Everything is going to be all right after all."

* * *

Merde. Fletcher was on to her. Sweat formed on Colette's upper lip, but she urged herself to stay calm. Maybe he was just playing with her, trying to rattle her. "Who am I? I'm the new Megan. You don't like?" She tried an innocent look, but she wasn't good at selling that and Fletcher wasn't buying.

"You're not Megan. Megan would never get a tattoo. And she's about as interesting in bed as a soggy noodle."

Dammit. She should have pleased him less and conned him more.

"And your American accent sucks." Fletcher lifted his leg off her and sat cross-legged beside her on the bed. "I repeat, who are you?"

Colette assessed the situation. Sex wasn't going to distract him this time. She'd have to tell him something. "I'm a new friend of Megan's," she said sheepishly, lowering her eyes for effect. "We ran into each other in Paris and freaked out. We couldn't believe we looked so much alike." She glanced up through her fluttering lids but couldn't read Fletcher's expression. "I'd always wanted to see the United States and she wanted to stay in Paris a while longer. We thought it would be cool if we switched places for a few weeks."

He stared at her intently. Colette held her breath. "Try again," he said, flattening his hand against the mattress. "Megan never mentioned a new friend. Besides, she wouldn't have traded cell phones with anyone. Hers rang in your backpack a little while ago."

"Oh, no, that was mine," she said hastily.

"You have 'The Sound of Music' as your ring tone? I don't think so."

This guy with the television-host face and stallion cock wasn't as dumb as he looked. Colette scooted back in the bed and pulled the covers up to her neck, searching for a lie close enough to the truth for him to believe.

"You can't con a con man." He glared at her. "Give me the truth this time, or you're out of here wearing exactly what you've got on."

Which was nothing. "Okay." She heaved a long, laborious sigh. "You're too smart for me to fool." She considered an eye-batting for emphasis, but that would probably be too much. "The truth is...I'm in a little trouble with the law."

Fletcher's ears perked. "What kind of trouble?"

She waved a hand in a nothing-serious gesture. "A few arrests for shoplifting. A couple of minor scams. But last week I...I got into the bank account of the guy I was living with and relieved him of most of his cash. Turns out he's good friends with the chief of police. So the whole damn Paris police force is looking for me."

She stole a glance at Fletcher to see if he was buying any of this. His eyes were fixed in attention and a grin was spreading over his face.

I'm glad you're amused. "When I saw Megan," she continued, "and noticed the uncanny resemblance, I figured this was my opportunity to get out of the country and start over."

"So you 'relieved her' of her passport and plane ticket." Naked and cross-legged on the bed, Fletcher absent-mindedly stroked his genitals.

"I switched bags with her." If she stuck close to the truth, maybe she could avoid entangling herself in her own lie.

Fletcher licked his upper lip. "And what did you plan to do when you got to the States?"

Nothing. I would have been gone already if not for your girlfriend's clingy family. "Get a job, start a new life. But then Megan's family saw me at JFK and of course, they thought I was her, and to keep them from calling the cops, I just went along with it and--"

"You've met the family? Jeez." Fletcher lay back against the pillow, an expression of amazement on his face. "You've got balls, babe." He patted her pubic area. "Figuratively speaking, that is."

Colette let out a slow breath. If he were going to call the police, he'd be on the phone right now. "Look, I'll make a deal with you. Let me get dressed and out of here--I promise I won't take anything with me--and give me time to get out of the state, and I swear you'll never see or hear from me again."

"That's a good deal for you." He fondled his genitals again. "What's in it for me?"

She pushed his hand away, and took over the stroking of his growing erection. "A nice little goodbye gift." She danced her tongue over her top and bottom lip.

From the headboard of the bed, a phone rang. Fletcher pulled away from her ministrations and stretched for it.

"Don't answer that," Colette pleaded, but he'd already jerked the phone out of its handset.

"Hello," he said coolly. Then, "Megan!"

Merde.

"How are you, babe?" He cooed into the phone. "Where are you? I'm here in your apartment, waiting for you. What!" His tone changed. "Oh my god, that's terrible. Did you report it to the police?"

Shit.

"Calm down, baby," Fletcher said into the phone. "Everything will be all right. What? No, there's nobody else here. I've been here a couple hours." A pause. "Sweetie, you're being a little ridiculous, don't you think? Your mother was probably just being...your

143

mother." He chuckled. "Okay, okay, I'll check the closets."

He laid the phone on the mattress and pointed, first to Colette's mouth, and then to his rising cock.

Outside of disconnecting the phone, which wouldn't help, since Megan would just call back, Colette had two options. One: she could throw on her clothes and make a dash for it, hoping Fletcher's condition would keep him from following. But that wouldn't prevent him from phoning the police. Two: she could service him as requested and continue to listen to what was becoming a very interesting phone conversation.

Quietly but intensely she gave him the best meaning of lip service.

Fletcher held one hand against her head, and with the other, picked up the phone again. "Jeez, Megan, your bedroom closet is a holy mess. A bear could hide in here."

A mess? Colette had found it rather well organized. Either this guy was a neat freak, or he just enjoyed playing the alpha dog.

"No, nobody here. Nobody in any of the closets. Are you satisfied? Look, don't worry about your mom, she was probably having one of her off days. You know how she gets. Just tell me what you need and I'll FedEx it to you right away."

Colette lifted her head but he gestured for her to resume her ministrations.

"Right. And your school ID. Got it. Yes, I've got a pen. I'm writing down the address."

But of course he did no such thing. He lay right where he was, stifling the grunts of pleasure Colette elicited.

"God, I miss you, babe." Fletcher bucked under Colette's

mouth and touch. "Talk to me. Tell me how much you miss me. How much you want my cock inside you."

The man was a real piece of work.

"What do you mean it's not a good time?"

Colette would have chuckled if she weren't close to gagging from the huge impediment in her mouth.

"I'm touching myself, imagining I'm with you." Fletcher started breathing harder and faster. "Oh, yes. That's it. God, Megan, just thinking about you is getting me off. I want you home, soon. I'll go by your parents' place and straighten out your mom and I'll send you that stuff right away."

Focused on her task, Colette heard a beep, then a phone bouncing to the floor. Fletcher grabbed her hair and slammed her head down all the way to the gag point. Then, with a groan that could have been heard in Paris, he came.

She swallowed and wiped her mouth with the back of her hand.

Fletcher sat up, his breathing still rapid. "Bitch!" he spat out. "You didn't just steal her passport and ticket. You left her without any goddamn money."

"Bastard!" she retorted. "You asked her for phone sex with your dick in my mouth."

A slow smile spread over his face. "I guess we're just two of a kind, aren't we?" He lay back on the bed and pulled her down on top of him, stroking her back and buttocks with a caress that seemed almost affectionate. "I've been thinking about that arrangement you suggested. About me not calling the police."

"Yes?" Her heart leaped. The blowjob must have clinched the

deal.

"But I have a different proposition for you."

Colette snorted. She'd accepted too many propositions from men, and what had she gotten? Robbed of fifty thousand dollars and wanted by the international police. "Been there, done that."

"Actually," Fletcher said, squeezing her buttock, "it's more of a proposal."

"Proposal?" She lifted her head to look into his face. "My English is not that good, but doesn't that mean--?"

"I want you to marry me."

Chapter Fifteen

"Excuse me?" Colette stared at the grinning, naked man beside her. She'd stranded his girlfriend in Europe, and as a reward, he wanted to marry her? The blowjob hadn't been *that* good.

"I meant, Megan is going to marry me."

Fletcher rolled out of bed and padded into the living area toward the pile of clothes strewn on the floor. Colette slipped into Megan's robe while Fletcher pulled on his black silk boxers. What was he up to? He obviously had no intention of helping Megan get home any time soon.

Wordlessly he walked into the kitchen and wrenched a pizza out of the full freezer. After he'd set up the oven and shoved the pie inside, he turned to face Colette. "You stayed at Megan's parents' house last night?"

She nodded, wondering where this was going.

"Nice place, huh?"

She was beginning to catch his drift. "They seem very...comfortable."

"They're filthy rich." He leaned his elbows on the counter. "The old man owns a string of wholesale liquor outlets. I work for him. I should be running the damn place. But he'll never promote me to upper management until I'm part of the family."

Colette moved to stand beside him and ran her fingers along his pale chest. "So why haven't you proposed to Megan?"

"I have. She's dragging her feet. Wants to wait a while before we even get engaged, let alone married."

"You love her, I assume."

His chortle confirmed what she'd already guessed.

"So you want to marry this girl for money and power, to have access to the family inheritance and, I don't know, I'm guessing...a trust fund?"

He winked. "You catch on quick, baby."

"Not planning to knock off the parents and brother for good measure are you?"

He laughed, heartily. "Nice thought, but no."

"And what do I get out of it?"

He parted the sides of her robe and poked his finger between her thighs. "I won't call the police on you."

She swatted his hand away. "Not good enough. I want in on the scam."

His chuckle evoked a mustache-twirling villain in a melodrama. Reaching for the kitchen phone, Fletcher punched in numbers and calmly said, "City Police, please."

Was he expecting her to run? Or fall to her knees and beg? Colette closed her robe tighter and folded her arms across her chest.

"Yes, I'll hold." He glared menacingly at Colette.

She glared back, holding her ground. He was bluffing. He needed her as much as she needed him. He probably hadn't even phoned the police, but some random number.

A man's voice came on the line. Colette heard a 'Hello. Hello?' Fletcher held the phone loosely in his hand, maintaining his intimidating stare.

After what seemed like forever, he hung up. "Treat me right," he said with a salacious smile, "and I might be willing to share twenty percent of that trust fund."

"Half."

He grinned. "A woman after my own heart. Or lack thereof." Apparently he found that outrageously funny. The grin graduated to a chortle and then a full out belly laugh.

Fletcher slipped his arms inside her robe and pressed the stirrings of an erection against her. "So it's you and me, babe. Partners."

Colette trusted him as far as she could throw him, but she didn't have much choice. Even if he didn't alert the police, she wasn't going to get very far without money.

The Sound of Music chimed a few feet away. Megan's phone.

"Answer it," Fletcher ordered.

Colette fished it out of the backpack, checked the display, and groaned. "Hi, Mom."

Fletcher stood at her ear, listening to both sides of the conversation. Megan's mother was semi-hysterical, going on and on about a phone call she'd received from a strange number. Colette's stomach muscles twisted.

"She sounded so much like you, Megan," the woman fretted. "I could have almost sworn--"

"I'm sure it was just some scam, Mom. Playing on your sympathies, on the fifty-fifty chance you actually have a daughter. Did this person ask you to send money?"

"Why, yes, she did."

"There you go." Colette took in a breath. "I'm glad you called me, Mom, but there's no need to worry. I'm perfectly fine. If you see that strange phone number again, just don't answer it."

"All right, dear." Mrs. Chandler signed off.

"Nicely done," Fletcher said, nipping at her ear.

She sighed. "Do you really think we can pull this off? Mama Chandler already suspects something. And brother Don could be a problem. On the two-hour car ride this morning, he actually noticed that my hair has auburn highlights, which, apparently, your girlfriend's doesn't." Unusually observant for a straight guy. The only other man who'd ever commented on Colette's hair was her friend Jacques.

"Megan's is totally mousy brown." Fletcher ran his fingers through her hair, grunting his approval. "Don't worry about Don. We can take care of him."

She had visions of shooting or slashing. "How?"

"We'll be pro-active. Invite him here for dinner tonight. Cook his faves. Feed him bullshit. Don't worry, I'll coach you. By the time I'm done, you'll be more Megan than Megan." He planted a quick kiss on her cheek. "And Donnie Do Right will report back so favorably to Mom and Dad they'll be convinced Megan's phone call was just some scam artist trying to fleece them."

150

Instead of us two scam artists trying to fleece them. She fluttered her lashes. "Whatever you say, Darling."

He winked. "So what do I call you? What's your real name?"

Colette hesitated.

"On second, thought, I'd rather not know." He captured her in his arms and nibbled on her ear. "I wouldn't want the wrong name to slip out. Better to think of you as Megan."

Whatever rings your bell. But how long could this charade go on?

Despite Colette's best efforts to avoid the security cameras in the embassy, she'd undoubtedly been caught on at least one. The police should be searching for a woman who matched the photo. If they found Megan and the gun, no one would believe she wasn't Colette. They'd be so busy congratulating themselves on having caught a dangerous terrorist they'd just lock her away with little chance of her seeing daylight in the near future.

Of course, Megan's future would be even more severely curtailed if Cyrus and his Community got to her first.

But in that case, 'Colette Marchand' would be officially dead, and the police would stop looking for her as well. She smiled to herself. She'd planned this better than she'd thought.

When the oven timer dinged, Colette let Fletcher see to the pizza while she went to 'freshen up.' In the bedroom, she checked the most recent caller ID on the landline phone. The area code was definitely France, and looked like the same number Megan had called her parents from earlier.

Attempting damage control, she blocked calls from that number, and then did the same with Megan's cell phone. The smell of pepperoni drifted in from the kitchen, torturing Colette's empty stomach. She glanced out the doorway. While he was still separated from his pants, she'd block the number from Fletcher's cell as well.

At least she didn't have to worry anymore about Megan calling her parents. Mrs. Chandler would block that number herself.

You are so clever, Colette. She smiled smugly at her reflection in the mirror. Then her pride deflated like a spent penis. *Email.*

She found Megan's laptop on the small desk, opened it, and searched for her email account. The ditz's login and password came up automatically, so there was no challenge at all to signing in. Hurriedly she replied to a few of the emails from friends asking about Megan's trip. *Lovely time, so much to tell you but super-busy, catch you later.*

Then she changed the password. If she and Fletcher had any shot at pulling off his get-rich-quick scheme, she'd have to keep up credibility with Megan's contacts as well as severing Megan's means of communication with them.

* * *

Yes! Megan set down the phone and wrapped her arms across her middle, breathing easier than she had in what seemed like a week instead of a day. "He'll do it!" she exclaimed. "Fletcher's going to send my paperwork!"

"That's wonderful, Megan." Paul leaned against the door to the bathroom, towel in hand, his shirt still open. A tantalizing mat of dark chest hair peeked out between the button rows.

"*You're* wonderful. It was your idea to call him." She danced around the hotel room, two-stepping her way to the window and back toward the bathroom, grabbing Paul's hands and drawing him into the center of the room.

"I don't dance," he protested. But he whirled her once around the small bedroom, his hand splayed against her back. His bare chest brushing her thin tee shirt.

"Thank goodness for Fletcher!" She stopped inches from the bed, her body still spinning, a tornado of emotions spiraling inside her. "He was at my house waiting for me."

"I'm sure he's anxious to have you home again." Paul stood facing her, holding her hand at arm's length.

"Of course he is. And I--" She would be glad to see Fletcher, wouldn't she? Accept his proposal? Marry him? She sank onto the bed, suddenly tired, but her mind swirled with uncertainty.

"Megan." Paul sat beside her, not too close, but near enough for his presence to crowd her space. "If you don't mind my asking, why are you with this guy? And don't tell me it's because he 'looks after' you. A dog will do the same."

She stared at her hands. She could tell him she *did* mind his asking. That it was none of his business. But that sounded defensive. Inhaling, she dug deep inside herself for a truthful answer. "Fletcher provides the strengths I'm missing."

Paul studied her silently, as if she were a computer program he was trying to decode. Finally, he narrowed his brown eyes and asked, "What exactly do you feel you're lacking?"

Half a dozen weaknesses jumped to mind, but she picked the most obvious. "I'm too trusting. 'Naïve,' Fletcher would say."

Paul folded his arms over his chest but made no comment.

"I just expect good things to happen, and when they don't, I'm not able to deal with it. I don't think things out. I have a hard time making decisions." Frustration walled her stomach. "I've been out of school a year and I still don't feel independent."

He crossed a leg over the opposite thigh. "So, when you were expecting to get on a flight home, but instead were robbed of your money and passport--and phone...?"

"I couldn't handle it. I just wanted my Mom and Dad to fix it, but I couldn't reach them."

"So you sat down in the middle of the sidewalk and cried?"

"Of course not. I'm not a child." Where was he going with this? "Will you stop playing psychiatrist and tell me what you're getting at?"

He smiled in that gently arrogant way. "Megan, you may not be used to adversity, but you did deal with it. When I found you, you were attempting to seek help at the American embassy."

She shrugged. "That was my last hope."

"It was a capable, responsible, decision. Isn't that the mark of an independent person? Why do you refuse to see that?"

Was that what she'd been doing? Denying her strengths?

Paul placed his palm over her hand. "I may be overstepping my bounds on this, but I'd say that without Fletcher to put you down and tell you how incompetent you are, you are actually quite a competent, quite plucky lady."

"Thanks. I guess."

"If you haven't achieved the independence you so desire, it might be because Mum and Dad have made it too easy for you to rely on them, and Fletcher has sensed your insecurities and played them to his own advantage."

He *was* overstepping his bounds. Paul had no right to judge a man he'd never met. And yet...

Yet he'd succinctly and accurately summed up a side of Fletcher to which Megan had been, perhaps intentionally, blind.

She stared into Paul's moist brown eyes. Had she really met him only yesterday? It seemed he'd always been a part of her life.

Flinching under her gaze, he stood and cleared his throat. "Forgive me if I've spoken out of turn. I'm sure Fletcher has many good qualities. It's fortunate that you were able to contact him and that soon you'll be on your way home."

"Right." She rose from the bed, as if propelled by some force, and stood opposite him. "Home." But she wasn't thinking about her apartment, or Fletcher, or even her family. She was focused on the big, imposing man in front of her. A man whose presence she would sorely miss.

Paul's breath hitched. His tongue swept his upper lip. "Good old Fletcher," he said.

"Yes." She imagined tasting the moisture on that agile tongue. "Good old Fletcher." She scanned Paul's face, from his school bus yellow hair, to his serious eyes, to his Grecian nose, to the dark patch of stubble on his cheeks. She wanted to remember every part of him. Her gaze drifted to his bared chest. Every part of him.

His hand brushed hers. As if her wrist were a string, he reeled her closer, then kissed each of her fingers in turn, drawing them into his mouth like succulent morsels.

A sensuous yearning hummed through her, touching her deepest parts. She laid her hand on his chest, stroking his hot skin with her moistened fingertips. Wondering what he tasted like.

She stood on her toes and wound an arm around his neck, inhaling the faint scent of his cologne. Her lips gravitated toward his.

Grasping her chin, Paul raised her face and touched her mouth with his.

It was a sweet kiss, at first. Tender and delicate, a simple meeting of two souls. His hand solid against her back, his tongue tracing the outline of her lips. Softly. Taking his time. Soothed yet aroused by the warm, gentle strokes, Megan closed her eyes and leaned into the kiss, supported by his strong arms.

Her mind shut down. Her body relaxed. She gave herself over to feeling, tasting, touching. With her feet barely touching the floor, she felt adrift and yet secure, as serene as if she were floating in a peaceful ocean. As if this was where she was meant to be.

Paul didn't rush. He didn't plunder. His tongue ventured easily and naturally inside her mouth, exploring and stroking. Megan touched his tongue with hers, then closed her lips around it as if she'd captured something that had always belonged to her. She hugged his neck to bring him closer, deeper. His body heat warmed her. Moisture sizzled from every pore of her skin, all over her body. *All* over.

This was insane. And not just because she was supposed to marry someone else. This kiss, this embrace felt too good, too... ordained. And that had to be a mistake, a celestial mix-up. Paul Bernard was one of those people who come into your life at the moment you need them, and leave just as abruptly when their purpose is over.

She pulled back. "What are we doing?"

He jerked up his head. His eyes were glazed as if he, too, had been lost in the moment. "What does it feel like?"

Sensuous. Arousing. Unsettling. "Wonderful. But we just met yesterday. We barely know each other." Blood thrummed through her fingertips. "We're probably just responding to the drama of our situation. What we're feeling now...it may not last."

"Does that matter?"

She stared into his earnest eyes. The simple question answered more than it asked. The past was irrelevant, it said, the future uncertain. Tomorrow she could be on a plane home. Or locked in a Paris jail. The only thing they could count on was today. Tonight.

She stood on her toes and framed his face with her fingers, her heart pulsing in her chest. Up to this moment, every decision she'd faced had been made with the future in mind. Tossing aside those shackles freed her to embrace the present. And the present was standing in front of her, erasing thoughts of everyone and everything else.

She touched the tip of her tongue to Paul's lips. He sucked it inside his mouth, kissing her deeper this time, and harder. His fingers forked through her hair. Megan tingled all over with an urgency she didn't remember feeling before, but was anxious to give herself up to.

She'd never felt so alive. Fletcher might think he knew her but he was wrong about one thing: she was *not* frigid. Her throat was dry and parched, the missing moisture pooled inside her panties. Her body was an itch that yearned to be scratched.

Paul slipped his hand under her tee shirt and caressed her back. His touch was cool to her feverish skin but warmed her in places that had been cold for so long. She smoldered inside as his lips brushed her neck. Her hands and mouth moved frantically, tugging his shirt off his shoulders, kissing his hard stomach, walking her fingertips up his chest.

It wasn't enough. She wanted him skin to skin.

She tugged her shirt over her head and tossed it to the floor. "Touch me."

Paul palmed her cotton bra, tucking a finger inside to stroke a stiff nipple. She let out a whimper of desire, then opened her legs and leaned into his rising erection.

He squeezed her breast and groaned.

Straightening, she grabbed at his jeans, unsnapping and unzipping in a raging, relentless fever. Reason fled. All she knew was that she wanted him. Now.

Paul cupped his hand over hers. "Let's do this right," he said with shallow, strained breaths. "Make it last." He brought her hand to his mouth and licked her palm. "We have all night."

Megan tempered her own erratic breathing. He wanted to stop? She glanced at Paul's intense, passionate eyes. No, not stop. Slow down. She'd never known a man who'd postpone his own pleasure to maximize hers.

Separating their bodies, he walked toward the mini-bar. "I'll open a bottle of champagne." He gestured toward the white terry robe hanging from a hook outside the bathroom. "Why don't you get comfortable? Let's savor this."

She barely breathed through the words. "Actually, I think I'll take a quick shower."

A cold one might be in order but she didn't want to deny the new feelings that overwhelmed her. She grabbed the robe, darted into the bathroom and stepped into the shower. What had gotten into her? She'd nearly ripped off the man's clothes and had her way with him on the floor. She used to be a lights-out- after-ten-o'clock- behind-closed-doors kind of lover. She hadn't been this aroused since the first time she and Fletcher--

Fletcher. How could she marry him after this?

No matter what happened tonight, she couldn't. Paul had figured out within five minutes of meeting her what Megan only now forced herself to acknowledge. She didn't love Fletcher. Deep down she must have known that, but something weak inside her hadn't believed she deserved better.

But she did. She was worthy of a man who would value her, respect her, love her. And even if tonight turned out to be just...tonight, she could never marry Fletcher.

The shower needles prickled her breasts. Her nipples ached. The truth was...she had *never* been this aroused. And she'd never known a man who promised to take his time. Savor her. *Slow Hand.* The Pointer Sisters' tune hummed in her head. She yearned for the easy touch of a man who would pleasure her all night.

A tap sounded on the bathroom door. "Megan?"

She turned off the water, stepped out of the tub, and quickly wrapped a bath towel around her torso. "Yes?"

"I ordered dinner. There was champagne in the mini-bar but it's not quite cold enough. I'm going down the hall to get some ice. Be back straightaway."

"I'll be here." Her voice, intending to sound sexy and inviting, came out in a weak croak.

After drying herself, she wrapped herself in the fluffy robe and stepped out into the bedroom. Paul had made a space on the desk for a room service tray, and set out two glasses for the champagne.

In front of the mirror, Megan opened her robe and stared at her body. Not so bad. Not as thin as Colette, but some men did like a little meat on the bones. Would Paul make the comparison when he held her, made love to her? Or might he...?

A knock sounded on the door. Had he not taken his room card? Megan smiled and wrapped the robe around her again. She'd have to scold him about his carelessness with his identity cards.

She stood on her toes at the door but couldn't see out the peephole. "Paul?"

"Service des chambres."

Room service. She tied the belt on the bathrobe and opened the door.

Two policemen stood in the doorway. Megan could barely translate their heavily accented French. "Get dressed," they ordered. "You are coming with us."

Chapter Sixteen

Paul hummed to himself as the ice cubes rattled into his bucket. His heart pulsed with the unrestrained urges of a teenager. Not from sexual deprivation--thanks to Colette, those needs had been well taken care of. Leaving his body sated but his soul empty.

Tonight he wanted more than physical satisfaction. He wanted to make this night special. Romantic. A mind-and-body connection that had been missing from his life for a long time. He didn't just want to hear Megan's orgasmic screams. He wanted to see her smile. Her guileless, ingenuous smile not only lit up a room but had sparked dormant embers inside his heart.

Don't fall for something you can't have. In a matter of days, Megan would be back in Kansas with Auntie Em and Toto.

But tonight...

Rounding the corner from the vending machine room, he stopped short. Two policemen were walking through the hall toward the elevator. Handcuffed between them, wearing jeans, a hooded sweatshirt, and a frightened expression, was Megan.

The breath sucked out of Paul's lungs. His first instinct was to run to her, but he squelched that. The cops would just arrest him too, and then, how could he help her?

He ducked back around the corner, his heart pounding

erratically. How had the police found them? He'd been careful to take several trains in various directions before heading back toward the hotel. He'd kept his distance from Megan so as not to call attention to them, but perhaps some astute bystander had recognized them and phoned the police?

He stood helplessly in the hallway, clutching the ice bucket to his chest. He couldn't go back to the hotel room. They might have left a man there to wait for him. Nor could he go to the police station to bail Megan out.

Not without a lawyer.

*   *   *

"You sure we can pull this off?" Standing barefoot in Megan Chandler's galley kitchen, Colette stared at the raw chicken breasts lying in the baking pan. "I can't cook."

"No worries, neither can Megan." Fletcher smacked her bottom as he passed. "This baked chicken dish is the only one she knows how to make. And her brother loves it." He reached into the grocery bag for the salad fixings they'd bought this afternoon. "You will literally have him eating out of your hand."

An image that was both disturbing and stimulating. Traveling the New Jersey turnpike this morning, Colette had intended to feign sleep to avoid conversation, but she'd found Don Chandler's Doctors without Borders anecdotes more interesting than she'd expected. He didn't have that 'I'm-doing-my-part-to-help-the-little-people-of-the-world' attitude that most rich do-gooders wore like a crown of thorns. He seemed to genuinely enjoy meeting diverse people and sharing their cultures. And his long, lithe body and charming smile hadn't been at all hard to look at.

"Don is very attached to Megan and vice versa," Fletcher said, as he mixed the white cooking wine with the spices. "He's always looked out for his little sister. And she's always looked up to him. He's the paragon of virtue who thumbed his nose at running his father's profitable business and went his own way. Megan admires Don for that. She wants to get out from under her parents' wings as well, but so far, she hasn't had the balls."

"So far?"

Fletcher grinned wickedly. "You're gonna grow them for her. She's going to announce to her family that she's marrying a great guy whether they like it or not, so they'd better like it."

"The great guy being...oh, right. You."

"Don't piss me off, little Megan." He pinched her breast. "You need me more than I need you."

Gritting her teeth behind a forced smile, Colette poured the sauce over the chicken as directed. "So why isn't Megan just falling over herself to marry this great guy?"

Fletcher let out an exasperated sigh. "I could get her there on my own, eventually. But I'm tired of waiting. Megan gets full control of her trust fund at age twenty-five. But--and she doesn't know I know this--if she marries, she gets it sooner."

"What's your time frame for this fake engagement and wedding? I have places to go, people to see." And people she never wanted to see again.

"I'm thinking Saturday afternoon might be nice for a wedding."

"*This* Saturday?" Three days could set a record for even the simplest of weddings, but the timeline suited Colette just fine. Every day she delayed she was risking discovery by the international police, Megan's family, and possibly, Megan herself.

"I can probably stall Megan with dumb excuses for a few days about why I haven't sent her stuff, but I can't keep her overseas forever." Fletcher opened the package of fresh rosemary and sprinkled several stems over the chicken breasts. "Or do you have a better idea?"

Not to have Megan come back at all? "We could elope," she suggested.

"Megan would never elope." He set the oven temperature, covered the pan with foil, and slid it onto the rack. "She'd want her family there, so we have to do the whole formal thing. But we'll make it as quick and simple as possible." He closed the oven door. "Now, let's go over your notes again."

For the next hour, he grilled her on all things Megan Chandler. Where she'd gone to school--private schools from middle school on, who her best friends were--Amber Leonard since sixth grade, her favorite colors, favorite foods, favorite music. It wasn't that much different from learning lines. The bigger challenge was perfecting Megan's walk and talk. If she forgot a biographical detail, Fletcher would back her up. She hoped.

"Now, let's see that big brother hug again," he cued.

Obligingly, she moved toward him and put her arms around him gently.

"Closer than that," he coached.

She moved in.

"Tighter. A big, soppy bear hug."

Colette squeezed her breasts against his chest.

"Whoa. Too damn tight. You're giving me a boner. Wouldn't want to do that to dear brother Don." He put his arms on her shoulders and pushed her back. "You suck at this. I'm guessing you don't have a brother."

"Not one that I'd claim." Involuntarily, she grimaced.

"Gave you a hard time as a kid?" He grinned. "Big brother teasing, got you in trouble?"

She pursed her lips. "Step-brother, actually. He raped and abused me from the time I was ten years old."

"Wow." The grin slid off Fletcher's face. "Did you tell your mother?"

"My mother?" She turned away to focus on the translucent lace covering the window. "She was always too drunk to notice, or if she noticed, she didn't care."

"Wow," he said again. "So what did you do?"

She pressed her hands against her sides and took a few steps toward the living room window. The sounds of Fletcher's quiet breathing behind her indicated he had not moved from his spot.

"I left home when I was fourteen," she said heavily. "Hooked up with a hot guy with a hotter motorcycle." She pressed her palm to the warmth of the windowpane. "Enjoyed my freedom for a while, until I got knocked up." She whirled to face Megan's boyfriend. "Hot guy split the day I told him."

"Yeah, we're all dogs, aren't we?" Fletcher sank his butt into the sofa, apparently really into her story. "What did you do about the kid? Abort it?"

"No." She took several sharp breaths. "I had it. Had *her*." She swallowed hard. "Her name was Emma."

He was eating this up. "Was?"

Colette pressed her palms against her stomach. "She was five months old. I checked her crib one night and she wasn't breathing. She wasn't sick. She didn't choke. She was just cold. Dead. The only person who ever really loved me." A tear welled in her eye.

Was there a little moisture in his eye too? "Wow, that's really some sob story." He cocked his head. "Is any of it true?"

"Not a word." She twisted the tear into a wink. "But I had you going there, didn't I?" She posed provocatively. "I told you I was a good actress."

He jumped to his feet. "Damn straight you are. I think you and I just might pull this off, Megan babe." He nipped a kiss on her neck. "I'll set the table while you hit the shower and dress. Wear something school-girlish. Don still thinks of Megan as his baby sister."

"Sure thing, boss."

In the camouflage of the shower stream, Colette let the tear that had escaped and the others lurking behind her eyes flow freely. She hadn't thought about Emma in a long time. She hadn't let herself remember what it was like to be vulnerable, to care, to cherish someone else more than your own skin. But she'd never forgotten the touch of her baby's soft little hand, the pure trust in her eyes when she'd looked up at her. For the first time in her life, Colette had known love. And then, after five short months, it had been taken from her. Emma had been Colette's sole reason for living. She'd never had one before that. And never since.

* * *

It was dark. Damp. The cot--or whatever it was she was laying on--felt like cold stone. Megan touched her cheek. A sticky, dried substance met her finger. She touched her tongue to the side of her cheek and recognized the iron taste of blood.

Had she been injured? She felt no pain. The last thing she remembered was being blindfolded and pushed into a vehicle. Had the police drugged her? Beaten her?

She squinted into the blackness, expecting her eyes to adjust to the dark. But they didn't. Unless she wiggled her fingers, she couldn't even see her hand in front of her eyes. What time was it? How long had she been here? What kind of cell was this?

She reached into the pocket of her sweatshirt for the gun, then remembered the police had taken it from the hotel room, finding the backpack she'd stashed under the bed as easily as if it were in plain sight.

They hadn't allowed her any privacy, not even the chance to go into the bathroom to dress. The French had a reputation for lechery, but the police? Were they really that concerned that she might jump out the fifth story window, or did they just enjoy her mortification as they ogled her?

She reached down to feel the floor. Good lord. She was *on* the floor. And it was not only cold, but slippery.

She tried to sit up, bumping her head against something hard and damp. Where was she? How would Paul find her? Would he even try to find her?

Be back straightaway. The last words he'd spoken before disappearing from her life, possibly forever. She stared into the darkness, holding tight to the last image of him. Hair wild and unruly, breath irregular, hard chest exposed to her eager touch. Megan's skin tingled with memories of unfulfilled desire. If Paul hadn't interrupted the embrace, they would have been making passionate love when the police burst in. And would have both been arrested.

Her chest caved to her stomach. Had the police found Paul at the ice machine, arrested him as well? Were they questioning him now?

What would he tell them about her? That they had the wrong suspect? That Megan was an innocent look-alike, used by Colette as Paul had been used? Or, tired of running, anxious to end his own ordeal, would he tell them they'd captured his ex-girlfriend, the nefarious embassy bomber?

Her blood chilled. No. Paul would never do that. Megan wrapped her arms around her chest. He cared about her. He would never desert her. He'd promised.

Chapter Seventeen

Paul lay restless and awake in Jacques and Marcel's guest room, the bedside clock ticking in rhythm with his pounding heart. Two a.m. Six hours since Megan had been taken. Three since Marcel had grudgingly dressed and gone out into the night to represent her and, hopefully, secure her freedom.

"They won't guillotine her," he'd grumbled. "We quit that some years ago. It'd be best to wait until morning when the police are at full staff. We don't even know where she's being held."

How could they? Even if they let her use a phone, Megan couldn't call and let them know where she was. Paul's cell phone was gone. She didn't know Jacques or Marcel's numbers. She didn't even know their last names. Paul bit down hard on his lip. Until a few hours ago, she hadn't known his.

"She's probably scared out of her mind," he'd persisted. "And hungry." The room service dinner he'd ordered was doubtless sitting undisturbed outside the hotel room. He pictured Megan wolfing down bread with water, wearing sackcloth and ashes.

Okay, that last image was probably a little extreme. But Paul couldn't bear to think of Megan locked up in prison like a criminal. Besides being frightened and uncomfortable, she probably felt abandoned.

Marcel had refused to take him with him to the police station, claiming Paul would be no help, and would likely get himself jailed for showing up. He was right, of course. But Paul couldn't stand to wait for her release a minute longer than necessary. He needed to see her safe. He needed to see her, period. It had taken every bit of his restraint not to 'pull a Megan' and dash out after Marcel, heedless of the consequences.

He swung his legs over the side of bed and pulled on his pants, trying not to think about Megan naked behind the shower curtain, her body warm and waiting for him. If he'd only allowed nature to take its course...

You'd probably be locked up with her. Sighing, he padded barefoot into the study alcove and booted up the laptop Jacques had made available to him. He expected to see the latest on the embassy bombing as the top story, but it was literally, apparently, yesterday's news.

If the police believed they'd arrested Colette, wouldn't that have gone viral by now? Were the police being cautious, waiting until morning to announce they had a suspect in custody? Or had Megan convinced them of the misunderstanding? Might she even have been released by now?

His heart jumped in his chest like a rugby player who'd made a critical goal. If so, she'd head back to the hotel. It was paid up for the night and her room key would still work. Paul was halfway to the bedroom for his shirt and shoes when he stopped in his tracks. Maybe there was no story because the police were sitting on it, hoping Paul would return to the room where they'd grabbed Megan. What if there was someone waiting there now to arrest him?

* * *

Colette stared across the dining table into Don Chandler's luminous blue eyes, a perfect match to his sky blue Ralph Lauren

170

polo shirt. Peeking out of the vee neckline was a thin sprinkling of golden brown chest hair one shade darker than the thick blond hair that swept over his forehead. The man was a virtual Ken doll, except, presumably, anatomically correct. If not for the fact that he was Megan's brother, which made him *her* brother-for-a-week....

"Megan, honey." Under the table, Fletcher tapped his foot against hers. "Shouldn't we tell Don our good news?"

She turned to the dark-haired man beside her and cooed into his ear. "Of course, Fletcher darling." She plastered a blissful smile onto her face before turning back to Megan's brother. Reaching across the table, she placed a sisterly hand on Don's. "Fletcher and I are getting married."

Don Chandler's eyes widened into ovals. His mouth formed a perfect circle. "Wow," he said at last. "This is so...well, not exactly sudden, but so...soon."

Megan and Fletcher had been dating a year. And they weren't even officially shacked up. How long did Don think his sister was supposed to wait? She lowered her eyes decorously. "When Fletcher proposed to me last month, I wasn't sure I was ready for the big commitment, but after three weeks away, I missed him so much, I realized how much we were meant to be together."

Colette faced her 'fiancé' again, and planted a long lingering kiss on his lips, then held up her left hand, proudly displaying the cubic zirconium they'd purchased this afternoon for her 'brother's' appreciation.

Don stood and walked around the table. "Well, then, congratulations, you two." He pumped Fletcher's hand and pecked Colette's cheek. "So when's the wedding? Got a date yet?"

"We were thinking this weekend."

Don's eyes bugged out like two blue ping pong balls. *"This*

171

weekend? As in, three days from now?"

She fluttered her lashes and paraphrased a line from When Harry Met Sally. "When you want to spend your life with somebody, you might as well start as soon as possible." Thank goodness for American movies.

"But it could be months before we can book the church. And don't women have to fuss over buying a dress, flowers, bridesmaid's costumes, etc?"

"I don't need all that," she said serenely. "We just want a small wedding with the family. You'll be the best man and Amber will be my maid of honor."

"We can have the ceremony outdoors, maybe a park, or a garden at the club," Fletcher suggested.

"Well," Don said as if he'd swallowed his tongue. His cheeks puffed out in deep exhalation. "Fletcher, how about you pour us a little wine or champagne to celebrate?"

When Fletcher headed to the kitchen, Don grabbed Colette's arm and steered her to the living room sofa. "Meggie," he said when they were seated, "Are you sure about this?"

If eyes could sparkle, Colette put every last effort into making hers do exactly that. "As sure as I've ever been of anything in my life."

Don gripped her shoulders with his hands and drew her so close, she could count the grey flecks in his Mediterranean blue eyes. "Megan. Little sister. I love you so much. I want more than anything in the world for you to be happy." He flicked a stray hair away from her face. "But you've got to tell me the truth. Are you pregnant?"

Pregnant! Colette could have slapped herself. Why hadn't she thought of that? She lowered her eyes, blinking demurely until a tear or two trickled out. "I'm sorry, Don, if you're disappointed. I should have been more careful. But it's not a bad thing, really. Fletcher and I love each other. And we're ready and willing to love this child we made together."

When Don didn't speak for a minute, Colette thought she might have poured it on a little too thick, but finally he locked her in his arms and held her close. Close enough for Colette to drink in his alluring after shave.

Too soon, he released her. "I'll call the club tomorrow and see what we can arrange on short notice."

"Oh, Don. Thank you. I love you so much." She kissed his cheek from the corner of his eye down to the curve of his lips. "I want you to be happy for me. For us."

"I am." He gripped her shoulders again but held her at arm's length. "I'm so happy for you, Meggie." He blinked furiously. "And so excited."

He walked her back toward the kitchen where Fletcher waited. "You treat my sister right, now, or you'll have to answer to me." He winked as if to assure Fletcher he was just teasing, and then patted Colette's stomach. "And take care good of my niece or nephew."

Fletcher's face paled one shade lighter than normal before he recovered. "Of course I will." He kept up his sickly smile until Colette closed the door behind Don and locked it. Then he turned to her.

"You told him you were pregnant?" Fletcher stared in disbelief as he stripped off his white short-sleeved dress shirt and headed toward the bedroom. Leaving the dinner dishes for someone else, presumably Colette, to clean up. "What in hell possessed you to make that one up?"

"It was his idea." Colette unzipped her navy pleated skirt and let it drop to the floor. "I just went along with what he already guessed."

"Great," he grumbled. "Now he thinks I irresponsibly knocked up his sister. That's sure to get his blessing."

"I said it was my fault." Colette fumbled with the tiny neck loop on her buttoned down shirt. "It makes the most sense, you know. Why else would we be in such a huge hurry to get married?"

"Yeah, you're right." Fletcher unzipped and stepped out of his jeans. "I should have thought of that myself."

"Damned straight."

He reached for her collar, slid his finger into the loop, and released it.

"Thanks." She was going to start on the buttons, but Fletcher continued his way down her shirt undoing them, as if she were some china doll he'd gotten for Christmas and couldn't wait to undress.

"Whoa." He spread the opened shirt to reveal her bare breasts. "No bra?"

She shrugged. "You told me to dress like a schoolgirl."

"So you thought you'd poke your tits in brother Don's face." He pressed the thin cotton material to her breast, through which the outline of nipple and aureole was clearly evident. "You little tart."

"Don't be ridiculous. Saint Don would never think of his sister that way."

"He's not the one I'm concerned about." He pinched her nipples, hard. "You're hot for him, aren't you?"

She tried to look indignant. "Of course not." She danced both breasts against Fletcher's bare chest. "Besides the obvious problem

174

with that, why would I want him when I can have you?"

He grinned. "I'm right. I saw you ogling him at dinner. You want the saint in your pants." He sing-songed like a child on a playground. "Megan's hot for her brother. Incestuous little slut." He palmed her breasts and suckled each one. "And you can't have him. That's just tearing you up, isn't it?"

The taunt didn't deserve an answer. Instead, Colette cupped Fletcher's package and stroked him until he hardened against her palm. "Tear this up."

He slammed her against the bedroom wall. His erection set her juices into pulsation mode. Colette grabbed at his underwear, he at hers. Before either could step out of them, he was inside her, thrilling with no mercy.

"Slut."

"Bastard."

His tongue invaded her mouth. His fingers dug into her buttocks. Colette met his thrusts with wild abandon. What was it about this man that fueled her passionate aggression? It definitely wasn't his fine character. She couldn't remember ever disliking a man so thoroughly. And yet, her body couldn't get enough of him.

She came, twice, and then he pulled out, still fully hard, and led her to the bed. Colette sank exhausted onto her back and wrapped her legs around his butt as he plunged inside her once again. When he released with a war cry, Colette came once more, her body clinging to his in a bath of semen and sweat.

"So?" he said after he'd rolled over onto his back and his breathing slowed to normal. "Were you thinking about Don when we were doing it?"

"No," she answered truthfully. She hadn't been thinking at all.

"Were you thinking of Megan?"

"God, no." He turned to his side and propped himself on his elbow, studying her body as if he'd never seen it before.

"Why are you staring at me like that?"

"I like looking at you." He caressed a clammy breast. "I enjoy seeing you naked."

"You've seen me naked—or a variant of me—for over a year."

"Not even close."

"What's different?"

She was expecting a lewd paean to her sexual talents. Instead, he answered seriously. "With Megan, I always had to be on guard. Considerate of her *feelings*." He said the word as if it were an epithet.

"What about *my* feelings?"

"You?" He chortled. "You don't have feelings." He pinched her nipple, then laved it with his tongue. "And even if you did, it wouldn't matter. In this situation, between you and me, I'm in control."

"And how do you figure that?"

He spread his thumb and pinkie in the universal gesture for talking on a cell phone. "Hello? Police?"

She snickered. He wasn't going to turn her in. Fletcher was so proud of this grand scam he'd hatched he'd probably cut off his left ball before he gave it up. But Colette wondered if he'd thought it all the way through.

She palmed his chest. "So let's say we make this happen.

Darling. We fool the family until Saturday, we get married, we split up Megan's trust fund. Then what?"

"What do you care? You'll be gone, on your way to Wherever. And don't tell me," he added quickly. "I don't want to know."

"I'm not leaving until I get my share of the money. And that may take time."

"So we'll go on a honeymoon. Niagara Falls. Or whatever American tourist trap your little French heart has been dying to visit. And wait until the trust busts open."

"And then what?" She'd be on the first plane out of the country going anywhere without extradition, but.... "What do *you* do once you get your money?"

He grinned. "Then I kill you."

She almost choked.

"Figuratively speaking, of course." He bent his leg and rubbed his knee against her shin. "I invent some boating accident or something, and I come back all distraught and grieving because I've lost the love of my life."

He *definitely* hadn't thought this through. "And what happens when the real Megan comes home?"

He stroked the five o'clock shadow on his upper lip. "I'm surprised and shocked, as is everyone else. Delighted of course, to have her back, and horrified that a ruthless con woman--that's you-- duped me into believing she was Megan."

"Oh, sure. Throw me under the bus."

"Why not?"

One thing she had to admire about this con artist, he was

totally upfront about it. "Faking a death can be difficult and risky," she said. "And how would you explain the missing money?"

"You stole it," he said promptly.

"Only half of it?"

Colette imagined the wheels turning in his handsome head. One. Two. Duh. By answering Megan's phone call, he'd limited his options. Now that Megan knew that Fletcher knew she was stuck in Europe, she'd eventually figure out his involvement in the scam.

"I guess I'll have to disappear too," he said when it all had sunk in. "Maybe you can recommend a good safe haven." He kissed her on the lips, not with his customary forceful ardor, but slowly and sweetly. "It's late. I've got to go into the office tomorrow to dance the razzle-dazzle for Megan's old man, and you've got to buy a wedding gown."

Colette turned to her side, away from him, for sleep. Fletcher spooned against her back, resting his arm on her breasts and his leg between her thighs. Surprisingly tender.

She closed her eyes and immersed herself in the sensation of his cradling touch. Imagining Don Chandler's limbs caressing her, she stroked the slim fingers cupping her breast. Hungrily she nestled into Fletcher's chest, fantasizing Don's cool skin against her back. What would it be like to live a normal life with a man who truly loved her?

Starry-eyed dreamer. Even if she weren't pretending to be his sister, a man like Don Chandler would never look at her twice. He was refined, cultured, polished, all the things Colette could never hope to be. Maybe if she'd made different choices, maybe if she hadn't gotten pregnant at fifteen...

But the past couldn't be changed. She could never have a man like Don. A man who was good and kind and loving would want a woman of similar inclination. If the self-sacrificing St. Don ever married, it would likely be to a wealthy, well-born, sophisticated woman who smoldered on his arm at parties and turned to ice in his bed.

* * *

"The bed wasn't comfortable?"

Paul lifted his head from where it had dropped onto the keyboard, blinking at the first rays of daylight and at Marcel standing over him.

Marcel! Paul jumped out of his chair and looked around, behind, and through the lawyer, but Megan wasn't with him. "Where is she?" he croaked.

"I don't have her," Marcel said. "She wasn't there."

"Not as Megan Chandler, perhaps." Paul rubbed his eyes. "Did you also ask for Colette Marchand?"

"I did."

"Maybe she's being held at another station." Marcel had said he'd go to the police station closest to the Hotel Denise.

"I've checked the databases for the entire city of Paris." Marcel tossed his brief case on the floor. "Your lady is not in police custody."

Chapter Eighteen

Light shone on Megan's face. Was it morning at last? Slowly she opened her eyes. But instead of sunlight pouring in through a high, barred window, a flashlight traversed her body from head to foot and back again. Everything outside its sphere was still dark as pitch.

"*Venez avec moi.*" She flinched at how close the voice was to her ear. "*Serus vous attendez.*"

She pulled herself to a sitting position. That strange phrase again. Serious attention. No, '*attend*' meant 'wait.' Serus waits. She converted the sounds she'd heard to French lettering. Cyrus. A name. Cyrus is waiting. But who was Cyrus?

Cool air hit her midriff. Her shirt had hiked up, and the sweatshirt was... Megan groped the floor and found it. She vaguely remembered taking it off in the night to use as a pillow.

She reached for a wall to brace herself, but there was no solid wall, only some sort of 3-D collage of spiny, spiky, hard things wherever she touched. Cold. And damp. Were they shells? Bones?

"*Maintenant.*"

Slipping her arms into the hooded sweatshirt, Megan rose to her knees, then pushed her palms against the ground and hoisted herself up. Her sandals skidded as she fought for balance.

"Dépêchez vous."

She tried to peer into her jailer's eyes, but the flashlight's glare in her own blinded her. The man--it definitely was a man--pointed the beam at the floor and pushed her to walk ahead of him. Weak and weary, her bones heavy inside her skin, Megan blinked and shakily followed the circle of light on the damp stone floor. *"Quelle heure est-il? Où suis-je?"*

No response from her captor. Maybe he wasn't wearing a watch, but he ought to be able to tell her where she was. If this was a cell, there didn't seem to be any bars. And if this was a dungeon...

Wet gravel crunched under her feet. One foot slid sideways and threatened to topple her. Megan grappled at the wall to right her footing. The flashlight beam followed her arm and lit up a whole array of...skulls!

Megan gasped as her fingers clutched an uneven row of teeth in a hole that had once been a mouth. She was in the Catacombs!

She'd heard of this underground labyrinth in what had once been a limestone quarry. In the eighteenth century the overcrowded cemeteries of Paris were emptied out and the exhumed bones brought to this subterranean ossuary. The remains of over six million people, stacked in piles, sometimes in artistic patterns of skulls, femurs, and other large bones. They gave tours of this place, and Megan had thought she might take one if she had extra days in Paris.

Be careful what you wish for. But this part of the catacombs didn't look like anyplace a tourist would go. There was no electricity, and, as far as she could tell, no path. She was totally at the mercy of the flashlight held by this--well, he didn't look like a policeman. When he redirected his lamp, a quick glimpse of his clothing revealed jeans and a sweatshirt, not the dark blue uniform of a Paris gendarme. Megan stifled a dry groan.

181

An impatient nudge in her back--from the flashlight? A gun?--kept her walking forward. To where? Was she walking out of the labyrinth or deeper into it? Who was this man and where was he taking her?

She didn't dare try to escape, not if he had a gun. Or even if he didn't. She'd heard the twisted hallways of the Paris catacombs covered two hundred miles. If she ran off alone, she could be lost down here forever.

The man grunted in French for her to turn right. Even with the warning, she almost smacked her head on another pile of severed skeletons. Was that what had caused the bleeding on her head? Or had he—they--beaten her? Knocked her unconscious?

She moved on in the pitch blackness whichever way her captor prodded, her hand out in front of her in anticipation of obstacles. Her feet fought for traction at every step. The distance seemed long, but that was probably because she moved so slowly. Megan guessed they hadn't walked all that far from the place where she'd slept, when, at their final turn, a lighted room appeared out of the darkness.

A huge candelabrum holding seven or eight candles stood in the center of the room. Beside it, a bearded, turbaned man sat on a throne of cushions. She made out almost a dozen shadowy figures standing in a semicircle against what might have been walls of bone. Several stooped their heads to avoid a low overhang in the cavern, but Megan was able to walk in at her full height.

The turbaned man scrutinized her for a full minute, and then addressed her in French.

"What have you told the police?" he asked.

The police? So these people were definitely not them. Who were they, then? And how did she get from police custody to this place? "I didn't tell them anything," she said in her broken French.

"They took me away in a car, and the next thing I knew, I woke up here."

Mr. Turban--was he Cyrus?--chuckled. At his gesture, the man who'd brought her to this room shone his flashlight on two men at the wall wearing police uniforms.

The same men who'd hustled her from the hotel room. But if they were the police, then who were--?

Gulp. They weren't policeman. They'd impersonated the authorities to bring her here to this gang of...of...

"But you did talk to the police, didn't you, Colette?" Cyrus's sardonic smile displayed a mouth of cigarette-stained teeth. "We saw them go into your apartment."

Paul's apartment. Megan's blood chilled. If he had gone back there... "I'm not Colette," she said in English. And in case he didn't understand, she translated, "*Je ne suis pas Colette.*"

Cyrus laughed. And just like in some B Mafia movie, all his men laughed after him.

And as if she were watching the movie, instead of entrenched in it, Megan suddenly comprehended the plot. She was being held underground by members of The Community. This was the cell Colette belonged to. Murderous, embassy-bombing terrorists.

Her knees knocked together and her bones rattled with fear. If they thought she was Colette, they weren't behaving like they were welcoming her back into the 'family.' Their objective was to debrief her, and then--

Omigod. They intended to kill Colette. Kill *her.*

* * *

Paul gulped in a big breath, but his lungs barely inflated. An invisible force had sucked all the air out of the room. If the police didn't have her, then who had abducted Megan from their hotel room? His mind danced a macabre jig as it reviewed the events of the last few hours. His lungs collapsed. "The Community," he gasped. "Who else could it be?"

Marcel handed him a teacup and saucer with the teabag still in it. A confused expression ringed his eyes. "You think the terrorist cell captured Megan?"

"You have a better idea?"

The lawyer took a seat next to the desk and set his own teacup on a tile coaster. "Why would they want Megan?"

"Because they think she's Colette."

"Wouldn't they already have Colette? If she did bomb the embassy, wouldn't she have gone back to wherever their cell is to hide out?"

"Not necessarily." Paul sipped his tea, letting the warmth open his compressed lungs. "Since she went to the trouble of stealing Megan's passport and plane ticket, I'm guessing Colette fled the country."

"Instead of reporting in. So they sent men out looking for her, dressed as policemen so she wouldn't resist. Makes sense." Marcel stroked his goatee. "But how would they know she was at that hotel?"

Paul winced. "Near my apartment, Megan was accosted by a dark-skinned man. Probably Arabic," he realized now. "He called her Colette. We got away from him, but..." He swallowed. "He could have followed us to the hotel."

Damn. Paul had kept a close eye out for anyone who looked

like they could be police, but he'd paid little attention to the dozens of dirty-jeaned, sweatshirt-hooded young bucks who frequented the subways at all hours. *Stupid, irresponsible blunder.* "What if he told his buddies where 'Colette' was?"

Marcel frowned. "But surely they'll release her once they realize she isn't Colette."

"You think they'll believe her? You didn't, not at first. I didn't, and I lived with Colette for half a year." A gnawing sensation ate at Paul's gut. "Even if they did believe her, you think they'd just let her walk away? If she's been to their hideout? If she's seen their faces?"

He jumped to his feet, fear filling his mouth. This was no longer a case of mistaken arrest, where the worst that could happen was a few days of false imprisonment. Megan's life was in danger.

He ran to the guest room, grabbed his shirt, shoes and jacket, and dressed hurriedly.

"Are you crazy?" As Paul dashed to the door, Marcel folded his arms and blocked his path. "It's not safe for you to go out there. Everyone in Paris has seen your face on television."

Paul jutted out his chin. "I have to find Megan." He tried to ease Marcel aside, but the man stood his ground.

"And how do you plan to do that? If the police haven't found the terrorist cell, how can you?"

It was a logical question but for once, Paul had no logical answer. "Hell if I know."

"And what if by some miracle you do find her?" Marcel persisted. "You don't even have a weapon. You plan to overpower a gang of trained killers with just your good looks and your bare hands?"

The gun in the backpack. Megan had stashed it under the bed in the hotel. Maybe it was still there. Paul nudged his shoulder against Marcel's. "Let me pass."

Again Marcel refused to move. "Have you considered that you may be risking your life for nothing? Megan, even if they think she's Colette, is no longer of use to the terrorists. She might already be--"

"Don't say it." Fear and anger pounded in Paul's chest. "I can't sit here and do nothing! If there's a chance, even a small one, that Megan's alive, I've got to try to save her. Now get the hell out of my way!"

He was about to shove Marcel bodily when a voice rang out behind him. "I'll go with you."

Paul turned. Jacques stood barefoot in the foyer, wearing blue striped pajama bottoms and a white vee-necked tee shirt. All of five feet six or seven inches, he looked about as formidable as a puppy.

"Thanks, but I'll do this alone. There's no need for anyone else to endanger himself."

"Okay, so you're set on being a hero. A dead hero, if you don't plan this out better." Jacques tugged Paul's denim jacket off his shoulders. "You're wearing a jacket two sizes too small for you. You speak French with an accent. And you look like a school bus exploded on your head. Even if you weren't wanted by the police, you'd attract attention."

"I don't care. I just--"

"He's right," Marcel said. "You need a wing man. Colette's disappeared and now Megan's gone missing. We don't want to lose you too."

"*Merci, mais non.*" He turned to Jacques. "You'd be a lot more help staying here. In case Megan finds her way back to your flat." It was a slim hope, but slim was all he had right now.

"I'll be here," Marcel said. "Working from home today."

Undoubtedly because he'd been out all night on Paul's behalf. He scanned the lawyer's bloodshot eyes, feeling guilty for having doubted the man's friendship. These blokes barely knew him, yet they'd gone out of their way to help him and Megan.

"Give me just two minutes to get dressed," Jacques said, already headed to the bedroom.

Seeing his chance, Paul sprang for the doorknob, but Marcel backed his butt against the door. "You have no phone," he reminded Paul. "It's not safe for you out there alone. Either take Jacques with you, or..."

"Or what?" Was he threatening to fight him? On his college wrestling team, Paul had easily taken out men twice Marcel's size.

"Or I call the police the minute you go out the door."

Paul sucked in a breath. He no longer worried about being arrested. But the police would never believe a cockamamie story about Colette having a double, and in the time he'd spend trying to convince them, Megan could be--

He swallowed. "Two minutes."

* * *

Megan couldn't stop shaking. Her knees wobbled, her toes clenched, and her lips quivered so much she could barely form words. *"Parlez-vous Anglais?* I'm an American," she tried desperately to explain. "I never met Colette, but she switched identities with me and I found out I look exactly like her." She wasn't sure Cyrus understood English, but if she tried to muddle through in French, she might accidentally say the opposite of what she meant. "The police think I'm Colette, too, but I ran away from them and they never questioned me."

Cyrus exchanged a look with some of his men. Megan tried to read his expression. Was it This-woman-is-crazy or Nice-try-Colette-but-I'm-not-buying-it? She held her breath, praying the turbaned leader would believe her. But she could manage barely a spark of her trademark optimism.

"So you're not Colette?" Cyrus said finally--in English, thank God. He stroked his beard with a sinister smile.

"No." She allowed herself one relieved breath. "My name is Megan. I'm an American tourist. I--"

"Salim." The leader turned to one of the henchmen on his right. "Why don't you have a talk with Colette—er, Megan--and convince her to tell us what she knows." There was a hard, grating edge to the word 'convince.'

The man to whom he'd spoken reached into the pocket of his jeans, pulled out a pistol, and cocked it. Megan choked on her one breath as he walked toward her and shoved it in her back. Hopes crushed in her chest of ever seeing her family again. He was going to take her out into one of these dark caverns and kill her. If she was lucky. If she wasn't, he'd rape her and beat her first.

"*On y va, ma chérie?*" He stood only a gun barrel's length behind her as he nudged her out of the 'room' with his knee in her butt, his breath hot on her neck. The hand not holding the weapon pointed the flashlight straight ahead, using her left shoulder as a brace. As they shuffled into the darkness, he pressed his lips against her neck.

"*Pourquoi m'a-tu fui, ma chérie?*" His teeth nipped at her flesh.

Megan gasped. But not from pain. That voice. That cocky,

Don Juan attitude. "You!" Against all good judgment, she whirled around. His face was shadowed but in the reflected glare she caught a glimpse of dark brown eyes and skin, and a sparse mustache on a smug upper lip. It was the man who'd accosted her outside the bakery.

"Bien sur, c'est moi." Propping the gun now under her chin, he wrapped his flashlight arm around her neck and forced his mouth on hers. His tongue flickered around the teeth she clamped together like an iron rail. "Colette," he hissed, and bit her on the lip.

When she cried out, he shoved a ruthless tongue inside her open mouth. Megan squirmed, receiving for her troubles a hard thrust to her chin from the gun.

He withdrew his tongue and spat at her.

She wiped her mouth. "You're Colette's boyfriend, aren't you?"

Instead of an answer, he slammed her into a wall of sharp spikes, then shoved her forward again.

"You're a real piece of work, you know that?" she threw back over her shoulder. It didn't matter if he understood English or not. It didn't matter if he believed her or not. She'd seen their hideout, and Cyrus's face. If they were willing to kill one of their own, if this man Salim would kill his own girlfriend, they'd have no sympathy for an innocent bystander.

She was going to die.

She'd heard that when people were drowning, their whole life flashed in front of them. But only one image flooded her consciousness. Paul Bernard's.

He was the last person she'd remember, the last good soul to show her kindness before she'd ended up in this place of death.

Would she have done the same for a stranger, endangering her life to help someone in need? Megan had never intentionally hurt another human being, but she hadn't gone out of her way to make the world better, either.

She wished she had more time, another chance. She thought of all the things she'd meant to do someday, when she was settled and on her own, when the time was right. One desire shot to the top of her list. To see and touch Paul again.

Her ankle twisted at a wet spot on the gravel. Megan stumbled, grappling to regain her footing. But the wall of bones that should have halted her fall was...not there. Screaming as one foot hovered in the air and the second threatened to slide after it, she clutched at her captor's jacket.

Salim grabbed her waist and hauled her back to solid ground.

Megan labored to catch her breath. She'd heard there were drops in the caverns, some, hundreds of feet down. The air just to her right was colder and smelled--different. She shivered. She'd come this close to death. And instinctively fought against it. She'd wanted to live.

Now, she made it a conscious choice. Though it seemed inevitable that this terrorist would take her life, Megan would not give it up without a struggle.

His body rigid against hers, Colette's boyfriend guided her forward, eighty-five more shuffled steps. Counting them made her feel she had some control over her situation. *Right*. Control. Even if she were to miraculously escape from this murderer, there's no way she'd run back the same way they'd come, into the arms of a dozen more murderers.

A gurgle of water trickled from somewhere. Salim pointed the flashlight to the left and yanked her into another, seemingly endless cave hallway.

They walked twenty-two more steps before he stopped and slammed her against a smooth, not bony wall. "*Maintenant*," he said, "*Parlez*." He thrust the flashlight into her face.

Now he wanted to talk? She blinked from the sudden glare. "I'm not Colette," she said wearily. "I didn't bomb the embassy. I'm an American tourist stranded in Paris." She met his gaze. "Your turn."

"Pourquoi m'a-tu fui?"

Why had she run from him? "Because I don't know you."

"Tu ne me connais pas?" He shone the flashlight in her face and grabbed her hand. *"Tu ne connais pas ceci?"* He rubbed her fingers against his mouth. *"Ou ceci?"* He placed her hand on his chest. *"Ou--?"* He dragged her hand down his body.

This man was definitely Colette's lover.

Which meant he knew her body well.

Which meant Megan had a small but plausible chance.

His right hand embraced her thigh, walking up her jeans to cup her buttocks. His left held the flashlight. Where was the gun? Had he propped it in his waistband? Set it on the floor? Unless she knew exactly where it was, even given the opportunity, she wouldn't be able to grab for it.

While his hands were busy, Megan quietly slipped her fingers under her shirt and deftly unhooked her bra. Go for the flashlight or gun? She'd have less than a second to decide.

When he pushed his body up against hers, Megan shouted out, "Salim!"

He jumped back, startled, pointing the flashlight at her chest.

Megan lifted her sweatshirt and tee and flashed her breasts. "No tattoo. I'm not Colette!"

For an instant, he stood dazed, staring. In that second, Megan grabbed the flashlight and ran.

Twenty-two steps. She turned off the flashlight to make herself less of a target as she ran and rammed her head into the end of the corridor. Wincing in silent pain, Megan turned to the right and hurtled her body forward again.

She heard footsteps behind her, then a gunshot ricocheting off ossified calcium. Megan ran faster, the pain of her twisted ankle escalating with every step. And then she realized. She was running the wrong way! Even if she were able to sprint ahead and lose Salim, she was running right back to the terrorist cell.

A gunshot whizzed by her ear. Megan choked down the aroma of singed hair. She didn't bother to blink back her tears because she couldn't see anything in front of her anyway. She staggered against a jagged wall, but kept running.

The next shot hit her in the leg. Pain sliced through her calf as the bullet ripped her skin apart. Megan's heart rattled and her breath gave out. He was going to keep on shooting her like a dog until she dropped. And then drag her body to his buddies as a trophy. And, God forbid, if she were still warm and breathing...

Seventy-eight steps since the turn. On sheer adrenaline, Megan pushed herself forward six more and made her decision. If she was going to die anyway, it would be on her terms. Not as a sniveling dog, but as a conscious, determined woman.

At step eighty-five, she slid to the left, said a silent final prayer, and jumped into the abyss.

Chapter Nineteen

"So what's the plan?" Jacques asked as they boarded the train and settled on a long bench seat. "Are we going to storm the terrorist stronghold and rescue Megan in the confusion? Or just find where they're holding her and then call the police for backup?"

"You watch too much television," Paul grumbled. It was barely seven and the train wasn't crowded. He scanned the car for anyone who looked foreign, especially if they wore jeans and a hoodie, but he saw only a handful of early commuters in business suits, and a couple of homeless blokes.

He turned to Jacques. "We're not storming anything. Marcel is right. If the police haven't found the terrorist, there's no way we can. Our only hope—Megan's only hope—is that whoever has her figures out she's an innocent bystander and releases her."

"But I thought you said--"

"Never mind what I said."

Jacques shot him a pitying glance. "You've really fallen hard, haven't you?"

"Excuse me?"

"You met this girl two days ago. How have you developed feelings for her so fast?"

Paul drummed his fingers on his knees. "The only feeling I have for her is a sense of obligation to help someone in trouble."

Jacques's brow lifted, then his eyes hardened. "Until recently, you felt the same sort of devotion for Colette. You even defended her to the police. What did this woman do to transfer your loyalty?"

"Megan did nothing." Paul's muscles tightened. "Colette destroyed my trust and any feelings I may have had for her when she used me to attack my country and murder my friends." He clenched his fists at his sides. "I will not rest until she pays for that."

After two stops they disembarked and caught a train going back the way they had come, then switched again for one going in the first direction. "A precaution," Paul explained. Not that he cared anymore if the police were following him. Still, when they got out at the station for the Hotel Denise, he lingered on the platform, waiting to see if anyone else lingered too.

When no one did, he moved slowly toward the exit and cautiously up the stairs, Jacques close beside him.

"You should have at least let me touch up that hair," Jacques said as they hit the sunlight. "Next time you steal somebody's theatrical makeup, be sure you know how to use it."

"Sorry about that. I was desperate." Paul tightened the hood of his own tan windbreaker, which Marcel had found on the floor of the laundry room after they'd fled.

Jacques pouted. "I can't believe you actually thought we would call the police."

He didn't inform Jacques that Marcel had threatened, less than an hour ago to do just that. Instead he shrugged. "Until I realized the police were following my phone, it was the logical assumption."

"Nice place," Jacques asked when the hotel came into view.

"This is where you stayed last night?"

"Yes. The room's paid up until checkout time today. I'm hoping, if she got free, that Megan made her way back here." His plan, formulated on the train, was to retrace Megan's steps for the last two days. Not a very good plan, but all he could think to do. If she were looking for him, which she surely was, she'd go to the places they'd been together or that she'd mentioned to him.

"Wait here," he commanded Jacques, as they passed through the quiet lobby, peopled by only the desk clerk and a few tourists on their way to breakfast.

Jacques accompanied him to the elevator. "And what if there's someone waiting for you in the room and they drag you out a back exit?"

Paul sighed. "Fine. Come up to the floor."

At the fifth floor, he motioned silently for Jacques to stand where Paul had been when he'd come back from the vending machines and spotted Megan being dragged away. Then he took a deep breath, walked to room 515, and inserted his key card into the lock.

The green light flashed. Paul turned the doorknob and eased stealthily into the room.

It appeared to be empty. The maid hadn't yet visited. The bed, though made, was rumpled where they'd sat. A towel lay on the spread.

His gut tightened. Megan had been in the shower when he'd left. He closed his eyes, envisioning her nude body wrapped in this towel, waiting for him to return.

And then murderous assassins had burst in.

His fists clenched so tight his fingernails drew blood. Paul strode to the bathroom, and after checking behind the shower curtain to make sure no one was hiding there, rinsed the blood from his palms.

The towel he used to dry his hands had faint yellow stains. From the hair dye, no doubt. And now there were bloodstains on it too. The last thing he needed was housekeeping noticing the blood and alerting the cops.

He grabbed the towel and headed back through the bedroom, nearly tripping on a black strap peeking out from under the bed.

The backpack. Paul yanked it out and opened it. No gun. The terrorists must have found it. Or... He closed his eyes in prayerful hope. Maybe Megan had managed to hide it in her sweatshirt.

He stuffed the towel in the backpack and slung the bag over his shoulder. Opening the hotel room door, he found Jacques standing just outside.

"What took so long?" he demanded. "I was getting worried."

"She's not here and neither is the weapon."

They rode the elevator back down to the main floor. "I just need to check on a package that may have arrived," Paul explained to Jacques.

"What's in the package?"

"Megan's boyfriend Fletcher promised to send a picture ID and other documents so she can obtain a new passport."

At the mention of the boyfriend, Jacques raised an expressive brow. "She couldn't reach her mother?"

"She did, but her Mum hung up on her. Colette is apparently

answering Megan's cell phone and has convinced the mother that Megan is safe at home and some scam artist is trying to sell her a Your-daughter-is-stranded-in-Europe story."

Jacques chuckled ruefully. "I wish I could say that doesn't sound like Colette, but actually, it does."

Emerging at the lobby, they headed to the front desk.

"You should let me do the talking," Jacques whispered. "They'll respond better to a Frenchman."

"There's nothing wrong with my French." Paul strode up to the counter and cleared his throat to get the clerk's attention.

"Mon épouse et moi y avons séjourné récemment," he began.

"You may speak in English," the clerk said.

Paul ignored Jacques's amused grin. "My wife was expecting some mail delivered, but we checked out before it arrived. I'd like to pick it up for her, please."

The hotel clerk looked up and scrutinized Paul's face for a long, breath-holding minute. "Name?"

"Megan Chandler."

"What dates was she our guest?"

Damn. Of course she wasn't registered under her own name. Paul threw out a recent date, then another. "I don't remember exactly," he said irritably. "Can you please look and see if there's a package?"

None too graciously, the clerk excused himself, disappeared behind the desk, and returned empty-handed. "There's nothing here, sir," he said dismissively and turned to wait on another customer.

Paul's cheeks heated. "Now see here," he began, but Jacques cut him off.

"I've got this," he said assuredly. Sizing up the other desk clerks, he walked up to a young man who even to Paul's unschooled eye looked decidedly gay, and began chatting amiably in French. The animated conversation revealed that they'd both grown up in the same neighborhood and attended the same high school.

Or not. Jacques might well have been employing his acting skills to draw the man out. But the end result of minutes of time-wasting chit-chat was the same as Paul's.

"The package hasn't arrived," Jacques told him.

"Thanks," he said sardonically. "I already got that."

"But my new friend Philippe said he'd call the minute it comes in." Jacques held up his cell phone. "I told you I'd be useful," he said as they exited the hotel. "How were you planning to leave a contact number if I wasn't along?"

Paul had to admit he'd not thought of that. And suddenly he felt overwhelmed. He was used to things making sense, damn it, one logical step following another. This whole adventure--no, misadventure—had plucked him out of his comfortable world and into some spy chase movie.

"Where to now?" Jacques asked as they descended the Metro steps.

"The Musee d'Orsay."

"That painting?"

Paul nodded. "I want to see it. According to Megan, after she saw that portrait everything went to hell in a hand basket."

"Excusez-moi?"

"English idiom. It means her life utterly deteriorated."

When they arrived at the museum, Paul let Jacques lead the way. "I remember it being on the second floor," the actor said as they climbed the stairs of the high-ceilinged entry. After several rooms of early twentieth century portraits and landscapes, they turned a corner and....

"There it is."

Paul stared at *Mademoiselle Adele Jarreau.* Which could have just as easily been titled Miss Megan Chandler. The resemblance was remarkable. If Megan were dressed in period costume, he wouldn't have been able to tell the difference.

He studied the painting from all sides, amazed how the subject favored Megan from every angle. He envisioned Adele Jarreau with her hair down, swinging casually from her shoulders like her young American descendant. Then he pictured Megan dressed in formal finery, wearing this upswept hairdo. Classically beautiful.

"It really looks like Colette, doesn't it?"

Colette? Paul blinked at Jacques. Of course it did, but when he looked at that face, he saw only Megan.

Jacques backed away from the painting and sat on the bench in the middle of the gallery. "Colette used to wear her hair long, you know."

Paul joined him on the bench. "Really?" Since he'd known her, Colette had kept her hair closely cropped.

"She looked so much better with long hair," Jacques said, his eyes still focused on the painting. "Why would she cut it?"

That did seem odd, especially if she were trying to look like Megan. "Exactly when did she cut it?"

Jacques considered. "About six months ago, I guess."

"Just before I met her." Paul's mind swiped at puzzle pieces just out of his grasp. "Which is probably about the time you and she saw that museum portrait."

"So?" Jacques cast an I-don't-get-it look.

He pressed his palms to his thighs. "Megan thinks that after seeing this painting, Colette might have searched for family members on the Internet. What if she found Megan? Her exact double. Except for the hair."

Jacques looked utterly confused. "But Megan has long hair. And back then, so did Colette."

"Megan has long hair *now*." Another piece of the puzzle locked into place. "But maybe she had short hair in her Facebook profile photo, or wherever Colette found her. Who knows how long ago that was taken? If Colette invited Megan to Europe to frame her for the embassy bombing, she would have cut her hair to look like Megan's picture. But by the time she arrived in Europe, Megan's hair had already grown out."

Jacque's mouth dropped open. "Colette framed Megan? I thought it was Nicole who suggested Megan take that tour."

"Colette *is* Nicole." He was sure of that now. Colette must have spied on Megan when her group first arrived in Paris, then purchased the wig and an identical backpack. "She wore the wig as a disguise during the bombing. Then she met Megan here, as Nicole, wearing the yellow scarf wrapped around her so Megan couldn't see her face."

"Then 'Nicole' drugged her, and stole her identity." Jacques shot to his feet, a disturbed look on his face. "If Colette is Nicole," he said slowly, "what if she's also Megan?"

Paul chuckled.

"No, I mean it. What if there's no Nicole, and no Megan? Colette bombed the embassy and she was on her way to meet up with her terrorist group when you confronted her. In an attempt to get away, she fabricated this elaborate story to get us to believe she was someone else."

Paul blinked. "You're serious?"

"Colette's a damned good actress," Jacques said without a trace of a smile. "And she was the best student in our class at improv."

Paul couldn't dispute that. Colette could charm a man out of not only his briefs but his senses.

"It could be true," Jacques persisted. "You said you found your security badge in the backpack. What if there was only one backpack? What if Colette stashed the gun, and your badge, with her cosmetics and magazine, then pretended some mysterious woman had drugged her and switched bags with her."

As a programmer and problem solver Paul would normally embrace the simplest explanation as the most likely. But even though he'd known Megan only two days, and not even in the Biblical sense, he was cocksure she and Colette were two different people. "Colette has a tattoo," he said dismissively. "Megan doesn't. Megan is more fully rounded than Colette, by about nine kilos. And what about the hair?"

"We already agreed Colette wore a wig," Jacques answered promptly.

"Because she was trying to look like Megan. Whose hair is

real."

"Are you sure? I was in a play once where the lead actress's wig kept sliding off. They used special glue to--"

"It's not a wig."

"Oh?" Jacques raised a prurient brow. "And you know this because...?"

Paul ignored the innuendo. "Megan isn't wearing a wig. She did not gain nine kilos overnight. And she has no tattoo."

"Tattoos can be removed."

"Not within a few hours and certainly not without some scar or skin discoloration." The dragonfly on Colette's breast had definitely been there the morning of the bombing. And if he hadn't been convinced of its absence in his ten second scrutiny of Megan that night, yesterday's more thorough exploration of those luscious breasts would have definitely persuaded him.

"But--"

"Jacques, I saw two men dressed as policeman drag her away. If they were in fact terrorists, and Colette is one of them, why the subterfuge?"

The actor shrugged. "Perhaps that was a scheme to fool you into thinking she'd been arrested. Colette actually went willingly, with her friends."

"Dammit, no." Paul rose from the bench. "She didn't need a ploy to get away from me. I went to my flat yesterday to try to retrieve my laptop. If she were Colette, she would have simply waited until I left and then walked away. Instead, Megan came running after me."

I was afraid you wouldn't come back. A lump knotted Paul's throat. He shouldn't have left her, not even for a minute. Now he might never see her again.

"You think she made up everything she told us?" He pointed to the portrait of Adele Jarreau. "Megan said it all started when she saw this painting."

"That doesn't mean she was here that day. Colette saw this painting, months ago, with me."

"Then let's walk through her story. See if the details hold up."

"A dramatization," Jacques exclaimed merrily. He positioned himself in front of the Jarreau portrait and lowered his head, as if he were getting into character. Then he looked up and stared at the painting. "'*Mon Dieu*! This woman looks exactly like me.'"

If Jacques were portraying Megan, not Colette, she probably would have said *Ohmygod* instead of Mon Dieu, but Paul let that ride.

"I'm stunned," Jacques continued. "Amazed. Then I look up and see a woman wearing a yellow scarf. "'Nicole!'" Taking small rapid steps, as a petite woman would, Jacques darted out of the room.

Paul went after him, summoning the particulars of the story Megan had told Tuesday night. "The woman doesn't stop for her. Megan tracks her through several galleries until she disappears into a bathroom."

With Jacques at his heels, Paul wound his way from gallery to gallery until he reached the wall and windows at the rear of the museum, then retraced his steps back through the Adele Jarreau gallery toward the front.

"I didn't see any bathrooms," Jacques challenged.

Paul approached a docent seated on a hard chair at the side of the room. "*Excusez-moi. Ou est le toilette?*"

"*En bas. Le lobby.*"

Paul frowned. He distinctly remembered Megan mentioning regaining consciousness in the bathroom stall, discovering her watch missing, and then dashing down one flight of stairs to the lobby. If there were no bathrooms on the second floor...

His gaze fell on a curtained doorway, above which hung a sign stating *Employees Only* in French and English. Paul tugged at Jacques's sleeve, and beckoned him outside the room.

"That curtain," he whispered when they were out of earshot of the docent. "Megan said she followed the woman in the scarf through one like that."

Jacques narrowed his eyes. "For someone who didn't appear to be listening, who in fact challenged everything the lady said that night, you seem to recall a lot of detailed information."

"Information is my business." Paul peeked into the next room, where the matronly woman still sat, studying her fingers and every so often, the patrons. "You think you can distract her? Get her out of that room?"

"Of course." Jacques grinned. "Distraction is *my* business."

Paul waited while Jacques approached the woman, asking her in French about, of all things, the portrait of Adele Jarreau. The woman replied and pointed, keeping her seat, but Jacques charmed her, looking petulant and helpless, until she got up and walked with him out of the gallery.

With the curtain unattended, Paul dashed through it. He found a hall like the one Megan had described, with doors marked Private, and presumably locked. Toward the end of the hallway he saw a water fountain and flanking it, two bathrooms. He opened the door to the Ladies room cautiously, prepared to claim if confronted that he'd mistakenly entered the wrong rest room.

No one was inside. Paul examined the toilet stalls scrupulously, looking for--what? Blood? A torn piece of clothing? A syringe? Something, anything, to indicate signs of a drugging or a struggle. Something to prove Megan's story wasn't a lie.

Behind one of the toilet seats, wedged between the porcelain and the wall, he saw a button. A brown leather button matching the ones on Megan's trench coat. Of which one had been missing. It must have popped off when Colette attacked her.

Paul fingered it delicately as if he'd found a treasure. Not that he really needed proof that Megan was who she'd said. She and Colette might look alike. But Colette had never looked at him the way Megan had, as if he were some kind of hero. As if he were essential to her world.

The matronly docent, who'd resumed her post, glared at him as he emerged from the curtain, but Paul strode away nonchalantly as if he had every right to be there. He found Jacques back at the Jarreau portrait.

"Everything happened just the way she said," he declared, pulling the button from his shirt pocket.

Jacques stared at it uncomprehending.

"It's from Megan's trench coat," Paul explained. "I noticed one was missing when I first found her on Embassy row."

"So Megan Chandler is a real person," Jacques mused. "Well, that's good news. And bad news."

"How so?"

205

"Good because I know you're falling in love with her. Bad because this means Megan's life is definitely in danger."

Chapter Twenty

Megan awoke to the sound of gurgling water, her aching back and limbs submerged in a moving stream.

Was she alive? Or was the floating sensation Heaven?

Or Hell? The cold water brought back her earliest memory. She was three years old, separated from her mother in a thunderstorm. The flood waters reached her knees and obscured the curb. Batted by the winds, she slipped into the street, where rushing waters propelled her small body forward.

Mommy! She fought to hoist herself back onto the curb, but the force was too great. Megan saw her mother running after her, desperately trying to grab her, but the powerful waters swept the little girl onward. Surging toward a storm drain.

Strong arms grabbed her waist, lifting her to safety out of the rainwater river. A giant of a man--or so he'd seemed to a three-year-old, clasped her to his sturdy chest, then stepped onto the curb and handed her into her mother's welcoming arms.

Was she just having a nightmare? Megan tried to open her eyes, but everything around her remained black. She raised an arm and touched her lids. Her eyes were already opened.

Darkness. Catacombs. She was alive! She wanted to shout for

joy at having survived the jump, but celebration seemed premature. Alone in the dark, she might be surging helplessly toward her death.

The flashlight. She patted her stomach. Miraculously, it was still in the sweatshirt pouch where she'd placed it. Did she dare hope for another miracle, that it was waterproof? Once that would have been her optimistic first assumption, but she no longer held much faith that things would go her way.

Pointing it in front of her, she flicked on the switch. A beam of concentrated light outlined the walls and waterway of her prison. Megan's heart leaped. At last her luck was changing.

Or not.

Now that she could see, the view in front of her struck terror in her overwrought heart. She wasn't drifting in a meandering stream. The accumulated rainwater was rushing faster, plunging toward a point where it just seemed to...drop.

Her heart stopped. She was almost to the crest of what would become a waterfall and wash her over the edge down to another chasm. And today there was no strong man to help her. If there was any hope of survival, she'd have to save herself.

Shoving the flashlight back in its pouch, she said another prayer, then turned to her side and reached out. Her right hand caught on a protruding bone, then slipped as her left hand dug into another. The left hand held. The right found another grip. Willing all her strength into her arms, Megan pulled her body to the wall. She dug a toe in one hole, then scrambled up the column of bones until she could plant both feet in dry places.

She breathed.

Now what? She was momentarily safe from the rushing river, but she couldn't just hang here. The light glowed in her pocket strong enough to see her immediate surroundings, but it was too faint to tell if there was any dry land behind or ahead of her. Wincing from pain and exertion, she pressed most of her weight behind her right hand, and reached with her left for the flashlight.

Ahead of her, there was only wall-less cavern beyond the drop-off. Behind her...

She swallowed, praying wishful hope wasn't making her eyes see what her brain wanted. Just a few feet back the way she'd been, she thought she saw the grotto wall twist sharply to the side. The water bypassed the turn, rushing straight ahead.

She'd never make it. That few feet would require meticulous hand and foot placement, testing every handhold, resting every few inches. And what if that catacomb oasis really was just a mirage? Her arms already felt wrenched from their sockets, her leg was bleeding from a bullet. What if she used her last ounce of strength and then just dropped off into the floodwaters anyway?

She was so tired. It would be so easy to just--

No! She couldn't give up now. She hadn't died when she dropped from that ledge. Nor had Salim killed her. Grabbing another handhold, she tugged herself forward. She would not die today, not in this place, this way. She could save herself.

Her right foot felt for a toehold, slid, and recovered. Ignoring pain, focusing on one action at a time, Megan hand-walked her way toward the place where she thought she'd seen dry ground. Clock minutes had no meaning, only the number of transfers. The eighth time she moved her hand and footholds, the shape of the bone wall curved subtly. She caught her breath. Reached for the flashlight. And looked down.

The ground three feet beneath her was puddled and slushy, but there was ground. Megan's lungs filled with breath. Tears of joy welled in her eyes. Was this how Noah felt when the Ark stopped pitching and rested on Mt. Ararat? Drawing on her last ounce of adrenaline, she propelled herself forward one more handhold, and then jumped.

She landed on her bottom, her fingers digging into the dirt. The damp earth smelled like countryside after a summer shower. Megan scooted backwards a few more feet to dry safety. Ahead of her, the rolling waters rushed on.

Breathe.

She aimed the flashlight at her leg where she'd been shot. The blood had mostly washed away in the current, and there was no great hole revealing bone or tissue. Hopefully just a flesh wound.

Fractured bones? How would her brother Don determine that? Deliberately, she exercised each one of her moveable parts: neck, fingers, arms, legs, knees. Every twitch brought a scream of pain, but everything moved. Nothing seemed broken.

The effort had exhausted her. She wanted to lie down and rest. But just because she was alive and viable didn't mean she was out of danger. Instead of instant death she might face a slow one of starvation.

How long and how far to an exit? This pathway might go on for miles and then dead-end. But what choice did she have? If there was any way to escape this cavernous prison, she wasn't going to find it sitting on her butt.

She turned off the flashlight to save battery, and, keeping one hand on the wall of bones at all times, trudged forward.

* * *

At the Mayfair Hotel, the desk clerk wouldn't or couldn't tell Paul if Megan Chandler had been a guest there. But at least he confirmed that an American tour group had stayed three nights in the last week.

Over a lunch of soup and sandwiches, Jacques called Marcel to see if Megan had shown up at their flat. She hadn't.

"I've got a class at three," Jacques said reluctantly. "I hate to leave you but--"

"I'll be fine." Truthfully, he'd appreciated Jacques's company, but this wasn't his quest.

"You're exhausted," Jacques said. "Why don't you go back to the apartment and get some sleep? We can start again tomorrow."

Like he could sleep with Megan in danger. If she was alive, she might not be tomorrow. Paul was determined to search every place he knew she'd been, anywhere she might have gone to look for him. His rational mind didn't hold much hope of finding her. But his rational mind would have to take a back seat on this.

Emerging from the Metro alone at the Boulevard Voltaire, Paul kept watch for anyone who might be following him, but the shoppers and strollers all looked intent on their own business.

At the small café near the station, he ordered a croissant and questioned the girl behind the counter. Yes, she'd been here since early this morning and no, she hadn't seen anyone of Megan's description. On a hunch, Paul asked about a dark skinned man who may have been wearing a hoodie, but the clerk hadn't seen him either.

Nearing his street, he scanned the curbs for any suspicious vehicles. If the police were still staking out his flat, it wasn't likely they'd be sitting out front in official police cars. But the few parked vehicles all seemed to be unoccupied.

He made a wide berth around his own street, ducking into the alley behind it. Anxiously, he studied the passing pedestrians on the boulevard. It was probably foolish to hope Megan had come here. She didn't even know which building was his, not even which street. And why would she want to return to the place where she'd been attacked by that man?

A sense of hopelessness settled around him. What if he never saw her again? What if--

Something hard crashed into his skull. The world spun around him and he dropped to his knees and one hand in dizziness and pain.

He blinked to clear the fog. Warm liquid oozed down his cheek. Paul hauled himself up to see a dark-skinned man wearing a ball cap and a jean jacket, pointing a pistol at his chest. The man looked familiar. And so did the gun.

"*Ou est Colette?*" the man growled, ramming the side of the gun at his face.

"*Je ne sais pas. Où est Megan?*"

The guy looked caught off guard. "Maygan?"

"*L'autre fille.*"

Dark eyes swam in confusion. Then they narrowed on Paul, assessing his interest. "I give you Maygan if you give me Colette," he said in badly accented English.

Paul swallowed, tasting a trickle of blood. "I don't have Colette," he answered slowly, his mind racing. He wasn't wearing a hoodie, but he was sure this was the man who'd accosted Megan, mistaking her for Colette. If he was part of that terrorist cell, he had to know where she was.

Paul's heart galloped to keep up with his brain. "I do know where Colette is," he said in simple English. "I will tell you if you give me Megan. Megan is innocent. She knows nothing of Colette or your people." He tried to control his voice from screeching, his pounding heart from jumping out of his chest. *"Ou est la fille Américaine?"*

The man tucked the barrel of the gun under Paul's chin, then slowly walked it down his chest and over his stomach, pausing an inch above his jewels. Uncomfortable *déjà vu*. When he looked down at the weapon, Paul recognized it as the gun from Megan's backpack.

"Maygan." The smile that cracked the terrorist's lips was unlike any Paul had ever seen, subtle and eerie, and skin-chillingly cruel. *"Est morte."*

Megan dead? The air whooshed out of Paul's lungs. From somewhere deep inside him a warrior cry raged through his internal organs. Acting without plan, from only his anger and pain, he swung the backpack at the man's head to catch his attention and then punched him in the gut.

The man yelped. Paul grabbed the gun from his hand. Howling in grief, he slammed it across the assholes's lying mouth and kicked him between the legs.

The terrorist struggled to retrieve the gun, but he was no match for Paul's size, or for his rage. Punching with one hand, pistol whipping with the other, kicking repeatedly, he beat the son of Osama into a bloody freaking pulp.

"Not so brave without this, are you?" He pointed the gun at what had moments ago been a decent-looking face.

The guy yammered curses in Arabic.

He planted a foot on the man's stomach and held it there until the weasel gasped for breath. Then he leveled the gun at his skull, and rammed him into unconsciousness.

Megan dead. The words swarmed in his brain but Paul couldn't think, couldn't feel. Moving solely by instinct, he took the towel out of the backpack and wiped the blood off the gun, then with a clean corner, scrubbed it again with a vengeance, intent on erasing the fingerprints. His fingerprints. Megan's fingerprints. And, undoubtedly, Colette's.

Holding the gun by the towel, he knelt and placed it in the palm of the terrorist's hand and closed his lean brown fingers over it.

Sirens wailed in the distance. Someone must have heard the ruckus and called the police.

Panting, Paul got to his feet and wiped his hands on a clean part of the towel, then shoved it back into the bag. Hands on his knees, still breathing heavily, he looked over the scene one last time. Had he left anything incriminating?

No, but he should. From the bag's zippered pocket, he took out his British Embassy security badge. Holding it by its edge, he placed it in the pocket of the terrorist's jacket.

Megan dead. Paul shuffled to the Metro station, frankly not caring whether the police arrested him or not. No one seemed to take notice of him or his bloody cheek. At the subway entrance he descended the stairs and waited for a train. Any train. What did it matter where he went? Megan was dead. He'd failed to protect her.

A train roared into the station. Its brakes screeched in his ears and air puffed at his face, but he heard and felt nothing. His emotions had been used up in that alley. He was numb. Dead inside. A useless, worthless human being.

Paul shuffled onto the train, shoved by hordes of passengers anxious to get home to waiting loved ones. He found one empty seat, and sat unmoving on the cold plastic, his heart barely beating. Time slowed like the plodding rhythms of his heart and breath. While Paris went about its day as usual above him, Paul rode aimless and unfeeling in a never-ending tunnel beneath the earth.

The crowds thinned. With the car almost deserted, Paul's brain began to recover its focus. His old friend Logic gripped his shoulders and propelled him forward.

The terrorist hadn't known Colette had a look-alike. Paul had glimpsed that in his eyes, a moment of unscripted confusion. He didn't know there were two women until Paul had told him. Only then, sensing Paul's concern in the second girl, had he announced she was dead, taking apparent pleasure in hurting him.

What if he'd lied? What if Megan had escaped?

The Community had kidnapped Megan all right, the gun was proof, but they'd thought they had Colette. Their minion was a loose end, a woman who knew too much about their operation. Paul didn't doubt they'd planned to eliminate her. But...

A gleam of hope infused Paul's body, washing away fear and darkness. If the terrorists had killed the woman they believed to be Colette, then why was that man still looking for her?

Chapter Twenty-one

How long had she walked? Minutes? Hours? Time was meaningless in here. When her legs wouldn't hold up her body any longer Megan stopped to rest and renew her strength, then soldiered on. Again and again. Rest and repeat.

She was lying on the hard ground, breathing shallowly when she heard the voices. Was she dreaming? Megan reached for the flashlight.

It hadn't been turned on for so long, the sudden onrush of light nearly blinded her. Raising a weary arm, she pointed the beam at the ceiling and then the long hallway ahead.

The voices stopped. Had they seen her flare? "Hello?" she called out, surprised by how weak her voice sounded. *"Allo? Il y as quelqu'un la-bas?"*

It took a while, but then she heard voices again, and responding flashlights. The sounds were still faint, although the tone sounded like shouting. She kept her flashlight on and made her way toward the lights and sounds.

Was she nearing the entrance to the catacombs? Were the voices from some tour group? Her heart sped up in anticipation, her hunger, thirst, and pain forgotten.

The voices got clearer. Men's voices. Megan's heart stopped.

What if they were the terrorists? She'd just invited them to recapture her.

She shut off her flashlight, cursing her naiveté. Stifling her breath, she listened for approaching footsteps. The cavern was silent except for the distant jabbering of voices in what sounded like French. Were they friendly voices? Should she risk calling out again?

"*Allo?*" she yelled frantically, and turned on her light, unable to bear the suspense.

"*Ici.*"

Her flashlight beam hovered on a human being. Two. Three. Dressed in jeans and tee shirts, wearing ball caps, not keffiyahs. There didn't seem to be a guide, or a defined tourist path. The three men were loaded down with an array of semi-professional photographic equipment. When one of the young men reached out to her, Megan collapsed in his arms.

Cataphiles. Madame Richard had mentioned on their tour-- good Lord, had it only been days ago?--the urban explorers who illegally toured the catacombs, entering through the sewers, Metro, or manholes.

One of the young men shoved a leather-wrapped canteen next to her mouth. Megan couldn't remember water tasting so cold, so clean, so good. It spilled onto her chin but she lapped it up.

"*Ca va?*"

She nodded her thanks and wiped her mouth with her sweatshirt sleeve.

They asked, in French, by which passage she'd entered.

She hesitated. To say she was drugged and dragged here by

terrorists would likely elicit only laughter and disbelief. Even if she got the vocabulary and tenses right. *"Parlez-vous anglais?"*

When all three nodded, she explained in English that she'd gotten separated from her tour group. "I got lost, and I fell." She didn't mention how far down, but pointed to her wet clothes. "I am so glad to see you guys." However they'd gotten in here, they had to know how to get out. "Where is the exit?"

One of the men who'd been crouching beside her got to his feet. "I'll show you." He helped her up and put his arm around her waist. "Back in a second, *mes amis.*"

If she hadn't been so exhausted, Megan might have paid more attention to the wink he gave his friends. She did notice, however, the double length of rope stretched along the floor of the cavern. The way out. Dragging one foot in front of the other, Megan kept her flashlight beam pointed at that symbol of life.

"This way." The man nudged her to the left, where the cave formed a natural alcove.

She couldn't tell how far back this opening went, but there was no rope trail in it. "But--"

He grabbed her hair and pressed his mouth hard on hers while slipping a hand under her shirt.

Seriously? After all she'd suffered to come this far, this close to freedom? Had she survived terrorists and floodwaters only to allow some pathetic Romeo to take advantage of a woman he thought a weak, helpless damsel? Rage gave Megan a boost of pure adrenaline.

She opened her mouth and as a nasty tongue weaved inside, she bit down hard. At the man's yelp, she shone her flashlight in his eyes and shoved her knee into his groin.

When he doubled over, she ran back to the rope path and turned in the direction she'd been heading. After a few minutes, she stopped, panting, and aimed her light behind her. Had he followed?

Apparently not. The scum was just looking for easy fun. He hadn't even taken the trouble to chase her. Megan trudged forward again through the seemingly endless corridor until she saw, up ahead, a pinprick circle of light.

She switched off the flashlight to make sure she wasn't looking at a shadow of her own lamp.

No, it was there. Either a flashlight far off in the distance or...the exit to this cavernous underground prison.

Megan's heart opened. The optimist that still lived inside her wanted to cheer. But the realist she'd become in the last few days cautioned her to keep her wits about her.

Positioning her feet firmly on the rope path, she moved in the almost-darkness toward the small spot of light. The farther she walked, the bigger it got.

Ouch! Something grazed Megan's head. She switched her flashlight back on. The catacomb's ceiling had gotten lower. The space between the craggy roof and floor was narrowing. And the walls were closing in tighter.

She bent her head and stooped. Finally, she was forced to get down on her knees. The space in front of her was as round and wide as one of those concrete tunnels at a playground, about the size to accommodate a ten-year-old child. But it was filled with that welcoming circle of light.

Megan got into semi-fetal position and pulled herself on her elbows and knees through the crawl space. She couldn't help thinking of the old joke. *When I finally saw the light at the end of the tunnel, it turned out to be a train.*

Maybe it wasn't a joke. She could swear, as she crept closer to the guiding light, that she heard the rumbling wheels and screeching brakes of an approaching train.

When she dragged herself through the last feet of damp ground, her hands and stomach landed on hard concrete. Megan blinked into the glare of overhead electric lights. She was in a Metro station!

Dazed, she hauled her feet out of the tunnel and tried to stand upright. Her legs refused to hold her. A wall behind her caught her back and she slid down, her legs outstretched in front of her.

Passengers scuttled past on the platform, to and from trains. Nobody seemed to notice her. Were they used to disheveled people crawling out of a hole in the ground or was she imagining all this? If this were an illusion, she'd prefer breathing in the salt of ocean waves on a quiet beach to inhaling cigarette smoke and body odors on a subway platform.

On the other hand, the familiar sights and sounds of the Paris underground were wonderfully...normal. Her body shivered. Then blossomed into full-blown shaking. Megan's eyes filled and her breathing hitched. She'd made it out. Alive.

Through blurry eyes she glanced at the round station clock hanging near the sign announcing Track 2. Five thirty-five. A.m. or p.m.? What day was this?

Bracing one hand against the wall behind her, she pulled herself to her feet. She was dizzy, weak from hunger, and every muscle in her body ached. But she was alive! She wanted to run up the stairs and outside to embrace the fresh air, but she could barely stand, let alone walk, and running was totally out of the question.

She shuffled instead to an empty bench, and sat before her breath oozed away. As she sat unmoving, hypnotically watching trains roll in and out, the light traffic milling around the platform increased to a steady trickle, then a human wave. Tired-looking people dragged coats and brief cases behind them, pushing their way into overcrowded subway cars.

Evening. Exhausted commuters eager to get home.

After the umpteenth train pulled away, she stared at the name of the unfamiliar station printed on the tile wall beyond the tracks. She had no idea where she was. Paul would never look for her here. She'd have to find him.

But how? Would he still be at the hotel? Megan closed her eyes and begged her brain to focus. Finally she remembered the name of the Metro station near the Hotel Denise, then picked up a discarded Metro map from the sticky platform floor and plotted her route.

Arriving at her destination, she forced her weary feet to climb the exit stairs, her heart leading the way. Hoping to see Paul again. *Please,* she prayed silently.

As she emerged into the open air, Megan almost choked at the beauty around her. The flickering lights of Paris at night rivaled the wonderland of stars above. The smell of coffee and the scent of *pommes frites* wafted from the cafes. God, what wouldn't she give for a crispy French fry right now.

Wait. Inside one of the sweatshirt's zippered pockets she found a few coins, change from the ten Euro note Paul had given her to buy croissants. In the other pocket, damp but still legible, a three day Metro pass. And the key card for the hotel room.

She bought a small order of fried potatoes and savored each bite as if it were caviar, then trudged with slightly more energy toward the Hotel Denise.

Her key card didn't open the door. Megan pounded on it to no avail. No one was inside. The room card had been rekeyed.

Paul had checked out.

Her hopes dashed like floodwaters against the craggy catacombs walls.

Had he gone back to Jacques and Marcel's? She pressed her fingers to her temples but as hard as she tried, she couldn't conjure up the name of the station near Jacques and Marcel's apartment. She'd been too freaked out to notice even the street name when they'd arrived there in the taxi, and when escaping through the laundry room, they'd fled through the back alley.

And of course she didn't know either's last name.

Would Paul go back to his own apartment? Perhaps the police were no longer staking it out. Maybe he would risk going there anyway, in the hopes that she'd try to find him there.

She ran back to the Metro station and boarded the line for the Boulevard Voltaire. As the rhythmic, rumbling rolling of the wheels against the tracks soothed her almost to sleep, Megan envisioned a romantic reunion. She'd walk into the café where she'd bought the croissants. Paul would be sitting calmly at a table, waiting for her. As soon as she crossed the threshold, he'd sweep her up without a word into his strong arms. Holding her close, and warm, and safe. She could almost taste the croissants on his lips.

Embarking at the station, she ran up the steps to the street, energized and hopeful.

The café was closed.

Tears trickled down her cheeks faster than she could brush them away. Maybe he'd waited around as long as he could, and then left. Or maybe he'd gone back to his flat.

She headed in the direction she'd seen Paul walk that night. He'd turned into a street about two blocks north of here. Or was it three? Megan scrubbed a hand against her wet cheek. Even if she found the right street, how would she know which apartment house was his?

Assuming he'd even come back here. Maybe he wasn't even looking for her. What had gone through his mind when he'd come back from the ice machine to find her gone?

That she'd just walked away.

Cold air passed through her lungs. Surely he knew she wouldn't leave him. She'd made a damned fool of herself running after him when he'd told her to stay in the hotel room. And last night...

She clamped her eyes shut in a vain effort to hold back the flood of tears. Last night apparently hadn't meant the same to Paul as it did to her. He'd been swept up, as she had, by the moment, the drama, the danger. There'd been possibilities, once-in-a-lifetime possibilities, but no promises. And when the moment had passed...

Sirens blared a short distance away. Megan looked up and down the street she'd guessed was Paul's but there were no moving vehicles. Across a small yard between the buildings, she saw flashing lights in the alley behind them. A police car drove out of the alley and careened onto the boulevard.

Megan lowered her head until the vehicle barreled past her, then whirled to catch a glimpse of it driving away. A man sat in the rear seat of the paddy wagon, his head covered by a ball cap but he seemed tall. Paul?

Excitement turned quickly to despair. Had he indeed come looking for her and been apprehended? The hunger and pain and exhaustion and fear Megan had kept at bay erupted into an anguished wail.

Now what? If she went to the police station, they'd assume she was Colette and arrest her too. She couldn't help Paul. She couldn't even help herself.

She was back to square one. No money, no documents, no friends. But now that she'd had a friend, the pain was ten times worse. The world, she'd learned, could be a cruel place, but she'd met one person whose kindness made up for all the others. And she'd caused him nothing but grief, stirring up his peaceful world and endangering his life.

A raindrop landed on her nose, then another on her eyelid. Great, another shower. The inclement weather which was becoming far too normal mirrored Megan's mood.

She was out of options. She'd have to spend the night in the Metro station, like the homeless person she was. If she survived the night, she'd go to the American Embassy in the morning and throw herself on the mercy of her American compatriots. Maybe she could even urge them to help Paul.

But she couldn't do any of that until morning. Megan descended the stairs of the Metro once again, inserted her pass, and boarded the train for the RER line to the Champs de Mars station. She'd seen the underbelly of Paris, but she'd still never enjoyed its crowning glory. Before she was killed by terrorists, or arrested—or, please God, boarded a plane for home—she was determined to see the view of Paris by night from its most famous landmark.

If the Paris police found her and arrested her, she'd tell them the truth and pray they believed her, but even if they didn't, she'd be better off in a French jail than with the terrorists. At least the police wouldn't kill her. And maybe she'd get to see Paul again.

The rain pelted her again as she left the station but as she neared her destination, it slowed to a drizzle and then, as she approached the Eiffel Tower, it stopped.

Megan gazed up at the architectural wonder. It was so much more beautiful at night, twinkling like an array of stars.

The line of tourists outside was short. Rummaging inside her sweatshirt pockets, Megan handed over the last of her remaining Euros, and clambered inside the elevator with the last load of tourists for the night.

Gazing out over the beautiful city of Paris with its hub of boulevards and lights, she took in a calming breath. How could one not be an optimist when the world was so full of wonder? A sense of serenity enveloped her. She wasn't going to be arrested. Or killed by crazed terrorists who thought she was Colette. Megan rubbed her entrance ticket against the faded metro ticket as if they were the heels of ruby slippers. She was going to make it home safe.

There were only a few people milling on the grounds below the tower, probably lovers strolling along the Seine. The crowd on the viewing deck was light as well. Without having to jostle or push her way to the rail, Megan allowed the Paris landmarks and city panorama to refill her optimism as she slowly circled the platform to take in every view.

Only a few clusters of stragglers remained, a couple of giggly teenagers here, a family of four there. At the north side of the platform a lone man stood savoring the landscape, or perhaps lost in thought. He wore a tan windbreaker. Its hood covered his hair, but as Megan neared his position, the hood slipped back.

She gasped. A shock of school bus yellow hair embraced his head like a floppy rag doll. When he turned to face her, her breath whooshed out of her chest.

A smile lit his face. "It's about bloody time you got here."

Chapter Twenty-Two

"I feel like a damned debutante." Colette stormed into the apartment loaded down with a plastic dress bag, a shoebox, and another bag crammed with hosiery, a strapless bra, and underwear.

"You bought a dress. Good." Fletcher beamed as if he were the efficient, well-organized wedding planner instead of the nervous, eager groom. He glanced at his watch. "And in record time. If Mama Chandler had gone with you, you'd have been trying things on all afternoon. How did you convince her not to go with?"

"Did I have a choice?" Colette draped the hanging bag over a barstool and dumped the rest of her purchases on the floor. She'd fooled Megan's mother on the phone, but exposing herself to the woman any more than absolutely necessary was committing scam suicide. "I told her it would be a simple wedding with a plain dress and no fanfare, and since she doesn't drive, it wouldn't be worth her trouble to come out here."

"Good call," Fletcher said with an admiring smile.

"Of course, Don helped too." She kicked off her shoes and sank into the sofa next to Fletcher. "Since we told him we didn't want Mom and Dad to know about my 'pregnancy' until after the wedding, he's keeping her occupied so she won't figure out the truth." She slapped his jean-clad knee. "Or the truth as we've devised it."

Normally Fletcher would have grabbed her hand and repositioned it on his crotch, but not this time. "So you've been chumming it up with St. Don?"

"Well, somebody has to. You were the one who said we needed him to make this happen, and he flat out doesn't like you."

"And that feeling is reciprocated." Changing the subject, Fletcher brightened his dour expression into a flirtatious smile. "So model the dress for me."

"I can't do that!" Colette made a mock-horrified face. "The groom can't see the dress before the wedding."

"Don't give a crap about the dress," Fletcher smirked. "Just want to practice taking it off you."

Did he actually think they'd be going off on a honeymoon together? "Fletcher, this ends when we get the money," she reminded him. "You go your way, and I go mine."

"Maybe not."

Uneasiness roiled Colette's stomach, but she tried to keep it under control. Was he about to pose some new threat? Had he been following the international news and guessed who she really was? "What do you mean?"

He crossed his arm over her waist and pulled her onto his lap. "We're a good team, you and me." He lifted a brow seductively as his fingers squeezed her breast. "And we're definitely compatible in the bedroom."

No argument there. She didn't like the man but his dexterous touch was already setting things in motion in the parts of her that did like parts of him.

"So why don't we keep a good thing going? Move someplace

far away, set up new identities, maybe." He nibbled at her lobe and then swirled his tongue inside her ear. "Make a life together."

Together? Her and him? Colette sat up straight and eyeballed him. "Why would I want to make a life with you? You're a thief, a scoundrel and a dirt bag."

"Oh, and you're Joan of Arc?" He slid his hand inside the back waistband of her jeans, splaying his hand over bare skin bereft of panties. "We're two of a kind, baby."

So? She forced a light laugh. "Are you trying to make an honest woman out of me?"

"Nah." His hands slid upward along her back to where a bra hook might be, if she were wearing a bra. "Honest women are a turnoff. I like a woman who wants the same things I do."

Colette yanked her shirt over her head and offered her exposed breasts to his mouth. "Screw unto others before they screw unto you."

He sucked on each pert nipple, then rubbed his face in the crevice between her breasts. "That's what I'm talking about."

Colette slid off his lap onto her knees, unsnapped the front of his jeans, and lowered his zipper. Fletcher opened his legs.

"So do we have a deal?" he asked as she gently rubbed the outside of his briefs. "After the wedding, you and I stay together?" His arousal pulsed against her hand.

He was serious? Colette stopped fondling and raised her head to his face. "God, no. I'm no saint, but I do have standards. And you are the last man on earth I'd want to set up housekeeping with."

Lowering her head to the business at hand, she freed his erection from its prison, and stroked it from base to tip. "Let's just stick to what we're compatible at." She took him in her mouth and sucked hard on his magnificent length.

His gurgle didn't sound like a groan of desire. "No thanks." He extracted his penis from her mouth and shoved her backwards. "I'm nobody's charity case."

Colette landed on her butt and elbows. Fletcher pushed off the sofa, crammed his still-hard member into his briefs, and tried without much luck to zip his jeans.

"I'm going back to my own apartment," he announced, tugging the hem of his shirt down to cover his open zipper. He strode to the door. "I'll see you at the country club Saturday at two. Wear underwear." He jerked the front door open, banging it against a ceramic wall tile that crashed to the floor.

She dashed after him. "But what about the rehearsal tomorrow?"

He turned to flash hateful eyes at her. "Why don't you have brother Don stand in for me?" He slammed the door behind him.

Topless, horny, and unsatisfied, Colette got on her knees, and not in a good way. *You are a piece of work,* she reproached herself as she picked up the broken ceramic pieces. *You just hurt the feelings of a man who doesn't even have a heart.*

* * *

Megan stretched languorously between cool, crisp sheets that caressed her body like a lover's touch.

She froze in mid-stretch. Was she dreaming? Or awake? Alive or dead? Lying on hard ground, a concrete floor, or... Heart pounding, she opened her eyes.

She was in a bed. In a small room with a stubborn ray of sun

229

poking between dark curtains. She sat up, clutching the bedcovers to her chest. "Where am I?"

"You're safe." Paul's voice reassured. He sat at a small secretary desk in a corner of the room, a laptop propped in front of him. Wearing jeans but no shirt or shoes. "We're at Jacques and Marcel's. You don't remember coming back here?"

"Vaguely." She recalled flinging herself into Paul's arms at the Eiffel Tower, sputtering her tale of catastrophe between sobs. And then there was a taxi, and....that was all she remembered.

She let her head fall back on the pillow and slipped once again inside her cool cocoon. "What day is it?"

"Friday. Noon. You slept twelve hours."

Not nearly long enough. Megan peeked under the covers. No wonder the sheets felt so smooth against her skin. She faced Paul, her lips tight. "Where are my clothes?"

He chuckled. "In the dustbin. Those jeans need burning. Your underwear is drying in the bath."

"That's not what I asked." She sighed. "Okay, it was, but it's not what I meant."

He grinned. "You don't remember that either? I was amazing, wild and wanton. And your orgasmic screams--"

"So, nothing happened." Same old Paul, same dry wit. She started to grin back but her dry lips cracked with the attempt.

His gaze turned serious. "What kind of a cad would I be to take advantage of a barely conscious woman?"

Relief surged through her. Not because she hadn't been molested. Because she hadn't missed the experience. "So you're saying I undressed myself?"

"I did help," he admitted. He studied the ceiling over her head. "In a situation like that, a gentleman averts his eyes and performs the duty quickly."

"Really." She rolled her eyes.

When he focused on her again, his grin sneaked out. "Pity I'm not a gentleman."

A warm flush spread over her body, but not one of embarrassment. Picturing Paul's eyes roving over her body, she swished under the covers, letting the sheets rise and fall again to brush her breasts. Imagining his hands--would they be rough or soft?--—touching her. And his lips...

"How's your leg?"

Her mood sobered as the memory returned. Gunshot wound. Bleeding. Pain. She crooked her leg and reached down to discover gauze bandaging rolled around her leg below her knee.

"Marcel patched it up for you but if it's not better by tomorrow, I'll take you to see a doctor."

She sat up and looked around the small bedroom. A desk, a dresser, a door that might be a closet, and little else.

He pointed to the small door. "Need to use the loo?"

Indoor plumbing sounded positively luxurious. Megan tucked the sheet around her for modesty and swung her legs off the bed. She took three faltering steps before her knees buckled.

Paul was at her side instantly, lifting her with one arm at her back and the other on her waist. "You're still weak from your ordeal." He extricated her from the tangle of bedclothes. "Let me

231

Linda Steinberg

help."

Gratefully she accepted his arm. "I am a little...a little..." Words flitted through her brain and escaped, but no matter. She didn't need to talk to make herself understood to Paul.

Making no mention of her bared backside, he guided her toward the small bathroom which contained only a toilet and a wash basin, waited outside the door, and then escorted her back to the bed. "There's tea on the bed stand, still hot."

Megan glanced at the teapot but waved aside his efforts to pour for her. "Not now, thanks." Her stomach was empty but she wasn't sure she could manage the effort of swallowing. She sank into the luxurious mattress, her bones as light as if she were floating.

Her eyes closed. Her mind drifted. She was in a dark, wet place. Rushing water echoed in her ears, drowning her thoughts, even her ability to think.

Panicked, she opened her eyes. And returned to the comfortable bedroom. Paul was still at the computer. Hearing her gasp, he got up and stood next to the bed.

He touched her hand, his skin cool to her palm. "Are you hungry? I can fix you--"

"Don't leave." She grabbed his wrist. "I mean..." God, she sounded pathetic. "I'm still feeling a bit..."

"It's okay." He sat at the edge of the bed, atop the covers, and wrapped his arms around her bare shoulders. "I swear I will never let anything happen to you again." Brushing a straggly lock off her forehead, he kissed her brow. His breath fanned her face like a tropical breeze.

She reached up to caress his cheek. A three day stubble of dark beard contrasted with his yellow hair. The blanket covering her

232

breasts dipped an inch, but she ignored it. "How did you know where to find me?"

"Something you said the other day. I'd run out of places to look and the Eiffel Tower was my last hope."

He'd searched for her. A tear formed in Megan's eye. "I was afraid you'd been arrested."

"I thought the same about you at first, when I saw the men in police uniforms dragging you away."

"You--" She gasped. "—saw that?"

"I wasn't about to rush two armed policemen. I knew I couldn't help you if I got arrested too, so I came here for help. Marcel spent all night at the police station trying to bail you out but they had no record of apprehending you. That's when I realized those guys must have been terrorists."

She swallowed. "Please thank Marcel for me."

"Thank him yourself when he gets home. Without him and Jacques...." He ran his hand over her brow and across her hair, as if he'd lose her again if he didn't keep touching her. "How did you ever manage to escape the Catacombs?"

She sat upright, readjusting the sheet under her arms. "I didn't tell you last night?"

He pressed a hand against her back. "You said you woke up in the Catacombs and you were led to the terrorist cell. And that the man who accosted you the other day shot you in the leg when you ran away from him." His Adam's apple quavered. "Then you nodded off in my arms."

Megan drew in a long breath. Although she dreaded reliving the experience, sharing it with Paul made it seem less terrifying. He listened, really listened, this time. When she told him of her jump into the black cavern, he flinched as if he were leaping with her.

"My God, Megan," he said, when she'd described crawling out into the Metro station. "You are an amazing woman. I hate that you had to endure all that alone. I should have been with you."

"You were." At the moment of almost certain death, it was Paul's image she'd clung to. She licked the corner of his upper lip, then pressed her mouth to his.

His kiss was tender, if a bit cautious. Megan dropped her hands and held them stiffly at her side, aware of his body so close yet not touching hers. Gently his tongue traced the outline of her lips and then flickered inside, warm and wet and probing. Megan's breaths commingled with his, eager and erratic.

The sheet slipped to her waist.

As if she were a present he'd gingerly untied and was suddenly eager to unwrap, Paul tossed aside the remaining covers. Cupping her bare bottom in his large, cool hands, he lay on his side and cocooned Megan against him. Snuggling close, she flattened her breasts against his chest. "I was afraid I'd never see you again," she whispered.

Lightly calloused fingers drew arousing circles in the hollows of her back. "And you're supposed to be the optimist?"

She giggled, throwing her thigh over his jeaned hip. New jeans, by the feel and smell of the denim. Squeezing her butt cheek, he ground her against his pelvis. His erection strained against her, teasing her pleasure spot. Megan's aches and pains receded into memory, shunted aside by potent stirrings of desire.

Paul rolled her to her back and knelt between her legs. His mouth commanded her lips, tasting, touching.

Eagerly she met his tongue with hers.

Rough hands teased her body with light, unhurried strokes. Her nipples rose to attention as he flicked each with his thumb, palming her breasts until they were putty to his touch.

And then his mouth was on her breasts, tongue caressing her hot flesh, teeth pinching her inflamed nipples. Megan whimpered and arched her back.

He placed one hand under her bottom while the other explored her body, stroking, caressing, teasing its way down between her legs. When his thumb touched her pleasure spot, Megan moaned with unrestrained eagerness. But when he scooted lower on the bed, bent his head, and pressed his lips to her tender nub, she panicked.

"No!" She clamped her legs together, almost clipping his chin.

He raised his head. "You don't like it?"

"No. That is..." She gulped. "I don't know."

He raised a brow. "You've never--"

"Once." Fletcher had promised her the experience of a lifetime. But he'd acted like he was doing her a favor for which she should be grateful, and an obligation was implied. She'd tensed up, and whatever mysterious delights he'd hinted at remained a mystery to her.

Paul smiled, not in a mocking way. "Do you trust me?"

"Of course."

"Then relax. Close your eyes and imagine yourself on a cloud, drifting aimlessly. Don't think about anything." He bent over her again and kissed her stomach, swirling his tongue inside her belly button.

She giggled.

He sucked the moisture from her navel, then licked and kissed his way across her stomach, gradually traveling south, toward the apex of her thighs.

Don't think about it. Don't think. Don't--

Ohh. Her heartbeat quickened as his mouth lightly touched her in that special spot. Without conscious effort on her part, her thighs opened. Paul pressed them outward and held them apart, wedging his body between them.

Her mind fought against his hold, urging her to struggle, yell, escape. But her body had other ideas. It arced to feel his mouth hard and firm against her mound, his three day stubble scratching places she hadn't known she itched.

And his tongue. God, why hadn't it felt like this before? Her throat dried, forcing out cold, erratic breaths. All her body's moisture pooled in one place. She couldn't remember ever being this aroused. Megan bucked and twisted helplessly under the magical teasing of Paul's mouth and lips. Her hands fisted in his hair, holding him captive to her one overpowering need. *Don't stop. Please don't stop.*

His lips sucked the moisture they'd created as one smooth finger, then a second, slipped inside her. Submitting to sensation, her body quivered with relentless pleasure, crested, and exploded.

It was thrilling. And momentarily fulfilling. But it wasn't enough. Desire still raged within her. Every pore of her skin cried out for his touch. "I want you inside me," she whispered hoarsely, and reached for him.

Sitting, Paul unhooked his belt, dragged it through the loops, and tossed it to the floor, then unsnapped his jeans and kicked them in the same direction. He lay on the bed beside her wearing only black briefs.

Megan ran her hands over his chest from nipples to navel, and then cupped the hardening mound inside his briefs.

He groaned at her touch. Encouraged, she stroked him gently until his calm breaths hitched in short gasps. When she dipped a finger inside the waistband of his briefs, his erect organ sprang out and pushed into her palm.

A thrill of feminine power surged through Megan. She tugged his briefs down to his hips, and kissed the tip of his organ.

"Oh God." Paul wriggled out of his briefs, then grabbed her and deftly rolled her to her back. Megan squealed in anticipation as he straddled her, then slowly lowered his body.

He was warm and heavy and comforting, like a protective blanket. Megan sighed as her aching nipples connected with his skin. She opened her legs, inviting him between her thighs.

His body, eager and hungry as hers, slammed against her sore, aching chest. Megan flinched.

Paul drew back immediately. "So sorry, love." Fervor still burned in his eyes but his jaw muscles tightened as he eyed the purpling bruises on her chest and arms. "You're hurt worse than I realized. Perhaps we should wait...?"

"Wait until what?" Frustrated gasps issued from her dry throat. "Until the police find us and arrest us? Or the terrorists discover I'm still alive and try to remedy that situation?" She understood now the fragility of life, how quickly it could be snatched away.

Her body tingled, craving his touch. "I just spent two days in hell that I want to forget." She rubbed a finger along his unshaven jaw and traced the outline of his lips. "Please make me forget."

He hesitated just an instant, then made a desperate grab for the nightstand drawer. Finding what he sought, he lay on his back and smoothed on a protective sheath. "You get on top."

She straddled him tentatively. She could count on one hand the number of times she'd had sex with Fletcher in this position, and even from underneath, he'd managed to dominate the act. The control Paul was obviously ceding to her filled her with a delicious sense of freedom. Hovering over his pulsing member, she leaned down to kiss his flat male nipple, fanning her hair across his chest. Then took the tight pebble between her teeth and lightly nipped.

He groaned and grabbed her bottom, centering her over him. As he pushed her down, Megan braced herself for the painful twinge that usually accompanied the first thrust.

But there was no pain. Maybe because she was so wet. Or so eager to know him inside her. Or maybe it was because Paul fit her so well. It seemed her body had been shaped especially for him, as if they were two puzzle pieces that didn't just align, but that clicked into place in a perfect match.

His eyes met hers in a silent smile. His hands held her steady, but allowed her free rein. Megan relaxed, finding her rhythm. With each thrust, she fit around him tighter, drawing him deeper. As she rocked against him, her palms pressed against his stomach, Paul's breathing quickened. His fingers dug into her butt cheeks, guiding her as he moved beneath her at an ever increasing pace.

Megan took her cue from him and rode him harder, that feeling building again, almost there... She gasped and exploded with pleasure. Once, and then again, as he rocked and released inside her. Drowning in bliss, Megan collapsed against his stomach, sweaty, spent, and sated.

She could have fallen asleep right there, safe in his arms. But Paul gently eased her to the mattress and turned on his side, his chest lightly grazing her breasts, his chin caressing the top of her head. The rhythm of his breathing matching hers.

Megan's every muscle exhaled and relaxed in euphoric haze. This was how it was supposed to be. A meeting of minds and bodies in perfect harmony and trust. "I love you," she whispered to Paul's chest.

He stiffened beneath her lips.

Uh-oh. "I shouldn't have said that," she backpedaled hastily. "I was just...you know...overreacting to the drama of the situation." She lifted her head to read his expression, but his face had turned into a poker mask. "It's not like I'm expecting some happily-ever-after." She forced a chuckle.

His fingers gently caressed her back, drawing spirals up and down her spine.

She wished she could fold herself up and disappear into the mattress. Why couldn't she have kept silent and just enjoyed the aura? And yet she couldn't seem to stop. "After all, I'll be going home in a few days and your life is here in Paris. We'll probably never even see--"

"Megan." Mercifully, Paul ended her pitiful pretext. He smoothed a damp hair off her brow and forced her to meet his eyes. "Don't over-analyze this. It was special. It was real. And it was right, at least for now." He kissed her eyelids. "Let's just enjoy the moment. After what you and I, especially you, have been through, it's all we can ask for."

Simple, straightforward, and so true. But the irony tasted bitter on Megan's parched lips. The last time they'd been together, she'd insisted that desire was merely a knee-jerk response to a shared temporary trauma, blah, blah, blah. And Paul had apparently believed it. But while her brain was busy elsewhere, Megan had fallen head over heart for him.

She turned her back and wrapped herself in the covers,

pressing the sheets against her wet eyes. How could she have leaped so irresponsibly off this emotional cliff? Paul Bernard was a good man, a valiant protector. Someone who never shirked his duty and always did the right thing. He'd stood by her and, at great risk to himself, gone out of his way to help her.

He just didn't love her.

Chapter Twenty-three

It boggled his mind. With his laptop perched on Jacques and Marcel's dining room table, Paul's fingers trolled over the keys but his mind lingered in the back bedroom. Physically, Megan and Colette were almost identical. Yet Megan's body had felt softer, warmer, more in tune to his. Colette's lovemaking was as flawless as a professional's but Megan's almost-virginal enthusiasm had lit his jaded sex drive afire. Her eager enjoyment had brought a first-time magic to an act that for him had been solely physical far too long.

He reminded himself that there was seven years difference in their ages. Perhaps that why he felt this compulsion to shelter and protect Megan.

But that wasn't all he felt. The lingering stirrings of his body reminded him how womanly she could be, her eagerness arousing and peaking his desire. Megan was not a vulnerable waif. This afternoon hadn't been wrong. It had been exactly what they'd both needed.

So why did he feel as if he'd disappointed her, made promises with his body that his heart couldn't keep?

I love you. Her words taunted. Allison had said those same words once, but she hadn't meant them either. Not in the same way he had. Not enough to marry him, not if it meant leaving her home and family and accompanying him to his post in another country.

And he and Allison had been together three years. Megan had entered his life three days ago. They barely knew each other.

It was Megan, after all, who'd insisted a relationship based on whirlwind drama was impractical. Her romantic declaration had to have been a heat-of-the-moment expression, a glad-to-be-alive outpouring of emotion. She was grateful to be safe and warm. Grateful to Paul for helping her.

Fuck gratitude. He clenched his fist. He'd rather a woman use him for sexual release, or even to steal his security card, than mistake gratitude for love.

* * *

The next time Megan awoke she was still in the soft bed, still naked, but alone. "Paul?"

No answer. Wearily she propped herself on her elbows, rose to a sitting position, and dangled her legs over the bed.

Standing was painful, but she managed. At the edge of the bed lay her bra and panties, a pair of men's exercise shorts, and a purple golf shirt. Paul's? She sniffed the shirt, but it didn't have his scent. And it would have barely fit over half his magnificent wide chest.

Probably Jacques's. Guilt panged at the realization that she'd not only endangered Paul, but involved his friends as well.

She wrapped herself in a sheet and stepped out of the bedroom into a narrow hallway adorned with a red and gold Oriental rug. Two other doors fronted it. The master bedroom held a four poster bed covered by an ornate bedspread and mounds of satin pillows. Pretty tasteful for a bachelor apartment.

The other room was a full bath with a shower. Gratefully, she turned on the water and stepped in.

The shower needles stung her bruised body, but the pain was worth the liberating cleansing. Megan threw back her head to let the hot water rain on her face. If a few tears mixed with the warm stream, well that would be expected, wouldn't it, after the nightmare she'd been through?

After dressing in the clean clothes, she walked barefoot over a bride-white fur rug to the main living area of the apartment. From a dining room furnished with a large oval mahogany table and a matching buffet and hutch, came the sounds of a clicking keyboard. Paul sat with his back to her, hunched over his laptop.

She took in a breath. "Good afternoon."

He startled, then pushed his chair back from the table and turned to face her. He wore his jeans and shirt, but the shirt was unbuttoned, taunting her with the memory of his warm, broad chest. "Feeling any better?"

"Yes." What was she supposed to say? *You rocked my world in bed but then made me feel like the morning's garbage?*

He grunted and went back to his typing as if they were casual friends instead of having just shared the most intimate connection between a man and woman.

Physically intimate. The emotional connection, at least for him, just wasn't there.

How could she have been so stupid to blurt out those words? Of course she'd made him uncomfortable. She'd known Paul mere days. He must think her the most desperate ditz on the planet.

What did she know about love, anyway? She'd almost convinced herself she loved Fletcher, for heaven's sake.

It might have made her parents happy to see her settled and married to a man who would take care of her. It would definitely have made Fletcher happy to gain access to her family's money. But in the last three days she'd learned two important things about herself.

One: She didn't need anyone to 'take care of' her. She'd taken care of herself, hadn't she, with a little help from some new friends, in a situation she would never have believed she could survive.

Two: she was not the passionless 'ice queen' Fletcher had labeled her. Something wonderful had happened to her this morning, releasing a place inside herself she hadn't known existed. With Paul's heart beating next to hers, she could have sworn the earth had moved for both of them, that this accidental adventure had been purposely ordained by the heavens to bring them together.

Okay, so she'd been as wrong about that as she had about the Tooth Fairy, but now that she knew such feelings existed, she could never enter into a passionless relationship again.

She smoothed the purple shirt over her stomach, as if that could keep her still-raw emotions inside, and moved closer to Paul. "Were you able to discover any more about my family?"

He stopped typing and turned to her, grinning. Damn, she was going to miss that grin. "I found a marriage certificate. Sophia Adele Dubois and John Wendell Jameson were married in Calais in nineteen forty-five."

"Yes! That's my grandmother. They came to the United States right after the war ended."

Paul crossed his leg over his other knee. "Your mother's name was Elizabeth Dubois Jameson?"

"Y-yes." Excitement faded to caution. She'd told him Mom's middle name but she'd never mentioned the Elizabeth part. How private was one's private life when anyone with a computer could learn almost anything about you? "You found her birth certificate?"

"And that of her two older brothers. Peter and Joseph?"

Uncle Pete and Uncle Joe. Paul had learned as much about her family in a few hours as she had in twenty-three years. "Wow, you really are a geek."

"Thank you," he said, accepting it as a compliment.

She raised her gaze from his dark-haired chest to his dark beard-stubbled face. "Too bad you couldn't find out anything about Colette."

Paul's eyes twinkled. "Who says I didn't?"

Her heart fluttered. "But if my grandmother's twin sister died in the war, the French line would end there. You said so yourself."

"What if she didn't die in the war?"

Megan blinked.

He paused--waiting for a drum roll?--and then said dramatically, "The sister, Marie Dubois, died in nineteen eighty-two." He spun his laptop around.

Megan stared at her great-aunt's death certificate. "But what...? How...?"

Paul invited her to pull up a chair next to his. "Marie Dubois was active in the French resistance. She was arrested near the end of the war and sent to Auschwitz concentration camp." He scrolled through his typed notes and then looked up. "Your grandmother probably assumed she was killed there. But when the Allies invaded the camps, she was set free."

Megan's breath hitched. "Why wouldn't she have contacted my grandmother then?"

"She may have tried to, but your grandmother—her sister—

had already married and moved away. Marie wouldn't have known what last name to search under."

Megan let out a long breath. So Marie Dubois had survived the war and lived into her sixties. "Can you find out if she married and had children?"

"Done and done." He clicked to another tab on his screen. "I couldn't find any marriage record. But she did give birth to a son, in nineteen forty-six. Pierre Dubois."

"So he's my mother's first cousin." Megan's eyes widened. How excited would Mom be to learn she had a cousin and family in France.

"Was. He died in 2010. Apparently of cancer."

As suddenly as she'd gained a cousin, she'd lost him. Megan frowned. "Did he have any ch--"

"Yes." Paul clicked to another screen. "Pierre married Yvette Marchand in 1970 and they had one daughter a year later."

Her eyes riveted on him. "Named?"

"Colette."

Colette Marchand! Megan jumped up from her chair. "Colette is my second cousin! She uses her mother's maiden name instead of her father's." She hugged Paul's neck, breathing in the scent of a masculine soap.

"Hold on, we're not there yet." He extricated himself from her arms, then re-seated her in her chair. "That woman would be in her forties now. Colette's not even close to thirty."

"Then...?"

Paul paged to another screen on the laptop. "Your second

cousin, Colette Dubois, never married." His eyes twinkled. "But, like her grandmother Marie, she did have a child out of wedlock, when she was just fifteen years old." He showed her the name on the birth certificate.

"Nicole Dubois." Megan took a deep breath. "That has to be Colette. She used the name Nicole Reneau when she friended me on Facebook. With you--and Jacques--she used Colette from her mother and Marchand from her maternal grandmother."

"And I wouldn't be surprised if she's used other aliases in the past," Paul said.

"And the present." Wherever she was, Colette was undoubtedly using Megan Chandler now.

"The Internet is amazing, isn't it? If we'd had the World Wide Web back in the forties, your great-aunt Marie and your grandmother Sophie might have been reunited."

"And my mother would have known her French family." Megan counted on her fingers. "Marie, Pierre, Colette, Nicole. Four generations."

"Five, actually."

She squinted at him. "There's more?"

Paul's shoulder brushed against hers. "When she was fourteen years old, Nicole Dubois, alias our Colette, gave birth to a daughter. Emmeline Dubois."

"Oh my God." Megan gasped. "Maybe that's where she's gone. To find her daughter." The child must be fourteen years old herself by now. If Colette/Nicole had given her up for adoption...

"Sadly, no. That baby died at five months," Paul said.

Despite her animosity toward Colette the terrorist, Megan felt a pang of sympathy for the teenage mother who'd lost her child.

"What baby?" A bell tinkled as Jacques entered by the front door, carrying two cloth grocery bags.

"Apparently Colette became pregnant as a teenager and gave birth to a daughter," Paul explained. "The baby died in infancy of Sudden Infant Death Syndrome."

"Mon Dieu." Jacques plopped the bags onto the dining table.

"You didn't know?" Megan asked. "She never told you she'd had a child?" Jacques had known Colette several years and they were apparently quite close.

Jacques shook his head and turned to Paul. "You?"

"Apparently I didn't know anything at all about Colette. Not even her real name."

The front door opened again. "Have you heard the news?" Marcel asked, dumping his briefcase on the dining room floor.

"What news?" Megan asked in unison with Paul and Jacques.

"They have a suspect in the Embassy bombing."

"Colette?" Megan and Paul exchanged glances.

"No, a man." Marcel unlocked his cell phone, angled it so they could all see it, and then scrolled to a photo of a man lying next to a garbage dumpster. "The police found him unconscious in an alley."

Jacques reached for the laptop Paul had been using and pulled up the image and the accompanying news article. "The fingerprints on the gun he had in his pocket," he translated from the French, "identify him as Salim Hussein, a known member of the Community terrorist organization."

Salim? A squeak escaped Megan's throat.

"The bullets matched the ones used in the embassy shootings." Jacques's face brightened. "Does this mean Colette is innocent? Maybe she entered the embassy using Paul's security card for some other reason, and then left before the real killer entered."

Megan glanced at Paul to see if he shared the same opinion, but his expression was blank.

"Or maybe she and this Salim committed the crime together," Marcel mused.

Megan forced herself to study the photo. The olive-skinned face was bruised and bloodied, but she'd recognize those eyes anywhere. Her stomach wrenched at the memory of him touching her, hurting her. "That's the man who tried to kill me!"

Jacques eyes widened. "In the catacombs?"

She nodded, her stomach cramping at the memory of his leering gestures, his slimy touch. "That gun. It must be the one he shot me with." Her mind jumped and twisted. "It's Colette's gun."

Paul straightened in his chair.

"I had it with me in the backpack when we went to the hotel. Those people found it and grabbed it." She swallowed. "Actually, it was probably his gun in the first place. He must have given it to Colette."

Paul flinched but didn't comment as she described to Jacques and Marcel the man who'd accosted her outside Paul's apartment. "He was Colette's b--" Stealing a glance at Paul, she rephrased. "He knew Colette and naturally, he assumed I was her. When those goons took me, he was the one assigned to...make sure I didn't get out of the Catacombs alive."

Jacques and Marcel nodded sympathetically without asking intrusive questions. Either they wanted to spare her from recounting her experiences, or Paul had filled in his hosts on the details she'd shared with him.

She dared herself to glance at the photo again. "Oh my god. Paul. This place looks like an alley near your apartment house."

"Really." He scanned the picture noncommittally. "It does at that. I guess most alleys look the same though, don't they?"

Megan recalled the shrill sound of police sirens as the paddy wagon rushed by her. "Maybe that's the man I saw arrested yesterday on the Boulevard Voltaire." She turned to Marcel. "When did this happen?"

"Yesterday afternoon," he replied. "About four-thirty."

Right about the time she'd been there.

Jacques turned excitedly to Paul. "You might have seen it too. You must have been there about that time, if you went there after we left the hotel."

Megan stared at Paul. "You went to your apartment?"

"You went to my apartment?" he asked her in the same instant.

"The hotel," Jacques said. "I almost forgot. I went by there today after my class but Megan's package still hasn't arrived."

"Package?" Marcel asked. "What package?"

Her documents. In the trauma and excitement she'd almost forgotten but Paul obviously hadn't. Megan tried to remember what day she'd asked Fletcher to send her birth certificate and picture ID. Wednesday. And today was Friday. If he'd sent them overnight mail, wouldn't they have arrived by now?

Ignoring Marcel, Paul turned to Megan. "Are you sure Fletcher understood the urgency of your situation?"

"I'm sure. He seemed very upset when I talked to him but a bit...overwhelmed." Maybe he couldn't get to the bank. Or find her safe deposit box key. Or...

"Fletcher." Marcel looked at Megan. "Your boyfriend?"

Ex-boyfriend as soon as she got home. This morning, even if a one-time thing, had convinced Megan she deserved better. "He promised he'd send my proof of American citizenship in the overnight mail."

"Perhaps there was a hang-up with the post," Marcel offered. "A wrong address, not enough postage."

Not likely. Fletcher didn't make mistakes like that. She was the one who tended to be careless.

Jacques raised a brow. "Does he know about you and Paul?"

She stole a quick glance at Paul, catching his gaze on her, and then turned back to Jacques. "There is no me and Paul. We're just friends."

"Um hum," Jacques said, rolling skeptical eyes. He offered his phone to Megan. "Try calling Fletcher again."

She took the phone, her heart beating rapidly. It was ten in the morning in New Jersey. Fletcher didn't usually go out on sales calls until the afternoon. Had he gone back to his own apartment or would he still be at her place?

She dialed her home phone number, but it rang four times and then went to voice mail.

"Try email," Jacques suggested.

Megan sat in the chair next to Jacques's laptop and brought up the Gmail site. She tried to sign into her email account but…. "Something's wrong. I can't connect."

Paul leaned over her, his chest brushing her back. "The Internet's up. Must be something with your logon or password. Is the Caps lock on?"

She checked it, then rekeyed her password. Still denied.

"Let me have a go at it. What's your password?"

"Password."

"Yes. What is it?"

"That's it. *Password.*"

He shot her a You-can't-possibly-be-that-dumb-look and nudged her aside.

"Well, I have nothing to hide," Megan protested. "And I can't remember dozens of complicated passwords." She got up while he did whatever computer geeks did to make things work again, but though he tried her user name and password several times, she was still locked out.

"Looks like your password's been changed," he said.

"How could I have changed my password? I haven't been online in a week."

He shrugged. "Do you have another email account?"

"No. Why?"

"I tried resetting your password, but it won't send a new one to my account."

"Some computer genius you are," she grumbled.

"How about Facebook?"

Facebook. Of course. She could contact not only Fletcher, but her brother and all her friends. Somebody could get to Mom and Dad, explain what had happened. Megan's hand shook as she slid into the chair and logged into her Facebook account.

The page didn't come up.

She let out a wail. "What's happening?" Megan fought to hold the tears back, but what was the point? She gave them free rein. What had once been her world had been rung through a wringer so tight it wasn't even recognizable. How could all these misfortunes happen in just a few days?

Paul put his arm around her, but even his strong presence failed to comfort her.

"It's like I don't even exist. Megan Chandler disappeared into thin air. Just like--"

Nicole. Nicole Reneau whose Facebook page had vanished without even a puff of smoke. Nicole Dubois. *Colette.*

"Colette!" she screamed. "She erased my Facebook page and email."

"Why would she want to do that?" Jacques stared as if she'd lost all her marbles.

"To keep Megan from contacting anyone at home and alerting the authorities that her passport had been stolen." Paul seconded Megan's opinion. "To buy herself time. If Megan's password is so transparent, she could have logged into her pages from anywhere and changed those passwords."

"Can you change them back?"

"Are you asking me to hack into your accounts?" he smiled slyly.

"Can you?"

"Maybe. But it would take time." He motioned for her to get up and again took her place at the laptop. "Everyone here but Megan knew Colette. Let's try inputting some passwords she might use."

They tried her birthday, various combinations of Nicole, Colette, and her year of birth, as well as roles she'd played and favorite dialog of her characters. Even '*merde*' brought no results. It was painfully obvious that none of these people knew Colette nearly as well as they'd thought.

Finally, Paul typed in "Emmeline," and the magic door opened. Three weeks' worth of Facebook messages, pokes, and likes bounced to life. Megan stared, at first in delight, then in dismay, at the messages from her friends and family.

Oh. My. God. The string of posts jumped out at her like blinking cursors, each one more ominous than the last.

"Congratulations!" one read. "I'm so excited for you and Fletcher."

"Marriage is a great institution," a buddy from graduate school wrote, "but who wants to live in an institution—LOL."

And yet another, from her best friend Amber. "Girlfriend, I'm so excited to be your maid of honor. I'll be at the country club Saturday with lots of love and good wishes."

Country club? Saturday? *Marriage???*

She couldn't breathe. Nausea curdled her stomach. She opened her mouth to scream, but no sound came out. Only her heart thudded noisily in her chest, its ominous rhythm repeating, *Colette stole your life. Colette stole your life.* The proof that she'd been right all along offered no consolation.

She glared at Paul. "I told you days ago Colette was in my apartment but you wouldn't believe me! You said I was overreacting."

His face was ash white but he answered calmly, coolly. Logically. "I didn't say I didn't believe you. Just that your theory made no sense. And it still doesn't. Besides the obvious risk of your family discovering her deceit, why would Colette want to marry Fletcher? Is he rich?"

Not yet. Fury pushed past the nausea and forced out the words. "No. I am. At least my family is. Colette wouldn't want to marry Fletcher, he'd want to marry her--that is, me."

"How long have you dated him?" Jacques asked. "Has he proposed to you?"

"About a year. And yes, three weeks ago. I told him I'd tell him my answer when I returned from Europe."

"Odd that he proposed just before you left," Marcel said. "Why the hurry?"

She'd wondered that herself. Fletcher had seemed so determined to put a ring on her finger before she left home. As if he were afraid, once out of his control, she might get away from him. As if he might lose—

"My trust fund," she gasped.

The floor grew unsteady beneath her feet. Megan swayed and tottered. If Paul hadn't grabbed her arm, she might have fallen into the hole that seemed to have opened under her. "I gain access to it, when I'm twenty-five. Or when I marry, if earlier." She swallowed. "I didn't think Fletcher knew about that clause."

Paul led her to a stuffed arm chair. "Apparently he does," he said dryly.

She sank into the cushions, still holding his arm. "So when Colette showed up, pretending to be me, she must have given him the response he wanted."

"She's fooled everybody into believing she's Megan," Jacques said excitedly.

How could that have happened? Fletcher was neither naïve nor gullible. And he was so hot-blooded, it wasn't plausible to think he hadn't yet had sex with the imposter.

That thought almost made her gag. "Fletcher knows me well enough to know I'd never get a tattoo," she said. "But Colette has one. There's no way he wouldn't notice."

Marcel stroked his mustache. "Then how could Colette fool him?"

A stone dropped to the pit of Megan's stomach. "Maybe she didn't."

She gripped Paul's arm so hard her fingers left marks on his skin. Fletcher knew she was stranded in Paris without a passport. He hadn't mailed her documents. How could he have supposed she'd gotten home without them?

Her throat tightened so, she could barely breathe. "They're...in this...together!"

Chapter Twenty-four

A fist jabbed into Paul's upper arm.

"Hey!" He rubbed his arm.

Megan growled. "You and your damned logic. I knew in my gut that Colette was there, but you said that didn't make sense." Her chest heaved like an out-of-breath runner. "Not everything makes sense!"

The contents of Paul's stomach leaped to his throat, then slammed back down again. He gagged on guilt. If he hadn't been so cocky, if he'd paid more attention to Megan's bad vibes instead of making her feel like a silly child, if he'd alerted Interpol that Colette might be in New York or New Jersey, maybe they would have captured Colette by now. Instead...

Megan shot out her other fist. He grabbed both her wrists and pinned her arms to her sides. "Calm down before you self-combust."

"I don't want to calm down!" She flashed tsunami blue eyes. "And don't patronize me. I was right and you were...stubborn and arrogant. Admit it."

Paul eyed their hosts, both looking unsure as to how to respond, or whether to respond at all. He nudged Megan in the direction of the kitchen. "Let's get you some cold water."

He poured her a glass from the fridge and admonished her to drink slowly. Megan swallowed it with one gulp as if it were pain-killing whiskey and slammed the empty glass on the counter.

"Another?" he asked.

Instead of water, she reached for the half-full bottle of red wine he and the boys had availed themselves of last night and filled her glass with a shaky hand. "I'll have this."

She downed the wine, then poured another glass, as Paul watched helplessly. What had he done? His eyes-wide-shut affair with Colette had not only caused the murder of his friends and betrayal of his country, but threatened to destroy the life of an innocent woman he'd come to care for more than he wanted to admit.

Do not go there. With his track record, falling for Megan could likely kill her. Almost had. "I'm sorry," he mumbled. "I should have listened to you."

She raised a brow, as if surprised by his apology. "So you admit you were stubborn and arrogant?"

"Don't push it, Megan." He poured another glass for himself. "We need to focus our efforts on going forward."

She swilled her second glass of wine. "Colette didn't just steal my identity, she stole my life. Everybody I know, even my family, thinks she's me."

Except for Fletcher. Paul would bet English pounds sterling that the boyfriend had wasted no time getting the woman he presumed to be his girlfriend naked. And when he literally uncovered the truth, he'd used the situation to his advantage.

How could Megan ever have fallen for such a scheming opportunist?

258

And you're smarter? He downed the red wine without tasting it. Considering what he now knew Colette was capable of, he was damned lucky she hadn't taken an ice pick to his head one night while he slept.

"Facebook," Megan said, an intense determination in her eyes. "My family and friends are all there. And I can contact them now." She headed back to the living room but Paul caught her arm.

"Don't."

She struggled to free her arm, jamming her elbow into his chest. "I have to tell Amber. She'll believe me. Somebody has to believe me..."

"Megan. Look at me." He released her wrist and spoke slowly, deliberately, as one would a child. "That page doesn't belong to you anymore. Colette owns it. She'll see everything you post."

She blinked, swallowed, and then recovered her resolve. "So let her. It's my word against hers. My friends have known me a lot longer than they have her. They don't know her at all."

None of us did. "You're missing my point." He pulled out a kitchen chair and straddled it. "If Colette knows we're on to her, she'll run. We've got to keep her there, playing her game, until you can get there and confront her. With the police."

Megan let out a wail. "The wedding's tomorrow. Even if I had a passport and ticket in my hand, I couldn't get there in time. It's too late." She choked on a sob. "I'm doomed. A woman I never met has ruined my life." She flung herself onto his lap and sobbed against his chest.

Mine too. If he hadn't been so clueless, he might have trusted Colette less and guarded his security card more. If he hadn't been so logical, so... stubborn, he might have done something to prevent Colette's machinations from hurting Megan.

He held her close, tears he couldn't express welling inside him. Now there was nothing he could do to help her. Unless.... He drew in a breath. "Megan, I can fix this. Trust me. I have a plan."

She stilled and looked up at him, tears washing her cheeks. Suspicious eyes flashed. "What plan?"

Paul pulled her to him, locking her arms around his waist. And kissed her.

Probably due more to surprise than passion, Megan opened her mouth. But before she could close it, Paul darted his tongue inside. Using only the gentlest touch, he took control of her mouth, capturing her tongue, surrounding her lips with his. She quivered, unclenching her fingers. Her hands caressed his back. When her breathing slowed to a steady, serene rhythm, he let go of her hands, and gently pulled away.

Megan let out her breath on a sigh and opened her eyes. "That was your plan?"

He shrugged.

She licked her upper lip. "If you were trying to calm me down, why didn't you just slap me like they do in those old movies?"

"I didn't want to slap you. I wanted to kiss you."

And damn him, he wanted to do it again. Megan's passionate outpouring had him so turned on he could barely think straight. But he forced himself to focus on the facts that now seemed apparent.

Fact one: Colette was living in Megan's apartment and had hooked up with her boyfriend Fletcher.

Fact two: Fletcher had proposed a marriage scheme to gain control of Megan's trust fund and Colette had gone along with it. Why wouldn't she? After committing murder, identity theft and fraud must seem like child's play.

Fact three: Given facts one and two, no passport documents would be forthcoming from Fletcher.

Fact four: If Megan were to get home, they'd have to find another option.

He'd have to find another option.

* * *

Friday morning, for the first time in many months, Colette woke up alone. She smiled. And stretched, spreading her arms the width of the queen sized bed. For once, she didn't have to attend to some man's morning lust and pretend to be awake enough to enjoy it. She could stay in bed for hours if she liked, take a long, languorous shower, or even a bath. Without Fletcher watching her every move, she could spend her day as she wished, go wherever she wanted.

She could go wherever she wanted.

Kicking off the covers, she sprang out of bed, dashed to Megan's closet, and tore open the black backpack. To the clothes already stashed, she added handfuls of panties and tee shirts from Megan's drawers, and then charged around the apartment looking for candidates to add to the treasures she'd liberated from the parents' home.

There wasn't a lot. For someone who loved art so much, Megan owned only a few prints and cheap reproductions and her curio shelves held mostly photographs. Her jewelry box looked much more promising. Although the beads and bangles were probably costume jewelry, the case also held a diamond tennis bracelet, several rings whose stones might have been expensive gems, and a gaggle of necklaces which, at today's gold prices, were worth rescuing for the chains alone.

Colette stuffed them all in the backpack amid the clothing, then showered and dressed. She might be crazy to walk away from this wedding and lose Megan's sizeable trust fund. But it could take weeks, or longer, to turn those assets into cash, and every day she lingered, the risk of discovery increased. Particularly tomorrow. No way would she be able to avoid Mama and Papa bear at the wedding, even with Fletcher as her wing man.

Fletcher. Even if they pulled this off, she'd still have him as a partner. And after his sappy proposition yesterday, he wasn't likely to hand her half the money and let her go on her merry way. She'd be stuck with him indefinitely. *Non*, after Salim's betrayal, she was determined to finish this alone. That trust fund, tempting as it was, came with too many strings attached.

After one more foray through the apartment, she slung the backpack over her shoulder, plucked the Lexus key ring off the kitchen hook, and bolted down the stairs to the parking lot.

The sun shone brighter today than yesterday, and the birds who'd chirped annoyingly at her window now seemed to be singing with her in congratulatory spirit. Colette stashed her bag in the passenger side of the Lexus's floorboard and entered "JFK airport" into the GPS. Rolling down the windows, she switched on the radio and sang "We Will Rock You" with Queen as she barreled down the road.

Freedom! She wouldn't miss one thing about this provincial little burg. Well, maybe one thing.

She glanced at the Cartier watch on her wrist. The wedding rehearsal would take place in half an hour. Colette visualized herself on Don's arm as he stood in for Fletcher. Then imagined herself as a true bride, with him as the groom.

You can never have him. Men only want you for one thing. Well, Fletcher wanted her for two things. Her body *and* the money he presumed they could steal together.

Face it, you have champagne taste in men on a beer budget. The only currency she had to offer was her body, and in a few years, even that wouldn't be worth much.

If only she'd lived a different life. But with a slut as a mother and a brother who'd abused her as if she were his personal toy, what else could she expect?

Megan's life. If by some quirk of fate she'd been born into Megan's side of the family, she could have rich, honorable doctors throwing flowers at her every day.

When she'd trolled the Internet after coming upon Adele Jarreau's portrait, she'd been merely curious to know if she was descended from that woman and the painter Dubois. That search had led her to seek other members of the Dubois family. Discovering the American branch, specifically, Elizabeth Dubois Jameson Chandler, had led her to her daughter's Facebook page.

Megan's Facebook page. Another woman who looked exactly like Colette. Finding Megan the exact week the Community had 'offered' her that damned-if-you-do-dead-if-you-don't assignment had blown her mind, and given birth to her 'perfect' escape route.

Perfect, right. She almost wished she'd never seen that Facebook profile.

Before getting on the highway, she pulled in at a quick stop market for coffee, a croissant, and a newspaper. Back in the car, she unfolded the paper over the steering wheel and flipped to the international news section. It was only a page, but it still took a minute before she noticed the very short article at the bottom. "Paris. Suspect arrested in British Embassy bombing."

Her breath caught in her throat. She scanned the one-column report in the blink of an eye, but the article made no mention of the arrested person's name or physical description. Still, it had to be Megan. Maybe she'd attempted to actually leave the country and been arrested at the airport.

Colette leaned back against the leather seat and let out a huge sigh. They'd stop looking for her now, at least for a little while. Megan was bound to protest her innocence but it would take some time before the authorities sorted that out, if they ever did. More likely, they'd be anxious to close this case and let Megan rot in prison for the rest of her life.

She laughed to think of Megan struggling in her place, Megan who'd probably never known a day's discomfort in her picture-perfect, coddled life.

Starting the engine again, Colette headed toward the New Jersey Turnpike. It was early enough in the day to catch a flight to...anywhere that had no extradition agreement with France. She might have dodged the bullets of the French police and Cyrus's terrorist troops, but she wouldn't feel safe until she was totally anonymous, totally free.

Which meant totally broke. She couldn't sell her pilfered jewelry in a street bazaar. She'd need a fence, and it would take time to find someone she could trust. Not to mention that her supply of American dollars was dwindling as fast as her euphoria.

A three million dollar trust fund. Colette caught her breath to realize what she'd be giving up. Of course, there was still Fletcher in the picture, but it shouldn't take too much effort to swindle him out of most of it. Or acquire all of it. She'd done much worse for a lot smaller payoff.

Which she had never received.

Cursing Salim with renewed vengeance, she revved the Lexus up to eighty miles per hour, as if the faster she drove, the faster she could escape from her situation. But she could never get away from herself. She was who she was, and would always be.

Three million dollars.

A cell phone rang in the backpack. Megan's. Colette dug for it and glanced at the display. Don. She bit her lip. She should have known better than to answer it, but she couldn't resist listening to his dreamy, toe-curling voice one more time.

"Hi, Don." She tried not to use her bedroom voice but she couldn't help a little breathy softness.

"Meggie? Where are you and Fletcher? We're ready to start."

Merde. "Fletcher is...he wasn't feeling well and asked if we could just do it without him. I'm...running a little late."

He emitted an irritated grunt. "How soon will you be here?"

Ten minutes past Never. "Give me twenty minutes."

"Okay, hurry. Amber just drove in from Boston and she's anxious to see you. I love you, Meggie." He clicked off.

Amber. The best friend. Yet another person Colette did not care to see.

But if she didn't show up for the rehearsal, Don would call Fletcher. Who'd know she'd bolted. And call the police.

Without a confirmed ticket in hand, Colette had no idea how long she'd be stuck in airport waiting areas. What an ironic joke if she were arrested in the same mode and place as Megan.

But Fletcher thought her guilty only of scams and misdemeanors. With Megan in a Paris jail, Colette was safe--for the moment--from the long arm of the international police. Dared she risk a few more days on this colossal con?

265

Three million dollars.

Swerving across two lanes, Colette exited off the next ramp and made a u-turn back toward the country club.

Chapter Twenty-five

"Thanks for meeting me." Paul tried to keep his tone light as he squeezed his frame into the narrow booth at the back of the noisy cafe.

Roger nodded, glancing about nervously. "Your photo's all over the news, mate." He twisted a finger through one of his unruly blond curls.

"They didn't even get my best side," Paul cracked but the humor fell flat.

Roger flagged a waiter and ordered a *croque monsieur* without even looking at the menu. He turned to Paul. "The same?"

Paul grunted affirmatively. He hadn't come here for the food.

Roger drummed his fingers on the scarred table top. "Jesus, Paul," he said when the waiter had moved on. "What in the bloody hell is going on?"

"What have they told you that's not been on the news?"

Roger checked the empty booth next to them. "That your security card was used in the bombing. Did you know? Had you lost it?"

"Of course I didn't know." He frowned in annoyance that his

friend would doubt him, but got past it. Roger was just trying to make sense of something that made no sense at all. He leaned forward and lowered his voice to a whisper. "You know that hot babe I was seeing?"

"Oh man, yeah." Roger licked his lips, grazing his pencil-thin mustache. "Colette, right? Whatever happened with that?" His face contorted. "Bugger, she's not the photo on the security tape?"

Paul nodded ruefully. "Apparently she lifted my badge. I want to find her and bring her in so I can clear my name."

"What trouble we bring on ourselves for a hot piece of tail, eh?" Roger clicked his teeth against his tongue. "What can I do to help?"

This time it was Paul who checked to assure there were no eavesdroppers before speaking. When he told Roger what he needed, his friend visibly retreated to the far edge of the booth. "I can't do that," he muttered. "If I were caught..."

He'd be sacked and arrested immediately. Paul's stomach muscles clenched into a ball. "I'm sorry to put you in this spot. I'd never even consider asking, but I'm desperate."

Roger narrowed his eyes. "Why do you need to leave the country so quickly?"

A glimmer of hope stirred. "I think I know where Colette is. Since Interpol took my passport, I can't prove my innocence until I've produced the guilty party."

"Why can't the local police bring her to justice?"

"She's using an assumed identity. They won't find her as long as she has everyone around her fooled."

"But you can locate her because...?"

268

This wasn't going to work. He should never have been so brazen as to think it might. He didn't want to lie to his friend, but the more he told Roger, the more trouble he exposed him to. "Never mind, I made a mistake asking." He stood. "Just please honor our friendship by not speaking of what I've said to anyone." He threw down a handful of Euros to cover the meal.

"Paul, wait."

He stopped, his heart in his throat, Megan's life and safety hanging on his friend's words.

"Sit."

He did.

Roger shook out his blond curls in a gesture of resignation. "I can't do what you ask. But I will...help you do it yourself." Roger reached into his pants pocket and passed something under the table.

Paul felt hard plastic scrape against his knee. His heart beat double time as he reached down and drew up Roger's British Embassy security badge.

"You'll have to search through the files of deceased British citizens to find one of the appropriate age and description. The materials you'll need are in a locked drawer at the left side of my desk."

Something jingled under the table and Paul grasped a key ring with two keys. The other was presumably for the door to Roger's office.

"I'll need these back tonight," his friend admonished, "as soon as you finish the passport."

"Two passports."

269

Linda Steinberg

Roger quirked a pale yellow brow.

Paul held his breath. Had he gone too far? Would Roger rescind his offer? He kept his gaze steady. "I'm taking my nephew with me."

Roger was silent a long time. Then he groaned in exasperation. "How old is your 'nephew?'"

"About sixteen." *'About?' You're asking him to help you forge a passport for a nephew whose age you don't even know?*

Suspicious brown eyes bored into him. "I warn you, if this is for Colette--"

"Oh God, no. I would never do that. I'd never betray my country. It's--"

"Don't tell me any more." Roger held up his hand. "On the strength of our friendship, I'm going to trust you." He sighed. "I hope you know what you're doing."

"I do."

"Are you coming back?"

"I am. Hopefully with the suspect in tow."

"And your 'nephew'?"

"Has committed no crime. Just needs passage to the States." Dammit. He'd said too much. If Roger knew where they were going, he'd be obligated to tell that to the authorities if they questioned him. "That person is an innocent bystander caught up in this whole mess," he explained, hoping he wasn't making things worse. "I don't want to know."

Roger fell silent as the waiter approached with their food and slapped the plates down on the table. "Just so you know," he said after the waiter left, "If you get caught, I'm throwing you under the bus. We met for dinner, and you must have stolen my security card while I was paying the check."

"Understood." Relief tightened Paul's throat. "You're a good friend, mate. If there's ever anything I can do..."

"Just one," Roger said as Paul rose to leave. "Don't get caught."

* * *

Trust me, he'd said. If she had a dollar for every woman who'd believed that from a man and ended up disappointed, disillusioned, or dead, Megan would be the richest woman in the world.

"So what do you think?"

She reached for the mirror Jacques held out to her. "Oh my god. It's so short!" Megan twirled to see the back of her head in the full length mirror in the master bedroom. She grasped at the clipped strands of hair next to her neck. "I look like a boy."

"That's the idea, as I understand it," Jacques said. "Paul believes you have a better chance of getting out of the country in a disguise."

Apparently Paul had confided more in Jacques than he had her. An hour ago he'd texted someone on his phone, grabbed his jacket, and, promising to return soon, whispered some instructions to Jacques as he dashed out the door. "What did he tell you of his 'plan'?"

"Nothing, except to cut your hair and buy you clothes."

She hooked her thumbs in the belt loops of the newly purchased jeans and tugged them up. Boys' jeans with no tapered waistline, they kept slipping down to hug her hips. "These pants will

271

fall down to my ankles, like those rappers wear them," she fretted. Realizing how whiny she sounded, she hugged Jacques' neck. "I appreciate your help, but you have to admit, I do look hideous."

"She looks perfect." Paul appeared in the doorway. Ignoring her as if she were some department store mannequin, he spoke to Jacques. "Great job, *mon ami. Formidable.*"

"My photographer friend was busy this afternoon but she lent me this," Jacques said. He pointed to the camera and tripod in the corner of the room. "It's not state of the art, but it'll do for a passport photo. They all look like mug shots anyway." He clasped a hand to his mouth. "Oops. Did I say a bad thing?"

"Not unless it's prophetic," Paul assured him.

Passport photo? So he proposed to disguise her as a boy, and...and what? Smuggle her out of the country with a fake passport? "Whatever your plan is--and I'm not sure I even want to know--it won't work. There's no way I can get to New Jersey by tomorrow."

"The wedding's not until three o'clock." Paul smiled in that assuring way that said he had everything under control.

Nothing was under control. "It's a nine hour flight from Paris to New York."

"But there's a six hour time difference." That smile again. The one that made her want to trust him despite all her senses telling her to trust no one. "If we leave tonight, or even early tomorrow morning, we'll arrive in America before noon."

We? Her heart throbbed in her chest. "You're...coming with me?"

"Of course." Paul looped his arm around her waist as if that were the most natural position in the world. "Colette stole your boyfriend, which, if you ask me, is no great loss. But she attacked my country and killed my friends. I won't let go of this until she's locked away."

Of course his motive was to punish Colette. Still, Megan shuddered with relief at not having to go through this alone. *My hero.* She stood on her toes and wound her arms around Paul's sturdy neck. "Thank you."

When she tilted her head back her lips just naturally found his. And his tongue slipped inside her mouth as smoothly as if that were an instinctive trip.

Dammit, she did trust him. He was the only friend she had left in the world. Megan moved her lips over his, drinking in Paul's essence. So, he'd summarily dismissed, at first, what to him must have seemed a silly emotional argument. The man had never listened to his gut. But his heart was listening now. And hers rebounded with joy. Closing her eyes, she wound her arms around his waist and slipped one hand inside his shirt to caress the smooth skin of his back.

"Ahem."

She jumped back, having completely forgotten Jacques was standing right there.

"You two need to get a room," Jacques grinned. "Oh, wait. You have one just down the hall."

Paul actually blushed. "No time," he said in a rational, all-business tone. "Let's get these photos taken."

"Marcel!" Jacques called to his partner. "We're ready."

Marcel entered the bedroom and tugged the photographic equipment to the center of the room, then drew the curtains. Jacques positioned Megan to face the camera, lifting an arm here, turning a cheek there.

"Wait," Paul said. He stared at her breasts and frowned.

Megan felt her own cheeks flame. She folded her arms across her chest. "Something wrong with my boobs?"

"Not a damn thing. Hence the problem." Paul walked all around her chair as if she were a museum exhibit. "We need to strap those puppies down."

She blinked.

"And lose the bra. It shows through your shirt. In the back," he added when she looked down questioningly. Paul turned to Jacques. "Did you buy those boys' undershirts I asked for?"

Jacques handed Paul a package and then he and Marcel quietly left the room and closed the door.

Megan swallowed. Could she really go through with this? "This is so risky. What if I can't pull it off? What if get strip searched?"

Paul's lips twisted into a grimace. "If you follow my lead, that shouldn't happen." He softened his tone. "The authorities will be looking for a woman, possibly a woman traveling with a man. As a man and boy traveling together, we might not even rate a second glance."

He'd thought of everything. Megan took in a deep breath. "Tell me what I need to do."

Paul reached for a roll of gauze on the dresser, probably the one used to bandage her leg, and nodded toward her shirt. "Become a sixteen year old boy."

"I'll do my best." Megan stripped down to her waist and closed her eyes. "But I've never been so mortified in my life."

He chuckled wryly. "You had your identity stolen, you've been shot, and you jumped into a ravine and lived to tell about it. I think you can survive this small indignity."

Paul unrolled the thin, gauzy material and indicated for her to hold one end at the side of her breast. Then he carefully wound it around her, back to front to back, wrapping her like a mummy. "Suck it in," he directed, as the material got tighter around her breasts.

Megan winced from the pressure, shrinking herself concave. At least he wasn't touching her directly with his hands. Although her nipples, damn them, responded as if he had.

If Paul noticed, he had the decency not to mention it. After packaging her from décolletage to ribs, he pulled the end of the gauze strip taut.

"Ow!"

"Sorry." He tore off a piece of white tape. It screeched like fingernails on a blackboard. Gently he taped the tail of gauze and tucked it in, then handed her the undershirt and boy's tee shirt.

She quickly slipped them over her head. "Paul?" she said as he opened the door to admit the others.

He turned to face her.

"You're not worried?" She tried to still the beating of her heart. "Not even a little scared?"

"Frightened out of my mind, actually." One side of his mouth turned up in a lopsided smile. "But if we succeed, and this all turns out well, I'll deny I ever said that."

Megan smiled, a little bit of the tension seeping out of her muscles. "You don't have to do this, you know."

275

"I know."

While Marcel took her picture, Paul extracted something from his shirt pocket that looked like a security badge and showed it to Jacques. "Can you make me look like this?"

Jacques chuckled. "You want those Harpo Marx curls?"

"Regrettably, yes."

Megan inched closer to see the photo. "This is a British embassy badge." She raised a brow at Paul. "Whose is it?"

"A friend's." He didn't explain further and Megan didn't ask. She wasn't sure she wanted to know any more about Paul's plan. She closed her eyes. Blind trust. Fletcher would have called her naïve to trust a man she knew so little about. It was true they hadn't had much time to get acquainted. But the one thing she knew for sure about Paul Bernard was that she would trust him with her life.

"Your hair's too short for that style," Jacques asserted. "We'll need a wig."

He procured one resting on a mannequin head from the large bedroom armoire, and like her mother's salon beautician, wound the hair around large rollers. Paul shaved the initial stages of a robust beard, leaving just a whisper of growth under his nose. Jacques filled in the mustache with an eyebrow pencil a shade darker than the corn yellow wig.

"I liked your beard," Megan said ruefully, thinking about their passionate afternoon.

Paul didn't answer but his eyes twinkled. He knew exactly why she'd liked it.

When he set the wig on his head and smiled for the photographs, Megan tried not to laugh, but couldn't suppress a giggle. The look was natural enough, for that guy in the photo maybe, but Paul's hard face just didn't match the soft look.

"Good enough for government work," he said wryly, when Marcel showed them the digital images on the camera.

Megan examined the photos. She did look like a boy. Which, she reluctantly acknowledged, was a good thing. She felt one step closer to getting home.

Adrenaline pumped through her veins. It was exciting to be part of this flurry of activity, everyone coming together for one purpose. But... "Aren't we missing something? Like the passports the photos need to go into?"

"Don't worry about the passports," Paul said. "Just leave that to me."

Fear shot through her adrenaline rush, reminding her that whatever Paul was planning was probably illegal. She couldn't imagine logical, by-the-book Paul ever breaking the law. He'd probably never even had a traffic ticket. Yet here he stood, ably directing the operation as if he were an MI6 operative instead of a programmer.

And despite all rational thought, Megan found his quiet heroism thrilling. And arousing.

While Marcel printed the photos, Paul stepped into the other room and returned wearing a corduroy jacket and a tie. He took the two sets of passport sized photos and shoved them into his jacket pocket. He breathed audibly. "Wish me luck."

"*Bonne chance*," Jacques and Marcel said in unison.

Megan's breath stopped in her throat. "Where are you going?" The American Embassy was closed at this hour. The British Embassy was probably not even operating. Was he planning to meet some unsavory underworld character to buy counterfeit passports? Or-- She gasped and dug her nails into her palms. "Please, please don't do something dangerous."

His brown eyes gleamed with determination. "You want to go home? You won't get there by clicking your ruby slippers." He looked down at the shoes Jacques had purchased for her. "Or your Converse sneakers."

Nor over his dead body. "We'll find another way. Call the American police. Call Interpol. Whatever you're planning, it's too risky."

Intense eyes bored into hers. "I need to do this, Megan. I need to see the look on her face."

Megan clenched her fingers. "So this is about honor? You feel like Colette made a fool of you and this is your personal payback?"

"It's not just that."

Not *just* that but it *was* that. "This is crazy. Let the authorities handle it. We know where Colette is. Let them apprehend her."

"And what if they don't get there in time? What if paperwork or jurisdictional issues prevent them from stopping that wedding? You could lose your trust fund. Or, at the very least, have to jump through legal hoops to restore your identity."

"I don't care about the damned trust fund. Not if it means you getting in trouble. Or hurt. Or d--" Oh God, he could be risking his life. If he tried to break into a government office and was caught, the guards would shoot first and ask questions later. She grabbed his arm. "Please, Paul, don't do this."

He uncurled her fingers from his forearms. "All my life I've played by the book and let the 'rightful authorities' fight my battles for me. I never served in the military. I chose to serve my country, but all I've done is sit behind a desk and enjoy living in Paris. I need to do this." He headed toward the front door. "Don't try to take it away from me."

Megan wanted to rush ahead of him and spread-eagle herself against the door to prevent him from leaving. But watching Paul's determined stride, she got it. She understood what he needed. And why. In this past week she'd taken risks she never would have imagined she'd have the courage for. And despite the sheer terror, she'd discovered a sense of fulfillment. Freedom. Joy.

She drew in a long, hard breath. If she could survive the catacombs, then somebody must be looking out for Paul too.

"I'll be careful. I promise." His lips brushed her cheek. "It'll be all right," he whispered.

Megan lifted her chin to his face. His brown eyes exuded the quiet confidence he'd displayed all morning but his lips, when they met hers, imparted the same desperation Megan felt.

"It'll be all right," he repeated, as if to convince himself.

Chapter Twenty-six

The sun was low in the western sky as Paul exited the Metro station and approached the British Embassy. Until recently he'd walked this way every day, almost on automatic pilot. But this evening it all seemed different and sinister. The bombed out section of the second floor, his workplace, was no longer burning, but the blown out windows and blackened walls twisted his gut into knots.

He took a calming breath to slow his heartbeat from its current hundred kilometers a minute. Circling the locked front gate, he went round to the employee entrance.

Would a guard be posted there tonight? Paul urged his legs to keep moving, but as he neared the door, they froze. Perhaps he could have a peek in a side window, and if a security guard was stationed at the entry, wait until the bloke left his post to relieve himself.

You're stalling, Bernard. Even if he could manage that timing, the wait could take hours. He didn't have hours. If they were going to get to America in time to stop this bogus wedding, he had to accomplish his mission straightaway.

He drew in another deep breath, and pulled open the door.

A guard was at the desk, but not one Paul recognized. The man looked up from his book as Paul entered, but didn't make conversation. With a polite half-smile, Paul flashed Roger's security badge and printed his friend's name on the sign-in sheet along with the time of arrival. Six forty-six.

The guard glanced quickly from the card to Paul's face, then compared the name on the clipboard to his list of authorized personnel. Nodded. And went back to his book.

Paul swiped Roger's badge into the slot.

No bells or sirens went off. Swallowing a mouthful of saliva, he passed through the metal detector and emerged on the other side.

Walk slowly. Nobody called in to work after hours would be in a hurry to get to his desk. Heart pounding with every step, he rounded the corner and strode purposefully toward the bank of offices along the back wall, stopping at the one labeled Roger Glade, Passport Control Manager.

Roger's key easily opened the door to his private office. Paul entered, turned on the light switch, and locked the door behind him. Setting the keys on the large desk, he reached into his pockets for the gloves Jacques had given him and slipped them on.

He settled noiselessly in the executive desk chair and turned on the computer. Its quiet boot-up was a deafening roar against the eerie silence.

Second desk drawer on the left. Inhaling deeply, Paul inserted Roger's key and tugged it open. Yes! Inside were the promised paper and passport covers, as well as Roger's passwords.

After logging in as Roger, he brought up the database of British citizens in France, then filtered to deceased Britons, then sorted by gender and birth date. The task felt like digging up graves, but he did find a handful of males who would have been in their thirties or late twenties today, even a couple of his approximate height and weight.

Finding a boy born fifteen to twenty years ago proved to be a much more difficult task. The closest were two children who'd died as infants, one who'd be twenty-five today if he'd lived, and another who'd be thirteen.

Megan was twenty-three, but a twenty-five year old man with no beard stubble and a soprano voice might cause suspicion. The thirteen-year old seemed the better option.

He was assembling the passports with the photos they'd taken that afternoon when he heard footsteps in the corridor. The security guard must be making his rounds. Paul froze in his work. And held his breath.

A key turned in the lock.

Shit. Hastily he pulled off the gloves, but there was no time to stuff them in his pockets. He shoved them on the chair between his legs just as the door opened.

He forced himself to look up and meet the guard's eyes. Another man he didn't recognize who, hopefully, wouldn't recognize him. "Evening," Paul said quietly.

The guard returned his greeting. "Everything all right here, Mr. Glade?"

Swallowing his relief, Paul nodded. The security guard paced around the office, then stopped beside the desk. He gaped at Paul with a befuddled expression, as if he were trying to remember something. Or someone.

Keep calm. "Something I can do for you?" Paul asked in a measured tone.

The guard broke his stare. "Not at all, sir. Have a nice evening. Prudent of you to keep your door locked." And with that he left, locking the door from the outside.

Paul waited a full minute before allowing himself to breathe normally. Then he hurriedly finished the passports, shoved them into his jacket along with the gloves, and logged off the computer.

After locking Roger's office door behind him, he glanced at his watch. Seven thirty five. The halls were quiet. Logic dictated that he get the hell out as soon as possible, but morbid curiosity got the better of him. Stealthily climbing the stairs, Paul headed instead to the bombed out area that had once been the embassy's data center.

Yellow police tape circled the small area that had been more of a home to him than his walk-up flat. Clutching his stomach at the sight of what was left of Will and Ian's desks, he dropped involuntarily to his knees. Though it had been years since he'd attended church, he prayed for the souls of his mates in the hope that they'd died instantly and without suffering.

His shoulders shook. He tried to tell himself he was not responsible for this, but he knew better. He'd foolishly trusted a woman who'd appeared to be an air-headed coquette, and his negligence--make that horniness--had enabled Colette to commit this horrible act.

And now he'd not only aided a terrorist, but was a criminal himself.

He could barely walk for the knocking of his knees or breathe for the heaviness in his heart. After descending the stairs to the main floor, he checked his watch again. Seven fifty-two. He'd been here just over an hour. Too long to report, if asked by the guard at the desk, that he'd just come in tonight to pick up files or a forgotten object, but not long enough to warrant coming in to the office for work.

He'd seemed a taciturn fellow. Maybe he wouldn't ask.

Paul was striding toward the exit when he heard footsteps

behind him. *Breathe. Act normal.*

A dark-haired man wearing khakis and a polo shirt came abreast of him. "You working late too?"

Paul forced words out of a dry throat. "Yes. It's all quite a horrific mess, isn't it?" He averted his face and continued walking, at a normal pace, but his height allowed him the long strides necessary to distance himself from his companion. Disguise notwithstanding, his photo had been broadcast on the news. He didn't dare take chances.

Dogging his steps, the man stepped in front of Paul and faced him with a chilling, quizzical stare. "Are we acquainted?"

Damn. "Not as yet." Paul stuck out his hand. "Jordan Fowler. I'm temporarily assigned here."

"Martin Weems." After shaking his hand, Weems cocked an eyebrow. "You must be with that lot brought over from the Portuguese embassy to assess the security situation."

"Yes, that's right." Paul hid his relieved sigh and said a silent prayer of thanks. He'd been frantically devising a cover story when Mr. Weems had graciously provided one for him.

Although if he *were* on a security assessment teams, he would have reported the helpful Mr. Weems precisely for divulging that information.

"You've been issued a security badge, of course." Martin Weems stared at Paul's chest.

"Of course." Paul looked down at the buttons on his shirt, from which an identification badge would have normally hung on a lanyard. The one in his pocket had another name on it. "Damn. Must have left it at my desk." He retreated with a smile and a wave, intent on hanging back until Mr. Weems departed.

"Don't bother, mate." Paul turned round to face him and his blood chilled. The convivial Mr. Weems pointed an automatic weapon at his chest. "I know you're not here from the Portuguese embassy. Because *I'm* from the Portuguese embassy."

* * *

Megan sat on the sofa facing the entry, her legs curled under her, her eyes trained on the front door.

Footsteps tread almost silently behind her. "He'll be okay," Jacques assured her. He handed her one of the two glasses he held.

Taking the wine, she forced a smile. "Do I look worried?"

"Holding your head so as to keep it from falling off gives you away a bit."

Her involuntary laugh helped dissolve the tension. A little. But all the wine in the world wouldn't make it disappear until Paul returned safely.

She made room for Jacques to sit beside her. "Why did you take me in? You didn't know me at all and you barely knew Paul."

Jacques took a sip of his wine. "You were in trouble."

Megan was almost too touched to speak. How strange that the people she'd counted on in life had failed her, whereas complete strangers had put themselves out for someone they'd never met.

She sipped her wine, slowly this time. "How long have you and Marcel been together?"

"Five years." A sweet blush came over his face. "The best five years of my life."

It must be nice to be able to say that so definitively. "When did you know that...you loved him?"

Jacques grinned. "The first night we met."

Love at first sight. Was it possible? "I've only known Paul three days," she mused, barely realizing she spoke aloud.

"You can learn a lot about a person in three days. Especially under the circumstances you two have been through."

"But that's not real life. It's the day to day experiences, over time, that tell if two people are compatible."

"You were with your American boyfriend for a year. Did that tell you that you were compatible?"

Undoubtedly a rhetorical question. "But it seems so...irresponsible to have feelings for someone you've only just met." Megan had never been a live-for-the-moment person. In all her twenty-three years she'd never once cut class on a whim, taken off on a spontaneous road trip with no planned destination, or had unprotected sex.

She'd never before had a one-night stand. Or even slept with a man she hadn't known at least a few months.

But everything had changed this week. For her.

She fingered the stem of her wine glass. "Do you think he's still in love with her?" she blurted out.

"Colette?" Jacques chuckled. "You're assuming that he did, at one time, love her." He placed his hand on the top of her head and pulled her against his shoulder. "Colette is—was—a breath of fresh air. Impulsive. Unpredictable. Paul needed that kind of excitement in his life. But he's too smart and serious to lose his heart to someone like her."

Paul had said as much, but he hadn't sounded convincing. "Do you think he's capable of feeling...something more...for any

286

woman?"

"I hardly know the man, Megan. But I've seen his eyes when he looks at you. Give him time."

"We don't *have* time!" She dug tense fingers into her palms. Even if Paul's efforts were successful and they did manage to stop the wedding, once Colette was apprehended, Paul, having done his duty, would turn right around and fly back to Paris.

You're getting ahead of yourself, Megan. The most important thing right now was for Paul to come back tonight, safe.

* * *

Shit. Shit. Shit. The blood drained from Paul's face as he slowly raised his hands above his head. "I do work here," he said, staring at the gun. "I can explain."

Explain how? He tried to think, but when Weems spoke into a radio and called all units for backup, Paul's gut took over.

With a high, swift kick he hadn't practiced since his wrestling days, he knocked the weapon out of Weems' hands. Before the man could react, Paul slammed him to the ground, thumping Weems' head on the hard marble floor. He was unconscious.

The security guard from the desk came running up, fumbling for his weapon. But Paul punched him in the stomach before he could draw it, then pummeled the poor man who was only doing his job until he doubled over and slid to the floor. Paul grabbed his gun and ran.

To where? He couldn't go out the way he'd come in. In a matter of minutes, the building would be surrounded.

The emergency exit. The staff had been schooled on escape routes in the event of a terrorist attack. Paul ran, zigzagging, to the back of the building, as a bullet whizzed by his head. One of the men he'd disarmed had recovered.

Paul thought about returning fire, but shooting to disable was more difficult than shooting to kill, and he'd lose precious seconds taking aim.

Another shot rang out. The bullet grazed the wall beside him. Paul's heart pounded so hard he'd swear it bruised his ribs.

The exit, if he remembered correctly, was through a locked storeroom closet. When Paul paused in front of it, his ear buzzed as if a giant fly had flown past. A bullet singed the sleeve of his jacket.

He whipped out Roger's badge and inserted it in the lock. The door clicked open. Breathing heavily, Paul slipped through and slammed the door behind him.

He stood in a narrow corridor with floor-to-ceiling shelves on either side. They held supplies, toilet paper, old printers and computer equipment. Paul grabbed as many heavy objects as he could and shoved them one atop another against the door. Hopefully that should hold back his pursuers for a few minutes.

About ten feet on, a dozen steps took him down a short flight of stairs. The room narrowed even more. There were no lights. Paul had to stand sideways to press his body through the dark passage. Was he underground? Where did this thing lead?

Behind him, he heard a loud rumble. Like furniture being moved. Or desktop computers, printers and fax machines.

He was almost out of time. Where the hell was the exit? His heart stopped as several pairs of footsteps pounded the floor of the corridor above him.

His shoulder bumped against something hard. Metal. A door. Paul pushed but it didn't open. He groped for Roger's badge and felt for the card key slit in the lock. Swiped the badge.

The door didn't open.

They must have shut off the electronic card readers.

Sweat beaded on Paul's forehead. His life flashed before his eyes. Was it over? Would they take him into custody or just shoot to kill?

The footsteps were on his level now. Shots fired. Bullets zipped through the dark.

His fists clenched around something hard. The gun. Paul backed away from the door and aimed at the knob. Zing! Another two shots and the lock snapped.

The door was heavy but with all his weight against it, it heaved open. Paul ran into the night like an escaped felon, tearing through tall shrubs and bushes. Shoving the gun into his pocket, he headed in the direction of lights and voices.

Rain pelted his head and obscured his vision, but he ran blindly up the sidewalk and into the street in front of a yellow vehicle with a lit sign on its dome. A taxi.

The cab screeched to a halt six inches from his body. Paul grabbed the door handle and hauled himself into the back seat. "Rive Gauche," he panted, trying not to look round to see if cars were following.

The Left Bank was not his destination, but he hoped they might lose any pursuers crossing the bridge. Paul made small talk in French with the driver, trying to act like someone out for an evening stroll caught unexpectedly in the rain, instead of a fugitive from the police.

When he deemed it safe to stop, Paul directed the driver to let him out at a Metro station. Slipping the gun out of his jacket and into a covered trash can, he bought a ticket for cash and hot footed it underground.

The trip back took half an hour longer than if he'd taken the taxi all the way. After changing trains twice, he scanned the platform for uniformed officers before stepping out of the train's sliding doors. As he jogged up the steps to street level, Paul searched for police cars.

He let out a ragged breath. No sign of any law enforcement officials. He wiped his temples with his jacket sleeve, suddenly exhausted. Shaking. Adrenaline had taken him this far, but now his energy flagged and he thought he might collapse. Forcing his feet to move, he trudged to Jacques and Marcel's flat. His ribs ached. And a dull pain throbbed in his side.

He'd barely knocked on the door when it swung open, and Megan lunged into his arms. "Thank God you're safe," she exclaimed, then took a step back. "What happened to your face?" She ran her hand over scratches he hadn't been aware of.

"I'm fine." He reached into his inside jacket pocket and slapped the two passports onto the entry table. "It's done. I'll just wash my face and we'll get the hell out of here."

He started to walk down the hall, but felt suddenly unsteady. Megan grabbed his arm. He almost knocked her down with his weight, but she kept her hold, and threw her other arm around his waist.

"I've got you," she said as he regained his balance. "You're okay."

He was definitely *not* okay. But gazing into Megan's luminous, I-believe-in-you eyes, he knew he would be.

Chapter Twenty-seven

Megan clutched the back seat door handle and held on for dear life as the purple Peugeot swerved around a traffic circle. A typical Frenchman, Marcel drove fast and changed lanes like a racecar driver. Hopefully he wouldn't kill them all before they arrived at the airport.

She scooted closer to Paul. "Test me on my cover."

He blinked as though he'd been lost in thought. "Huh?"

She opened up the authentic-looking passport and scanned the page with her picture on it, memorizing the data. "I'm Timothy Briggs," she said mimicking a British accent. "I'm thirteen years old. Born in Sussex." She closed the passport. "How's my accent?"

"Tolerable."

She shrugged. "I live in Lyon with my parents. You're my Uncle Albert Warner. You're taking me to New York for a three week vacation."

"Holiday," he corrected.

"A three week holiday." Sweat formed on her upper lip. "What if I mess up and say something American? What if they don't believe my accent?"

"What?" He returned from outer space again. "Just let me do the talking. Don't speak unless directly spoken to." His eyes glazed over once more.

"Paul, are you sure you're all right?" All he'd told them about his ordeal was that he'd run into someone at the British Embassy who might have recognized him. When she'd questioned him about his cuts and bruises, he'd claimed he'd fallen on his way to the Metro. "Is there something you haven't told me?"

"Bugger all, Megan," he said irritably. "I'm just feeling a little stressed, that's all."

"What time is our flight?"

He glanced at his watch. "The last flight to JFK leaves at midnight. But we don't have confirmed reservations. We're listed on standby."

"We don't have seats?" Megan's hopes crashed around her like breaking waves.

"It's early September and tourists are going home. All the planes are fully booked," he explained. "The earliest flight I could get leaves tomorrow at noon."

"That's too late!"

Paul nodded. "They said they sometimes have last-minute cancellations. That we could go to the airport and try for one. The sooner we get there, the better our chances of getting on a flight."

She bit her lip. What if they didn't make it? What if everything Paul had gone through—whatever that was—was for nothing?

Pull up your big girl panties, Megan. And paste a smile on your face. The last thing Paul needed was a whiner. She had to be positive. And make him think that way too. If they believed in success, it was more likely to happen.

Leaning against the window, she pillowed her head with the faded blue duffle Jacques had pressed on her, filled with boy's tee shirts and underwear, as well as several changes of dressing for her leg. Paul had insisted that traveling without checked baggage was suspicious enough; going through without carry-ons could turn a red flag neon pink.

When they arrived at Charles de Gaulle airport, Marcel stepped out of the car and shook hands with Paul. They hugged.

"Thanks for everything," Paul said. "When I get back, it's dinner on me at Le Jules Verne."

"That's overly generous," Marcel said visibly touched. "But thank you."

Megan was impressed too. Although Marcel probably made a good salary, dinner at the expensive restaurant atop the Eiffel Tower probably wasn't an everyday occurrence for him and Jacques.

"Not nearly as generous as what you've done for Megan and me," Paul said, a hint of a tear in his eye. "You guys went above and beyond for someone you hardly knew."

"And we'd do it again," Marcel said passionately.

"I'm glad you said that," Paul said, looking sheepish. "Because I need one more favor."

Marcel raised an amused brow.

Paul took the envelope the passports had been in from his jacket and wrote an address on it, then drew a picture ID card from his pants. Before Megan could get a good look at it, he slipped it into the envelope. "I know it's a lot to ask, but would you mind delivering this for me? Tonight, if at all possible."

Marcel grinned. "If you'll do us one more favor and get this young 'gentleman' here home safe."

"Will do." He hoisted his almost-empty gray duffle bag over one shoulder. "Let's go, Timmy."

Did teenage boys embrace older men? Megan took a chance and hugged Marcel as tight as was decent. "Bye, Uncle Marcel. Love to Uncle Jacques."

She fought tears as the Peugeot drove away. This was happening. They were really going. For three days all she'd thought about was getting home, and now that she was, she realized how much she'd miss the friends she was leaving behind.

"Tim?" Paul coughed loudly.

Megan took in a deep breath. *Showtime.* She followed Paul into the terminal, but when she'd taken just three steps, cool air hit her lower back. *Damn these boy jeans.* They'd ridden down again while she was in the car. Megan set her duffle down and yanked at the waistband, undoubtedly looking like she had an itch she couldn't reach.

"What the hell are you doing?" Paul frowned.

"Don't ask." She hiked up her jeans with clammy hands, then headed to the security line and stood quietly behind Paul. He'd changed out of the corduroy jacket he'd worn earlier back into a black tee shirt and his tan windbreaker.

"Remember. Don't speak unless you have to," he growled into her ear.

Megan nodded, trying to keep her heart from jumping out of her chest. *Think positive.* She called up her old optimism mantras. Inhaling deeply, she pictured herself gliding easily through the security line, onto the plane, and alighting at JFK airport to the sound of cheers and the confetti of a ticker tape parade.

Okay, maybe that last part was pushing positive thinking a little too far.

Paul handed his passport to the airport sentry who looked at it, grunted, made a little tick mark on his boarding pass with a highlighter, and waved him on.

He did the same for Megan. She let out her breath as she passed beyond him, eager to catch up with Paul, but then--

"Timothy Briggs?" The airport official was staring at her.

She nodded, her heart in her throat.

"Wait here, please." He spoke into the blue-tooth phone wrapped around his ear. "I have him."

Her heart sank into her stomach, twisted like a pretzel. Should she try to ramrod her way through the security station, which would undoubtedly set off all sorts of alarms? Or run out of the terminal, into the relative safety of the Paris streets?

She stole a glance at Paul, who was almost to the conveyor belt, removing his shoes. He had to be as panicked as she, but his gaze was calm, willing her to stay composed.

A sky cap ran up, weaving through the corded lines, to the sentry's podium. Carrying a blue duffle bag.

The sentry checked the tag Megan had hurriedly thought to loop through the handles. "I believe this is yours, Mr. Briggs? It was found near the curb."

And probably examined. Thank goodness she'd stuffed in those pairs of boys' underwear. "Oh, yes, thank you." With a breath that had her lungs racing for cover against her chest wall, she grabbed the bag and raced to Paul's side. In view of the authorities, he gave her a patronizing, uncle-like smile.

Ignoring the reproach, she stepped in front of him and plopped her duffle on the conveyor belt, then placed her baseball cap in a tray and started untying her tennis shoes.

Would they make her take off her hoodie? The sign dictated that she should. And two young men in the line ahead of her removed their jackets and stuffed them in one of the plastic trays before walking through the metal detector.

Megan's heart thumped in her chest and she imagined her breasts growing as she breathed. But if she didn't comply and had to be asked personally, she was more likely to be carefully scrutinized. Sighing, she slipped out of her oversized sweatshirt and held her arms casually in front of her chest. *Don't act like you have something to hide and maybe no one will notice.*

While she waited to walk through the metal detector, she saw something that throttled her heart even more. Beside the metal detector, another security station consisting of a glass cage scanned a white-haired passenger who stood spread eagled with his arms pressed to the sides.

Her breath caught in her throat. She'd gone through that X-ray machine at JFK. It captured a picture of you--all of you--even inside your clothes.

Her stomach cramped as she stared at the machine. Not everyone was asked to go through that station. The young mother with a baby, yes. The businessman, no. It seemed random. Or was there a numerical pattern? Megan tried to remember how many persons in front of the elderly gentleman had gone through without being pulled from the line. Two? Three?

She watched the white-haired man exit the machine. The

young man next in line passed through the normal scan. One. Nor was his buddy called out of the line. Two.

Paul pushed his way in front of her and set his shoes and duffle ahead of hers on the belt. Thr--

"Sir, come this way, please."

Without a glance at her, Paul walked to the X-ray machine as he was bidden and stepped inside the glass cage. Apparently he'd been monitoring the pattern too.

Megan walked through the regular metal detector without incident, picked up her bags, and met Paul at the small circle of chairs where he was putting on his shoes. They didn't speak, but as their eyes met, she read in them exactly what she was thinking. *Whew. Close call.*

At the gate, they put their names on the agent's standby list and waited. And waited some more. After the flight had almost completed boarding, the gate agent started calling names. One by one and two by two, standby passengers rose from their seats and joined the line of passengers still waiting to board. Megan looked at Paul uneasily. He shrugged. She sipped at the coke he'd bought her and waited some more.

Finally the door to the jet way closed. They were the only two passengers left in the waiting area.

"I'm sorry, guys." The gate agent looked at Paul. "That's the last flight to New York. You're welcome to come back in the morning and try again."

Megan sprung out of her chair, and despite Paul's admonitions to avoid speaking, asked the agent, "What time is the first flight?"

"There's one at six-fifteen. And another at nine-thirty."

Nine-thirty would cut it too close. They really had to make the six-fifteen to have even a shot at stopping this wedding. Which meant getting back here by four-fifteen.

It was just after midnight now. By time they took a cab back to Marcel and Paul's, they'd get only a couple hours sleep before heading back to the airport. And they'd already imposed enough on their good friends. Megan surveyed the empty chairs. "Can we stay here overnight?"

Paul stood as if to shush her, but the agent answered readily. "Not here. But there's a lounge area down that way." She pointed to an escalator.

A lounge. Perfect. In Megan's flying experience, that meant comfortable sofas, a bar, and a buffet of fruit, pastries and mini-sandwiches. She grabbed Paul's arm. "Let's go, Uncle Bert."

Paul raised a skeptical brow, but allowed her to lead him down the escalator to the waiting area the agent had spoken of.

And that's all it was. A waiting area. Instead of comfortable couches, there were two rows of plastic chairs facing one another, each chair hitched to the ones on either side of it. Instead of a bar and buffet, two vending machines. At least there were bathrooms in the vicinity.

Paul plopped into one of the sunshine-orange chairs and propped his feet on the chair in the opposite row. Megan sat beside him, but her legs were too short to reach across, so she folded them under her.

"Welcome to the Charles de Gaulle Hilton," Paul said.

"It's just for a few hours." But after only thirty seconds, her bottom was already getting sore from the hard chair. She should have realized they wouldn't be admitted to the nice lounges with a coach ticket. An unconfirmed one at that. "We have no choice." She turned to him. "*I* have no choice. *You're* free to leave now if you want to back out."

He chuckled without mirth. "You know me better than that."

Did she? She knew that Paul wouldn't renege on a plan he'd committed to. But she wasn't sure why. Was it just his British stiff-upper-lip, duty-God-and-country upbringing that compelled him to stay the course? Or had he developed feelings--*any* kind of feelings--for her?

Moot question, she reminded herself. Paul wouldn't allow feelings to interfere with what he perceived as his duty.

Although the fluorescent lights burned bright overhead, this part of the airport might as well be closed. The ticket counter was deserted, as was the long hallway as far as Megan could see. A few pilots and flight attendants appeared sporadically, heading to a restful night's sleep at their homes or crash pads. She and Paul were the only occupants of the waiting area. It almost seemed like they were the last people on earth. Except that the end of the earth would undoubtedly be dark and silent, without the Big Brother lights and annoying strains of Muzak.

The large room was getting stuffy. The ultra-economical French must have turned the air-conditioning down for the night. Megan slipped out of her sweatshirt but held it in front of her, just in case. When she turned her gaze to Paul she caught him holding his side and wincing in apparent pain.

"What is it?"

His face changed immediately. "Nothing. Just nerves."

He'd said that earlier but this time she wasn't buying it. "What are you not telling me? What happened at the embassy?"

He sighed irritably. "Like I said, I may have--"

"Tell me the truth." Her stomach muscles twisted. "My God, Paul, what have you done?"

"Look, Megan, I'm tired. Why don't we try to get some sleep?" He smashed his duffle bag into a pillow, and then yanked off his jacket. "Did they turn off the a/c? It's hot as hell in here." He lay down on his side.

Megan stared in horror at his black tee shirt. It was stained with blood.

Chapter Twenty-eight

Christ. Paul stared at his blood-stained tee shirt and nearly lost it. The top of his head seemed to separate from his brow. No wonder he'd been feeling so weak and wobbly.

He looked up at Megan's horrified face. "You were...shot?"

She was freaking out. He couldn't let that happen.

"Possibly." Despite his own panic, he'd have to keep calm. Act as if gunshot wounds were a normal part of his experience.

"My god, we've got to get you to a hospital right away."

"It's just a flesh wound, Megan." *That's it, calm and composed. Don't let her see you fall apart.*

"How can you be sure? What if there's a bullet inside you?"

"If there was, I wouldn't have made it through the metal detectors." He pressed his hand against his side. The blood was fresh. Maybe he'd opened the wound when he'd stretched his arms in that security machine. It seemed like just after that, the pain had gone from a dull ache to Kill-me-now.

"Take off your shirt," she said. "Let me look at it."

"What are you, a nurse?" He was purposely derisive. He didn't want her poking around his wound. There wasn't much she could do anyway.

"I was a candy striper." Her lips set in a line. "I've seen gunshot wounds before." She reached for her blue duffle bag and unzipped it.

"Not here."

"Okay."

She pointed toward the restrooms. He shrugged off her helping hand. "I'm not an invalid. I can walk."

"Do it, then."

He grumbled, but headed to the bathroom. He was about to remind her they should go in the Men's, but Megan didn't need reminding. Finding no one inside, he stripped off his tee shirt and tossed it in the sink. Megan grabbed a handful of paper towels, doused them with water, and cleaned his wound.

It wasn't as bad as he'd feared. He'd been afraid Megan might faint but she didn't look the least bit unsteady. "I feel like a turkey being dressed for dinner," he groused as she patted him dry.

"You might have been killed tonight." Her blue eyes twinkled. "I think you can survive this small indignity."

He couldn't help grinning. She'd mimicked not only his words but his accent. God, he loved this woman.

Had he just said that? Thankfully, only to himself. But even thinking it was unsettling. They were almost at the finish line of their adventure; it wouldn't be wise to complicate things now.

Megan reached into her duffle bag and drew out ointment, gauze and tape. "So what happened tonight?" she asked as she deftly dressed the wound. "Whose security badge did you steal?"

"I didn't steal it." He tried not to flinch as the ointment touched his ragged skin. "I 'borrowed' it from a friend." He told her everything, from his meeting with Roger, to his entry into the embassy building, to making the passports, to his unfortunate confrontation with Martin Weems and his narrow escape. Megan made no comment, just stared at him with some mixture of shock, dismay, and admiration.

"I thought candy stripers only fluffed pillows and emptied bedpans," he said when she'd finished.

"My dad's diabetic. He cut his foot badly at the beach last year. My mom is squeamish, so I changed all his dressings for him." She started to pack up the supplies, but he stopped her.

"We should change your dressing as well. Take down your pants."

Peeking out the doorway to make sure no one was about, Megan unzipped her jeans and stepped out of them. Paul's mouth watered at the sight of bare legs and thin panties, but he focused on the task. Megan's wound was looking much better. He changed the dressing, tossed the old one in the trash, and watched her tug on those hip-hugging jeans again.

"I could have just rolled up my pant leg," she said.

Busted. "I know."

She giggled, and it was all he could do not to grab her, kiss her, and have his way with her against the wall.

What the hell was that about? He'd lost blood, was sick with worry about the ongoing ordeal, and his pecker was still sending randy thoughts to his brain?

Megan placed her hands provocatively on her hips. "You need to have your head examined," she said, "for doing what you did tonight."

At least it wasn't for the thoughts he was having right now. Any therapist—at least any male therapist—would have declared those perfectly normal.

She moved a step closer to him. "You know what you are?"

"A blithering idiot?"

She smiled. "That too." She stood on her toes and melted his eyes with the warmth of hers. "You're a freakin' hero." She planted a brief but stirring kiss on his lips.

Paul's head felt light again. But not from any loss of blood. He was losing something else. His objectivity. His judgment. And maybe his heart.

* * *

Megan bolstered her duffle at the small of her back and turned sideways in the hard plastic chair, resting her head against Paul's shoulder. He felt so comfortable. Maybe too comfortable. She stretched her legs across two other chairs to the other side. "If we pull this off, once the police have Colette in custody, what are your plans?"

He adjusted the duffle bag between them, bracing it against his side. "I'll have to turn myself in to the authorities." Although there was no one within hearing range, he lowered his voice to a whisper. "I committed a crime. My government doesn't look kindly on forged passports."

She snorted. "That's nothing compared to what Colette did."

"It's a crime nonetheless."

304

"If it's a crime to help someone in a desperate situation and put a murdering terrorist in jail, then something is very wrong with the justice system." She let her legs drop to the floor and turned to face him. "You won't go to jail?"

He shrugged. "Don't know. I've never broken the law before."

And he wouldn't have done so now, but for her. "Have you never done anything illegal or unethical in your life? Steal candy from a drugstore, copy a classmate's paper, cheat at cards?"

"I cheated at cards once," he admitted.

"And?"

"I lost anyway. So I never tried it again."

She couldn't help giggling. "I know so little about you."

He winked. "I'm a man of mystery."

And he was likely to remain that way. Even if they stayed awake the rest of the night, there was no way she could learn all she wanted to know about Paul Bernard in just a few hours.

"We've got a long day ahead of us," he said with a yawn. "Why don't you try to get some sleep?"

So much for staying awake and sharing stories all night. Using her bag as a pillow, Megan cradled her head against his thighs and stretched out. She didn't want to sleep. She didn't want to miss a moment of the short time they had left together. But she closed her eyes and listened to Paul breathe, very much aware of the warmth of his flesh through his jeans.

* * *

Paul opened his eyes and immediately covered them with his hands. What was that harsh light? His neck hurt. He rotated his head

305

to shake out the kinks and focused. Airport lounge. Well, what did he expect from sleeping sitting up in a hard chair?

Megan still lay with her head in his lap, her breathing slow and serene, stretched out artlessly like a Renoir nude. *Beautiful,* was the thought that came first to Paul's mind. The second thought, *why was he imagining her nude?*

Probably because of the erotic dreams he'd been having with her cuddled in his lap.

She stirred. A lock of tousled hair fell across her forehead, the baseball cap having long since fallen to the floor. Her eyes opened. When they met his gaze, she smiled.

That smile damn near melted him. "Morning."

Immediately she sat up and jumped to her feet. "What time is it? Have we--?"

"Relax, it's not that much into morning. It's only four o'clock." The terminal was still quiet except for the soothing sounds of the janitorial crew in another hallway, swishing their vacuums against the floor.

She sank back into her chair. "I had a dream."

So did I. It involved me getting you out of those boy clothes and making sweet love to you all night.

"A nightmare, really." She scrubbed at her eyes. "I dreamed we made it to New York on time and we exposed Colette and everything went back to the way it used to be."

He slipped his arms into his windbreaker. "So what's nightmarish about that?"

"The wedding went on." She grimaced. "I married Fletcher."

He let out a laugh. After the tension of the last few days, he deserved a good laugh.

Megan stared into his eyes. "You knew I wasn't in love with Fletcher even before I did. How?"

"It was obvious, lo--." He swallowed the end of the word. He never had before. He called lots of women 'love'. The appellation was meaningless, casual. Or it always had been. But now he was uncomfortable letting it pass his lips, because his feelings for Megan were no longer casual.

She tugged at his jacket sleeve. "But how could you tell? How was it obvious?"

About Fletcher, she meant. "The way you talked about him. The look in your eyes whenever you mentioned him."

"What look? Wistful? Dreamy?"

"Lifeless."

Thank goodness she hadn't asked him to describe *his* dream. It was all he could do to keep his arms at his sides. His hands ached to touch her, to feel her skin under his fingers. He knew there was no way Megan would marry Fletcher now. But would she ever think about *him*, once there was an ocean between them?

"Paul." Her voice was breathy, just like in his dream. "Have you ever been in love?" Almost shyly, she stroked his cheek. "I mean, really in love?"

Damn, this was worse than asking about his dreams. Paul fought the memories he'd struggled to keep buried, but they won. He closed his eyes and took a deep breath, allowing the pain back in. "Yes."

Peaceful silence filled the room. But not for long. "That's all you're going to say?"

He opened his eyes. It was more than he'd told anyone else in Paris. But after the trust Megan had placed in him, he owed her some of himself. And the truth was, it felt good to open up to someone. Why shouldn't he trust her? They were like strangers on a train. In a few days, Megan would be out of his life as if she'd never entered it.

"Her name was Allison." He closed his eyes again and saw her as she'd been that last day. "She was beautiful, and quite bright, and our families traveled in the same social circle." He let his mind go back to happier times, when he'd thought his future set, his world secure. "We dated three years. Everyone said we were a perfect match."

Megan twined her fingers through his. "So what happened?"

He released her hand and stood, pacing between the two rows of chairs to the end of the line and back. "When I was offered this post, I asked her to marry me. She didn't want to move to Paris."

Megan's eyes widened. "Who wouldn't want to live with y--in Paris?"

"Perplexing, isn't it?" A sour taste tinged his mouth. "Allison didn't want to leave her family and friends and the social scene she wished to become accustomed to." He drew in a long breath. "I believe she did love me. She just loved the London townhouse, summering in the Cotswolds, and wintering on the Riviera more."

A familiar pang strafed his chest but this time, diminished by sudden warmth. Megan's head pressed against his chest and her arms encircled his waist. "I guess neither of us has been lucky in love, she whispered. "I almost married a con artist who was only after my money."

As much as he missed her warmth, he pulled away and sat her back in her chair, taking the seat opposite. The terminal was stirring.

Security agents were arriving and hastening to their posts. "I'll see your con artist," he challenged," and raise you a murdering terrorist."

She giggled.

God, he was going to miss that laugh. So natural, lacking in agenda, delighting in simple pleasures. Appreciating *his* dry sense of humor.

Voices carried from a distance as passengers began lining up at the escalator. "We should go to the gate," he said.

Megan hoisted the strap of her duffle bag over her shoulder. "Pau—Uncle Bert?" There was as yet no one close enough to hear them, but Megan apparently sensed the need for vigilance just as he did.

"Yeah?" He almost took the duffle bag from her but reminded himself that a teenage boy would carry his own pack.

Her face shone with earnest concern. "You can still back out. Go to the hospital. Or home. Or turn yourself in to the people at your embassy. At least they know you here. They won't throw you in jail like a common criminal."

But he was a common criminal. He hadn't just committed fraud; he'd resisted arrest, picked off a security guard's gun, and damn near shot the good guys who were trying to protect his embassy. "I want to see Colette brought--"

"--to justice, I understand. But I won't have any trouble identifying Colette by myself, since she looks so much like me. Why do you need to be there?"

His breath caught in his throat. Megan didn't need him anymore. "If you don't want me to go with you--"

"Of course I do." She touched his arm, then drew her hand

back. "You saved my life and I want everyone in my family to know it. But if you were to stay here in Paris and wait for Colette to be extradited, your embassy would clear you and you'd have your job and your life back. There's no need to sacrifice yourself."

"The deed is already done, Megan."

"So you forged passports. For a good cause." Her lips passed disarmingly chose to his cheek. "I hope you know *me* well enough to know I'd never implicate you. So why stick your neck out any farther than it already is?"

He was tired from a day of desperate decisions, tired from a night of little sleep. Too tired to think up a witty response. So he told her the truth.

"I'm a dull, boring guy who's played it safe all his life." He rubbed his thumb across his cheek. "I lived six months with a psychotic murderer and didn't even know it, just kept plodding along on my straight line. Until the day I ran into you outside the American Embassy."

"Literally." She smiled.

His eyes moistened but he fixed them unfalteringly on hers. "I've pumped more adrenaline in the past few days than in the last thirty years. It's been dangerous, and terrifying, but it's also been...fun." He made no attempt to suppress the smile that started on his lips and spread across his face, down his neck, all over his body. "You brought excitement into my life, love. Made me feel...alive. And I guess I'm not quite ready for that to end."

Chapter Twenty-nine

Different gate. Same scenario. They waited for the flight to be called, bags clutched in their hands as the ticketed passengers shuffled through the boarding lines. Megan's ears filtered out the erratic squawks from speakers throughout the terminal, listening only for the gate agent who would pronounce their names. She was physically exhausted and mentally drained, but the thought of finally confronting Colette, and picturing the shock on Fletcher's face, charged adrenaline through her like a stick of lit dynamite.

She beamed positive vibes at the plane on the tarmac. If all went well, in a few minutes they'd be on it and taking off.

"Mr. Warner."

It took a second for the name to register with Megan, but Paul stood stiffly and headed toward the agent.

The woman didn't smile. "I'm afraid you won't make this flight. Coach is completely booked and everyone has checked in."

No! Megan rushed to Paul's side. "Please, we have to get to New York. Today. Now! My uncle is very sick, and I'm taking him for treatment in New York. We've been here all night and he's not doing well. Isn't there anything you can do for us?" She'd ride in the lavatory if they'd let her.

The agent studied Paul's face, which was appropriately drawn and haggard. Sweat beaded his forehead. Megan held her breath as the agent scrolled through her computer screen and announced, "There are two seats available in First Class." She glanced at the plane, which was revving its engines, and at the jet way, where an attendant was closing the door. "Normally we'd ask you to pay for an upgrade but--"

"Thank you so much," Megan said, flashing a grateful smile. She held out her hand for the boarding passes as if they'd been incontrovertibly offered. The positive vibes must have worked, because the agent yelled at the gate attendant, "Hold the plane," and printed out two crisp, beautiful boarding documents.

And as simply as that, the anxiety was over and they were on the plane. Megan leaned back in the spacious leather seat and grinned at Paul sitting beside her. "Can I breathe now?

"Soon." He craned his head forward. "They're getting ready to serve the champagne. That's a good sign we'll be taking off momentarily."

Though it might be premature, Megan exhaled a deep sigh. She reclined her seat stage by stage, trying to decide which position she liked best. Even when traveling with her family, she'd never flown first class. And to think she'd been willing to make the nine hour trip in the lavatory!

She stifled a giggle envisioning Paul's large frame squeezing into the lavatory with her. But that made her think about the "mile high club" which proved many couples had managed to fit together quite nicely. She turned her head to the window so he wouldn't see her blush.

At the flight attendant's admonition, she sat fully upright. The middle-aged woman with silvering hair and the figure of a twenty-year old held out a tray. "Champagne or orange juice?"

"Orange juice for him," Paul said, lifting a champagne flute from the tray for himself.

Megan picked up an orange juice, though she'd much rather have had the champagne. When the flight attendant moved down the aisle, Paul whispered. "You didn't have to make up that sick uncle story. I could have paid for the upgrade."

He was worried about a little white lie after all the illegal things he'd done last night? "You've already spent too much of your money on me." Even a one-way coach ticket booked at the last minute had to cost more than a thousand dollars--each. "And how would you have paid for that upgrade?"

"With my cr--" He paled, apparently realizing that Albert Warner didn't have a credit card. And that Interpol was probably monitoring any purchases on Paul Bernard's account.

Oh no. A hard knot twisted Megan's stomach. Her eyes trained on the airplane cabin door, half expecting a policeman to enter and haul them both off the plane. She leaned in close to Paul's ear. "How did you pay for these tickets?"

Unpredictably, he smiled. "Marcel's credit card." He slouched down in his seat so his mouth was at Megan's ear level. "I wrote him a check for the amount and asked him to hold it until this is all over."

"Smart." Megan let out a shallow breath. "Lucky you had your checkbook with you."

"I don't. I always keep one check in my wallet for an emergency." He grinned. "I think this constituted an emergency." He took the baseball cap she'd stuffed into her seat and crammed it back on her head.

Megan fought tears. Three days ago she didn't have the money to make a phone call. But three men she'd met only this week had reached into their hearts and pocketbooks, at great risk to

313

themselves, to help her. "I promise I'll pay you back as soon as I get home."

With her parents' help. But they should be happy to repay the man who'd brought her home safely, shouldn't they? A cold vise gripped her chest. What if her parents didn't believe her? Would she have to engage in a shouting match with Colette to prove she was really Megan?

Paul held up his champagne flute. "Consider the ticket my parting gift."

Parting gift. That made his feelings painfully clear. He'd get her safely to New Jersey, then be done with her. "I can't let you do that," she said stiffly.

"Please. I have sort of a trust fund myself," he admitted.

"Really."

He set his glass on the beverage tray next to him. "Not a trust exactly. Family money set aside for me. But I don't like to use it unless I have to."

"Why not?"

He cocked an eyebrow. "Because I'm a grown man. I live off what I earn. Isn't that what you want for your life?"

"Well, yes." She just hadn't been very successful at it so far, allowing her family to spoil her for far too long. Mom and Dad had kicked in to pay part of her apartment rent so she could live in a nice part of town. Don often took her to dinner, and Fletcher...well, at least she'd be rid of that self-centered scam artist.

She hadn't spoken aloud, but Paul seemed to read her thoughts. "You're still young. You'll get there." He started to reach for her hand and then drew back. "This will be over soon," he said quietly into her ear. "You'll have your life back in a few hours."

She tried to take heart in that, in seeing her parents and her brother again. Her friend Amber, for the first time since college. But Megan couldn't help thinking about Paul's earlier words. Once she was back in her old life, he'd return to his.

Unless he was arrested and thrown in jail.

He picked up his champagne glass again and raised it toward her. "To getting your life back."

Think positive thoughts, Megan. "And yours." She clinked her glass to his and took a long slow swig, imagining champagne bubbles tickling her tongue and sliding languorously down her throat. Surely once he explained the situation, the authorities would release him. She focused on Paul's warm brown eyes. How could anyone think him a terrorist? The man was a hero. They should put up a statue in his honor, name a wing of the British Embassy after him.

Which she'd never get to see.

After the flight attendant picked up their empty glasses, Paul stretched out his legs and closed his eyes.

She was going to miss those eyes. They'd calmed her when she was so frantic she'd thought her world would explode. They'd aroused her when she'd almost convinced herself she didn't have it in her to enjoy making love.

Nine hours to New York. Megan cradled her hands in her lap. The moment she'd so looked forward to was almost here. But when this traumatic adventure ended, so would her time with Paul. She almost wished these nine hours could stretch out for days.

The captain's voice crackled over the intercom, alerting the crew to take their seats and prepare for takeoff. The plane backed slowly away from the gate and taxied down the runway. After another few minutes of waiting, it wheeled off with a roar, gained speed, and lifted off into the sky.

Paul opened his eyes, grinned at her, and pressed his fingers against hers in a surreptitiously low high five.

Chapter Thirty

They sailed through Passport Control like plastic boats through a child's wading pool. Paul let out a slow breath. For once, Megan had listened to his sage advice to keep silent. When the agent stamped their passports and said, "Welcome to the United States," she'd just smiled demurely and headed brusquely through the *Nothing to Declare* door.

Once in the main terminal, he let her take the lead. She dragged him by the arm to the Air Train. The light rail took them above the traffic-clogged streets to Jamaica station where, unhampered by bulky luggage, they hopped off and transferred to the Long Island Railroad, heading into the city.

"We'll take this to Penn station where we'll catch the New Jersey transit train," Megan explained, "then get off at the station nearest my house and take a cab to the country club."

"Wouldn't it be simpler take a taxi the whole way?" Paul was already missing the convenience and ease of the Paris Metro.

"Takes too long. What time is it?"

"Twelve-forty five." He frowned. With the wedding starting at three, they couldn't afford to miss any connections.

Though neither of them had slept much on the plane, Megan orchestrated their transportation with the energy of a hyperactive child, her eyes shining with anticipation. If she'd seemed a bit helpless in Paris, now that she was on her own turf she was a capable woman intent on a mission.

"Have you ever been to New York?" she asked as the train rumbled across the bridge and into the heart of Manhattan, passing skyscrapers that looked like Lego buildings.

"Yes. But not in a long time."

Her querying look requested details.

"I used to live in Washington D.C. when I was a kid," he explained. "My dad worked at the British embassy."

"Ah, the family business."

He nodded. She didn't ask what his father had done for the Embassy, and Paul didn't volunteer the information. People tended to act strangely when they learned his father had been Ambassador to the United States, and was a personal friend of the queen.

They alit at Penn Station in midtown Manhattan to transfer to the New Jersey transit commuter rail. The huge underground station Paul remembered from his childhood didn't seem quite so large nor its platforms as long as they had twenty years ago. Nor so clean. The smells of urine, pizza, and unwashed bodies wafted from the horde of homeless lingering on the platform and waiting areas.

Another fond memory corrupted. When he was ten, Paul's mother had often taken him on the train from Washington into the city, for an afternoon at the Museum of Natural History, or Carnegie Hall, or Madison Square Garden. Just Mom and him, without the nanny or his older sister. He remembered them as the best days of his childhood.

While Megan studied the timetables, Paul walked to a bank of telephones and extracted a business card from his wallet. He had no

American money but if the machine accepted Euros...

No. No coins at all. Only credit cards.

He hesitated only a second. Agent Moreau would undoubtedly be tracking his card and place him in New York, but that didn't matter now. In fact, it was the point.

The Interpol agent was away from his desk, but Paul left a message with his department. Hopefully they'd make it to the wedding site on time. If they believed him.

Catching sight of Megan frantically waving to him, he hitched his duffle bag over one shoulder and went to her.

"Where's the sodas?" she asked as they ran to the platform.

Had he said he'd get sodas? "Sorry, just went to the loo."

It was barely one-thirty when they boarded the train and settled into their seats. The striking New York skyline gradually fell away, replaced by views of fields and farms. At another time, the trip would have been relaxing, but today Paul's nervous thumbs dug ridges into his seat, as if pressing harder would make the wheels roll faster. Sweat formed on his upper lip. The dull ache in his side grew more acute with each mile.

Across from him, Megan changed her seat from the aisle to the window, then back again to the aisle, practically bouncing with nervous energy. The silent question lay between them: would they make it on time?

They disembarked at the Princeton station and Megan raced to the front of a line of taxicabs, taking two steps to each one of Paul's. When they scrambled into the third cab and slammed the door, Megan gave the driver directions and Paul dared look at his watch. Two-forty. They'd made good time. Letting out a sigh, he leaned back against the leather seat. If their luck held they should arrive at the country club in a matter of minutes.

He hadn't counted on Saturday afternoon mall traffic. The taxicab inched its way forward, stopping at every red light, sitting through some of them twice. Paul checked his watch again.

"You're not helping," Megan snapped. "You can't make the time go any slower and we can't move any faster."

He was making her nervous. Or rather, more nervous than she already was. Disregarding their disguises, he pulled Megan into his arms and whispered, "We'll make it. It'll be all right."

Paul had no idea if he was prophesying the truth or spouting a lying platitude, but Megan relaxed in his arms.

He cleared his throat. "However, if you know of an alternate route..."

Megan sat up and leaned forward to talk to the driver. "Take the old farm road, please." She gestured, and the cab arrowed off the main highway onto a poorly paved road that ran between an orchard and a dairy farm. Cows looked up from their grazing with bored expressions as the taxi bounced across potholes and swerved to avoid dark piles of manure.

But the detour saved precious minutes, and they arrived at the country club at ten before three o'clock.

The parking lot was full, making Paul wonder how many 'dear friends' Colette had invited to this farce of a wedding. But then he recalled rich Americans' penchant for golf. Most of these vehicles undoubtedly belonged to players out on the links.

While Paul paid the driver, adding a generous tip to thank him for taking Euros, Megan charged inside. He caught up with her at the reception desk in the lobby.

320

"The Chandler wedding," she demanded. "Where is it being held?"

The man working reception looked down his nose at their jeans, tees, and tennis shoes.

"We're with the caterers," Paul said quickly.

Raising his nose as if to point the way, the man gave them directions to the kitchen. "The Chandler wedding is in the garden area," he added impassively.

Megan headed off in the direction he'd pointed, but suddenly jumped into an alcove and hid behind a pillar.

A man exited the restroom, running a comb through his moussed hair. A member of the wedding party, Paul guessed from the white ruffled shirt and gray tuxedo. Their eyes met and he was about to make a casual comment about the weather or weddings, but the man brushed past him as if he weren't there, his dark eyes narrow and focused.

Megan emerged from behind the pillar, her face ashen white. "That was Fletcher," she gasped. Her body shook and panic shone in her eyes.

Paul almost caught her in his arms but controlled his impulse. "You can do this."

"Oh, I definitely can do this." She swallowed visibly, her blue eyes fortified with molten steel. "I *will* do this."

She stepped out into the lobby, reached for a courtesy phone, and dialed the operator. "I need to call 9-1-1," she said authoritatively. "There's a public disturbance at the Vista Ridge Country Club."

He looked around at the quiet gathering. "But there's not."

"There will be," she assured him. When the local police came on the line, Megan offered the anonymous tip that a sought-after international terrorist had been spotted in the country club gardens. She gave enough information about the Paris embassy bombing to be taken seriously, then hung up when she was pressed to give her name.

She faced Paul, her hands shaking. "Do you think they'll show? They won't think it's just a crank call?"

"They'll definitely think it's a crank call," he predicted. "But they'd be derelict in their duties if they didn't check it out."

Between Interpol and the local police, there should be plenty of manpower—and firepower—to apprehend the 'bride and groom.' If he had to, Paul could restrain Colette on his own, but Fletcher was a big guy. No way could he capture both, even with Megan's help. Too bad he hadn't brought along a pair of Colette's furry handcuffs.

They slipped out a side doorway and into the courtyard, which led to a manicured garden bordered by two rows of trees.

For a small wedding, it was quite festive. A string quartet played Mozart in muted tones. Champagne flowed like the Thames, and fancy little hors d'oeuvres with toothpicks were passed by waiters to the arriving guests. Paul looked around but didn't spot the 'bride.'

They stood at the back, trying not to call attention to themselves. "Do you want to make this dramatic," he whispered to Megan, "and wait until the pastor asks if anyone objects, or jump right in?"

"Jump right in," she answered immediately. "As soon as all the parties are assembled within grabbing range."

Paul chuckled. The waif he'd met four days ago had turned into a tigress. Fortunately, he happened to like tigresses.

The music drifted away. The pastor strode to an arbor of vines overhanging an arched trellis. He stepped up to the podium which served as the altar. "Please take your seats. We're ready to begin."

The music struck up again, a somber march. Megan shivered beside him and emitted a strange sound. Paul looked up to see the groom and another handsome bloke, this one slim and blond, moving toward the ivy-twined arbor.

Megan gasped. "My brother Don is the best man."

Though he wasn't touching her, he could almost feel Megan's heart galloping. Was she distressed that her brother had fallen for the scam Colette and Fletcher had perpetrated? Or was Don Chandler involved in the deception as well?

From their vantage point at the side, they could see both men clearly. Paul couldn't keep his eyes off the man Megan had almost married. Besides his attractive facial features, now that he was in public, he wore a white-toothed, megawatt smile.

If he and Paul were standing together at a Ladies Choice dance, it was obvious which one would be picked. But it wasn't Fletcher whose arm Megan now held in a death grip. And when Paul faced her, he saw no wistfulness in her eyes. The look she fastened on her ex-almost-fiancé was pure revulsion.

Paul kept her behind him, partially hidden by a tree, as groomsmen in tuxes appeared and bridesmaids carrying bouquets walked up the aisle. He checked his watch. Three-fifteen.

The quartet struck up "Here Comes the Bride." And it was Paul's turn to suck in his gut and restrain himself from running out and wringing Colette's neck. Not for what she'd done to him. Nor even primarily for the deaths and destruction she'd caused. But for the hell she'd put Megan through.

Her arm linked through an older gentleman's, presumably

Megan's father, she wore that fake smile of which he'd often been the recipient. Beaming like a virginal bride. Instead of what she was, a bitch in perpetual heat.

When Colette and Mr. Chandler reached the arbor where Fletcher and Don waited, Paul glanced at Megan. Her jaw was set like finely chiseled rock. She stepped forward.

He grabbed her arm. "Not yet," he whispered.

Unless the station was next door, the police hadn't had time to get here yet. But where was Interpol? He'd told them three o'clock sharp. Had they not believed him? Had the person who answered the phone even relayed his message to Agent Moreau?

Perhaps this was a bad idea. Paul considered retreating, waiting for the police at the country club entrance, going directly to the station if they failed to show. But just as the music ended and the pastor opened his Bible and was about to speak, plucky, intrepid Megan Chandler strode up to the arbor and said loudly, "Stop the wedding!"

Whispers started at the front rows and reverberated back like a rave in a concert hall. The plot twist of many a movie, rarely encountered in real life.

The pastor tried to take control as the crowd murmurs intensified. "Please, everyone, remain seated." He turned to Megan, the real one. "Young man, what is the meaning of this? Who are you?"

"It's me, Pastor Ray." She doffed her baseball cap. "I'm Megan." She pointed at Colette. "This woman is an imposter."

Paul edged closer.

Fletcher blinked at the 'young boy' in the short haircut as recognition dawned. "M-Megan?"

The pastor looked from Megan to Fletcher to the 'bride' whose face had turned as white as her dress. But bless her tainted soul, Colette didn't break character. She looked at Fletcher all fluttery, her expression one of dismayed confusion.

"Megan?" An older woman joined the crowd at the altar and peered into Megan's face. "Oh, my God, Megan!" Mrs. Chandler clasped her daughter in her arms, casting a wary eye at Colette in the wedding dress. "Who is...how did she...?"

Megan's father dropped Colette's arm and came to stand by his wife and daughter. This was his first glimpse of the man's face but Paul doubted it was usually this red.

The pastor narrowed his eyes at 'the bride.' "If she's Megan," he demanded, "then who are you?"

Paul stepped forward. "Her name is Colette."

If it were possible for her face to blanch whiter, it did. "Paul!" She hiked up her skirt, preparing to run.

Paul grabbed her arm and blocked her escape.

Wide-eyed, Fletcher looked from Colette to Megan. And then hurled himself into Megan's arms. "Omigod, Megan, it really is you. She looks so much like...I had no idea..."

Megan elbowed him hard in the gut. "Don't pretend innocence, Fletcher, because I know better. I'm not sure whether she scammed you, or you scammed her, but you knew I was stranded in Europe and you definitely knew she wasn't Megan."

Paul couldn't have been prouder of her if she'd been awarded a medal for courage.

Megan glared at Fletcher, fisting her hands at her hips. "Do you really believe I would ever get a tattoo? Especially--"

Confronting Colette, she snatched at the lace bodice of the wedding dress and ripped a hole at the right breast. "—-there."

The buzzing among the wedding guests turned into shrieks, as if they were watching a circus act and the trapeze artist had just plunged to the net. Megan's father looked distraught and disoriented. Her mother paled as if she were going to faint.

"How much did she tell you?" Megan planted both hands on Fletcher's chest and shoved. "Did she happen to mention that she blew up an embassy and killed three people?"

Horrified gasps filled the garden. The guests scrambled out of their chairs and retreated to the edges of the courtyard. Some fled, as if fearing a bloodbath. Others couldn't seem to tear themselves away.

To Fletcher's credit, he looked revolted as well. But whereas most men would have backed away and escaped, he stood rooted to his spot. Frozen in fear? Or angling for a way to salvage his situation?

Paul couldn't let Megan have all the fun. He clutched Colette's arm tighter. "By the way, darling, your boyfriend Salim has been arrested. With his fingerprints identified on *your* gun. He's spilling his guts to the French police and Interpol as we speak."

Paul had no idea whether Salim had talked to the authorities or maintained his stone-faced silence, but the suggestion struck fear in Colette's eyes.

"Your boyfriend?" This from Fletcher. "The one you were living with whose bank account you stole?"

Finally, Colette broke character. "I didn't steal anybody's account! Salim the Scumbag stole mine." She jabbed her finger at Paul's chest. "This is the guy I was living with."

Since no gunshots had been fired, nor bombs exploded, people moved in closer to the fray so as not to miss a single sordid word. Sweat lined the pastor's upper lip. "Would everyone please take their seats?" he begged.

"You!" Fletcher turned to Paul, and then pointed to Colette. "*You* slept with *her*?"

"Many times, friend." *That* was what he cared about? The bloody fool didn't even ask about Paul's relationship with Megan. Before the thought could occur to him, Paul opened his mouth prepared to change the subject, but he wouldn't have been heard anyway over the crowd's raucous laughter.

"Ladies and gentleman, please!" The pastor had lost control of the situation ten minutes ago but kept trying to contain it. "Please take your seats so we can sort this out."

"We'll sort it out at the station." A pair of uniformed policeman rushed to the altar, handcuffing Fletcher and Colette together. Paul noticed two more standing at the edge of the courtyard, guns drawn. Paul let out a relieved breath. Talk about your nick of time. His knees felt weak but he kept his balance. It wasn't over yet.

As the officers led Colette away, she turned her head and screeched at Paul. "You can thank your ass you slept with me! If I hadn't screwed your brains out that morning, you'd be lying in a morgue with your buddies now."

He flinched, but kept his voice level. "Sounds like a confession to me."

The pastor closed his book and looked helplessly at Megan's father, who stepped up in his place. "Show's over, folks. Sorry for the inconvenience, but there will be no wedding today."

The guests dispersed, a few to the exits, but most gathered in small circles, pointing and chatting. Several headed toward Megan and her family, but Mr. and Mrs. Chandler and brother Don formed a protective circle around her.

Paul edged away from the tender family reunion.

"Megan, honey, I'm so sorry," her mother sniffed into a white lace handkerchief. "It *was* you who called that day and said you'd been stranded in Europe. That...that woman--" She jerked her head toward Colette's departing figure. "--said it was a scam, that your-her—your cell phone had been stolen."

Paul took another step back.

"It *was* stolen. By her." Megan's teeth gritted visibly. "Along with my money, my passport and my plane ticket. I might be sleeping in the Paris subway right now if not for--" She grabbed Paul's arm as he was about to take another step back. "Mom and Dad, Don, this is Paul. Paul Bernard. He works for the British embassy in Paris that got bombed."

Confused, concerned faces stared at him. Either they hadn't heard about the bombing or they didn't understand how that connected him to Megan.

"Paul is...a good friend. He saved my life."

"Not true." Modesty prevented him from accepting the compliment. "You saved your own life."

"He found me a place to stay," Megan continued, "and kept me safe from the terrorists and the police who were trying to arrest me and--" She stopped, gasping for breath, her adrenaline charge apparently having finally run out. Paul's instinct was to take her in her arms and soothe her, but with her family now surrounding her, he kept his arms stiffly at his sides.

Her parents' mouths gaped open, their expressions escalating from concerned to horrified.

The brother's eyes roved from Paul's wild yellow hair to Megan's boyish haircut. Paul started to explain the reason for the disguise, but adding passport forgery to Megan's list of his stellar qualities would probably not win points with her family.

Mr. Chandler regained his composure. "Any friend of our daughter's is a friend of ours," he said formally, extending his hand to Paul. "Please join us at our home this afternoon."

"Thank you, sir."

Megan's father surveyed the garden emptying of guests and attempted a stiff-upper-lip smile. "Excuse me while I settle up with the Club for this grisly swindle."

Megan's brother took her arm. "I'm so sorry, Meggie," he said as they walked toward the garden exit. "I can't believe I actually fell for that...person's story. I wouldn't have thought you'd want to get married in such a rush, but then I assumed that was because of the preg--" His voice dwindled to a mumble.

Megan's eyes widened.

"Geez, I was a gullible jerk." Don slapped his forehead. "They led me to believe that you...that she..."

"I'm not pregnant!" Megan yelled. She turned to Paul. "You think maybe Colette--?"

"Absolutely not!" he assured her. At least not by him.

Don was suddenly full of questions for his sister. "Why didn't you call me? How did you get home without a passport? How did you meet this guy?" He raked a suspicious gaze over Paul.

"Long story. We'll tell you all about it when we get home." Megan hugged her brother, and then reached for Paul's hand, her eyes brimming with tears.

His heart filled with warmth. No matter what happened to him, it would be worth it for Megan to have her life back.

He didn't let himself dwell on what *his* life would be like with her no longer in it. Calmer, for sure. But Paul wasn't sure he could ever be content again with the predictable, routine life he'd once carved out for himself.

He twined his fingers through Megan's and squeezed her hand, an action that did not go unnoticed by Don.

But what the hell. As they passed in front of the two armed policemen who still stood guard at the exit, he pulled Megan into his arms. But before he could kiss her, the officers boxed them in and locked a pair of handcuffs onto her wrist and his.

Chapter Thirty-one

Megan looked down at Paul's arm dangling with hers between the two wooden chairs, their wrists once again cuffed together. The windowless room in the local police station was furnished with only a small wooden desk and another hard wooden chair like the ones they were sitting on. Behind the desk was a large mirror, undoubtedly a window from which they were now being observed.

Her pounding heart gradually slowed to normal cadence as the adrenaline oozed out of her. Despite the situation, she wasn't frightened. After the elation of seeing Colette and Fletcher hauled off to face their richly deserved fates, she felt strangely euphoric and relaxed.

For the first time since they'd been brought in here ten minutes ago, she looked up at Paul's face. "Thanks for coming home with me." She waved her free hand at their prison. "Sorry it came to this, but...it was kind of fun, wasn't it?"

He grinned. "I wouldn't have missed it for the world."

She returned a triumphant smile, twining her fingers awkwardly through his. "I didn't realize you knew about...about Colette and Salim."

"I didn't, not while it was going on. I figured it out when you told me about flashing your breasts at him in the Catacombs. I knew you wouldn't do something so random without a reason."

Megan stole a glance at the mirror. Whoever might be watching them was either scratching his head or having a good laugh, but she didn't care. Being arrested in her own country by people who spoke English seemed like a Sunday picnic compared to being held captive in the catacombs by terrorists. Despite the seriousness of her current situation, Megan felt impervious to peril.

"We both got duped," she admitted to Paul as if they were alone. "But I've learned my lesson. I'll never trust anyone again."

"Me neither," he said. But from the way his eyes met hers, Megan knew that he knew they were both lying.

She looked around the spartan office. *What happens next?* Would Paul go to jail? Would she? The policeman who'd cuffed them and brought them here had said little on the way over, just confiscated their passports, deposited them in this room and locked the door behind him, muttering something about Interpol.

Choking back tender emotions, she rattled her cuffed hand. "When this is over, do you think they'll let us keep these?"

He grinned.

She was going to miss that grin. Paul's wasn't an ear-to-ear, teeth-flashing grin. Like everything else about him, his smile was subtle, just enough to let you know he was amused, but making you wonder what thoughts he wasn't revealing.

The door behind them opened, and a man in a suit entered, carrying a laptop and a file folder. He set both on the desk. "I'm Detective O'Shea." He took the seat behind the desk and folded his arms. "Albert Warner?" He scrutinized Paul as if he were a hardened criminal. "A.K.A. Paul Bernard?"

"It's just Paul Bernard, sir." Paul's Adam's apple quavered.

"The passport is under a false name."

The officer shot him a Do-you-take-me-for-an-idiot-of-course-I-know-that glare. He turned to Megan. "And you are obviously not thirteen year old Timothy Briggs." He glanced at her chest. "It's Colette Marchand, isn't it?"

Megan's temporary euphoria plunged into a pool of grave reality. *Oh God, this wasn't happening.* "No sir, I'm Megan Chandler. Colette is...she's the terrorist you apprehended. She stole my passport and my identity."

The detective looked bored. As if he'd heard this story many times before.

"Please, sir, she's done nothing wrong," Paul said. "I forged the passports. Megan is just a victim in all this."

Detective O'Shea grunted. He opened the laptop in front of him and clicked through it. "I've learned from Interpol that the Embassy bomber suspect now in custody was beaten in an alley behind your apartment, Mr. Bernard. Several of your neighbors reported it to the police. And identified you as the assailant."

What?

Detective O'Shea turned the laptop around so they could see it, and pressed play on a video. "This was taken from a cell phone. I believe that's you in the video, beating our terrorism suspect."

Yes! She'd *known* Paul had to be responsible for Salim's arrest. But now he'd be brought up on an assault charge as well as forgery. She glanced at him, but he stared straight ahead like a military recruit, his face devoid of emotion.

Megan faced Detective O'Shea. "Even if that were Paul in the video," she said, using the hypothetical to avoid incriminating him, "you should give him a medal for helping apprehend a terrorist, instead of prosecuting him for it."

The officer ignored her as if she hadn't spoken. His cell phone rang. "O'Shea," he answered. After a minute of listening, he rose, unlocked the handcuff from Paul's wrist and clicked the cuff attached to Megan to the chair. "Please come with me, Mr. Bernard," he said as if that were a request instead of an order.

Paul stood. "What happens to Megan?" he asked.

"We're questioning the other young woman now. If she corroborates your story, Miss Chandler will probably be released."

But what about Paul? Megan craned her neck as the detective and a uniformed officer escorted Paul out of the room. Fear plunged to the pit of her stomach. Where were they taking him? Would they beat him? She'd seen way too many TV shows where the interview suspect 'accidentally' hit his head against the wall and bloodied his face.

She jumped up, upsetting the chair. The officers hadn't locked the door. She could drag the wooden chair with her, shuffle out the door, down the hallway...

Right. She'd be caught before she made three feet. Adding attempted escape to her crime of traveling on a forged passport.

Where were Mom and Dad? Don? They'd followed the police cars from the country club to the station. Why wouldn't they let her see them? Were they suspected of taking part in the terrorist plot too?

Her thoughts returned to Paul. She closed her eyes and saw him bruised and bloody, shoved into a jail cell, set upon by other prisoners. Sickened, she opened her eyes, but the images wouldn't go away.

This was all her fault. If he'd never run into her at the

embassy, he wouldn't have mistaken her for Colette and tried to help her, then turned on her, then helped her again, then...

She righted the chair and sank back into it. *Please let him be all right. Please let him be all right. Please—*

"Miss Chandler." The gray-suited policeman entered the room and unlocked her handcuffs. "You're free to go. Your family is waiting outside. I'll take you to them."

She jumped up and dashed to the door. Had Colette, then, 'corroborated' Paul's story? Confessed to bombing the embassy? As Detective O'Shea directed her around a corner, Megan nearly bumped into her mirror image.

Escorted by a uniformed officer, Colette's hands were cuffed behind her back. She glanced at Megan with the disdain one might accord a loathsome bug, then turned aside.

Megan didn't let her by. "Why?"

Colette shrugged. "You were a way out," she said without remorse. "Nothing personal."

Nothing personal? Rage churned in Megan's gut. "You think that justifies ruining my life?"

Colette narrowed her eyes, her cheeks pinched and taut. "*Ruined?* You're alive, aren't you?" Looking as if she wanted to spit, she moved on down the corridor.

Megan swallowed her bile. Colette could be executed for her crime. Not that she didn't deserve it. She'd murdered Paul's colleagues and would have killed him too, except for...

She gasped. If Colette's parting taunt at Paul was true, she hadn't tried to kill him. She'd tried to spare him. Megan blinked. It was hardly an argument for judicial mercy but her act revived

Megan's flagging faith in humanity just a notch.

"Megan!" Her mother wailed in high pitched hysteria as she entered the waiting area. Megan pushed away from Detective O'Shea and threw herself into her parents' arms.

"This has all been a terrible mistake," her father said. "You must be frightened and exhausted. Let us take you home."

"No." Not without Paul. "I can't leave yet."

Dad exchanged a look with her brother, then pried a weeping Mom off Megan and comforted her. "We'll wait here a while."

"Is it true that woman bombed the British Embassy in Paris?" Don asked. "And tried to pin it on you?"

"Yes." She sank into a plastic chair.

Her brother looped his arm over her shoulder. "Thank goodness you weren't arrested there. Things could have been so much worse."

"Sooo much worse." Someday, she should probably tell her parents about her experience in the catacombs. But not today. She glanced at her sobbing mother. *Maybe not ever.*

She wrung her hands, too tired to speak, not sure why she was waiting here. It wasn't like Detective O'Shea was going to come back and give her an update on Paul. She wasn't his wife. She wasn't his *anything*.

Finally she couldn't stand waiting any longer. She jumped up and ran into the maze of corridors she'd been led through, not sure where she was going, but determined to find Paul. Or someone who could tell her about him.

She found the room they'd been held in, but it was now empty.

Back in the corridor, she heard men's voices. One slightly familiar. One voice so familiar it made her heart ache. She ran toward them and saw Paul in cuffs, being led out a door toward a parking lot.

"Please." She begged Detective O'Shea and another man in plain clothes. "Where are you taking him?"

The men stopped. Detective O'Shea studied her as if trying to decide whether to respond. Finally he said, "To the consulate in New York City. An Interpol representative there will take his statement. If it jives with Miss Marchand's--assuming we get a confession from her--the charges pending for aiding and abetting a terrorist plot could be dropped."

Megan breathed a sigh that was only half relief. So Colette hadn't confessed yet. And this wasn't over. "What about the forgery charges?"

Paul glared at her.

What? She mouthed at him. *Like you thought they'd forgotten about those?* He'd readily admitted his guilt in that.

"That's up to the British government," Detective O'Shea said, "as that would have been an internal crime committed on British 'soil'. In fact--" Megan could have sworn he almost winked. "--no such charges have been filed as yet."

She breathed out the other half of her sigh. Surely the embassy wouldn't charge him. After all he'd apprehended two terrorists.

Detective O'Shea dropped the two fake passports in an envelope which he handed to the other detective, then spoke to Paul. "If Interpol clears you, you'll be issued a temporary travel document with which to return to France."

Megan's heart pounded with excited relief. He wasn't going to jail! Interpol would clear him, they had to. He'd go back to Paris a free man, probably get his job back.

She tried not to focus on the going-back-to-Paris part.

For the first time, she drank in Paul's gaze. Wondering if the longing in her eyes shone as deeply as that in his.

Detective O'Shea cleared his throat. "Let's give these two a minute alone," he said to his colleague. He gestured toward Paul's handcuffs and the other officer unlocked them. O'Shea opened the door to an empty room. "We'll be just outside."

Alone for the first time since they'd been arrested, Megan staring into Paul's deep, comforting eyes. She trembled. "I guess it's really over."

He smiled, sadly. "Something to tell your grandchildren."

That made tears well. *Be strong, Megan. Don't cry in front of him.* The last thing he needed was for her to fall apart.

She couldn't bear to see him walk away, but what was there to say? Should she ask for his email address? That seemed pointless. After what they'd been to each other, casual friendship seemed rather shallow.

They'd had their moment. She should let him go on with his life, pick up the pieces of hers.

Paul moved forward to embrace her, but she backed away. If she let him touch her, she'd break in half.

He opened his mouth to speak, and closed it again. Silently they stared at each other, Megan trying to memorize every detail of him. Though their bodies weren't touching, her soul reached out to him, and his serene warmth bounded back to her.

A rap sounded from outside the door. Paul turned to go. "Take care," he said in a tone that would have been distant if not for the catch in his voice. "Don't go chasing any women in yellow scarves."

No! It couldn't end like this. "I get a two-week break from classes at Christmas," Megan said without thinking. The words gurgled up from her heart. "How is Paris in the winter?"

He turned back slowly. There was nothing subtle about this grin. It lit up his eyes and left his whole face shining. "Cold," he said. "But I know a great way to keep warm."

And then suddenly, rightly, she was in his arms, his kiss promising all the warmth she'd ever need.

THE END

Dear Reader:

If you liked this book, please write a review to let others know. And I hope you'll enjoy my new Contemporary Romance, *Only With the Heart.*

Brian McKay hates Tinseltown. Everything in L.A. reminds him of his actor father, who deserted Brian when he was four. But when he needs funds to construct a model of his invention, a voice-activated hotel suite, he's forced into a business partnership with his spoiled half-brother Connor. Brian's got three weeks to complete and sell the product, then he's outta this town, and nothing can stop him. Except the distraction of a beautiful Beverly Hills do-gooder with a smile that can melt ice, and a heart big enough to embrace the whole world.

Special education teacher and day camp volunteer Paige Anderson is looking for a way to draw out her shy, visually-impaired campers. When she visits her friend Connor's design lab, she finds just the thing: a talking robot. Paige is even more intrigued by the robot's creator and programmer, a surly loner with a chip on his shoulder who needs drawing out even more than her campers. But when she finally succeeds in opening Brian up, she finds a soul that attracts her as no one ever has before, and a heart that demands more than she has ever had to give.

Excerpt from Linda Steinberg's *Only With the Heart:*

Someone was in the laboratory.

Setting aside his blueprints and sandwich, Brian flattened his palms against the metal desk and listened. Thirty seconds after the security beep, he heard the grinding of a gear.

He took in a shallow breath. He didn't expect Connor back from lunch for at least two more hours. And no one else had a key to the lab.

Possibly some street kids had broken into the converted warehouse, thinking it was unoccupied. Brian mopped his brow with the tail of his flannel shirt and silently exhaled. Slipping his feet out of his sandals so they wouldn't flop against the concrete floor, he threaded his way through the graveyard of electrical circuits and wires. As he passed the unassembled fileserver rack, he grabbed a four-foot metal rod and shouldered it like a baseball bat.

A rash of static crackled through the stale air. A raspy, inhuman voice grated. "Hellooooooo."

The intruders had activated Victor.

Clenching his weapon tighter, Brian stepped over a stack of computer science magazines, raised the pole and prepared to swing it at--

A woman? He lowered the pole to the floor.

The female hunched over the platform supporting the VICTR 001 prototype was blond, shapely, and definitely hot, though from her provocative position, he couldn't see her face. The feature that first drew his attention was her compact, heart-shaped backside.

An eyeful of tanned legs lured his gaze from the short, classy tennis dress to the spotless white sneakers with cheerleader sock pompoms kissing her ankles. Upper crust Valley girl. Connor's type.

She didn't turn or look up. Brian's military stealth training served him well. Though females rarely noticed him even when they were looking straight at him.

The woman reached a hand under the hem of her flared miniskirt. Skimming pink pearl fingernails over a bare buttock, she yanked a wedged cotton panty over the mouth-watering expanse of skin.

Whoa.

ABOUT THE AUTHOR

Linda Steinberg wasn't born in Texas, but she got there as soon as she could. Writing has been a passion for as long as she can remember. She started writing her first novel when she was living in Lagos, Nigeria, in longhand on school tablets, the only available writing paper, and hasn't stopped since. She writes contemporary romance, romantic suspense, and women's fiction featuring strong heroines with the wit and brains to solve their problems and formidable heroes who are more than a match for their tough women. A retired accountant, Linda now lives in a suburb of Dallas with her second time around sweetheart and enjoys reading, travel, family and friends. Visit her website at www.lindasteinberg.com.

www.ingramcontent.com/pod-product-compliance
Lightning Source LLC
Chambersburg PA
CBHW061323170626
46817CB00001B/289